BOOK # _023464_ MONTH/YEAR _7/05_

AUTHOR _T. W._

TITLE _P._

PUBLISHER _____

EDITION _____

YEAR _____

BOOK CONDITION _____

JACKET CONDITION _____

ISBN# _____

COMMENTS: _____

_____

_____

CODE _____ PRICE _____ US _12_

Tim Wilson was born and brought up in Peterborough on the edge of the Fens. He was a student on the University of East Anglia MA Course in Creative Writing, under Malcolm Bradbury and Angela Carter. He now lives with a word processor in a small flat.

# Purgatory

## Tim Wilson

KNIGHT

First published in 1993
by HEADLINE BOOK PUBLISHING

First published in paperback in 1994
by HEADLINE BOOK PUBLISHING

A HEADLINE FEATURE paperback

This edition published 2001 by
Knight an imprint of Caxton Publishing Group

10 9 8 7 6 5 4 3

ISBN 1 84067 380 X

Typeset by Avon Dataset Ltd., Bidford-on-Avon

Printed and bound in Great Britain by
The Guernsey Press Co. Ltd, Guernsey, C.I.

Caxton Publishing Group
20 Bloomsbury Street
London
WC1B 3JH

The pattern is familiar to us, at the end of the twentieth century — the transformation of society into an atomistic aggregation of mutually antipathetic strangers, in which whatever is not known is *ipso facto* a threat.

Michael Greenwood,
*Anglian Voices* (Introduction)

# ONE

## 1

Afterwards Michael could never remember what it was that alerted him to the fact that he was not alone.

He leaned back and closed his eyes as the train pulled out of the city. The mess of warehouses and coal tips with which all towns seem to advertise themselves to rail travellers was utterly familiar to him, and he had memories of being snug in bed just an hour ago which seemed worth re-creating. The train was not full, and he had a table to himself.

He was sure he did not even hear the man sitting down in the seat opposite him. Somehow his feeling of relaxation just seemed to leave him, as the temperature is supposed to drop in a haunted room, and he opened his eyes.

## 2

His new companion was watching him, hands gripping the edge of the table.

'All right?' he demanded.

Michael responded with a smile that he hoped was genial but also discouraging of further conversation.

Already, however, he suspected that he was out of luck. The young man had said 'All right?' with weird emphasis, rather as if it were a tailpiece to some belligerent admonition not to mess with him or else.

'You going to Cambridge?' the young man said, jerking the words out of himself.

'That's right.'

'Yeah,' the young man said, the emphasis all haywire again, as if he were ruefully admitting something, 'yeah, me too. See the old mum.' He uttered a short laugh, as explosive as a cough. 'You work there, then, Cambridge?'

'No, just visiting.'

'Yeah?' This as if visiting Cambridge were a matter for astonishment. 'What, got friends there, business, what?'

I'm not an unsociable person, thought Michael, really, it's just that it's nine o'clock in the morning and I wouldn't mind just sitting quietly for the journey and collecting my thoughts . . . 'No, well, what it is, I'm going to the radio station there to do an interview.'

The young man merely grunted, unsuccessfully trying to light an abbreviated roll-up. 'Mmm. The thing about the *radio* is, it's just like *there*, you can just like *listen* to it. I mean that telly—' All at once the young man was laughing – laughing like the sailor in an old seaside penny-in-the-slot machine, rocking from side to side, head thrown back, ha ha ha ha ha, loudly and hugely. 'Oh, God, that telly, I mean can you *believe* that?' There were tears in his eyes. 'It's just like, the people on it, they're just *zombies*, do us a favour, give us a fag.'

After a startled moment Michael handed over his

Rothmans and lighter. Across the aisle a petite black woman patiently going through a pop-up book with her infant daughter met his eyes for a sympathetic second.

'Nice lighter,' the young man said. 'Where'd you get that from?'

'It was a present,' said Michael.

From Kate. Funny how it could still hit you, at unsuspecting moments. It had been his birthday, and the first time he had clicked the lighter the flame had gone up like a torch, nearly taking off his eyebrows, and they had lain in bed helpless with laughter . . .

'What, you're going on the *radio*?' the young man bellowed, as if Michael had just that moment said so. 'What, you like done something special, you like *climbed a mountain* or something . . .' He was laughing again: Michael remembered a television puppet who used to laugh like that. Basil Brush, that was it. 'Oh, God,' the young man chuckled, shaking his head, 'them fucking mountains, man . . .'

Michael intercepted another wry glance from the black woman, who was now listening to her little girl read aloud. Why, he thought, couldn't I have had them sitting opposite me? Why did I have to get the Train Loony? He had a vague recollection of a comedian − he couldn't remember who, he had a terrible memory − doing a sketch about the Train Loony, who always sat at your table and told you he had a radio in his head. It was a very funny sketch. But when it happened to you . . .

'So what you going on the radio for, then?' Harshly interrogative now.

'Well, I've just had this book published . . .'

3

'Yeah, what's that, science fiction/fantasy sort of thing?'

'No, no, history.' He had a copy of *Anglian Voices* in the carrier bag on the table — he kept meaning to get a briefcase — and he passed it over.

' "Michael Greenwood",' the young man read out, with heavy inverted commas, as if the name were an impossibly unlikely pseudonym *à la* Groucho Marx — Rufus T. Firefly or Wolf J. Flywheel. 'Jesus, you write all this?'

'Well, no, I just edited it really, and wrote the introduction and the linking material. It's a collection of oral and local history, you know, the ordinary people of East Anglia down the years, in their own words.'

He watched the young man riffling through the pages, stopping to examine the photographs with which the publishers had liberally sprinkled it: halfway through production the money men had advised them to give it a popular format or else. Michael's feelings were mixed. Of course, history should be attractive and not elitist. He had always believed that. That, indeed, was what had made him compile such a book. He just wished he could forget the suppressed sneer on Geoffrey Selby's face as he had examined it in his office and casually pronounced: 'Very nice, Michael. Look very nice on the coffee table.' Whilst Selby's own publications, defiantly un-coffee-tabular, dense with erudition, stood ranged on the shelf behind him . . .

' "Michael Greenwood is a lecturer at Broadland University".' The young man was reading from the back flap, which also bore an author photograph — absurdly flattering, Michael felt: the picture made the most of his dark eyes and thick head of unruly fairish hair, turning him into an academic dreamboat. 'It doesn't *say* much about you, does it? Like it might say whether you're married, or got kids, or got *piles*' – he interrupted himself to laugh again, high and yelping – 'or what you like and what you don't like, look, do you see what I'm saying? Michael Greenwood likes doing *crossword puzzles* or Michael Greenwood likes playing *Monopoly* or Michael Greenwood likes playing, what, *Cluedo*—'

'There's not much to say, really,' Michael said, cutting him off. Probably unwise to interrupt the Train Loony: but there was something peculiarly unpleasant about having a stranger use your name so insistently.

'Listen, I'll tell you a good book to read, right,' the young man said. *'Lord of the Rings.'* He gave the word *Rings* such a bizarre Doppler effect that the little girl across the aisle looked up from her book in surprise. 'You read it and it's just like you're *there*, right. Just like this magical wo-ooorld.'

He gestured expansively. Never make eye contact, that was the rule. But there was no getting away from it with this man. He stared into your face all the time. His eyes were a very pale blue, in uneasy contrast with black curls and a curiously sunburnt face – the colouring, together with a sort of empty intensity of expression, reminded Michael of Mr Punch. He was probably about thirty, broad-shouldered and boxer-necked, but the too-tight pullover and skewwhiff shirt-collar were like the clothes of a young boy in the blessed interval between learning to dress himself and becoming self-conscious about his appearance.

'Steve,' the man said with sudden gravity, holding his hand out across the table.

Michael took it to shake, and found that Steve had, in schoolboy fashion, bent his middle finger so as to tickle Michael's palm.

'Ah, ha ha ha ha!' The Laughing Policeman act was back, so loud this time that the little girl craned round her seat to see. Michael no longer bothered to hide his annoyance. This, he thought, is going to be rather hell. Not for the first time, he wished he had taken a course in assertiveness training. Then he might have been able confidently but politely to say nice to meet you, but I want to get on with some work and not be disturbed . . . But he had never been able to pinpoint where assertiveness ended and rudeness began: and so he ended up in situations like this.

The ticket inspector had entered the carriage, and was disputing a youth's claim to be fifteen. 'You'll have to pay full fare, young sonny Jim, that's about the size of it,' he was intoning in sonorous I-thang-yew Ealing Comedy tones: a ticket inspector straight from Central Casting.

Steve shook his head in tremendous disgust. 'Always one bad apple that upsets the applecart,' he said, and went on shaking his head, longer than Michael had ever seen anyone shake their head before. He was just thinking it was going to go on and on like a perpetual-motion machine when Steve suddenly bounced up and down in his seat and tapped at the window.

'Christ, will you just – will you just *look* at that countryside, I mean those *clouds*, yeah? It's just like *God's glory*, God's glory, *God's glory* . . .'

6

*of remembering that it was the one when cancer robbed her of life.*

It didn't work, of course. But it helped not to be reminded of it.

'Here's the way I look at it, right,' Steve said, wagging his forefinger rather in the way Geoffrey Selby did when submitting a particularly rich and diverse nineteenth-century novel to a particularly dreary and reductive Marxist analysis. 'It's all sorted out after death, right, the good end up good and the bad end up bad, you see what I'm saying? We go to a different land when we die.'

Where, Middle Earth with the hobbits? thought Michael. But then, it was no worse consolation than he had from Geoffrey Selby, for example, who had sternly notified him that women in the Third World much younger than Kate were dying every day.

'I tell you what, mate,' Steve said solemnly. 'She's better off where she is. This world, it's just crazy, evil. You walk down the street, right, and look at the people's faces' – Michael should have been used to the sudden hyena laughter by now, but still he jumped as it burst forth again – 'I mean, look at their *faces*, man, it's like *crazy*, it's not *real* . . .'

They were passing through Attleborough, Michael noticed. Come on, Cambridge, he silently begged. A worst-case scenario of a derailment at Ely causing hour-long delays sketched itself swiftly in his mind before he dismissed it. Come on, he told himself. It won't be too long before the little Dalek voice comes through on the speaker saying we're approaching Cambridge, and then it will all be over.

'Listen, you reckon you're the great historian, right,'

Steve said. The transition to belligerence was startlingly swift. 'So you tell me this. All that with Cromwell, and the Roundheads and Cavaliers, how did *that* start? You tell me that.'

'Well, that's not really my period . . .'

'Look, man, you're a *history* teacher, right, you see what I'm saying?'

'Well, I mainly teach English Studies,' Michael said. His palms were damp. Why was he allowing himself to get so het up? 'That's really history as it relates to literature, the general culture of a period . . .'

Steve was wincing. 'Listen, I don't *care* about all that, right, your *English* and your *French* and your Indiana *Jones* . . . I want to know what it was all about, right?'

'It was about the attempt of a king to rule without Parliament, after the manner of Continental absolute monarchies, and to smuggle in an orientation of the national church towards Catholicism under the cloak of ecclesiastical reform,' Michael rapped out. He was using what he recognized as his professorial voice, as he very occasionally did to bring some of his more cloudy-minded students down to earth. Immediately he regretted it. Something came into Steve's eyes.

'You trying to bullshit me?' The odd prawn colour of his powerful neck deepened to red.

'Look, like I said, it's not my period,' Michael said. 'I can only tell you what I've read.'

Steve stared into his eyes for several pounding seconds. Suddenly a cherubic smile was on his face.

'Here's a good story,' he said. 'This is true. This bloke I know, he was driving down this country road, yeah, when this cat runs out and he runs over it. So he stops the car and gets out and he goes to the lay-by at the side of the road where this cat's lying and like twitching all over.' A mime followed, not notable for its brevity. 'So he thinks, shit, I'd better put the poor sod out of its misery, so he gets a wrench out of his boot and starts bashing this cat on the head.' Steve paused to fire off a fusillade of laughs, until Michael began to wonder whether that was the punchline. 'So anyway, then this woman comes running out of this house near the road saying, what you doing to my cat, you've killed my cat, and she's called the police and everything. So the police turn up, and the poor bloke's explaining that he accidentally ran over it and he's just trying to put it out of its misery. And then the copper takes him aside and says, "Have you looked under your car, sir?" So he does and there's this other cat all mangled up. And *that's* the cat he ran over. The one he's just bashed to death was this woman's cat that was an old dozy thing that used to go to sleep in the lay-by and was always twitching in its sleep. And there he was — there he was thinking — bashing it . . .'

This time the laughter went on and on. What they used to call laughing immoderately, thought Michael. He became aware that his buttocks were tightly clenched together. Perhaps, he thought, he could get up to go to the toilet and not come back, go and sit in another carriage . . . But that would mean taking his bag, which would be obvious; and besides, why should he be pushed around by this fruitcake?

'Any teas, coffees, soft drinks?'

A compellingly thin young man in an off-white jacket steered the trolley alongside them. 'Oh, yes, a coffee, white, one sugar, please,' said Michael, relieved at the distraction.

'Do us a favour, mate, buy us a coffee, I'm skint,' Steve said casually.

'Make that two, then,' said Michael, catching an ironical lift of the eyebrow from the thin young man.

'Packet of crisps as well,' Steve said. 'Cheese and onion.'

Michael nodded. Maybe a few comestibles would stop his mouth.

'Oh, haven't you got an ashtray?' said the thin young man. He had a droll campy accent, and he handed Steve the crisps in an arch way that made Michael want to laugh for the first time since the journey began. 'Don't tell me that one's broken as well. Honestly. Tell you what, I'll give you one of these cups, all right? Better than nothing. Better than a poke in the eye with a blunt stick, that's what they say.'

Steve, eating his crisps, gave Michael a glowering look as the trolley passed on down the carriage. 'Sick,' he said. 'Makes me sick. Sick-making. It's sick, man. They're sick.'

'It takes all sorts,' Michael said.

'Liquorice,' said Steve. 'Allsorts.' The blast of laughter was accompanied by cheese-and-onion shrapnel. Then Steve was choking. He made frantic gestures, which Michael at last understood as an instruction to slap him on the back. He leaned forward to do so, remembering at the same time who those broad, curiously hunched shoulders reminded him of. The tennis player, Bjorn Borg. Though Jimmy Connors seemed to have that build too — perhaps it was common with tennis players . . .

'All right, all right, what you trying to do, kill me?' Steve said. He took a deep swallow of coffee. 'Ah, that's the good thing about trains, mate, you get your *tea* and your *coffee* and your *toilet* . . . You drive a car, right, you get none of that. Do you? You've had it. That's right, ennit? You're screwed. You drive?'

'No,' Michael said, gesturing to his glasses. 'Sight's not good enough.' So he supposed, anyhow. Perhaps these Coke-bottle lenses would bring him up to scratch: the fact was he had never had the inclination to learn. People were often astonished. 'You've never *wanted* to drive?' they gaped. Nowadays, of course, you could fob them off with some flannel about the environment, instead of saying you just didn't like cars.

'I can drive,' Steve said. 'They taught me in the army. Teach you a lot of things in the army, man. But driving, that's like *dead*, you know. You don't see the countryside that way. See the countryside, you want to go on a pushbike, I'm telling you, it's just beautiful . . .'

Michael nodded, with a sympathy not entirely synthetic. It was rare to find any English person who could say the word *beautiful* without embarrassment, as Steve did. Why was it? The French could say *beau* and the Germans could say *schön* . . . and beautiful was after all one of the most, well, beautiful words in the English language . . .

Suddenly, like a stunning blow in the face, another train slammed past the window in the opposite direction. Michael, who had been gazing abstractedly out, jumped visibly.

'Boo,' said Steve, laughing. 'Man, you were miles away. What were you thinking about? No, go on, I'm

13

not being nosy. What were you thinking about?'

'Just about this interview, what I'm going to say and so on,' Michael said. 'Need to collect my thoughts.' Anyone else would take the hint and give you a bit of peace, but of course he was dealing with the Train Loony here.

'Say . . .' Steve picked up *Anglian Voices*. 'I wrote this book . . . with a pen. Ha ha ha, no no no. Thirteen quid, shit, man, do you have to buy it yourself?'

'No, you get free copies.'

'What, if you go in a bookshop and say I wrote that, they've got to give you it?'

'Well, no, the publishers send you copies through the post. The postman gives you some funny looks when he hands over the parcels.'

He should have known there could be nothing throwaway, humorous or otherwise, with Steve, who was brick-red and suspicious in a moment. 'Funny looks, what do you mean, what you on about?'

'Well, they're always wrapped in brown paper, with "Books" on the front, so I suppose he thinks they're dirty books, you see,' Michael said, with a mirthless chuckle of his own. Well, that went down like a lead balloon.

Steve was performing one of his impossibly protracted head-shakes. 'No,' he said, 'no, listen. That, right, you're only looking at pictures of these women. It's not like they're real women, just pictures of women, not like you're going out and doing things to these women.' He put a peculiar topspin on the word *women*. 'No harm in it. We've all done it.' Suddenly, like an escapologist who realizes the rope is burning through rather quickly and

14

that the straitjacket and chains are not enhancing his
chances of survival, Steve clawed his pullover over his
head and flung it on the seat beside him. 'Christ,' he
said, 'it's so bloody hot. Jesus. I've never known it this
hot. Aren't you hot? You *must* be, man.'

'It's pretty warm. I think the weather forecast—'

'Listen, the weathermen, right, they don't know
*nothing*. It shouldn't be like this in *May*, for crying out
loud. It's not right, there's something wrong, it
shouldn't be like this.'

'Global warming, I suppose.'

Steve took another cigarette from Michael's packet.
'It's man that's done it,' he said, fiercely morose all of a
sudden, smoking the cigarette between fingers and
thumb in the manner of schoolboys and Hollywood
Gestapo officers. 'All the evil in the world, that comes
from man. I tell you, there's a lot wrong with this world,
mate. Evil. Listen, I was walking round the Cathedral
Close the other day, right, and just looking up – there's
this cathedral all black against the sky, and it was just
*evil*.'

Evil cathedral, thought Michael. Evel Knievel. No,
whatever you do, don't laugh. They could be pretty
spooky places, after all . . . 'They can be pretty spooky
places,' he said.

' "Scooby-dooby-doo, where are you'',' sang Steve,
falsetto. 'Oh, it shouldn't be this hot, it's crazy . . .
How'd you get started in this history business, then? Tell
us about yourself. Come on.'

Michael told: at least, he thought, if he was talking it
meant Steve wasn't. They had passed Ely now, and
Cambridge wasn't that far off . . . Born forty years ago

15

in Cumbria, mother an infant-school teacher, father an accountant. Always fascinated by books, letters, the fragrance of the past, the footworn doorstep of an old cottage, the graffiti on a church pew. Went to York University, did his postgraduate work at Cambridge before going to teach at Broadland. Father died in meantime, mother was retired and living outside Carlisle, mostly in her garden. His dry narration concealed much feeling. For his parents, warmth, love and regret − his father, witty and imaginative, had been the polar opposite of the accountant of popular stereotype, and Michael never visited his mother in her vivacious retirement without a feeling of rage that his father's sudden collapse and death on a French holiday had deprived them of this time together. For himself, a filmy dissatisfaction which was not quite self-disgust, a feeling of wrong turnings taken, of effort unmade, which was all mixed in with Kate's death. Of course, he couldn't have prevented her dying: but the fact remained that most of her short adult life had been spent with him, and that meant that every slight quarrel, every impatient word, every faintest moment of unhappiness between them stood out in his memory like weals on bare skin. Yes, they had been few: but given that short time she'd had, any at all seemed blasphemy.

But he couldn't have known that, as Christine said. Robustly, Christine pointed out that any one of us might die tomorrow, but we couldn't live our lives on that premise, pussyfooting around each other, insuring ourselves against guilt. She was the more robust in that she knew that his guilt applied also to his relationship with her, and if he ever let it show too much, then . . .

All this went on in his mind while his mouth proceeded with a plain précis of his career — which Steve suddenly interrupted with a resounding groan.

'Bloody, bastarding hot,' Steve said. He snatched up his pullover. 'Don't *need* this,' he muttered, and springing out of his seat he pounded down the length of the carriage to the door, his gait a sort of rolling, hunched parody of casualness, and flung the pullover out of the window.

Oh boy. This was something to tell Christine when he got home, if she could believe it.

Steve was already stalking back. The other passengers were examining with great concentration newspapers, knees, anything that wasn't Steve.

'Don't *need* it,' Steve complained, crashing back into his seat and reaching for Michael's cigarettes. 'All these things, man, you don't need them. Tell you what I did the other day, I chucked all my tea and coffee and milk out, just chucked them OUT, man, your body doesn't need all that crap . . . I feel sorry for that dog.'

Michael hadn't seen a dog. He must have looked puzzled, for Steve said with whistling impatience, '*There*.'

Michael saw, in one of the seats behind him, a Yorkshire terrier sitting in a state of whiskery, contented tremble on its owner's lap.

'These animals, right, they should be fending for themselves, they should be running about out there,' said Steve, waving a hand at the wheat-green fen which, flat as Dorothy Gale's Kansas, was unrolling beside them. 'Hunting and breeding, wild and free.'

This man is a prat, thought Michael. The thought was

17

new. Up to now he had been engaged simply in trying to get through the journey with a minimum of trouble, and to put into practice his fairly firm view that it did indeed take all sorts. But really, the man was an irritating prat. Had he really thrown his pullover out of the window? Yes, he had really done that. Good grief.

Of course, did that mean there was no room for eccentricity in the world any more? Michael had remarked before that if you were upper-class and did odd things you were called eccentric: if you were poor and did odd things you were called a nutter. He had certain eccentricities of his own. A habit of coming up with whimsical theories: he had recently noticed, for example, that descriptions of characters in American novels always included their weight. 'He was a square-shouldered man, long-legged, a hundred and eighty pounds . . .' Perhaps it said something about American materialism. And then there was his inability to drive, perhaps that looked like eccentricity. He couldn't be sure, indeed, that he didn't deliberately cultivate a few eccentricities, just as he sometimes adopted the professorial voice as a sort of cloak . . .

Steve slammed his elbow on the table, fist upright.

'Arm-wrestle,' he said.

Oh no. 'Oh, no,' Michael said, sitting back in his seat, folding his arms. 'No, no. Forget it. Not my thing.'

Steve gave a long windy sigh and said, as if to a dull and insistent child, 'I'm not talking about the bloody arm-wrestling Olympic bloody world championship of the *world*, man, come *on*.'

I can't get out of it, Michael thought. Crazy, but I can't get out of it. Resignedly, he put his elbow on the table and grasped Steve's long-nailed tea-coloured hand. Maybe he should just lose, and get it over with: but it occurred to him that Steve was likely to fuss about him not trying, and besides, a bubble of suppressed annoyance had come to the surface of his mind, and it was really that that had made him take up the challenge, that made him want to resist, however ineffectually, this impossible man who had invaded him.

He was much weaker, of course. One glance at Steve gave you an impression of tense, unfocused strength, whereas Michael was a hundred and ninety pounds (as an American novelist would say) of scholarly slackness. His only power was in his brain, and he wasn't too sure about that nowadays. But he found himself gritting his teeth and pushing as if this were a challenge that actually had some point to it.

Steve's eyes glared into his. His grin, as in a child's drawing, seemed to reveal every single tooth in his head.

Michael imagined Christine watching him. The old Adam of macho confrontation coming out, she would say. Justly too. That was what was so irritating about this nuisance of a man, the way he forced you into positions you never wanted to take up.

'Playing with you, mate,' Steve said, and pushed Michael's hand down to the tabletop as easily as turning the page of a newspaper.

'Well, I told you,' Michael said, feeling the blood flow painfully back into his squeezed fingers. He had, without knowing how or why, a stung, humiliated feeling like that of a child which has mutinously pitted its strength against an adult's. I'm letting this meathead get to me, he thought.

'You want to look after yourself, sunshine, that's what you want to do, lift a few weights, get on a bike now and then.'

'I do ride a bike.' Look, Michael, just don't answer him and he'll be quiet.

'Yeah, what's that, racer?'

'No, just an ordinary bike.'

'Ah, if it's not a racer, it's *nothing*, man, it's not a bike at all. Is it?'

Michael ignored that one. He had just noticed something; the villages glimpsed through the window were beginning to look less like farming communities and more like the homes of politicians and TV personalities – more rustic in other words – so Cambridge couldn't be far off.

'Real bikes, racers, man, the *only* bikes. Listen, right, somebody nicked my bike the other week, can you believe that? In the middle of the day, man. That's how it's going. There's no discipline any more, there's no respect. Christ, if Churchill was around, man, he'd turn in his grave, the things you see these kids doing. Right, they sniff glue or some other crap, right, they don't know what they're doing, before you know it some homo's picked 'em up, where are you then? And then you get these girls, they're tarting theirselves up, they're just asking for trouble, do you see what I'm saying? *Naaaaah*' – the negative was a racing-car screech, and Michael saw someone further up the carriage hunch himself down in his seat in smug thankfulness that *he* hadn't got the Train Loony, lucky swine – 'nah, mate, keep yourself clean, that's my motto. Dirty water,' Steve darkly said, with a fastidious

20

gesture, 'dirty water, dirty water.'

Michael, who was nodding like a regional TV interviewer in an establishing shot, found his wrist grabbed. After a moment's alarm he realized that Steve was trying to see his watch.

'Is that waterproof?'

'Er – I don't think so.'

'Good job you're not a duck then, ennit?' Steven made a kazoo of his fingers. 'Wak wak! Time for a piss.'

He was off at a fast lope, in search of the toilet.

For several seconds the sheer bliss of finding himself alone, like the cessation of toothache, occupied Michael completely. Then there was a hideous hiss and crackle, and a little voice, relayed with all the clarity of one of Edison's least successful phonograph experiments, announced, 'Leddies and gentlebub, we shall shortly be arriving in Kinbridge, where this trin terbinates. Please ensewer you have all your beloggings with you when you live the trin.'

Michael had scooped his beloggings up in a trice. With a bit of luck, he could be on to the platform and away before his travelling companion was back from the toilet. Impatiently he stood by the carriage door while the train made an interminable, clanking, Murder-on-the-Orient-Express fuss about drawing into the station. Steve was right in one regard: it was hot for May. Michael was sweating in his jacket and tie. Why on earth had he worn a jacket and tie to go on the radio? It was like those early BBC wireless announcers who wore evening dress. They used to have ventriloquists on the radio too. Suzanne didn't believe him when he told her that. Actually that was a little before his time, but he had a habit, he didn't know why, of making himself seem slightly older than he was. Defensive maybe.

He stepped down on to the platform, almost buoyant now. Awful journey, but never mind. An announcer's voice was booming around the station, in the same costive tones as the one on the train. Why did they all talk like that? *Only applicants with severe adenoidal conditions need apply . . .* He glanced at his unwaterproof watch. Twenty-five minutes before he was due at the radio station. Time for a coffee, maybe, and a little think about what he was going to say.

He jostled past rucksacked students with terminal haircuts, realizing he was behaving like just that sort of busy-busy person he deplored. The sort who ran past you on the Tube escalators, my-gosh-my-life-is-*so*-important-and-frenetic. A prowl of taxis waited outside the station. Radio Cam, somewhere in the city centre presumably . . .

He gave a spluttering cough as the thump hit him right between the shoulder blades. Before he could turn round Steve had skipped in front of him and was laughing in his face.

'Never said ta-ta, mate! Thought you'd done a runner on me. Thought you'd been took up in an alien spacecraft, beam me up Scotty, psssheew.'

Michael equipped himself with the last smile he had left. 'Look,' he said, 'I'm in a hurry.'

'No, I won't keep you, mate, when you got to go, you got to go. Just do us a favour, give us a fag.'

'Here,' Michael fumbled, 'take them — take the packet.' He was supposed to be giving up anyway.

'Ah, cheers, you're brilliant.' Steve popped one in his

mouth, then stood snapping his fingers. '*Light*, mate,' he said at Michael's frown. 'Jesus, I don't believe this guy,' he humorously appealed to the world at large, 'he's just like incredible—'

'Here you go.' The cigarette was lit: that was it. He was damned if he was going to surrender Kate's lighter. 'Well, nice meeting you – I really must dash.'

Steve took hold of Michael's lapel. 'Listen,' he said, cigarette clamped between his teeth, lips moving round it, 'don't take any rubber fivers, all right? You take care.'

'I will. You too.' Michael reached up to loosen his collar, hoping the movement might subtly dislodge Steve's fingers.

The fingers tightened. 'And listen, good luck on the radio, right? Who is it, Jimmy Savile?'

'Oh, I – somebody local, I should—' Michael started to say, but Steve's laughter was already trumpeting out.

'Nice one.' Steve gave him a hearty slap on the shoulder and, thank God, turned and walked away.

As he made for a taxi Michael watched out of the corner of his eye, just in case Steve should come pouncing back with some idea of cadging a lift with him; but Steve's figure, with its dogged Foghorn Leghorn gait, went plunging on down the street, and was lost in the crowd even before it was lost in Michael's myopia.

Before the journey back, he thought as he climbed into the taxi, I must remember to buy the *Eastern Daily Press* and then hide behind it as soon as I'm on the train. Never mind if it's antisocial. Sanity's more important.

'Radio Cam, please.'

Cambridge, a university and a town fighting each

other for the same inadequate ration of space, with tourists exacerbating the conflict like refugees, was dusty and abrasive in the glaring sunshine. Cyclists wove and wobbled in the taxi's slipstream, unseasonable scarves flapping. A street theatre group did their best to make urban life even more uncomfortable. A don mouthed to a television camera in front of a venerable gateway covered in scaffolding. Michael thought of the featureless functional spaces of Broadland University more kindly than he was wont.

'Bloody Cambridge,' the taxi driver said. 'Bloody hole.'

Not another one, thought Michael. But the taxi driver contented himself with adding, 'I'm from Newmarket, myself,' and then, after a pause, 'Bloody hole as well.'

He wouldn't have time for that coffee after all, he decided as they drew up as near to the radio station as it was possible for a vehicle to get − only two streets away, not bad for Cambridge. He paid the driver and was about to make a neck-or-nothing dash through the traffic when a voice yelled at him, loud and shrill above the engine hubbub.

'Oi! Oi, there!'

Ten yards along the kerb a woman with wild white hair was waving a stick and gesticulating. The roar of a bus reduced her shout to something like 'Can of pork!'

My God, thought Michael, they're everywhere. He had just darted into a gap in the traffic when his mind doubled back. The stick − it was a *white* stick . . . Not *Can of pork* but *Can I walk?*

He dodged back the way he had come, to furious squeals of motor horns. One glinting bumper actually brushed his trouserleg before he made it to the kerb where the woman still stood with her white stick outstretched like a fencing foil.

'Hello, sorry about that, can I help?' he panted.

'Oh, are you there? I thought I heard a car door.' The woman extended her arm and Michael took it. 'We'll be a while, duck,' she said. 'They won't stop, not on this road.'

He was amazed, then angry, at how many cars flashed blithely past. 'Bloody cars,' he muttered. 'Bloody drivers.'

'Well, you can get run down by a horse,' the blind woman said temperately.

They got across at last, and with a cheerful 'Ta, duck' the woman went on her way. Michael followed the wing of a long, blank brick building until he came to a pair of glass doors bearing the words *Radio Cam* and a logo apparently representing a crown with a tennis ball on top. In the reception area he was invited to sit in the sort of low chair from which dignified rising is an impossibility, and a pleasant woman in flapping Scholls brought him a plastic cup of coffee. 'I'll take you in to Jane in a moment,' she said, gliding orthopaedically away. Michael, sipping, had just worked out that the logo was a stylized representation of the sun rising above King's College when he was summoned.

### 3

'Shortly I'll be talking to Dr Michael Greenwood, Lecturer in English Studies at Broadland University, whose new book *Anglian Voices* offers some remarkable

25

insights into the lives of ordinary men and women of our region down the centuries. That's coming up after the news: first this from Stevie Wonder.' The DJ raised her eyebrows in greeting to Michael as he tiptoed into the studio and then as the record began extended a hand across the baize table.

'Michael. Thanks for coming. Haven't quite finished the book. I was reading it on the train this morning.' She was young, small-boned, fair and brisk: her voice, fascinatingly, became less demotic and more posh when she was off air.

'That must have been nice,' he said. 'Reading on the train, I mean.'

'Bad journey?'

'You could say that.'

'I know, British Rail, it's hell, isn't it? Well, as I say, I've had a good stab at the book. Love the letters these rioting chaps sent to the parsons and squires and so forth, when was it, 1830? Surprising they could read and write in those days.'

'Probably something like one in three. A lot more people could read than write, which seems strange to us.'

'OK, perhaps we could begin by talking about that, literacy and so on, why it is that the history of the ordinary folk, as it were, is so scarce, and then we can move on to specific topics in your book. I'll just do the news, and then go on to introduce you.'

He settled himself in front of the big fluffy orange gonk of a microphone. He had been on radio before, pontificating about cuts in higher education a few years ago. How untechnological it all was, really: a thickly carpeted room, compact-disc players, microphones, a few wires, a clock on the wall. He was a little nervous, but fortunately that fraught, stifled feeling that his unwanted travelling companion had produced in him was subsiding at last; and once the interviewer began, he simply went into overdrive, as he did when delivering a lecture.

'. . . What I find particularly interesting, Michael, is the fact that East Anglia, which people, unfairly perhaps, think of as a backwater, was really at the cutting edge, as it were, of a lot of historical developments . . .'

'It's chiefly the Industrial Revolution that made us a backwater – temporarily, of course. And it's important to remember that the Industrial Revolution was at least partly pushed forward by another revolution, what's been called the Agricultural Revolution, of which Norfolk in particular, where I live, was the centre . . .'

It's important to remember . . . He could remember every significant date in the life of Charles James Fox, but with everyday things he was hopeless. He had definitely left the house this morning telling himself that there was something he must remember, but what it was he couldn't for the life of him think.

'. . . The stories of Mary Mann, practically unknown in her lifetime, are a real eye-opener,' he said. 'Reading those you're soon disabused of any idyllic illusions about country life in the last century . . .'

A real eye-opener. A vision of a disdainful Geoffrey Selby hovered over his shoulder. Peddling your crypto-nostalgic picturebooks, afraid of committing yourself to serious scholarship, afraid of *committing* yourself . . . Mind you, Suzanne said the Selby kids were right little snot-noses. Didn't prove anything, but it was comforting.

Suzanne, that was it – she had asked him to say hello to her on the radio. 'But you'll be at school when it's on,' he'd pointed out. 'I can get somebody to tape it for me,' she'd said. 'Oh, go on, Dad. And say hello to my friend Steph as well.' He had agreed, with a show of reluctance: but in fact he was obscurely flattered. Perhaps he wasn't such an embarrassing old fart of a father after all. Not that she had ever *said* he was an embarrassing old fart, but sometimes he did wonder . . . Geoffrey Selby, for example, took his children to rock concerts. And a right lemon he must look, Michael thought. Or was he getting a bit paranoid about Geoffrey Selby . . . ?

'Well, if you're anything like me, you'll want to hear more of these *Anglian Voices*, and you can in Michael Greenwood's book,' the DJ concluded. 'It's published by Morris-Trevor, priced twelve ninety-nine, and beautifully illustrated. Michael, thanks for coming in to talk to us.'

'It's been a pleasure,' Michael said. 'And can I just keep a promise and say hello to my daughter Suzanne, and her friend Steph.' The name *Steph* gave him a little impish idea: it seemed to flash above his head like a light bulb in a cartoon. 'And a special hello to Steve, my travelling companion on the train here – thanks, Steve, for making the journey sheer purgatory.'

The DJ laughed as she faded-in a record. 'How old's Suzanne?'

'Nearly twelve. Two days to go. That reminds me, I must look for a birthday present for her. There's a singer she likes called Seal, is that right? I don't suppose he's got a new album out or anything?'

'No, not that I know of. Is she into posters?'

'That's an idea. I'll have a look round. Thanks a lot.'

'OK, Michael. Thanks for coming. Have a nice trip home.'

He had a seminar to take at half past three: there was time for a mooch round Cambridge. He found a poster of Seal for Suzanne, added on his own initiative a new pair of headphones and, high-risk this, a pair of sunglasses of the sort that he *thought* she liked. The trainers she wanted – he called them, to her fury, plimsolls – she could choose herself: he couldn't even begin to understand the complexities of that fashion. Passing a roadside flower stall he thought of Christine and bought a bunch of carnations. Was this, he wondered, a concentrated form of the generalized sense of guilt that accompanied him as constantly as his myopia? On the train he had been thinking around that question of keeping faith with the dead: but there was after all the opposite side, the question of keeping faith with the living. A dead, much-missed wife was no excuse for taking Christine for granted, even if their relationship was that cautious, no-strings matter which she insisted on . . . Or was he being too analytical? Kate had once said jokingly that he had all the spontaneity of the Edinburgh Military Tattoo . . . Well, anyhow, the flowers were beautiful, and Christine loved flowers.

He ate chilli and baked potato in a student-haunted café to the sound of listless koto music. A woman in a flowered hat, dirndl skirt and red wellingtons stomped past the open door, loudly announcing, 'There's a funny

smell around here and it's NOT ME.' He participated in
the general cringe, but felt sad. Were there more of the
oddities and outcasts around than ever before? Or was it
simply that more people were driven out by society and
left to flounder on the margins? It was impossible to
think about it without tripping over your own hypocrisy.
Sympathetic tolerance of weirdos was a fragile thing: it
tended to break as soon as you had to sit next to one on a
train or the bus. It had been a bit mean of him to make
that crack about the dreadful Steve, but he had wound
him up so much . . . Perhaps that was how it began: you
got so wound up by other people that you ended up
deciding to annoy them first, throwing your clothes out
of the window, wearing red wellingtons . . .

He forgot, inevitably, to buy a newspaper to hide
behind on the journey home, but his only companion in
the carriage was a tweedy old man who was entirely
silent except for some appreciative suckings on his pipe.
Michael watched the countryside, thought of *Anglian
Voices*, thought of the articles he had written for
*Nineteenth Century Review* and *Journal of Romantic
Studies* — serious stuff, the stuff to make a name with, if
only it could be given the proper bulk. He thought of
William Cobbett, his hero, the great nineteenth-century
Radical writer and agitator, and the definitive biography
that was waiting to be written. *William Cobbett and the
Revolt of the Field*, by Michael Greenwood . . . By God,
he was going to do it. Sitting in that radio studio he had
felt — though *Anglian Voices* was worthwhile — that he
was only scratching the surface. He wasn't challenging
himself. Well, that was going to change. His life was
going to be different from today onwards.

*4*

The capital of East Anglia, though a large cathedral city of long history and for many years one of the most important towns in England, had had to wait until the nineteen sixties for a university, and then it had been placed right on the outskirts, practically in the Norfolk meadows. The self-contained campus environment had been the ideal at the time of its conception. By the time people had begun to think again, and to reason that a navel-gazing purdah was not the healthiest of attitudes for an educational establishment, the thousands of tons of concrete and breeze block had already gone up, and the University of Broadland was a *fait accompli*.

Michael had mixed feelings about it. Having caught a bus from the station straight to the university, he watched with a certain affection as the flat campus roofs – magnificently porous to the lightest shower – came into view. In the bright sunshine, you could see the rationale behind the place. An ultra-modern temple of academe, a machine for learning. Unfortunately Norfolk was not California, and in November – or even an average April – Broadland University was a Gulag with books, a Lubyanka with lectures.

'Michael, you old bastard,' a voice called as Michael crossed the main campus square which was called, in the university's solemn toytown nomenclature, The Square.

'Hullo, Peter. How's life?'

'Don't ask. Always the same near finals. Had one of my advisees rabbiting on at me for an hour this morning, saying he couldn't sit his exams because he'd split up with his girlfriend and he couldn't be expected to write a cogent essay on the Angevin inheritance when he was under emotional stress. Little turd'll be shagging somebody else before the week's out, that's what gets me.'

'Not that you're envious.'

'Just a deep shade of green, that's all. The buggers'll do anything rather than open a book, you know that? One smarmy little tyke told me he hadn't read up on his subject because reading was bibliocentric and oppressed the illiterate. What's he bloody taking a history degree for, then? Well, obviously, to fill in three years before he sheds his ideals and goes into his daddy's business, but you know what I mean.'

'I've never known anyone who hates his students quite as much as you do, Peter.'

'I don't hate them,' Peter Worrall said mildly. 'I just want to watch them being disembowelled over a slow fire.'

They climbed the steps of the English Studies building, Michael adjusting to Peter Worrall's pace — a broad-beamed amble that from behind gave him the look of a denimed tractor.

'Want to hear some gossip?' Peter said. 'It'll depress you, mind.'

'Everything you say depresses me.'

'Good man. This is a leak from the Dean's office. Horse's-mouth stuff. Memo went out to all arts and humanities faculties from the VC, saying there was a funding crisis and drastic action must be taken.'

'There's always a funding crisis,' Michael said.

'This is serious. What does he bloody look like?' Peter Worrall interrupted himself to gaze at a gaunt young

Anglo-Saxon in a slouch hat and dreadlocks which looked as if they would come off with the hat. 'No, this time it's serious. Not just an appointments freeze. They're talking about fifteen, twenty per cent cuts in staffing levels.'

Michael stared. 'How are they going to manage that?'

Peter's strawy eyebrows danced a jig. 'Somebody will have to take the Black Spot. Early retirements. Or they'll push up the student—staff ratio so much that people will just pack it in.'

'What do the AUT say?'

'They don't know, officially. Like I say, it's a leak. But there's quite a few people trying not to panic. Bit like that film *Alien* really, everybody wondering if they're going to get chomped next. Of course, the temporaries know they're not going to get tenure now, so they're looking round at some of the old farts who give lectures to empty theatres and wondering at the unfairness of it all. There's Muriel Weeks thinking she'll get the gentle push because she had a heart attack a couple of years ago. There's Geoffrey Selby thinking it'll be him because the cuts are a symptom of the global meltdown of capitalism and the running dogs of the dying establishment are bound to turn on the prophets of their downfall. A lot of frightened people, my friend.'

'Nothing like a bit of paranoia to start the week,' Michael said, more lightly than he felt.

'Well, you know what they say. Paranoia is when you think they're out to get you. Sanity is when you *know* they are.' Widening his eyes in mock horror, Peter trundled off.

Michael's seminar was on the agricultural riots of the

early nineteenth century. His students, he found to his surprise, were genuinely interested. It occurred to him that the plight of the long-dead farm labourers, confronting a world where their labour and old-fashioned skills were scarcely wanted, was not so very far off from them. For now they could cut those artful holes in the elbows of their cardigans and espouse poverty-chic: but they must know that the real thing lay in wait for some of them. History and English degrees nowadays were about as useful as the hand flail in the days of the steam thresher. The nerveless casualness and self-confidence that made students so frequently unattractive were probably defensive, he thought.

Fear and uncertainty. He was responsive to it because of his own submerged feeling of unease, called up by Peter Worrall's words. Of course, Peter was a confirmed gossip addict, though an unmalicious one. But he had hit a nerve. No one in the arts faculties, and probably the science ones too, felt safe. Engrossed in your studious world, you could forget that your security was a matter of precarious balance, liable to be overturned all at once.

'Heard you on the radio this morning,' one of his students shyly said to him as the seminar was breaking up.

'Oh, dear, did you? What did I sound like?'

'Well . . .' The young man fingered his earring. 'You could hear your accent more on the air, funnily enough.'

'What accent?' Michael said, indignation only partly feigned. He had gone through a stage, during his postgraduate research at Cambridge, of talking broad Cumbrian, saying 'ganning herm' and 'please thesel', chiefly as a reaction against the laminated accents that surrounded him. Now he just talked naturally, but even that — to a student body which he sometimes suspected to be simply the whole post-pubescent population of Kent, transported *en masse* — seemed strikingly quaint.

'Well' — the student grinned — 'touch of the Melvyn Bragg about it.'

'Christ,' Michael said.

'You were quite good though. Music was bloody awful, mind you.'

'Oh! Well, I don't understand these skiffle groups and jitterbugging and what have you,' he said, doing his old-fogey bit. That had started as a joke: now he found himself falling into it unconsciously. The trouble was, the students seemed to believe it.

His office was at the end of a long breeze-block corridor. The whole building was made up of corridors like these, feebly lit by fluorescent panels that gave off a glow like rotting matter. It was like being inside a termites' nest. He intended just popping in and picking up some essays for marking tonight: but when he opened the door he stopped dead.

'Oh, hell,' he said.

His wastepaper basket was overturned and its contents were strewn all over the carpet. He bent and picked up a torn plastic bag which, he seemed to remember, had contained the remains of a half-eaten sandwich.

'Michael.'

5

He turned to see Geoffrey Selby regarding him from the doorway. Selby had the office next door to his, an outstandingly unhappy arrangement.

'Oh, hullo, Geoffrey. Look, I'm afraid Nono's been in here again.' He gestured at the mess, trying not to look tetchy as he did so.

'Yes, I should think so,' Geoffrey Selby said. Nono was Selby's dog, a fat bull terrier named after an Italian Marxist composer. He came frequently to the campus with his master (or non-hegemonic trans-species companion, as Geoffrey would say) and waddled about the faculty building doing his own thing. As he had found a way of turning door handles, this included investigating Michael's office.

The trouble was, Michael couldn't complain. Not without laying himself open to accusations of being a bourgeois possessionist, laying an imperialistic claim to personal space, fussing about a dog overturning his bin when people in the Third World were dying of malnutrition. (Geoffrey Selby utilized the Third World as a sort of personal Mrs Grundy, to back him up in all his opinions.) And besides that, Michael did tend to leave his door unlocked, not only because he had no idea where the key was and there was nothing in the office but a desk and a telephone and a jar full of paperclips, but because, he supposed, of a hangover from his own sixties youth, which made him feel that a university shouldn't be like a jail. So all in all, after a glance at Geoffrey's expressionless face, he decided to let it go, and began shovelling the rubbish back in the bin.

'So,' Geoffrey said, watching him, 'how did the little chat on the radio go?'

'Oh, pretty well, thanks. Nice woman doing the interview, really done her research.'

'Mmm,' Geoffrey said. Meaning, Michael thought, that a glorified picturebook hardly required much research . . . Or was he getting paranoid again?

'Might get over to Cambridge myself at the weekend,' Geoffrey said. 'Take a look round the second-hand bookshops.'

'There's a thing about second-hand bookshops,' Michael said, remembering a little theory that had come to him on the train back. 'Have you noticed that any collection of second-hand books, no matter what size, even just a single shelf in a charity shop, will always contain at least one copy of *Jaws* and one copy of *The Moon's A Balloon* by David Niven?'

'The book as mass, culturally conditioning artefact,' Geoffrey said. 'Printed placebos to keep the people's minds off their miserable condition. The giant shark lurking in the waters below, externalizing the bourgeoisie's fear of proletarian uprising. Reminiscences of an English actor in Hollywood, decayed descendant of triumphal Victorian accounts of the rape of Africa — an imperialist people's last available form of colonialism.'

It was always difficult, until you met him again and had it confirmed, to believe that Geoffrey Selby really talked like this. But obviously Geoffrey was sermonizing on autopilot and had something else on his mind, for instead of pursuing his theme he cleared his throat and said, 'Yes, might as well drive over to Cambridge this weekend. Doesn't look as if I'll be seeing Jake and Roz.'

Michael paused. 'Problems?'

Jake and Roz were the children of Geoffrey's marriage, terminated in divorce (acrimonious, Michael had heard) a year ago. Geoffrey, stroking the curly, prematurely silvered beard which along with the matching hair gave him the look of a morose Pan, said, 'I'm not going to give you any nuclear-family, mummies-and-daddies shit, Michael. As far as I'm concerned the family unit is the prototype for the broader repressive structures of society. But I've bonded with those kids, I love them as autonomous individuals, and that means I'd like to be with them as much as possible.'

'Isn't Liz giving you access?'

'By law she has to. But hey, to hell with the law, that's just an enabling mechanism for the perpetuation of an exploitative system. What I'm saying is, she's being obstructive. It's like she wants to create this new happy-family unit, except with me out of it.'

Michael felt both touched and confused that Geoffrey should confide in him like this, when there was such a fund of intense dislike between them. Perhaps, he thought, Geoffrey just couldn't conceive of anyone not being profoundly interested in every detail of his personal life. Or perhaps he was really unhappy.

'Maybe she's not really aware of doing that. Maybe it's just that being with the kids all the time, she—'

'Oh, she knows what she's doing all right,' Geoffrey said. 'Of course, the marriage was a mistake. I mean embracing that institution was a mistake.' Michael did a mental double take at the idea of Geoffrey Selby admitting to a mistake: but then Geoffrey went on, 'Of course, it was the pressure of social convention that was responsible for that. Indoctrination by the politics of monogamy. Just been taking a seminar on Renaissance poetry, you know. There it all is, in Sidney, Wyatt, Spenser – that poisonous idea, the neo-Platonic myth of exclusive romantic love, the heaven on earth in the lover's arms. The root of all our troubles, emotionally speaking. Thank God I've seen through it.'

'Is it any good talking to your solicitor about it – I mean access to the kids and all that? You should be able to see them.'

'That's only imposing an authoritarian matrix on a situation already distorted by oligarchic values. Anyway, Michael,' Geoffrey said aggressively, 'I don't *own* those kids, you know. Some of us want to do away with that possessive patriarchy.'

'OK.' Michael shrugged. Why do I always back down like this, he thought, instead of telling him what a little toerag he is. I really ought to read up on assertiveness.

'I know it's different for you. I mean, I can understand you feeling possessive of Suzanne under the circumstances.' Geoffrey spoke with a sort of grudging contrition. About his attitude to Michael's being a widower there was always a certain vague resentment. It was as if by having a dead wife Michael had somehow copped out.

Disliking the subject, Michael said, 'You've heard these rumours about the cuts?'

'Nothing very surprising about it,' Geoffrey said loftily. 'The UGC have stopped even pretending to be anything but the tools of crypto-fascists. The only good thing that might come out of it is the clearing away of some dead wood. In terms of political correctness, some of the teaching by older members of faculty is an outrage. And it's to be hoped that the powers that be will

39

take a look at such things as publishing records, and unhealthy tutor—student relationships.'

Geoffrey made his characteristically abrupt, gliding, Ghost-of-Jacob-Marley exit, leaving Michael swearing under his breath. He was still swearing as he made his way across The Square, past The Pub, round the Student Union building and across the service road to the car park (which, curiously, was not called The Car Park) where Christine's van was waiting.

She was sitting with a brick-sized textbook propped open against the steering wheel, and chewing an apple. It occurred to him, still inwardly cussing as he was, that one of the things he loved about Christine's face was that it had no malice in it. It could express — as he well knew — volcanic fury, but never spite, thank God. Already the sight of her was doing its healing work on him: the elegant dark head, the large sceptical eyes, the pale skin and lithe frame were like messages from a better world.

'Hello, I caught the Big Broadcast,' she said. 'I taped it for Suzanne. Reception wasn't very good though. Who's Steve?'

'What?'

'This fellah you made a joke about on the radio.'

'Oh, him. Just some nutty bloke I met on the train, a real pain. Got you these.' He carefully extracted the carnations from his bag.

'Flowers, yet! What have you done to be sorry for, I wonder? Ooh, hurt look. No, they're gorgeous, thanks, lovey.' She took a sheet of xeroxed paper from her book. 'Seen this?'

It was a questionnaire, inviting students to record in

confidence any sexual harassment they had suffered from tutors.

'We've all got one,' Christine said. 'Really cracking down on it apparently. Some toad in Environmental Studies kept trying it on once too often.'

'So that's why Geoffrey Selby was dropping hints,' Michael said. He gazed at the blocks of student residences overlooking the car park, glassy pyramids that might have come from the cheese nightmare of a Babylonian temple-builder. Plastic bags containing cartons of milk hung forlornly from the windows. 'The old bastard.'

'I can always tell when you've been talking to him. The tips of your ears go red. What, because we're seeing each other that makes you a harasser in his eyes, does it?'

'I suppose it might look that way.'

'Oh, well, it *isn't* that, so it doesn't matter. Does it?'

'It shouldn't . . . It's just that I think Selby's got it in for me sometimes.'

'Now you're sounding paranoid. Let's get away from the old multistorey brain park, it has that effect on you after a while.' She started the engine. 'Anybody tries to harass me, they get a judo chop in the windpipe.'

A party of students in fancy dress crossed the service road in front of the van: Michael remembered that it was Rag Week. 'What are they up to?'

'Abseiling down from the Steve Biko Room, so I've heard. I'm supposed to be going on a sponsored pub-crawl with the Mature Students Society this week. I don't fancy it. They're such a bunch of pissheads when they get together, I shall end up wrecked.'

'I think I was supposed to be doing something for Rag Week. My Victorian Prophets group put my name down for some charity do, I seem to remember . . . Christine, do I remind you of Melvyn Bragg?'

'You should be so lucky,' she said. 'Home, James?'

The Norfolk city bore its burden of traffic better than Cambridge, but in the rush hour it was still a long business getting from the university to Michael's home close to the centre. As they waited in a long tailback on the ring road, with on their right a deep bowl of allotment land and playing fields rising to the distant spire of the cathedral, puncturing the skyline just as it did in the innumerable eighteenth-century watercolours of this view, Michael said, 'I ought to learn to drive really, shouldn't I?'

Christine looked at him in surprise. 'With your eyesight?'

'Maybe with the glasses I'd be fit.'

'But you don't like cars.'

'Well, no. But it would make things easier. I could take Suzanne to places. You wouldn't have to be always driving. And then it's not like public transport. A car cuts you off from people . . . Which is one of the things I don't like about it, at the same time as I can see its attraction.'

'Like a lot of isolated people going about in their little metal bubbles, I know what you mean. That's why Thatcher hated the railways. They're social, but she denied there was any such thing as society. Just complete fragmentation instead. A collection of strangers, all locked in their own cars and houses.'

'And families.'

'And families,' Christine echoed — scornful as
Geoffrey Selby, but with more reason. She did not often
talk about her marriage, which had ended five years ago,
but Michael had learned enough about it to know it had
put her off nest-building for life.

It was hard looking at her now to picture her as a
doormat: but he remembered her saying to him, 'Never
underestimate the power of a total bastard to destroy
your confidence'. It had been low to begin with, from a
childhood spent with a mother who said, 'Don't bother
your father when he's picking his horses', and a father
who had once snatched an Enid Blyton book from her
hands and putting his sneering face close to hers said,
'Books, books — you're *thick* really, Christine, don't
pretend!' Glad enough to escape into marriage after
leaving school, where extreme shyness had disabled her,
she presently found that her husband concealed her
father's swinish qualities behind misunderstood little-
boy eyes and a solicitous manner. The things he was
most solicitous about were the prompt appearance of his
dinner and the meticulous pressing of the workshirts he
wore in his succession of conspicuously manly jobs. He
had played the card of look-how-hard-I-work-and-it's-
all-for-you for all it was worth: it was when they were
living in Great Yarmouth, he with a job on the oil rigs,
that the worm had begun to turn. Christine found herself
in her thirties with a house containing every variety of
electrical appliance and a head full of little beyond the
price of smoked ham. Her husband saw, or chose to see,
her tentative venture into evening classes as rejection of
him; but Christine found she enjoyed education too
much to go along with his guilt games any longer, and

the remainder of their marriage was a destructive collision between her growing determination and his hardening stubbornness. Michael suspected the confrontation had become physical, though she never said as much. Since the divorce sheer hard graft had seen her through to the point where, based in her own flat, she could apply for and get a university place as a mature student reading politics: she still combined study with a part-time catering job at the Castle Museum and with voluntary work for a conservation group at weekends — hence the van with its odour of soil and sap and its rattling cargo of spades and trowels.

Her life was full and her experience of relationships was unhappy: it was no wonder that her friendship with Michael, begun at a university party, had progressed to something more serious only with the utmost slowness and circumspection, with a further obstacle in Michael's perplexity over the question of faithfulness to Kate's memory. Then, of course, there was the matter of student–tutor romances. Not that Michael taught Christine or ever would, she studying in a different faculty: but the image of the randy lecturer knocking off his students, though wholly invented by frustrated campus novelists, had a powerful hold on the academic imagination. The idea of anyone presuming to 'knock off' Christine Reed, who guarded her hard-won independence with feisty strength, amused Michael, but he was annoyed too. Geoffrey Selby must have known that when he inserted his sly needle of innuendo.

Theoretically, all this ought to have made their relationship a minefield. In practice, it worked. A crucial help was Suzanne, whose memories of her mother were

loyal if faint, but who straightforwardly accepted
Christine as a factor in her father's life. In fact she
admired everything about Christine, from her short,
sharp haircut to her collection of James Brown records.
Michael knew for certain there would be no jealousy
problems from the day when Suzanne quietly besought
Christine to 'get Dad not to wear such antwacky
clothes'.

'Got any food in, and am I invited?' Christine said as
they turned in to Sheeps Hill Road.

'Yes and yes. Well, burgers and chips, anyway.'

'Ooh, lovely. Had some awful pious bean stew in the
refectory today. All the Christians from Development
Studies were going, "Mmm, this is rilly gu-uuurd." '

Michael laughed. Christine loved college, but she saw
her fellow students with a very beady eye.

Sheeps Hill Road rose leafily up its steep slope. It was
a few minutes' walk from the city centre but as quiet as a
suburb except when a student party broke out in one of
the tall, grey-brick Victorian houses. In front of
Michael's house, two storeys and garret with crumbling
square-bayed windows, a peculiar car was standing in
the weed-grown drive.

'Looks like Fred's home,' Christine said. 'God knows
how he keeps that car on the road.' For several years
Michael had been letting the garret floor as student digs,
and the current tenant was a phlegmatic young West
Countryman called Fred who drove and cherished a car
from the days when cars had chassis shaped like ice
lollies and headlights like Dame Edna Everage's glasses.
This clapped-out curiosity was called a Ford Zodiac and
it was lime green.

The house resounded with a battle of amplified music. From Suzanne's bedroom came a stealthy pounding that was, Michael presumed, either Seal or similar. From Fred's top-floor bedsit — which had a kitchen so small that he called it a kitchenettette — flowed a surge of amorphous sound: Philip Glass or Steve Reich or another of the minimalist composers that Fred loved. Michael didn't dislike some of this music, but it did seem to him rather like dining off a whole plate of peas.

'Dad?'

Suzanne, with the physique of the young Bambi, somehow managed to descend from her room with all the galumphing noise of Oliver Hardy falling downstairs.

'How long will tea be, Dad? Only we've got a rehearsal for the school play at half past six. And Steph's here, can she stay for tea? And the school play's on Wednesday, you are coming, you won't forget, will you?'

'Hello, Dad, how are you? I'm very well thank you, what about yourself?' Michael said.

'All right, clever-clogs,' Suzanne said. 'Only you will come to see the school play on Wednesday, won't you?'

'When do I ever forget things?'

Suzanne did a big no-comment number and turned to Christine. 'You'll make sure he remembers, won't you, Christine?'

'Well, I'm coming. I should think I'll drag him along.'

'Great.' Suzanne attacked the stairs, then thundered back. 'Oh, how did the radio go? Did you remember—'

'Hello to Suzanne and Steph, yes, amazingly enough I did.'

'I taped it,' Christine said. 'I'll bring it round tomorrow.'

'What music did they play?'

'Oh, it was good stuff,' Michael said, 'you know, the Shadows, Freddie and the Dreamers . . .'

'Oh, *Dad*,' Suzanne said, exiting with a retching sound.

'Shout Fred and ask him if he wants to eat with us,' Michael called after her.

'How do you keep your sanity?' Christine said as the house vibrated around them.

'I think I've developed a sort of selective deafness,' said Michael, delving in the freezer. He did not say that there had been a time, just after Kate's death, when the terrible silence of the house had seemed the concentrated essence of grief. In noise there was life and hope.

Fred joined them for the meal, drifting downstairs with his finger in a theoretical physics textbook of terrifying incomprehensibility. Not for the first time Michael was filled with awe at what Fred studied and, presumably, understood: it deepened his suspicion that the members of the science faculties with whom he rubbed shoulders in the staff refectory were inhabiting such remote intellectual regions that they must look on the arts bods as so many children. Most baffling of all, you associated brains with urban weediness, and Fred, with his big-boned height, curly thatch and creamy vowels, appeared perfect for the part of an amiable shepherd in a television Hardy adaptation.

'What are you in this play, Steph?' Michael asked Suzanne's friend.

'The Tiger-lily,' said Steph, a study in corduroy and

47

hair. 'Don't get much to say. Not like *her*.'

Suzanne was the White Queen in the school production of *Through the Looking-Glass*. This, Michael thought, was something of a miscasting: with her acuteness and brisk unsentimentality she was a natural for the Red Queen. He saw her blush a little at Steph's 'Not like *her*'. He knew how much Suzanne enjoyed being in the play, how important it was to her — and he guessed that she had to pretend otherwise, because it wasn't cool. My God, he thought, do you have to worry about being cool when you're eleven nowadays? He was used to the vagaries of students, who could not sit on a chair with their feet on the floor but must, even at maximum discomfort to themselves, hoist them up on to the seat: but it was a pity you had to pose when you were eleven. Or was he being sentimental?

'Who's playing Alice?' Christine said.

'Oh, Tracey Betts, she's *gross*, she acts like this.' Suzanne paused, hamburger in the air, to perform a grotesquely convincing impression of an untalented brat acting surprised. Fred choked on his chips.

'Are the Selby kids in it?' Michael asked.

'Huh, they wanted to be the Walrus and the Carpenter but they were so rubbish they just had to be soldiers, and now they're not in it at all because their dad wouldn't let them be soldiers because he says it's, I don't know—'

'Militaristic?'

'Yes, something like that.'

Michael tried not to show the absurd sense of satisfaction this news gave him, but he caught a wry glance from Christine.

'Always had to be Shakespeare when I was at school,'

Fred said, placidly munching. 'Mm, nice this.'

'Change from sponge pudding, eh?' Michael said.

'Fred, you can't *really* eat sponge pudding every day,' Christine said.

Fred beamed and nodded. 'Beans on toast or something, and then a sponge pudding. When I was a kid I always used to love Heinz sponge pudding so much I said I'd have it every day when I was grown up. So I do.'

'Could you understand all that Shakespeare, Fred?' said Suzanne.

'Well, I was never very good at English, but no, I couldn't understand a word of it.' *Word* came out with one of Fred's richest Wessex *R*'s, and Michael saw Steph peeping through her hair with furtive adoration. Calf love of course, but did she know she was barking up the wrong tree? Fred had been with them for a year and a half now, and it had been quite early on that Michael had realized he was gay. He remembered winding himself up to talk to Suzanne on the subject only to find her interrupting his liberal platitudes with an impatient: 'Oh, Dad, I know he is, so what?'

'Will we have to do Shakespeare in English, Dad?' Suzanne said.

'Yes, and lots of it I should hope,' Michael said professorially.

'Groan groan,' Suzanne said. 'That stuff's so antwacky.'

'Where do they get that word from?' Michael said after the departure of the two girls, who had seized with whoops Fred's offer of a lift to the rehearsal in his lime-green chariot.

'I think it's Scouse,' Christine said. 'Probably from the TV.'

'It's a good word though.' He washed up, feeling twinges of tiredness running up and down his thighs. He would have to start using his bike more, he was getting lazy. Not driving had kept him reasonably slim when many of his contemporaries, who never used their legs except to get them from car to door, had turned into blancmanges; but all these buses were defeating the object. Bike rides, Cobbett biography, finally break with the cigarettes: there were some goals for him.

In the living room Christine had switched on the television, and the quiet sound of it, together with the lemony smell of the washing-up suds and the warmth of the cluttered kitchen and the sight of a pair of Suzanne's shoes and Fred's vast overcoat in the hall, combined to hit Michael with a wave of comfort. It was good here . . .

And with that sense of comfort, a tang of guilt.

Why? Because of Kate . . . no, because of the absence of Kate. Because she was shut out from domesticity for ever, in a cold grave, and it seemed wrong to revel in such cosiness when she could no longer share it. Indeed, there had been a time after her death when the sheer idea of domesticity had been intolerable to him, so redolent was it of what was lost. And this particular domesticity . . . a determining factor was the presence of Christine, who was one of those people who make themselves at home in the best sense of the phrase, who add something to any place they are in just by being there.

To make the domesticity complete . . . He had

shunned thinking about that, because of Christine's crucial independence and the tangle of his own feelings about Kate. Now he allowed himself to dwell on it a moment. And it was attractive, there was no doubt.

He could just see Geoffrey Selby's sneer, of course. *Really, Michael, how can you still be enslaved by the bourgeois myth of the nuclear family?* Well, all right, if that's what you wanted to call a divorcee, a widower with a daughter who had three times his own nous, and a gay lodger. Maybe he just wanted security too much — or was beginning to believe it possible again, for the first time since he had watched Kate's coffin being lowered into the ground.

He went into the living room. Christine was curled up on the settee, filling in the questionnaire she had shown him earlier.

'Some of this spelling's atrocious,' she complained.

'Probably written by English students,' he said, handing her coffee. 'Have you, ever?'

'Ever what?'

'Been sexually harassed at college.'

'Oh, well, you always get the odd lecher who looks at your legs in tutorials while he's pretending to go through your essay. But they're usually little shrimps who'd be terrified if a woman went anywhere near them.'

He glanced over her shoulder. ' "Have you ever been pestered by a member of staff to go out with him/her?" ' he read out. 'Hmm.'

Christine looked at his face and after a moment gave a shout of laughter. 'You? You practically tied yourself in knots before you could ask me if I'd like to go for a cup of tea in the snack bar.'

51

'Well . . .' He was laughing and flushing at the memory. 'I mean, how it might seem . . .'

'Who cares how it seems? Michael, you've been talking to that Selby effort, that's what it is. Listen. I spent most of my life doing things I didn't want to do because I let other people take control. Then I stopped. I decided I wasn't going to let anybody pressure me into anything any more. And I haven't. So stop worrying.'

'I seem to remember,' Michael said, sitting down by her, 'some Hollywood disaster movie where this cheesy man who's screwing his secretary says to her, "If I ever start taking you for granted, let me know." '

'*Towering Inferno*,' Christine said promptly. She was the scourge of trivia quizzes. 'Robert Wagner and that blonde woman. They got fried after having it off in his office.'

'That's right. As soon as you see somebody fornicating in one of those films, you know they've had it. Very puritanical morality really. I must work up a theory out of that. What was I saying?'

'You were saying something about taking me for granted. And *I'm* saying don't worry about it, because if you do I'll certainly let you know.' She tapped his knee with her fist. 'I'll make sure and let you know, lovey.'

'Of course,' he said, fumbling at what he wanted to say, 'it's not a question of commitment – not for me – what I mean is, it can't be too committed for me, and if you wanted to make it more committed—'

The telephone erupted with a shrill ring, leaving him floundering and Christine sitting with a surprised expression on her face.

'This never happens in Jane Austen,' he said, getting

up to answer it. Before he picked up the receiver he noticed a note to himself scribbled on the cover of the directory. *Ring Suttons re Wed.* What on earth . . . ? Then he remembered: he was scheduled to do a signing of *Anglian Voices* at Suttons, the bookshop on campus, on Wednesday. Though why he was supposed to ring them he had no idea . . .

'Hello?'

There was a moment's call-box clatter, and then the voice spoke.

'I'll give you fucking purgatory.'

Michael was idly looking at the drawing of the cathedral on the cover of the directory, and for a couple of seconds the thick snarl did not register on his mind. 'I'm sorry, who did you—'

A click, and the line went dead.

### 6

He was still standing there holding the receiver when Christine's voice faded into his consciousness.

'. . . Michael? Michael, who was it?'

He put the receiver down, his hand not quite steady.

'Wrong number, I suppose,' he said.

Christine was watching him closely. 'What did they say?'

He sat down beside her again and picked up his coffee: then set it down untasted.

'This chap said . . . well, I *think* he said, "I'll give you fucking purgatory." '

'Charming,' said Christine. 'Was that all?'

Michael stirred and nodded. 'Then he rang off.'

'Weird. Must have been a wrong number. Is there any more coffee?'

'Yes, I think . . .' He was trying to replay the voice in his head, but the sound of it somehow evaded his mind's ear in the maddening way of a perfectly familiar name that suddenly eludes the memory.

'Must have been somebody doing a wind-up, only they got the wrong number and rang off when they heard your voice,' Christine said from the kitchen. 'Either that or some nutter ringing numbers at random. I once had this woman ring up and just say in this little happy voice, "I'm born again." I thought, well, if you say so, love . . .' She came back with more coffee. 'Funny thing to say though. Purgatory. Didn't you say something like that on the radio today?'

Michael looked at her soberly. 'That's just what I'm trying to remember. Is that what I said? At the end — after saying hello to Suzanne and Steph, I mentioned this chap I'd met on the train—'

'And he made the journey sheer purgatory, yes, that's right.' Christine sipped coffee, then swallowed hastily at Michael's expression. 'What, do you reckon that was *him*?'

Michael struggled mentally to recover the timbre of that voice, those few curt words aimed at him down the crackling telephone wire. Aimed at him: for they had been spoken as soon as he answered. 'I don't know,' he said. 'When I was sitting there listening to him rambling away on that awful journey I thought, I'll never forget this voice, but of course you do . . .' The voice would not quite come, but a vivid image of Steve's staring Mr Punch face rose abruptly before him, the Red Indian complexion, the unmoving pale blue eyes. At the same moment he grasped what it was the brief phone call had made him feel. Invaded. This was what it must feel like to be groped in the street.

'Oh, but how could it be him?' Christine said. 'He doesn't even know you.'

'It's the only explanation I can think of,' said Michael. 'I mentioned this Steve on the radio and said he'd made the journey purgatory. If he heard the interview—'

'Oh, Michael, it's not very likely. Even if this fellah heard it, he's not likely to connect you with—'

'But that's just it, he knew I was going on the radio, he knew practically every bloody thing about me before we got to Cambridge. He was one of those people who just . . . you know, pumps you, wants to know everything about you.' He tried, hampered by his bad memory and his reluctance to summon up an unpleasant event that he thought he had finished with, to give Christine a summary of his encounter with the dreadful Steve: the hyena laughter, the pullover hurled out of the window, the arm-wrestling, the wild *non sequiturs* and bizarre religious bromides that were Steve's idea of casual chitchat. Even briefly rehearsing it gave him a peculiar depressed, stifled feeling, as if he were being locked in a confined space with Steve with the full glare of those eyes —

*did they ever blink? I don't think they ever blinked through that whole journey*

— eternally on him.

'God, what a pain in the arse,' Christine said when he had finished. 'Couldn't you . . . ?' He saw the question

55

forming on her lips, and saw her abandon it. *Couldn't you get rid of him?* 'No,' she said, 'that's the trouble with those situations.'

'I suppose it was a bit of a mean thing to say,' Michael said. 'On the radio, I mean.'

'Well, maybe, but after all, if you had to put up with that for the whole journey . . . You *do* think it was him, then?'

He shrugged. 'If you've got any ideas . . .'

'Well, these are my ideas.' Christine counted on her fingers. 'It was a wrong number, somebody messing about. Or just a crank call, they happen all the time. Or it was the chap you met on the train who heard you being sarky about him on the radio and decided to ring you up and say something nasty back, yah boo sucks to you too sort of thing, which wouldn't be all that difficult seeing as he knows your name and you're in the phone book. Or, here's another one, it was somebody you know winding you up. It is Rag Week, remember, Michael.'

He nodded absently. 'I would have apologized if he'd hung on a bit longer. I mean, Christ, if it upset him, I'm sorry.' He stared at the silent telephone. What a strange invention it was. In modern life it was as charged with emotional significance as were in former times the musical instrument, the church or the sword: but nobody painted pictures of it or wrote poems about it.

'You are the most guilt-prone person I've ever met,' Christine said, stroking the nape of his neck. 'If it really was this fellah, and he did get in a tizzy because he heard you say his name on the radio, then tough on him. You haven't exactly committed a great sin. Serves him right if you ask me. And now he's said his piece. *If* it was him.

Which I'm still doubtful about.'

*I'll give you fucking purgatory* . . . It was surely Steve's voice. But could he be sure? He hadn't even been listening properly. Woolgathering as usual . . .

'Don't be hurt when I say this, Michael,' Christine began.

'I'm hurt,' he said, coming up with a smile.

'No, really. All I'm saying is, maybe you're feeling a bit paranoid generally.'

'It's funny, Peter Worrall said something about that today. Paranoia is thinking they're out to get you, sanity is knowing they are. Something like that.'

'What made him say that?'

'Oh, bad news from the UGC. More cuts. This awful android we've got instead of Thatcher feels the same way she did about higher education, apparently.'

'Well there you are then. Honestly, Michael, I shouldn't worry about it.'

'Rag Week,' he mused. 'I did say I would take part in some stunt or other . . .' He couldn't match the voice he had heard on the phone with any of his students, but that didn't disprove the theory. After all, the Franciscan gentleness of Fred was by no means the rule: students could be the cruellest of the *Carnivora*, as witnessed by the numbers of the lonely and unaccepted who threw themselves in the artificial broad (called The Broad) at the back of the campus every year. Perhaps that was it. Student pranks. All the same, he didn't like it. The voice had seemed to rasp with horrible intimacy in the shell of his ear, like the buzzing passage of a wasp close to your head, making you flinch and panic . . .

'If it happens again, just firmly ask who it is, and say you don't find it funny,' Christine said. 'And you'll ring the police if there's any more of it. I'm sure it won't, though.'

'No.' He tried to shake off the hollow chill feeling that had come over him, looked round at the room with its books, records, cushions, mess: normal, everyday, reassuring. Then at Christine with her incisive eyes and fine-boned limbs that even in repose had something taut and alert about them. She smiled.

'As you were saying before you were so rudely interrupted,' she said.

'Yes . . . yes, that.' The mood that had prompted him to speak had been destroyed: the phone call, though it was just a stupid, unnerving little reprise of that morning's ordeal-by-train, had punctured his confidence. 'The thing is, I wouldn't say anything if it seemed like putting pressure on you. And I mean, I'm really happy going on just as we are . . .'

'So am I,' Christine said. She seemed to repent of the abruptness of this, and said, taking his hand, 'Look, Michael, I know what you're trying to say. And you're right, it needed saying. And now it's out, and I can say, Not yet. I love being with you, and this way I can do that and still bolt back to my little flat when I feel like I need to be on my own and just throw things about and scream and not change my tights or whatever. Perhaps the novelty of that will wear off, but at the moment it hasn't.'

'I do understand,' he said. 'As long as you know you're more than welcome to scream and throw things about here. Some time. Whenever.'

'Thanks.' She kissed him. 'And the tights?'

'We-ell . . .'

'So listen. I'm one thing in life you don't have to get paranoid about, got it? Serious, though, is this true about the cuts? I mean, they can't get rid of you, can they?'

'Well, I've got tenure. But nobody's safe any more. They're quite capable of making life so difficult for you that you just have to get out.'

'Christ. And there was me after your money. Well, it would give you more time for the writing. Your Cobbett book.'

'I must get started on that.' He remembered the euphoric sense of purpose that had come over him in Cambridge today; but that too seemed to have gone. Perhaps he was just tired –

*I'll give you fucking purgatory*

– and wasn't he, in fact, as Christine said, getting a little paranoid? Surely, deep in his heart, he believed *Anglian Voices* was a worthwhile book, never mind what Geoffrey Selby said. Surely, deep in his heart, he believed he was a reasonably good teacher and there wasn't a conspiracy to get rid of him. Surely, deep in his heart, he believed there was nothing discreditable in his having a relationship with a mature student who did nothing against her will.

Surely, in his heart, he believed that there had been nothing really to worry about in that stupid phone call.

Surely.

'Well, my lovey, I hate to go now I've eaten you out of house and home, but I've got that essay on Burke to finish,' Christine said, getting up. 'And what a burk

59

Burke was. Working himself up into a lather over that daft cow Marie Antoinette.'

Michael laughed. 'Put that in your essay. Shall I see you tomorrow?'

'I'll meet you for lunch. In The Pub.' A quick hug. 'I prefer you to Melvyn Bragg, by the way.'

When she had gone Michael felt, for some minutes, intensely and extraordinarily bereft. The house seemed spectrally quiet. He went out to the back garden to feed Suzanne's rabbits, named Matt and Luke after a defunct pop duo notable for the size of their ears. Then, after wandering around the living room performing a perfunctory tidy-up — it was his boast that you couldn't actually *see* any dirt in his house, and it was true, though if you had looked round the backs of chairs you would have seen plenty — he went upstairs to his study and switched on his word processor. He had a diskful of material on the life of Cobbett, the starting-point for that biography he was going to write. He scrolled through it, feeling increasingly like a man who has taken delivery of a lorryload of bricks and been told to build a three-bedroomed chalet-style home with double garage. He put on a tape of Schubert songs, the one that always sent Suzanne into a cruel mime of an eyebrow-wiggling tenor; and soon the cursor on the word-processor screen was winking at him unregarded and he was lost in melancholy listening.

> Leise flehen meine Lieder . . .
> Liebchen, komm zu mir . . .

The ring of the telephone by his desk slashed across

the music like a knife through paper.

Michael stared at it for several seconds. He found he was moving with a peculiar heavy slowness as at last he reached over and lifted the receiver.

'Hello?'

He tried to put his half-empty coffee cup down on the desk, clumsily tipped it over.

'Hello, Michael. Would you believe I just called to say I love you?'

'Christine.' He let out a slow breath.

'I know, corny or what, don't know what got into me. No, what I wanted to say was, well, about what you were saying earlier — I didn't mean to sound cool, offish. I mean, I have thought about it myself. Domestic bliss and all that. And just because the last time I tried it it was anything but bliss — well, that doesn't mean I don't think it's possible. With you, I mean. I'm not making myself very clear, am I?'

'Yes, I think so.' He grunted as he bent to dab at the spilled coffee with his handkerchief.

'Are you all right?'

'Yes — just spilled some coffee on the floor.' He scrubbed with the toe of his shoe at the mark on the carpet. Oh, well, it matched the others.

'Honestly, Michael, you're a mess! Anyway, that's what I wanted to say. Not no. Just let's give it a bit of time.'

His mood was transfigured by this phone call, and only someone who knew how cautious and guarded Christine normally was could have seen why. Those halting phrases had meant much. Elated, he turned back to his work, which now seemed full of potential; but he had scarcely resumed when Suzanne arrived back from the play rehearsal, and came in to talk.

This was how Michael and his daughter sustained their friendship. He would remain at the desk while Suzanne sauntered around the study, picking things up and putting them down, flicking through books, and talking to him. It was a ritual, and the casualness was the essence of it. It would not do for him to turn from the desk and face her, or for her to sit down and address him straight. That would be a confession on her part of the need to confide in her dad, and he remembered well the awkward self-consciousness of the threshold of puberty, the constant fear of somehow giving yourself away. But she did come, and she did talk to him; and it was only because he knew it would embarrass her that he refrained from telling her that this gladdened him more than anything in his life.

Tonight she was full of the play. 'You and Christine will come on Wednesday, won't you? *Steph's* mum and dad are going.'

He did not look round, but the emphasis of that phrase – connecting him and Christine with other mums and dads – made him start inwardly. He wasn't sure what he was feeling. Gratified, surely, but troubled too, perhaps because a glimpse of Suzanne looping her long fair hair back behind her ear, revealing a high cheekbone, reminded him intensely of Kate.

'We'll be there, I promise,' he said. 'Suzanne . . . what would you think about Christine maybe coming to live here sometime?'

'*God*, Dad, have you only just got round to that? Steph's always saying, how come Christine doesn't live

here? I say, don't ask me. Steph's mad on Fred, you
know, Dad. When he gave us a lift she just sat there dead
red in the face, not saying anything, I wanted to crack up
laughing.'

When she had gone Michael laughed softly to himself.
Yes, she should have played the Red Queen.

Suzanne in bed, and Fred aloft burning the midnight
electricity, Michael locked up the house, checked all the
electrical sockets — a pyrophobe habit of Kate's he had
caught — and went up to his bedroom. A soft sporadic
hum of traffic underpinned his thoughts, which were
quiet at last. Of course it was impossible to know what
Kate would have wanted for him, impossible that the
memory of her could ever take an uncomplicated,
unambiguous place in his life; but he seemed to have
come to some sort of mental and emotional
reconciliation at last. He realized just how tired he was
as he got into bed — so tired that when a flash of unease
flared up in his mind he could not be bothered to put a
name to it, and let it go.

When he opened his eyes he had the feeling of only
having slept a few minutes, but the clock by the bed said
two thirty. A beam from the headlights of a passing car
roamed across the ceiling, and for a confused second he
thought it was that that had woken him. Then a sort of
harsh tickling on his eardrums resolved itself into sound:
the sound of the telephone ringing.

Perhaps it would stop. He lay tense in the darkness for
a few moments, listening to it. A feeling stole over him, a
feeling that was a sort of distillation of memory.
Memory of the time when it was becoming apparent that
Kate's illness was something serious, the time when every

letter and phone call and hospital visit contained dread. The time when the world turned itself right round and showed a ghastly face.

That was what this felt like.

*Oh come on*, he told himself, and pushed himself out of bed.

He padded across the landing to the study. Blearily he saw his long, pale boxer-shorted figure reflected in the word-processor screen as he switched on the light. The telephone kept ringing.

*Christine it was probably Christine sorry Michael I couldn't sleep just needed to talk you know how it is . . .*

He snatched up the receiver.

'Hello?'

Fumble and click of money going into a call-box slot. Then silence.

'Hello, who is this?' Michael said. His own voice sounded strange to him, bare and chilled as his body.

*Not Christine you knew it wasn't you knew . . .*

'Ah ha ha ha ha ha ha . . . !'

The laughter burst from the earpiece, harsh and sudden as shattering glass. Michael nearly dropped the receiver.

'. . . ha ha ha *ha* . . . ah, ha ha ha ha ha . . .'

He knew that laugh. That loud, high-pitched, funless laugh that went on and on. An empty parody of a laugh that made you think of a seaside automaton, rocking back and forth, red wooden lips agape over carved teeth.

'Look—' He unlocked his voice with difficulty. 'Look, I don't know what—'

A grotesque raspberry cut him off. He seemed to feel the spit spraying obscenely into his ear.

'Listen, if this is who I think it is — '

*Steve a man called Steve I met on the train Christ what am I doing this Steve is NOTHING TO DO WITH ME he's got nothing to do with my life.*

Invaded.

' — I don't know what the hell you think you're doing—'

'Dad? Who's that?'

Suzanne's sleepy voice, calling from her bedroom. Something about the silence on the other end of the phone suggested that the caller had heard it.

'It's all right, love,' Michael said. 'Go back to sleep.'

'It's all right love go back to sleep,' parroted the voice on the phone. Then it gave a single blank titter. A second's breathing silence, and then Michael heard the receiver being softly put down.

### 7

He came awake, hardly aware that he had fallen asleep. Since the phone call at two thirty he had been sitting up in bed and blankly gazing at the same close-written page of a student essay, and had despaired of getting to sleep at all. But he must have dropped off at last, because here he was starting awake, and there was the student essay that had slid to the floor, and there was the clock radio saying four eighteen —

— and there was the sound of the telephone ringing again.

# TWO

## 1

There was somebody knocking at the door. It was a steady tapping, soft but persistent. Michael was eating sponge pudding in the kitchen with Suzanne and Fred. They both looked up at him.

'That'll be for you,' Suzanne said.

Michael got up from the table and went to the front door. Now he realized there was something peculiar about that knocking, something slurred and slushy, as if the hand that was doing it was wearing a mitten or a boxing glove.

*Christine?* he thought, and opened the door.

Kate stood there, dressed in her favourite black jeans, long fair hair dishevelled by the wind, smiling at him. No, she wasn't smiling. It was just that he could see all her teeth through the few tatters of flesh that remained on her skull. Her arm was still uplifted from knocking at the door, and now he understood that peculiar muffled sound. Not a mitten or a boxing glove, but a hand that had completely rotted away to a ribbon of skin over a nub of white wrist bone.

'I had to come back, Michael,' his dead wife said to him. 'We always come back.' The two symmetrical rows of teeth opened wide and a laugh came out, loud and staccato, automaton-like.

'Ah ha ha ha ha ha . . . !'

The handless wrist came up and began to claw at the death's-head face. The face came off like a latex mask, and Steve was there beneath it, hooting with laughter.

'Aaah — fooled you there mate! Got you there — got you — got you — ah, ha ha ha—'

The laughter broke off suddenly, and Michael saw that the other hand was intact and that it grasped some shining metal implement, and that it was swinging in an arc towards him.

## 2

A hideous grinding vibration rattled through Michael's head. It felt as if a drill was being applied to his left temple. He jerked his head, blinked.

He was on the bus. It was the braking vibration that he had felt, as he had nodded off against the grimy window. He rubbed his face with his palms and noted that they were almost at the university campus. My God, he thought, falling asleep on the bus! Only real geriatrics did that.

He felt the dream slowly lift off him, with an effect like drying water on the skin. He had dreamt of Kate almost nightly for a year after her death, but those had simply been dreams of soap-opera normality, dreams that she had never died at all, from which the waking to bereavement was like a body blow. Never anything like this.

But then he had never fallen into troubled dozes on the

bus before. He had never had crank phone calls in the middle of the night before, destroying his rest and making him feel like a zombie as he set out for work.

One crank call in the middle of the night, at least. The second time the phone had woken him, at four eighteen, it had stopped ringing just before he had got to it. In a way that had been more disturbing than the crazy laughter. He had exercised his mind tremendously in trying to reckon the odds on that one being a chance wrong number, something normal . . . He was unconvinced, and had taken the phone off the hook.

And had no more sleep after that.

Now, with the bus labouring up the service road to the university campus, with students, nasally drawling, lolling in the seats about him, with sunlight spearing the avenue of trees and glaring off the ramparts of academic concrete up ahead, Michael's chief feeling was one of intense annoyance. Apart from tutorials this morning, he had an important lecture to give this afternoon, the key lecture for those taking the early-nineteenth-century special-subject course, and he was hardly likely to do it justice if he felt like the walking dead.

A memory of that dream brushed him. Kate . . . her face . . . dear God . . .

No. The whole thing was just bloody annoying and stupid and irritating, and if that ridiculous Steve — Michael knew it was him — thought he was getting some sort of revenge for what Michael had said on the radio then he was a sad case and that was all there was to it. And if he tried any more of it then Michael would just take the phone off the hook. He was damned if he was going to worry his head over a prat like that.

*Easier to say when it was daylight and there were people around and you weren't sitting on your bed staring into the darkness with a tingle over your skin knowing there was somebody somewhere who was thinking of you with malice – a stranger a stranger for God's sake somewhere amongst all those thousands of people in the city . . .*

But that was just it. It *was* sad, to think of that man going to all this trouble just because of an exasperated throwaway remark. What sort of life must Steve have?

Michael came up against a perplexing blank when he tried to picture it; and it occurred to him that while Steve with his dogged questioning on that train journey had found out practically all there was to know about him, he knew next to nothing about Steve. Not even his surname.

Well, again, that was just it. Michael didn't *want* to know anything about him. He was just a weirdo who had popped up briefly in his life, like the hundreds of people who would inevitably pop up into your life – and pop out again – unless you lived on a desert island. Steve's refusal to accept that was what had been so unsettling about him in the first place: in Steve's particular fruitcake world-view, there was no such thing as a stranger.

*Strangers are just friends you haven't met yet*. Where had he read that little paste pearl of wisdom? It sounded like Patience Strong (and can that have been her *real* name?) but he could imagine it finding a place in the *Steve Dictionary of Nauseating Quotations*.

He got off the bus at the campus. The Square, a sunken cement amphitheatre opening on to a row of toytown banks and shops optimistically called The Street, teemed with students. Under the sun many of them, like sartorial plants, had blossomed into summer gear. Where, Michael wondered, did these weird varieties of shorts come from? He had never seen anything like them in the shops. And why were the legs of the male students always so extremely brown and hairy? He began to work up a little theory about it, and as always the effect of wandering through the inner country of his mind was a perceptible relaxation, a loosening of tight strings in his neck and shoulders.

'Excuse me.'

A young man was addressing him in a soft shy Scots.

'Excuse me, could you tell me the way to the Economics building?'

They must be interviewing for admissions, Michael thought, observing the youth's collar and tie and timid brown eyes. He pointed out the way, feeling slightly flattered that he had been picked out as the least intimidating feature of the human swarm around him, all so assured, so brightly invulnerable. And it *was* alarming, this place, at first. Close on ten thousand people thronging its walkways and terraces and corridors, all knowing what to do, all knowing where to go. He had worked here for years and knew many of the staff well and taught scores of students, and yet even he could walk around the campus some days and not see a single face that he recognized: just strangers.

He watched the young Scot climb the steps of the Economics building and, on entering, hold the door open for someone. Well, he would soon get out of that habit if his application was successful and he came here next year. Michael was always touched by the sight of these sixth-formers, so fresh and unmarked, issuing forth from suburban schools with football pitches and corrugated-iron bike sheds. They would never be as nice again. Within a year — within a few months, it happened that fast — they would have put on a new persona, taken to sitting on the floor whenever possible, be talking in that odd clenched-teeth manner, calling everything *amazing*.

*And propping up the world with their little fingers, when they can't even sew a button on*, as Peter Worrall would say. Michael didn't dislike them that much. He thought on the whole students were pleasanter than in his own undergraduate days, when virulent hatred of elders had been *de rigueur*. Now ageism had joined the proscribed attitudes, and they just pitied everyone over thirty instead of despising them.

In the English Studies building he took the lift to his third-floor office. This was another slob habit he would have to get out of, but what the hell. Stepping out of the lift he saw Geoffrey Selby's dog Nono waddling round the corridor corner. No sign of Geoffrey, though, that was one good thing. He paused outside Geoffrey's office door to look at the board by the nameplate. Most lecturers used these simply to pin up tutorial times or essay topics, but Geoffrey's was a veritable collage of clippings from newspapers and magazines and pamphlets that he felt should be drawn to the attention of the world. Today's additions: a *Guardian* report on the spoliation of Antarctica, and, hello hello, a copy of the sexual-harassment questionnaire with a little message from Geoffrey Selby declaring his full support for the project and urging students to report anything they knew or heard about unhealthy student–tutor relationships.

Is this a dig at me? Michael thought. Is the Beria of Broadland getting at me here? Shit, he really has got it in for me . . .

He felt a hot tingle crawling up his neck, and made himself stop. Hold on. Wait a minute. He'd had that prat Steve making nuisance phone calls, and that had tied him up into a bundle of raw nerves until the coming of morning and the reassertion of everyday normality had made him put the silly business into perspective. And now here he was starting to prickle with persecution again, just because of a note on Geoffrey Selby's Right-On Thought For The Day board. Hold on, Michael. Remember what Christine said about getting paranoid?

Christine. There was a Thought For The Day worth thinking of. Keep hold of that.

And maybe, just maybe, Geoffrey Selby was jealous. It wasn't likely, but it was a sufficiently cheering idea to restore Michael's mind to its hard-won state of calm.

He glanced again at the board, briefly considered drawing a pair of goofy teeth on the picture of Daniel Ortega, decided against it, and went into his office.

And had his state of calm explosively shattered.

### 3

Hilda, the faculty secretary, peeped smiling over the cactus plants ranged on top of her VDU. 'Morning, Michael,' she trilled, 'I'm reading a wonderful book, it's all about dragons—'

'That's nice,' Michael said. 'Hilda, do you know where Geoff Selby is?'

Hilda gazed in horn-rimmed alarm at Michael's glowering expression. 'He came in here this morning, he had a message in his piggy-hole, but I don't know whether he's teaching. Would you like me to look in the timmy-tables?'

'Please, if you would,' said Michael. He leaned his hands on the desk. He was out of breath from pounding down three flights of stairs. And he had only just managed to stop himself being sick.

'No . . .' Hilda studied roneoed timetables. 'No, he's not teaching. Perhaps he just popped out for a coffee.'

'Well, anyway, could you phone through to the caretaker? He'll need plenty of cleaning materials, tell him.'

'Is something wrong, Michael?'

'It's Geoff's bloody dog. It's crapped all over my office.'

'Oh, dear, poor thing,' said Hilda, whether in reference to himself or the dog Michael couldn't tell. 'I'll call George straight away. Is it messy, Michael?'

*What do you think?* he nearly said, but stopped himself: he liked Hilda, nursery talk notwithstanding. 'I'm afraid it is.'

Hilda paused with the telephone at her ear and pointed at the open doorway. 'Ooh! Who do I spy with my little eye? Isn't that Geoffrey?'

Michael turned in time to see Geoffrey Selby doing his Phantom-of-the-Campus glide across the vestibule and into the lift.

The lift doors had closed before Michael could get

there. Cursing, he ran up the stairs again and confronted Geoffrey just as he was stepping out.

'Come and see what your damn dog's done to my office.'

Geoffrey pursed his lips in his beard, looking more than ever like a puritanical satyr. 'Michael, is this really very important? I've got a tutorial to take—'

'So have I – fat chance with the bloody *state* my office is in – look – come on, look—'

Bundling Selby along, Michael pushed open his office door, holding his breath against the stink.

'There. See? Get the picture?'

The pile of dung was right in the middle of the carpet. It was not a small or tidy pile. Torn and crumpled papers – some poor sod's essay, Michael thought – added the finishing touch to the charming scene. The smell hit you in the face like a solid substance.

'Did you see Nono come in here?' Geoffrey said, stepping back and fishing for a handkerchief to press to his nose.

Michael stared at him. 'How many other dogs are there wandering round this building?' he said, almost light-headed with anger.

'None, to my knowledge,' Geoffrey said precisely. 'But that wasn't Nono, that I know.'

'Look, don't give me that crap,' Michael said. *And don't give me* this *crap*, he might have added if his sense of humour had been working. 'Maybe it's too much to expect you to keep your stupid dog under control, but can't you even *train* it?'

'Listen, I'm not in the business of *training* fellow creatures, Michael, I mean, I am totally not into imposing value systems on our ecological partners—'

'So you let your dog shit where it likes!'

'Certainly I would, rather than be a biological fascist. But as I was going to say if you'd let me finish, Nono of his own choice always goes outside to defecate, usually to the trees near the Senate building. He has never had such an accident in eight years.'

Selby's dry, superior tone ignited Michael's fury to such white heat that he could hardly speak. 'There is always a first time,' he said thickly.

'Well, this isn't it. Look, Michael, you're a historian, of a sort: remember the golden rule — facts, then interpretation. Take another look at the facts of this case.' Geoffrey nodded at the mess on the carpet. 'As I say, I don't believe in training Nono; and I certainly never trained him to use sheets of A4 as toilet paper.'

## 4

Geoffrey had noiselessly turned and gone into his office, closing the door behind him, leaving Michael staring at —

At *what*?

Michael felt his gorge rise. He moved away from the door, swallowing acid.

He had scarcely looked at the torn paper at first, assuming it to be just a secondary trick of the dog's, a little bonus, to rip up some essays as well as crap on the floor. But now he came to think of it . . .

He didn't *want* to think of it. God, no.

'George is on his way.' Hilda appeared, carrying a can of air freshener. 'Thought this might help. I keep it for when Professor Rudge comes into the office smoking his pipe – pooh!'

'Thanks, Hilda,' Michael said. 'No, I shouldn't have a look if I were you – it'll put you off your lunch.'

The caretaker arrived. He was a dour, unsurprised, bald man who came armed for battle with bin bags, sawdust bucket, disinfectants, mops, rubber gloves and face mask. 'Makes a change from sick,' was all he said before heaping sawdust on to the mess and beginning to clear up.

'I'm terribly sorry about this,' Michael said, lingering at the door.

George merely raised his eyebrows. 'Buggers should be shot.'

Both Selby and George had seen what in his first explosive anger Michael had failed to grasp. It was a *person* who did this . . .

A tramp, maybe? He dismissed the idea at once. The students might have a taste for carefully dilapidated clothes, but a real tramp would be pretty obvious wandering the corridors of Broadland University. And a real tramp would surely like to take advantage of the comfortable toilet facilities, if anything.

So horribly bizarre, so random. Yet it wasn't random. It was *his* office that had been visited, with his name on the door.

Well, that settled it. He was going to lock the place up in future.

But that couldn't alter the fact that somebody had been in there. Somebody had been in his office and –

*Got you there, mate!*

– invaded it.

77

Defiled it.

'I shouldn't use the room today,' George said, coming out. 'Disinfectant'll knock you out. Leave the windows open, it should be all right tomorrow.'

Michael thanked him and apologized again.

George shook his head resignedly. 'Rag Week,' he said, clanking away. 'Worst sodding week of my year.'

Michael seized on that idea. Rag Week . . . Students got up to some pretty off-colour tricks, after all.

But surely it would take real malice against him to make someone do something like this. And it was precisely that thought, the thought of a person who did seem to bear malice against him —

*I'll give you fucking purgatory.*

— that he was trying desperately to evade.

Because it was crazy. One trivial remark — it might trigger a nasty phone call or two, all right. But to go to all this *trouble*; you'd have to be a real nutcase. A lunatic.

The Train Loony, for example?

Michael regarded Geoffrey Selby's door, from behind which came the sound of a typewriter. After all, if he was looking for someone who had a grudge against him, he didn't need to look as far as an irritating stranger whom he had only met once in his life. He needed merely to look at the office next door.

Now it's me who's the lunatic, Michael thought. Geoff Selby was a horse's arse of the first order, and managed to reconcile a belief in universal brotherhood with being thoroughly nasty to practically everybody he met; but Michael just couldn't imagine him doing anything so insanely crude. And besides, what if Michael had come in just at that moment?

In fact, let's think about it. He *might* have come in at any time. Surely whoever did it must have known that?

And they still took the risk.

Christ, no. This thing *didn't* bear thinking about. He was going to have to find a way of forgetting it, of keeping the grisly thought from pouncing on him, if he was going to get through any work today.

Peter Worrall lent him his office for his tutorials. First up was a drama student who was unhappily taking some English Studies courses. She was a doll-faced patrician gasper who insisted on being called TJ. Her parents, instead of naming her Camilla or Sarah or Gemma as standard, had by some terrible aberration christened her Tracey, and the poor cow had obviously adopted the initials in a desperate attempt to deny the awful fact. (Michael went along with it, resisting the temptation of addressing her as Trace.) Then came Neil, an intolerable know-all who, almost uniquely for Broadland University, came from the North (Harrogate anyway). Then a brilliant bespectacled oddball named, incredibly, Inigo, six foot six and so maladroit as to be scarcely capable of getting through a door without mishap, but practically a don already in his grasp of history. Then Laura, whose father was a well-known television chat-show presenter and who looked so exactly like him that Michael always had a curious sense of being interviewed . . .

And though he tried to keep that pouncing thought at bay, Michael failed. He kept thinking of that abomination in his office with reference to these students, with their strident hairstyles and edgy, overemphatic, but fundamentally unsinister personalities. Rag Week? Surely not.

Yet how could you be sure what people were thinking about you, what enmity and resentment might lie beneath their blandly attentive faces? Michael always remembered the shock, a few years ago, of having a student ask to move to another seminar because he didn't get along with Michael. It was a thing that happened sometimes; and Michael hadn't been unhappy to see the back of him; yet still it was disturbing somehow to think of that dislike, silent, festering, unsuspected . . .

At lunchtime he met Christine in the campus pub. You would have thought that even Broadland University would have balked at calling this vast, melamine-filled hangar The Pub, but so it solemnly did. The haunch-numbing wooden seats, scarcely deeper than shelves, had perhaps been designed with some wild idea of making students sit with their feet on the floor, but if so the attempt had been a failure, and there they perched, score upon score of them. The only other fixture was a jukebox containing the essential corpus of student favourites, 'No Woman No Cry' and 'Walk on the Wild Side' and 'Light My Fire' and 'Born to Run', eternally revolving.

'Did you get any more funny phone calls?'

It was one of the first things Christine said to him, and it made him realize how much he needed to talk to someone about what had happened. He talked. When he came to the noisome gift left on his office carpet her eyes widened above her pint glass, and stayed wide for some moments.

'You're *kidding*.'

'I wish I was.'

'It *must* have been a dog . . . Mustn't it?'

'That's what I want to think. But . . .' He took a pull of beer. 'I'm afraid I don't think so.'

Christine was silent for some time, thinking. Pleased as he was to be with her again, Michael felt unhappy too. Having to talk about this business spoilt what should have been a good part of the day.

*And wasn't that perhaps the intention?*

'This Steve,' Christine said. 'You don't think he could be a student?'

'No. No, surely not. He would have said, when he found out I taught here. Wouldn't he?'

'What *did* he say, on that train? About himself?'

Michael frowned. 'You know what my memory's like. Plus I've probably repressed it because it was so bloody awful . . . I seem to remember him saying he'd been in the army. And there was a lot of wacko religious stuff. And his mother lived in Cambridge, because he was on his way to see her. But I'm sure he would have said if he was studying here. And besides . . .'

He was going to say that Steve surely couldn't be a university student because he was too thick. Not that he hadn't met some pretty thick students in his time, but even so . . . What stopped him from saying this, however, was a sudden intuition about himself, like being confronted with a mirror reflection in an unexpected place. Wasn't that why he had been so annoyed by the young man on the train: because he was so thick?

And had his face shown it? Had those unblinking

81

enamel eyes seen in Michael's face a lofty, clever-clever impatience?

It was not a nice thought.

'No,' Christine said, 'it doesn't sound as if he's at Broadland. It's just that it would have fitted in — you know, if he was on the spot. Handy for your office, I mean.'

They regarded each other soberly.

'But,' Christine said, 'I think there must be some other explanation. It is Rag Week, and some of the Hooray Henrys can be pretty gross.'

'The caretaker seemed to think that too . . . Do you think I'm jumping at shadows?' Michael said.

'Maybe a bit. I don't like those phone calls, though. That surely amounts to harassment. Why didn't you give me a ring last night, instead of sitting there worrying? You know I wouldn't have minded.'

'I don't know. I suppose because that would have meant acknowledging what was happening. Somebody, E.M. Forster I think, said the British public don't so much hate homosexuality as they hate having to think about it. That's the way I feel about this business.'

'Well, he wanted to wind you up, that's obviously why he made the phone calls, at any rate. The thing to do with these cranks is not let them get to you — I know it's easier said than done. The usual advice is not to respond when they ring—'

'Maybe I should, though,' Michael said. 'Maybe I should say something, try and talk to him—'

'But that would probably encourage him. I mean, if he doesn't get any response then he'll surely get bored with it. And if not, then the best thing to do is change your

number, go ex-directory. I doubt whether the police can
do much. I think that business where they trace where
the call's coming from is strictly for the films. Anyway'
— she stroked his hand, and suddenly gave him a warm
kiss on the lips — 'I can't see him carrying on with it, I
really can't.'

*Yes*, thought Michael, *but then you've got all your
marbles. And when you've heard this guy laughing in the
middle of the night you know he is definitely one
sandwich short of a picnic.*

A shadow fell across them. Michael felt breath on his
neck, and turned to find a hideously grinning face an
inch from his.

'Boo!'

Laughter rang out as Michael jumped in his seat. A
hand went up and peeled the grotesque face off —

*Like the dream just like the dream . . .*

— and there was the no more attractive face of Neil
from Harrogate, Michael's least favourite student.
Behind him were several of his fellows, similarly dressed
in masks and wigs and fancy-dress costumes, and
carrying yellow buckets.

'Collecting for Ethiopia,' Neil said, rattling the bucket
under Michael's nose.

'How much would it cost to send *you* there?' Michael
said, dropping money into the bucket with a trembling
hand, and cautiously accepting that he was not going to
have a heart attack after all.

'It's all in a good *cause*,' said Neil huffily, in his most
whiney toff-Yorkshire.

Christine looked her amusement. 'Dr Greenwood
displaying his celebrated rapport with the younger

83

generation,' she said when they had gone.

In spite of himself Michael felt his frown slowly break up and turn into a rueful smile. 'I'm getting as bad as Peter Worrall.' My God, he thought, I really felt like I was going to pass out then. I'm so jumpy.

'Speaking of the younger generation, I'm going to town this afternoon to get a present for Suzanne's birthday,' Christine said. 'I was thinking of that beanbag she wanted for her bedroom.'

'Christ, it's tomorrow, isn't it? I must get her a card. My memory's getting worse . . . Suttons is open, isn't it?'

'Yep. Don't get a Garfield one, by the way, I heard her say she's gone off him.'

'Don't tell me. Garfield's antwacky.'

They parted having arranged to meet that evening. In the campus bookshop Michael bought a Gary Larson birthday card (surely that wasn't antwacky yet?) and, his memory functioning for once, talked with the manageress about the signing session for *Anglian Voices* tomorrow. There was quite a stack of them on the New Titles shelf. Where would they be placed when they were no longer new? In the history section with Geoffrey Selby's tomes, like *Indignities of Labour: Engels and the Industrial Revolution* and *Bleak Houses: Studies in Cultural Hegemony*? Or next to *The Country Diary of an Edwardian Lady* and *The Coronation Street Story*?

His lecture was at three. To clear the fumes of The Pub, and the no less murky miasma of his mind, he took a walk through the water meadows behind the campus, crossing The Broad by the footbridge and strolling round Knightsford Park. A Norfolk worthy had bequeathed Knightsford Hall, a seventeenth-century manor, to the University of Broadland; and the park and house, partly used as a home for the Climatic Research Department and partly as a venue for official junketings, formed an unlikely annex to the sternly modern campus. Clouds passing across the sun made heliographs of the windows of the campus residences, pyramids of little glazed boxes, as private as open coffins.

He thought about his lecture, smoked a cigarette, and walked back to the campus by way of the Winfield Centre for the Fine Arts. A retailer popular with the middle classes had founded this place, which looked like an out-of-town DIY superstore and was filled with an outstandingly undistinguished collection of modern art. A walkway like a concrete Cresta Run on stilts led to the campus proper, through a strange silent hinterland of service buildings. There were boiler houses with huge black chimneys, mysterious acres of blank wall interrupted by still more mysterious grilles and metal doors that never opened, loading bays glimpsed as dizzy lifeless spaces below. Michael never liked it here: it vaguely reminded him of some nightmare of his childhood that involved being alone and lost. God only knew what it must be like at night.

Lecture Theatre One was the biggest of the university lecture theatres, as opposed to the faculty theatres, which were glorified classrooms. It was very big: you could have mounted *Aida* in it. Michael entered by the door that led straight to the stage. When Geoffrey Selby lectured he disdained this as authoritarian, preferring to enter by the main doors with the students and seraphically wend his way down the amphitheatre to the lectern. Geoffrey Selby also interrupted his lectures halfway through to go and sit down in silence at the side of the stage for five minutes, eating an apple. What a poseur, Michael thought, setting his notes out on the lectern with a small, not unpleasant flutter of nerves in his stomach. Selby, of course, lectured without notes. He said it should come from the gut. Michael thought that what Geoff Selby had to say came from quite another part of his anatomy . . . but anyhow, stop thinking about Geoff Selby, concentrate, this is a key lecture . . .

He looked up at the great bowl of banked seats rising to a gallery above. The theatre was still noisily filling up: half-full, he would have said, though beyond about the tenth row his myopia allowed him to see only a blur of moving figures, pastel colours bleeding into each other. He looked at his watch. Give it a few minutes. The familiar dilemma of what to do with his hands assailed him. He used to put them behind his back, until horrified by a glimpse of himself on a Broadland University promo-video looking like a minor member of the Royal Family.

They weren't usually this noisy: what the hell was the matter with them? He seemed to hear laughter among the hubbub too. He peered at the front row, saw someone leaning to whisper in a neighbour's ear. Saw a young man avert his eyes with a stifled grin. Saw a girl, red-faced, cover her mouth with her hand — her eyes fixed on the blackboard behind him.

He turned round.

The blackboard ran the whole length of the wall behind the lectern, and most of it was taken up with a childish, crude but extremely clear drawing in thick strokes of red chalk. His first thought was that it was something left over from the previous lecture — but what on earth could have been the subject? Freud? Anthropology?

And then he saw that the figures represented in the drawing had been labelled with the same vigorous red chalk-strokes. Above the man in spectacles were the words MICHAEL GREENWOOD. Above the naked woman with spiky hair were the words CHRISTINE REED. The man in spectacles, with exaggerated lavatory-wall explicitness, was penetrating the spiky-haired woman from behind, and both wore leering half-moon grins.

Michael's head swam. A rush of blood seemed to pound and thunder in his ears, echoing the commotion in the amphitheatre behind him. He had already snatched up the blackboard eraser when he saw that there was a third element to the composition. Away to the right, near the blackboard frame, a human skeleton had been roughly sketched, and above it were the words MICHAEL GREENWOOD'S WIFE.

5

'To speak of an age of transition is in one sense to beg the question. Any society and any culture at any given moment can be said to be in a state of transition: more telling is the intensity of that culture's consciousness of being so — whether the consciousness be "true" or "false" . . .'

He had been faced with two choices. One was to wipe

the drawings off the blackboard, turn and face his audience, wait for them to settle down, and then begin his lecture. The other was to walk out of the lecture theatre, run away, hide, rage and howl.

He had taken the first choice, but it had been a close-run thing. He had had to wait a long time for the assembled students to settle down; even in the best of circumstances he was poor at imposing authority on a theatre, as, for example, Muriel Weeks could with one paralysing glare over her bifocals, and all he could do was stand there and stare the audience out. For once in his life he was glad of his short-sightedness, mercifully eliminating detail as it did; but still he could see that quite a large proportion of the student body thought this the biggest hoot since the last Woody Allen.

*Bastards*, he thought. *They're all against me.*

Don't get paranoid . . . But Christ, who wouldn't?

'Age of Revolution. Age of Reaction. Age of Romanticism. Age of neo-Classicism. Can the age be all these at once? We have to remember of course that the very concept of a spirit of the age, in Hazlitt's terms, of the *Zeitgeist*, the set of emotional and intellectual preoccupations characterizing or indeed *expressing* one particular period in time – this concept is itself a Romantic one, reflecting Romanticism's view of itself . . .'

He was doing it, somehow. Somehow the brain and the mouth between them had set up a jury-rig and were going to get him into port. How much of it the audience were taking in was a different matter, but then it always was. At least he was going to deliver the damn lecture, in spite of the efforts of –

*Who?*

Rag Week. Don't forget that. One or two of the students seemed to have come straight to the lecture from some stunt or other still wearing fancy-dress, though given the whimsies of undergraduate fashion it was hard to tell. After all, Peter Worrall had had his car covered in shaving foam . . .

But by God, *this*! If this was youthful high spirits, then give him geriatric gloom.

He remembered Kate, during the beginnings of her illness, coming home from tests at the hospital and crying on his shoulder at the indignity of it all. 'I don't care what I've got,' she had sobbed, 'what I hate is being prodded and probed and – and *exposed* and *looked up* by the world and his bloody wife . . .'

Probed. Exposed.

Invaded.

That was how this felt.

And it was bringing Kate into it that made it so. He couldn't pretend he liked being publicly traduced in this way, but it wouldn't kill him; and Christine, if he knew her, would be robust in her anger. But Kate . . . Life had been so unforgivably cruel to Kate that this further cruelty to her memory filled him with an emotion he could scarcely define – indignation, sickness, despair, fury were all part of it.

Yes, whoever had done this had certainly got to him. Straight to the centre of the target. And there was no doubt that they had meant to. This one's for you, Michael.

'To account for the divergence between, say, the quietism of Wordsworth and the grand public gestures of Byron, the intensities of the Radcliffean Gothic sublime and the despiritualized world of Austen, we need to go further than simply saying that one is reacting against the other . . .'

Somebody was coughing, with irritating persistence. There was always coughing, of course, but this cough stood out — repetitive, unignorable. Someone up in the very back row, which with his vision was no more than a line of soft blots blooming and coalescing on his retinas. It was distracting to his already fragile concentration.

'The approach taken in Marilyn Butler's *Romantics, Rebels and Reactionaries*, which I strongly recommend . . . which I . . .'

He strained to see further up the vast receding slope of faces. That cough couldn't be other than intentional. In fact it was more of a splutter. More of a giggle.

*Admit it you don't think this is some sick Rag Week prank you think this is that damn moron Steve's work*

'. . . as I was saying . . .'

*Steve my God do you really believe that Steve is actually coming to the university and doing these crazy things to get at me?*

'. . . Butler's book includes a chapter on Gillray . . .'

Another spluttering noise.

*And what's more he's probably here now —*

'All right, who the hell's making that noise?' Michael burst out, slamming his hand on the lectern, feeling a flush flare on his cheeks. He advanced to the first row of seats, glaring up into the wavering, blurring recesses of the theatre. Startled faces looked up from folders, pens were still.

He scanned the furthest rows — scanned, Jesus, what

a joke, *scanned* with these eyes, like Mr Magoo, Colonel Blink the short-sighted gink . . .

A flash of compressed memory, of one of those sentimental old MGM cartoons, a baby mole who calls the junk heap outside his door his Fairy Palace because that's what his myopia makes it look like, then he strays out into the world, huckster weasel sells him a pair of spectacles, comes back and sees the junk heap for what it is – *oh my Fairy Palace it's gone* . . .

'Come on!' Michael shouted. 'Where are you? You know who I damn well mean. *Where are you?'*

Glances were exchanged. This wasn't the Dr Greenwood they knew.

'Well?'

A movement, near the back. Someone was standing up. A ripple of turning heads.

'I'll go and get a drink of water. It's not my fault if I've got a cold.'

A girl. She left the theatre with an affronted clop of heeled boots.

The ranks of faces watched Michael expectantly. After a moment he walked back to the lectern and with unsteady hands picked up his notes.

'Gillray, whose career brings together many of the contradictions of the period . . .'

He got through to the end of the lecture. There were no more interruptions: the distant spluttering ceased. If he did not feel as relieved about this as he might have, that was because he was sure that it had not been coming from the spot where the indignant girl had got up.

## 6

His office still reeked of disinfectant. There was a large damp patch on the carpet where the caretaker had scrubbed it. Michael didn't care to look too closely to see whether it had stained. He edged round it, got to his desk, sat down with his head in his hands.

He had come out of the lecture theatre none the wiser. How to pick out one person from that imperfectly seen mass flooding towards the exits?

It was the bloody uncertainty, the not knowing —

'Deep thoughts, or worries?'

Michael tried not to show he had jumped. 'Oh, hello, Peter.'

'Phew, bottles in here, doesn't it?' Peter Worrall came and perched his behind, ample as a Gro-Bag, on the edge of the desk.

Michael said, 'Peter, do you believe in motiveless malignity?'

'Of course I do. I've *lived* in Wales.'

Michael laughed. The sensation of doing so felt strange, as if his face had lost the knack.

'No kidding, mate,' said Peter. 'Five years at Bangor University totally destroys your faith in human nature, if you have any to start with. You know what they say about the Welsh — pray on their knees all Sunday and prey on their neighbours all week. Anyway, why do you ask? Geoff Selby being his usual self?'

'Oh . . . In the lecture theatre. A rather personal message left on the blackboard for me.' He didn't want to go into details.

'Yeah? Doesn't surprise me. Look out of the window,

Michael. What do you see? Students. We're surrounded by thousands of the bastards. And their one aim in life is to be as obnoxious as is humanly possible.'

'Well, OK, but this . . .' The crude, vivid drawings appeared on his mind's eye. 'This was pretty nasty.'

'That's what I'm saying. I mean, look at these little shits. Why do they come here – I mean the ones we teach? They come here because they're south-of-Watford middle-class, and an inseparable part of that is going to college. All you need is a couple of A levels, and with middle-class advantages that's like falling off a log. And they do English Lit or History because it seems easy: not many people can follow a page of theoretical physics, but anybody can read *Pride and Prejudice*. They're not interested in the subjects. Most of these tossers have never read a book in their lives except that little list of student classics: *On the Road* and *Catcher in the Rye* and *Lolita* and *The Magus*. Funny how that list never changes over the years, I mean the cretins actually haven't rumbled Kerouac yet – maybe you could work up one of your theories about it. The literary conservatism of students is in inverse proportion to their surface radicalism, or something like that. Anyway, you see what I'm saying. They come here simply to piss about and think they're God's gift for three years. But they know none of it matters, Michael. They're smart in that way. They know there won't be any consequences. Nobody gets sent down from Broadland. Nobody has their grant stopped. Nothing matters. So they behave like twenty-four-carat arseholes. And give them something like Rag Week and they go right over the top. They should all be stabbed in the eye with a burnt stick, if you ask me.'

Michael grinned. Warming his hands at Peter's cheerful cynicism took off some of the chill of fore-boding that had crept into his bones – though at heart he remained unconvinced.

'Forget about the bastards, Michael. Listen, we're having a bit of a booze-up at our place on Thursday night. Wedding anniversary.'

'Oh, I didn't know, congratulations. How many?'

'Seven. Whatever that makes it. One of those pathetic ones like cotton or paper or something. Good excuse to get shitfaced anyhow. So, do you and Christine fancy coming?'

'I'd love to. I'll have to see if Christine's got anything on, but I don't think so . . .'

Christine. That awful drawing, soiling what was good and real. Soiling it, crapping on it. Like his office floor . . .

Christine. If Steve was responsible, how did he *know* about her?

The chill spread through Michael's body again, clutching at his stomach. How did Steve *know* about Christine and Michael?

He tried to think back to the train journey. Steve had wangled all sorts of personal information out of him, almost without Michael realizing it, but he was sure he hadn't even so much as mentioned Christine. He just wouldn't have. It was no one else's business.

*And that's just it nothing's my own business any more . . .*

Invaded.

94

Spied on . . .

'Be good if you can make it,' Peter was saying. 'Haven't got really rat-arsed for ages. Better put it in there, I know your memory.'

'Eh?' Michael said, coming out of his thoughts.

Peter pointed to his desk diary. 'Put it down, mate. Peter Worrall's, eight thirty or whenever. I can promise you one thing.' He winked. 'No students allowed. See you later.' At the door he added, 'You know what we ought to have? A Rag Week for staff. When we inflict unimaginable tortures on the student body, culminating in a mounted pogrom on the halls of residence. I think I'll raise it at the next faculty meeting.' Smiling blissfully, Peter tractored out.

Michael scribbled a note in his desk diary and then sat pen in hand, gazing out at the open windows and flapping curtains of the campus residences across The Square, the smell of disinfectant scourging his nostrils.

Rag Week. Surely that made more sense. After all, there must be plenty of students at this university who knew about his relationship with Christine Reed. It wasn't the sort of thing you could keep secret even if you wanted to.

And the fact that his wife was dead?

Well, that was probably quite well known around the university too. Yes, a Rag Week prank surely made more sense. Of course, to talk of something involving such malice and cruelty 'making sense' was crazy, but *given* that malice and cruelty –

*Oh yes I've got to accept that because I can feel it touching me like cobwebs in a dark room.*

– then the Rag Week prank idea made more sense.

And besides, the alternative didn't bear thinking about.

## 7

He decided to walk home. It was about half an hour's walk to Sheeps Hill Road, but the spring weather was still remarkably warm and soft, a sort of meteorological equivalent of the colour pink, and he fancied the solitude in preference to the enforced company of the bus.

Besides, the route led past the cemetery, where Kate was buried, and he felt that she had been insulted today, and that he should go to her.

No doubt this was sentimental nonsense —

*My Fairy Palace! It's gone!*

— especially as he had no faith. He was an atheist or an agnostic, depending on who asked him the question. To some people, to profess atheism was to invite conversion — 'But how *can* you be?' — whereas agnosticism at least got you off the hook. He sometimes wished, given that you were always being exhorted to respect other people's faith, that they would respect his lack of it. After Kate's death he had tried desperately hard to believe that the essence of her still existed somewhere; he had wanted to believe it, indeed, because at one point it seemed the only way of preventing grief from turning into insanity. No good. She didn't exist for him, for Suzanne, for anyone who had known her: everything that she had loved and experienced in her life lacked her. If that wasn't oblivion, he didn't know what was.

And yet something made him go periodically to her

grave and concentrate on the memory of her. Lighting a candle against the darkness, if you liked. Registering a protest against the fact of death. Something.

The cemetery was large, in places quite old. One side of it was bounded by the ring road: a high stone wall and thick holly bushes divided the long-dead and the frenetically living, the smoke-saddened marble angels and the roaring lorries. The gravel paths were well kept, but here and there little eruptions of green spring growth disturbed the neatness. Like details from a didactic Victorian painting: *Resurgam*, I shall rise again.

Michael remembered his dream of that morning, and shivered in the bright afternoon sun.

Kate's grave, with its simple headstone, was well kept too. The clipped turf round about had that peculiar bright, almost artificial greenness only seen in cemeteries. Strange, the streets of the city thick with hamburger cartons, and here the dead reposed in hygienic cleanness. Something grim, indeed, about the sterility. Maybe the choked boneyards of Dickens' time had more of truth about them.

He should have brought flowers. Never mind. He hoped she'd understand.

As always, his eyes strayed to the neighbouring gravestones, read the names there. So bizarre, that she should be laid down for ever in the company of strangers. Even in death you couldn't avoid them. Dickens again – how did it go? 'What connection can there have been between many people in the innumerable histories of this world, who, from opposite sides of great gulfs, have, nevertheless, been very curiously brought together!'

He was being watched. From the top of a marble cross a blackbird was observing him. Every now and then it turned itself about and took up a new stance, as if it were posing for photographs.

Some people thought interment, rather than cremation, was archaic. Perhaps that, with his feeling for the past, was why Michael had chosen it. Neanderthal man laid his dead to rest in graves, and buried flowers with them. It fulfilled some need for continuity.

A cloud passed across the sun, erasing the long, stretched shadows of the headstones, and turning the grass a dun colour so that it seemed to have withered all at once. Michael realized that his mind was not focusing on Kate. Somehow she was elusive today.

In a way he preferred not to think of her spirit being around – not if it meant she could have seen that drawing on the blackboard this afternoon.

'I'm sorry, Kate,' he whispered.

After a few minutes he turned and began to make his way towards the gate. This was the oldest part of the cemetery, crowded with Victorian monumental masonry, rampant with ivy and moss that defied municipal manicuring. An angel, leprous with pollution, spread green-encrusted wings like some monstrous bat. Michael had just passed through its shadow when he heard the footsteps on the gravel path behind him.

He had, without really being aware of it, shed a few tears which were still on his face, and he didn't care to be seen; so he slightly quickened his pace towards the gate. The noise of the traffic, though it was only a hundred yards away on the other side of the stone wall, was curiously muffled here amongst the weighty tombs and urns and stelae of the city's past, and he was able to hear quite clearly that the footsteps behind him had quickened too.

*I'm alone* – the thought sprang up in his mind, swift and sharp and almost visual, like the image of the key you'd left at home on the table, the wallet you'd left on the bank counter – *alone in the city of the dead*.

The footsteps were running, and panic hit Michael like a blow between the shoulders, and he was running too, legs jerking into life, recalcitrant, scarcely obeying him . . .

He felt a tug on his jacket, and then hands were clutching at him.

Clutching, clawing, pulling, at his shirt, at his waistband, feverish, intimate – and weak.

He wasn't sure if he let out a cry as he spun round. He hoped not, for it might have further upset the little boy who was clinging to his clothes and wailing, more plaintively as he realized his mistake, 'Daddy! Daddy! Mummy, Daddy!'

Relief as well as pity almost made Michael hug the little boy, but he at once thought better of it. A cemetery, a lone man, a child – you couldn't be too careful. Crouching down, keeping the boy – no more than six – at arm's length, he said, 'Have you lost your Mummy and Daddy? Were you with them? In here?' He gestured at the cemetery.

Silenced by sobs, the boy nodded.

What a place for a kid to get lost, Michael thought. No wonder he's spooked. 'It's all right, we'll find Mummy and Daddy, I promise. Tell you what, I'll shout for them. What's your name?'

'Michael.'

No matter how ordinary your name, it was always a surprise when you found that somebody else had it. Michael Greenwood, after a moment's hesitation, climbed on to the lid of one of the giant Victorian tombs, stood up, and cupping his hands over his mouth shouted across the empty spaces of the cemetery. 'Hallo! Little boy called Michael over here, lost his mum and dad. Near the Knightsford Road entrance. Michael's mum and dad, hallo . . .' It didn't take long for even his eyesight to make out several figures hurrying along one of the gravel paths in his direction.

'*What* have I told you?' the little boy's mother barked, grabbing his hand and shaking him like a pillow, while two smaller children in her wake giggled.

'Cheers, mate,' the father said phlegmatically.

'It wasn't our fault,' the mother said, addressing Michael with apparent belligerence. 'He just runs off.'

'I know,' Michael said pacifically, 'my daughter was the same at that age—'

'Well, there you are then,' the mother snapped, hustling her brood off.

Oh, well, Michael thought, you can't expect a medal. At least his namesake gave him a little wave as he left.

*The kid wasn't the only one who was spooked, was he, sunshine?* he thought as he went out through the gate. *You lost your head yourself . . . And who was it that you thought was behind you?*

He was going to have to get a grip on this situation. Get a grip on himself, or he would be jumping at shadows. For instance, his neck was starting to tingle because he could hear a car pulling up at the kerb behind him, whereas that happened all the time, it didn't mean . . .

The car was crawling alongside him. He could see its bonnet from the corner of his eye, keeping pace . . .

A lime-green bonnet with fins. It was Fred's comical Ford Zodiac, and Fred was calling to him through the open passenger window.

'World of his own,' Fred said as Michael got in. 'Talk about the absent-minded professor. Good day?'

'Don't ask,' Michael said. Yet the shadows were already receding as he sank into the Zodiac's flatulent passenger seat next to Fred's big, calm Gabriel Oak presence. Motiveless malignity seemed a long way off, scarcely possible in fact.

'Oh, there was a phone call for you this morning, just after you left,' Fred said.

Michael's fingers fumbled at the seat belt. '. . . Yes?'

'Somebody from your publishers. Something about another radio interview. They want you to ring them back.'

'Not another one.' Michael relaxed and sat back.

'Be turning you into a media personality at this rate,' Fred smiled. 'Get on the telly, write one book every ten years, you're made.'

'You didn't hear the phone last night, did you, Fred?' Michael said. 'In the early hours.'

Fred shook his head. 'Dead to the world.' He looked with mild curiosity at Michael.

'Crank calls,' Michael said. 'Bit worrying.'

'Oh dear, oh dear,' Fred said, very rumbling, very *Archers*.

'It's difficult to know what to do. Reply, try to reason with him, tell him to piss off—'

'Don't encourage them,' Fred said. 'Worst thing you can do. That's what they want, to get a rise out of you, to know they've got to you. Gives them a kick.'

An uncharacteristic bitterness had entered Fred's tone. Michael glanced at him enquiringly.

'Had something similar once myself,' Fred said. 'When I was living in halls of residence. One of my neighbours, stalwart of the Young Conservatives, must have seen me going into a GaySoc disco or something, took exception to it. Went to the trouble of sending me a little gift-wrapped present through the post.' Fred swung the steering wheel negligently as they turned into Sheeps Hill Road, his handsome face reposeful as ever except for a slight narrowing of the eyes. 'It was a jar of Vaseline, with a note saying, "To be used in tight spots." '

'Little shit,' Michael breathed.

'Mmm.' The Zodiac's brakes howled as they pulled up in the drive. 'So I ignored it. It was either that, or pound the little tyke into hamburger meat.' Fred's large hands rested on the steering wheel a moment. Then he smiled. 'His room, by the way, was plastered all over with *Playboy* centrefolds. He doth protest too much, methinks.'

### 8

Christine came round in the evening. Suzanne, with both her birthday and the school play tomorrow, was being something of a pain — as restless as a long-legged, hair-

swinging fly — and they were both relieved when she
took her tapping Dr Martens off to bed.

They opened a bottle of wine and, kneeling about on
the living-room floor, wrapped Suzanne's presents. The
house was quiet but for a faint throb of minimalist pulse
from Fred's garret. Michael savoured the peace, not
wanting to disturb it; but what had happened in the
lecture theatre had to be told.

He told. Christine, who could ricochet around the
room like a firecracker when her temper was roused, was
surprisingly quiet.

'Perhaps I shouldn't have told you,' he said, breaking
the silence at last.

She shook her head slowly, eyes dwelling on the
middle distance. 'Of course you should.' She blinked as
if she were just waking up. 'Is there any more of that
wine?'

He passed her the bottle. She poured, drank, and then
looking at him at last said, 'This isn't just some casual
prank.'

He shook his head.

'This is real . . . persecution.'

'Yes.' There was relief, of a sort, in facing it.

'What are you going to do?'

'I don't know. None of it's certain. I *think* that this
guy Steve's behind it, yet I can't really believe it. I
mean, I'm sure it was him making those phone calls,
but as for the rest of it . . . It just doesn't make sense
for someone to go to all that trouble, over something
so petty . . . There's got to be another explanation.
But I can't think of it and I can't think of any way
of saying to the police that I'm being harassed when

I haven't got any real evidence.'

They were both silent for some time, though without unease. This was a good thing about their relationship: each recognized thought as a human activity. At last Christine said, 'Have you got a little tape recorder with a microphone?'

'Eh? Yes, I think — the radio in the kitchen, that's got one—'

'Put it by the phone,' Christine said. 'With a blank tape in it. And then if this Steve rings again, record the call. It's not much, but it's something. Something to show that you *are* being pestered. And if you do get anything at all, any other problems, go to the police. It's gone too far.' Anger rose belatedly to the surface. 'Bloody hell, my *name* used like that. What a bloody *invasion*—'

'That's what it's all about,' Michael said. 'Invading you.' He looked round at the low-lit room, Suzanne's presents in a tempting heap, the empty glasses, an open book on the floor. Again he was reminded of the time of the onset of Kate's illness — of looking about him and seeing all the familiar things shorn of their aura of security, subtly altered, distorted. The skull beneath the skin.

'Shall I stay tonight?' Christine said.

'It would be nice, if you'd like to.'

'I'd like to.'

He locked up the house while Christine went upstairs. He had always been a bit fastidious about this — 'Dad's all right, but he's a bit of a fart-arse' he had once heard Suzanne describing him to her friend Steph — but tonight he found himself, without knowing that he had done it, checking over the bolts and window-locks a third or fourth time. For some minutes he stood in the kitchen, motionless, listening because he was sure he had heard a noise, listening with his mouth open because he remembered (why could he remember things like this?) reading in a boys' adventure comic, thirty years ago, that your hearing was better with your mouth open, and so if you found yourself in a dark alley with the possibility of those archetypal flat-capped and mufflered assailants waiting to cosh you with slabs of apostrophed Cockney, then –

There was the noise again.

A perfectly familiar noise, a sort of clearing-the-throat noise made by his venerable fridge-freezer when it was about to swallow another hundred mega-units of electricity.

Michael closed his mouth with a snap. 'Bah, humbug,' he said.

Christine was already in bed when he went up. 'Get in here, Greenwood,' she said, smiling over the lip of the duvet. When he slid into the bed beside her he found that she was not wearing the pyjama-top she kept here for when she stayed the night. 'Too hot,' she said, snuggling up to him. Their kisses and caresses segued imperceptibly into something more detailed. 'Look at that, I'm under the doctor,' she whispered in his ear as he fitted himself on top of her. Their laughter, though it shook the bed, was only a brief interruption, and presently Christine's hands – God knew how she did it, but it was unfailingly marvellous – were finding places on his skin that he never knew were there, let alone suspected were so sensitive, and together they were spinning a delicious web of postponement and anticipation, and then –

He knew how it happened. He had pushed himself up and was stroking her from breast to hip with one hand, and the tactile sensation of her ribs – she was as slender as a girl – beneath his fingers revived a memory that for a second he could not place.

Then he knew it. The drawing on the blackboard. His dead wife's skeleton, observing himself and Christine obscenely joined.

The motion of his hips had become a dance out of time, a reflex. He was losing his erection. All he could see was that drawing, the childish clarity, the round eye sockets of the skull, the grins of the copulating figures . . . a blur of scandalized students, a snigger . . .

'I'm sorry,' he said, coming out with a dismal plop.

'Oh dear,' she said hazily. 'Must be the wine. Vintner's droop. Have to put a splint on it.'

They shifted, and she did some remedial manual work. To no avail.

They sat up, and each had a cigarette. The silence of the house flowed round them, viscous and oppressive. Michael stroked the white curve of her back.

'Well,' she said, 'you've got to admit that picture on the blackboard was . . . pretty to the point.'

He shook his head. 'Don't think that.'

She studied the glowing tip of her cigarette. 'I can't help thinking it. Michael, I . . . can't compete with a ghost.'

'You don't have to,' he said, hearing his voice come out edgy.

'Don't I?' She paused. 'If it's only that you're –

upset by this weird business—'

'Of course I'm upset,' he said, edgier still. 'And I don't like you being dragged into it and I don't like Kate being dragged into it, but they're two separate things, and it's him who's trying to bring them together—'

'And he's succeeding,' Christine said. 'And it's easy for him or them or whoever's messing you about, it's easy because that guilt's there to start with—'

'He's not going to succeed, do you hear, that stupid bastard's not going to succeed in fucking up my life . . .'

He saw the whites of her eyes widen. He was shouting and cussing, a thing he never did. *My God, he is succeeding, look what he's doing . . .*

'Don't take it out on me,' Christine said quietly, 'don't ever take anything out on me, Michael—'

The sound of the telephone snapped her words off.

Michael grabbed at his dressing gown, flung across the landing into the study. Anger, volcanic, gathering. He snatched up the receiver, realizing as he brought it up to his ear that he had forgotten –

*My memory!*

– to put the tape recorder by –

'All right, mate, how you doing? How you keeping? How's life treating you? How's business?'

*Steve* . . . That belligerent buttonholing matiness, unmistakable.

'. . . How's tricks, how's yourself, how's the wife?'

The laugh that exploded immediately after this was like a sort of convulsive fit. And yet so empty, such a shrieking mockery of amusement. Sometimes uncontrollable laughter could resemble uncontrollable sobbing: hilarity and grief met in a circle. Steve's laugh

107

instead had pain in it — the scream of agony, the battle yell, the exulting groan of a crowd at a public execution.

Michael thought for an instant that the strange colour before his eyes was a consequence of coming from darkness to light. But no. He was, literally, seeing red — it really happened . . . and he was barking into the receiver in a voice he hardly knew to be his own, words he had never planned, words that seemed to come from somewhere outside himself . . . 'Listen, you stupid, cracked bastard, I know who you are, I know what your stupid moronic fucking game is and you had better cut it out right now and crawl back into whatever shithole you came from because I am going to get the police on to you tomorrow and I am going to have them stitch you up so good and proper you'll wish you'd never been born, now have you got that in your thick fucking skull you mental *bastard*?'

A moment's silence on the other end of the phone was followed by a low, slow, arch, insinuating 'Wooo-oo . . . *ha-aard* . . .'

The receiver was softly replaced; but not before Michael had heard something different about Steve's breathing — something shorter, quicker.

He put down the phone, aware now of the sweat on his body, aware now of Christine watching him from the doorway. He did not need the sombre expression on her face to tell him that he had done a foolish thing.

# THREE

## 1

Steve went back to his bedsit in the late afternoon, after a busy day. He played his favourite record a few times, lay down a while. But he couldn't rest: he felt frustrated. There was nothing he could do here.

He looked at his notebook. 134 Sheeps Hill Road. That was an idea: he could go and check out the place where the Greenwood bastard lived. Think about him in there, bricking it. Steve had a laugh for a while and then got up.

In the hall he found Tommo and Adrian, with a puppy, a scruffy mongrel that trembled when you went near it. The puppy, it turned out, was Adrian's.

'I don't know why,' Adrian said. 'I was pissed. This bloke wanted to get rid of it and said I could have it for nothing so I said, go on then. I didn't know the fucker would start pissing everywhere.' He poked the puppy's rump. 'Fucking thing.'

'You can train them,' Tommo said. 'Just takes a bit of time.'

'Fuck that. I'm not arsing about trying to get some fucking dog to go outside for a piss. I've got better things to do.'

Steve just laughed and went out. These people cracked him up. They shouldn't get pets if they didn't want them! That was the trouble nowadays, people wouldn't take responsibility.

It took him over half an hour to walk to Sheeps Hill Road; but it was nothing, he was fit, he took care of himself. The sight of Greenwood's house was both interesting and frustrating. He knew Greenwood couldn't drive, he'd said so on the train, so the pukey old car in the drive must be somebody else's. His bit of stuff, maybe? He would have to find out.

There was a bus stop a little way down the road: Steve lingered there to have a good look at the place. The windows all had net curtains, except for the one in the roof, and there was a light on there, maybe a table lamp or a desk lamp or something. A bus came, but Steve waved it on as if it wasn't the one he wanted and continued his observation. Was that Greenwood's bedroom up there? Or maybe, being a smartarse, he had a study . . . His patience was rewarded when the light went off and a few moments later a tall, fair-haired guy came out of the front door, got into the puke-green car and drove off. So *he* lived there: where did he come in? Greenwood had said on the train he only had one kid. Maybe he lodged there: the house was pretty big for Greenwood and his sprog, and a lot of these places round here had students living in them . . . The puke-green car was back after a few minutes, and the tall guy went back into the house, using a key, carrying a small shopping bag. A few moments later the light in the roof came on again. Must be a lodger. Worth knowing: it was all worth knowing.

Someone came and stood at the bus stop with Steve, which made him nervous. He was conspicuous, he would have to move on. Would have been handy if there'd been an empty house nearby, somewhere he could get in and use as a lookout post; but no, it was all too lived-in, too straightforward, there were no possibilities.

It was that campus place that attracted him. That was where Greenwood and his tart hung out: that was where Steve could be invisible. He decided to go there again and suss it out some more. The evening was turning chilly after the heat of the day, but he didn't notice it, he wore the same clothes whatever the weather, the weather was inside yourself. He was surprised, when he got to the university, to find how busy it still was: people going to film shows and drama rehearsals and whatnot, others still working in the library; and of course, a lot of these students lived here, in those pyramid buildings.

Like the one that overlooked the English Studies building. He stood staring up at it. From there, he reckoned, you could see everybody who went in and out of the English Studies building, all day; and he was willing to bet that you could see Greenwood's office too, at an angle maybe, but well enough to tell if he was in there. If your eyesight was good, of course, not like Greenwood who was blind as a bat. And yet a four-eyed cunt like that got married and had a kid and then when his wife had snuffed it he was shagging this other woman with her lesbo haircut. It wasn't fair, when Steve wasn't a forty-year-old four-eyes and didn't go round insulting people on the radio and threatening them with a hammer – had that been Greenwood? Well, it came to the same thing – and yet he'd never had a girlfriend, they just

111

didn't want to know, even though that girl at Tesco's had led him on something chronic . . .

Someone came out of the security door of the residence building, a dark, slight guy in a sort of anorak effort and chinos. Steve watched him go down the walkway towards The Square. After a moment he decided to follow him. His feelings told him there might be something worthwhile here, and if not the following-game would be a bit of fun.

The dark guy went down The Street and drew out some money from the bank cash machine. Then he stood around as if undecided what to do. A group of students dressed as convicts, with striped overalls and footballs painted black tied to their ankles, went giggling by: something to do with this Rag Week business, Steve guessed. The dark guy watched them go by with a sort of wistful, timid smile, and then turned across The Street and went into The Pub.

After a minute or two Steve followed. He soon spotted the dark guy sitting on his own at a small table, with a half of lager in front of him. He had got a book out but he wasn't really reading it; he was glancing around at the groups of students in the pub – they were nearly all in groups: laughing and shrieking at each other. Steve went to the bar, got a shandy, then walked over to the jukebox. No Belinda Carlisle, no Taylor Dane: it was all this poxy trendy stuff. From the corner of his eye he watched the little dark guy.

His feelings hadn't lied. He could always spot the solitaries, the left-out ones, the people who didn't join in because they didn't dare and spent their life hanging around the outskirts. Sad cases really, Steve thought.

He went over and sat at the little dark guy's table with his shandy. The dark guy immediately switched his eyes to his book, clamping his lips tight. Steve noticed a packet of Marlboros on the table.

'All right, mate?' Steve said. 'Do us a favour, could you? Give us a fag.'

'Oh – yes, sure,' the dark guy said, proffering the packet.

'Cheers.' Steve lit up. 'Bit dead in here, innit?'

The dark guy made a sort of nervous nodding movement.

A great whinnying laugh went up from a nearby knot of students. Steve raised his eyebrows. 'I don't know,' he said. 'It's like they all seem to know each other, do you know what I mean? I mean, how do they do it?'

The dark guy gave his timid smile. 'It's difficult,' he got out, 'sometimes, to get to know people.'

Foreign, thought Steve. Foreign accent. Looked a bit like the people in Cyprus – curly black hair, smallish, dark complexion. Why didn't they go to their own colleges, instead of coming over here? Still, that didn't matter.

'You're right, mate, you're dead right,' Steve said. 'I mean, some people, they can just get along with anybody, do you see what I'm saying? It's like they've got no shyness or anything, they just go "Hellayow, how are yoooo?", it's just like "How do you dooo, what's your name, eeow, gosh . . ." ' Steve got carried away doing the posh voice, it was so funny it made him laugh, and he went away in his head for a few minutes. When he came back he found the little dark guy nervously laughing along with him. He got a grip on himself; this

113

was important, this might lead somewhere.

'No, mate, listen, what I'm saying, I'm not knocking them, it takes all sorts, doesn't it? That's what they say. You can't like judge till you've been there, the grass is always greener on the other side of the wall, do you see what I'm saying? You a student here, are you?'

'Oh, yes,' the dark guy said. 'I am reading physical sciences for a master's degree. What do you study?'

'Oh, I'm not here, mate, I'm just visiting like − well, I do this course part-time sort of thing, I'm not like actually at the university, I just sort of come here for the facilities. No, I'm on the dole, I'm afraid, mate.'

The dark guy nodded, looking concerned. 'There are a lot of people unemployed, I read, it's very bad. I think it's good that you are doing some studying too, that's a good thing.'

'Yeah, well, you got to use the time, haven't you? Stop the old brainbox going to pot, going to the dogs. Going down the drain, brain drain, good one!' Steve brought himself back from the edge of a laugh. 'It's a hard life if you don't weaken, but as long as you've got your health, that's the main thing, innit? What you drinking, mate?'

'Oh, no − please, let me get one for you,' the dark guy said. 'I, you see, I have a grant from home, so maybe I can afford a little better—'

'Oh, cheers, mate, you're great, wish they were all like you. Name's Steve, by the way.' He held out his hand.

'Pleased to meet you,' the dark guy said shyly. 'I am Georgiou Sofroniou.' So chuffed to have somebody to talk to, it was obvious: sad case really, thought Steve.

They had several drinks, and Georgiou (*Georgy-Porgy*, Steve thought to himself, *Hey there Georgy Girl*, and wanted to laugh, but he made himself stop, because this might be useful) talked about himself, prompted by Steve's questions. He was from Athens, he had come here on the university's Overseas Students Programme, he knew one or two other Greek students here but not very well, they were language students and lived a different sort of life to him, he liked England but found it a little cold and wet sometimes, the university was very good and he was working very hard, he wished his English was a little better, sometimes he got a little lonely but as Steve said it wasn't easy to get to know people, they all seemed to have their own friends . . . At last a sort of startled look came into his eyes as if he thought he shouldn't be talking about himself so much, and Steve rowed in.

'You live here then, on the campus like?' He knew that, of course; and it made him feel strong again, knowing. And he could feel God in him again, inspiring him.

'Oh, yes, I have a room in Borrow Terrace, it's just over there. It's very nice, everything you need—'

'Yeah? Cor, you're lucky. No, no offence, mate, I mean you should have it, you're working away at your physical training and everything, it's good stuff. Just I wouldn't mind a little place like that myself, you know, anything would do, only I'm stuck, you see. Had to leave my last place, just a bedsit, you know, but it was home, only they had to pull it down, you know? One of these manky old places, condemned sort of thing. So I'm stuck at the moment.'

115

'You are homeless?' Georgiou said, looking concerned again.

'Well, it's only temporary like, the council reckon they're going to house me, only it's taking ages, you know, you're just a number in the little red book, do you see what I'm saying? So in the meantime I have to manage best way I can.'

'That is terrible,' Georgiou said. 'I read about the homeless in England, how bad it is, it is very shocking in a rich country.'

'Yeah, mate, it's chronic.' Who was this little greaser to come here bad-mouthing our country? They could go back home if they didn't like it, he was fucking proud to be British even if nobody else was nowadays . . . But he mustn't say any of this, he must stay in control.

'Do you have no family?'

'No, mate, well only my mum, she's not here, she's in Scotland, she don't want to know. Still, there's always somebody worse off than yourself, that's what they say, yeah? Listen, I'd better be pushing off soon, you want another drink before they call time?'

'Er − no, I'm all right, thank you.' Georgiou hesitated. 'I'd better go too. It's been very nice talking to you, maybe we could meet up again . . . Unless you'd like to come back for a coffee?'

'Ah, cheers, mate, that's nice of you, I won't say no! Settle the old beer down, nice one.'

Georgy-Porgy was looking even more chuffed at having some company as he unlocked the security door and led Steve up some disinfectant-smelling stairs. Music was booming on all sides. 'Some of my neighbours are a little noisy,' Georgiou said apologetically. 'Usually they turn it down late at night, and, well, I don't like to complain—'

'Nah, mate, live and let live, I'm with you there, wish everybody felt the same,' Steve said. Second floor, no, third floor, better and better. They went along a long corridor lit by fluorescent lights. Looked like a prison, Steve thought. Cushy number though. And they had blokes and girls living together mixed in these places! — he had caught sight of a girl cooking in a big kitchen on their way up. No wonder these students were all so promiscuous, it was disgusting.

'I'm afraid it's a little messy,' Georgiou was saying as he unlocked a door at the end of the corridor and switched on the light. 'The cleaner came in just this morning, but I've made it untidy already.'

'Nah, mate, you can't call it home if it's all neat and tidy, you know what I mean?' Steve eyed the room. Fairly small, narrow wooden bed, desk, bookshelves, postcards stuck all over the walls, big window with curtains still open and —

Oh, yes. The perfect view, you could see everything, like God . . . Oh, yes, his feelings had led him right here, he had made a good move. Watch out, Michael bastard Greenwood, because Steve had God on his fucking side.

'You have a cleaner come in, you say?'

'Yes, once a week to clean the rooms. Is coffee OK? I'm afraid I don't have any tea—'

'Yeah, cheers mate, just the job.' He watched as Georgy Girl farted about with a little kettle and cups and then pulled in a carrier bag that was hanging from the window.

'It's where I keep my milk,' Georgiou said with his

little nervy smile. 'There is a fridge in the kitchen, but you can't put things in there because people take them.'

'Yeah? Jesus, that's terrible. I don't know, it's getting like it's just crime everywhere nowadays, people just don't have any respect, everything's just breaking down, like my bike, you know I had my bike nicked, can you believe that? I mean, I left it in the shed, man, if you can't leave your own bike in the *shed* without somebody coming along and nicking it—' All the rage of that time mounted up in Steve as he thought of it, the bike, the guy with the hammer, and he felt the blood rushing to his cheeks, his fists clenching . . . But he needed to be calm now, it was important. He forced himself to laugh. 'Yeah, crazy, crazy world, man, totally crazy.'

There were photographs all over the room, presumably of this dago-land where the guy came from, so Steve asked about them. Georgiou was more than happy to talk: Steve guessed that nobody ever came to his room for a chat like this. Pathetic really, but it was your own fault if you couldn't mix, that was his opinion. Georgiou talked about his home in Athens, raved about sailing in the Aegean, showed snaps of his family including some cousins in Australia (Christ they got everywhere), showed this great big lump of rock that came from some Greek island or other where he used to spend his holidays. It was a drag, but it kept him talking till late, and that was the main thing: it enabled Steve to look at the time and say, 'Bloody hell. I didn't know it was that late. I'd better think about where I'm going to kip.'

'Do you have somewhere to go?' Georgiou said, all anxious.

'Well, to be honest, mate, I am a bit stuck. I've been sleeping on mates' floors when I can, you know, but I think I've like imposed on them a bit too much, and at this time of night . . . Listen, you couldn't do us a favour, could you? Let me kip on your floor tonight?'

He watched the greaser carefully. 'Well,' Georgiou said, 'I'm afraid I don't have any other bed or anything like that—'

'Nah, mate, just the floor'll be brilliant, honest, I've been in the army, I'm used to roughing it a bit. Just as long as I can get my head down in the warm.'

'Well – if you are really without a place to go—'

'Honest, mate, I wouldn't ask otherwise, and you seem like a good sort of bloke, you know what I mean, some people don't give a toss for other people, that's the trouble nowadays. And listen, it's nothing funny, right, do you see what I'm saying? I don't go along with that queer stuff, no way, so you needn't worry about that. I don't snore' – he laughed, and let the laugh carry him along for a bit before coming back to himself – 'and first thing tomorrow, I'll be off.'

Georgiou was plucking his lip. 'Well – it's very bad having to sleep on the streets, that is bad . . . I have a sleeping bag, if you—'

'Ah, cheers, mate, you're brilliant! I tell you, if there was more like you, things wouldn't be so bad in this world, I mean that.'

Half-nervous, half-pleased, Georgiou began shifting furniture. 'If we move this chair over here, there'll be room for you . . . Of course, we are not supposed to have overnight guests, but I don't think anyone takes any notice of that.'

'Nah, course not.' You could say that again, Steve thought. These students were all at it, jumping in and out of each other's beds, it was no wonder there were all these single-parent families and AIDS and all the rest of the filth, they just had things too easy. 'Just nip to the loo, mate. Down the end of the corridor, innit?'

But it wasn't the toilet he wanted. He had seen a payphone in the downstairs hall, and he needed to call Greenwood.

Needed to, because he was so full of beans. He almost skipped down the stairs, calling out 'All right?' to a snooty-faced girl he passed coming up. Full of beans, full of the joys of fucking spring, that was him, and he just had to give Greenwood another little dig, another little jab. Remind him that the game was still on and that it was going to get a lot hotter. Give him a ring, joys of spring, ring-a-ding-ding. And that was funny because that was how he was starting to picture the situation, as a ring, like the rings they led bulls and horses round, except that it was Greenwood in the ring and the poor blind bastard was wandering round and round while Steve was leaning over the fence, now here, now there, and giving him a jab with the cattle-prod, now here, now there, they seek him fucking everywhere —

Steve burst into laughter. There was only one winner in this game.

Especially now he had himself a nice little gaff right on the campus, right where Greenwood and his tart spent their time, right in the middle of thousands of other young people who were the best camouflage you could wish for.

*Wonder what sort of day he had*, Steve thought. *Wonder how sleepy he's feeling.*

He didn't feel sleepy himself. Relaxed, though. Relaxed in a totally new way.

For the first time in his life, he was *in control*.

*Or was it the first time? Hadn't he been in control that time when his dad had lain there with tea soaking into his pyjama sleeve and begged with his eyes?*

Maybe. But this feeling was if anything even better. He had turned the tide of his life. It had always been running against him, but not any more.

He picked up the telephone receiver. There was a sticker on the wall above it — rape crisis again. Christ, these women were obsessed with it. Just frigid, in his opinion. And a gay helpline too, Christ, it made you sick. He dialled Greenwood's number and waited, listening, picturing Greenwood looking up in alarm, moving towards the phone . . . Smells of burning toast and sounds of thumping music drifted down from the residences. Come on, Greenwood, don't pretend you're not there. You're shitting it, aren't you? Well, it's not my fault, mate. You brought this on yourself —

'Hello?'

Bingo. Steve started to talk, asking him how his wife was, laughing, it was good stuff . . .

And then it started to go a bit wrong. Greenwood was coming back at him, shouting, swearing . . .

It was because he was scared shitless, of course, and that was good, that was what he wanted, he was getting a rise out of him.

And yet as Steve listened he felt his face flushing and that feeling of pressure building up in his head like when

121

he was starting one of his headaches and something was not right.

'. . . *stupid, cracked bastard* . . .'

Steve tried to laugh, couldn't.

'. . . *moronic* . . .'

*His dad crumpling up the school report* . . . *'Just stupid, Steven, that's what you are'* . . .

Greenwood was finishing his little tirade with some crap about the police. Of course, he was bound to say that, that didn't bother Steve, what was bothering him was –

*The barrack wall STEVE SHITFORBRAINS.*

– no, nothing was bothering him, he was all right, he was in control . . .

'. . . *stupid* . . .'

'Wooo-oo, *ha-aard*,' he managed to say, and put the receiver down. It jiggled slightly in the cradle as he did so.

He paced around the hall, windmilling his arms. He wished he had his football scarf with him, you gripped one end and flicked the other up at the ceiling, bonk bonk, it was good that, you could do it for ages, it made you feel better when things weren't right . . .

'Aah . . .' He had meant to laugh to cheer himself up, but it came out as a sort of groan. There was some sort of cupboard near the phone. He ran at it and kicked. He kicked a good big crack in the plyboard door, kept kicking until there was a gaping hole. The hole looked funny. He laughed.

He was all right. He was in control. He started back up the stairs, chanting under his breath.

Nothing had changed. The game was still on. And it

made it better if the opponent showed a bit of fight, didn't it? Course it did.

The sleeping bag on Georgy Girl's floor was comfy enough for him – he was used to roughing it a bit, people were too soft nowadays. For some time after he had got into it and the greaser had got into bed and turned out the light Steve talked, but he wasn't wholly sure what he was saying – it was just calming-himself-down talk, getting the heavy weight off his chest like he had to sometimes. At last the talk ran down, and soon Steve could tell from his breathing that Georgy Girl was asleep.

But Steve didn't want to sleep, yet. He was running over in his mind the events of the last two days, savouring his success.

The funny thing was, you could still slip back into trusting people: you could momentarily forget what they were like underneath. That was what had happened on that train yesterday when he had sat opposite Greenwood. Steve still believed in being friendly, you had to make the effort, else why were we put on earth in the first place? And really, things had seemed to go all right on that train. Steve still liked meeting people, finding out about them, seeing into their lives. Dr Michael bastard Greenwood was just another one to meet. Or so it seemed. Of course, several times he let it slip that he was against Steve; but then that was only to be expected, and Steve decided to let it go. He was going to have to start fighting back soon, but he didn't particularly want it to be yet. So the journey to Cambridge had come to an end, and he had said goodbye to the guy, and gone on to see his mum. It was a bit of a pain going to see her really. She had a nice little sheltered housing flat, she nattered to the neighbours, she didn't need him. In fact he suspected she was probably against him now: the other week she had said something about some relation of her neighbour's who was just turned thirty, 'and he's not married', which was clearly a dig at him. But it was his duty to go and visit her, and duty was one of those things that people didn't believe in nowadays which was why the world was in such a chronic state. Besides, he was short of money and she always gave him some: the dead old man had covered himself with so many insurance policies she had quite a bit salted away. Of course, she just slipped him the tenners so as not to be bothered with him, that was all it was. He knew her game. But he made the effort so his conscience was clear. And so he was sitting there in the living room of her flat and she was messing about in the kitchen making him something to eat (because she said he didn't eat properly, for Christ's sake, she was always *getting* at him) and he'd remembered that the guy from the train had said he was going on the radio. And so he switched on the old trannie his mum had on the sideboard, mainly to see if it was true what the Greenwood guy had been telling him, because he knew people were always fobbing him off with lies and he had probably made up all that stuff about going to the radio station, just to trick him. But there was his voice all right, going on about the poor people of Norfolk years ago and how they'd rioted and broken some farm machinery or something. It all sounded a bit anti. All right, maybe they were poor, but you had to have some sort of order, and anyway a lot of them were probably lazy, you only had to look at people nowadays, how easy they had things . . .

And then, just as the interview came to an end, just as Steve was about to switch the radio off, Michael bastard Greenwood issued his challenge.

'*Steve . . . thanks, Steve, for making the journey sheer purgatory . . .*' It was *on the airwaves*. He was being attacked *on the airwaves* for Christ's sake, that Greenwood was calling all the bastards' attention to Steve, giving the signal, let's get at Steve everybody!

Steve was shaking as he snapped the radio off. The rage in his blood was so great that he felt the vessels would burst, spraying the walls of the room with fountains of scarlet. He had to lock himself in the toilet for a few minutes, and do some chants and the special thing with his arms, a sort of windmill motion, that sometimes made him feel better. He laughed a bit, too, to cheer himself up.

He had known something like this was going to happen, of course. His feelings had told him so. It was all just forming a *pattern*, he'd have to be *stupid* not to see it –

*His father ripping up his school report. 'They're too soft on you, Steven. Lazy? You're just stupid, that's all. Stupid.'*

– it was a *pattern* and thank God he'd seen it. Yes, God was good. It had been building up all through school and the army and Tesco's and The Alders and the bedsit, you could look back and see it all rising up like the line on a graph right to the moment when Michael bastard Greenwood publicly crucified him just like Our Lord Jesus.

Except, thought Steve as he silently bolted down the dinner his mum had made him, except they'd made a mistake.

They'd pushed him too far.

*We'll see who's stupid, Mister fucking doctor university professor smartarse*, he told himself, and having finished his dinner and touched his mother for another twenty he set off for home. Eager, and feeling intensely alive. Because he had taken up the challenge, and he was going to enjoy it.

He didn't see Greenwood on the train back home. That was all right, he preferred it that way. It would be no good doing it yet, that would spoil the whole point. And he needed to have a good think. Some annoying bastard came and sat opposite him when they got to Ely and tried to talk to him − he couldn't *believe* it, the way they *picked* on him at every little opportunity − but Steve got rid of him. Just by staring at him. It really shitted him up, and Steve wanted to laugh. Yes, he could feel his strength growing. God was helping.

Back at the bedsit he put Taylor Dane on full blast and got the telephone directory from the hall and looked up Greenwood. Michael Greenwood. The conspiracy might be out to make him think he was stupid, but if he was stupid how come he had such a good memory? Maybe he sometimes forgot to have a bath or eat some dinner but what the hell, you didn't *need* all that stuff. He could remember everything about Michael bastard Greenwood. He liked to remember things that people said about themselves, liked to keep them inside himself, bits of knowledge. It gave him an advantage, and God knew he needed every advantage he could get with everybody against him.

There weren't many Greenwoods in the book, and only one M. Greenwood. There was the number, and the address too. 134, Sheeps Hill Road. Other side of the city.

He sat for some time on the bed with the book open before him, contemplating the address and telephone number, savouring the possession of them. There they were, he had them, and it was a good feeling, it was the best feeling he had had for a long time. A feeling of growing strength.

Then he reached for his notebook and pencil. He flipped through to find a blank page. Many of the pages were filled with prayers that he'd written out, descriptions of feelings, other things that had occurred to him. Here was a page with LEEDS UNITED written over and over again, filling the whole page. That looked good, he thought. A drawing of a naked woman, with long hair the way it should be, not like these hard women nowadays, you know what they needed. A page covered with squiggles. A page with the word *fuck* filling every space of every single line. *Fuckfuckfuck*. When had he done that? It was funny though. Steve threw back his head and had a good laugh. You could get carried away with laughing sometimes, your voice came out with all these different sounds, they were really funny, it made you laugh even more. At last he came back – that was the only way to describe it, you went away and then came back – and found a clean sheet of paper and wrote down everything he could remember about Michael bastard Greenwood. Steve had it all clear in his mind, but it was even better to write it all down and look at it.

Strength.

Purgatory. That was what Michael bastard Greenwood had said, that was what being with Steve was like according to Mr fucking smartarse doctor professor. And he had said, Steve, if you're listening, you're a pathetic shitforbrains who can't get it up. Imagine saying that on the radio, in the day, with kids listening, it was disgusting!

Was that what he had said? Maybe not those words, but his feelings told him that something like that had been said. Greenwood had definitely said *purgatory*, anyway. And Steve knew about that, it was blasphemous saying that. His dad had always warned about the dangers of Catholicism, but Steve was inclining more and more that way and he would have converted if that priest he'd talked to hadn't been against him. Purgatory. Fancy making a joke about that, that was the trouble, there was no *respect* any more . . .

And so he had gone out to the phone box on the corner near the parcels depot and for the first time dialled Michael Greenwood's number. And began it. The first two phone calls were great, hearing Dr Let's-hate-Steve's-guts Greenwood's voice, at first cocky, then unsure. The second time Steve just couldn't help laughing, it was so funny, the whole situation was just so brilliant. The third time, right in the small hours, didn't seem quite so good at first: Greenwood wouldn't answer, or he was slow getting to the phone, and by then Steve had seen a police car go cruising down the street and it had made him so nervous he'd put the phone down and hurried back to the bedsit. He was all for the police, one hundred per cent, but there were always the dodgy ones, the bent ones, who probably had it in for him and might start trumping up some charge and saying he was doing wrong. Which he wasn't, full stop. Because Greenwood had brought this on himself.

Steve had lived in the city for several years, but he had never been to the university before. When he had arrived there early that morning, after a few hours' sleep, he was surprised at how big it was. Surprised, and pleased. He'd thought of it like school, where you were always on show, where you couldn't hide; but this place was practically a town, with hundreds of people milling about everywhere. You could just lose yourself in the crowd. A few clocked him up in that snooty studenty way, but mostly they just seemed to accept him as part of the scenery. It was great: he was anonymous, free.

There was a map of the campus next to this horrible modern fountain thing, and he had soon worked out where Greenwood would do his stuff. Wandering around the corridors of the English Studies building, he was amazed again at how easy this was. You could just nose around, and no one took any notice. And on the main notice board outside the common room there was even a list of all the tutors, with their office numbers.

And there was Greenwood's office. With a little dull metal sign next to the door. *Dr Michael Greenwood*. Steve didn't know what he was feeling as he read that. It was a sort of exultation that made him want to laugh but there was something pure and quiet about it as well.

He felt strong.

There was no one in the grey corridor but himself. He tapped at the door. If there was any reply he would quickly slip away, because that wasn't part of the plan.

The plan was to get to know Greenwood's haunts, to spy on him, to see how the land lay, maybe give him a taste of what was to come if it was possible. Intelligence work in the war. But when he tried the handle and found the door was unlocked, he knew this was a chance not to be missed. This opportunity was literally Heaven-sent, and he said thank you to God.

In Greenwood's office. In his room, amongst his things. Steve was feeling stronger and stronger. Not much to see: a few books on steel shelves, a few papers, a poster of some old poet who Steve seemed to remember hearing had been a homo which was typical. Nothing in the drawers that was any use to him . . . but on the desk, that was different. There was a desk diary, and Michael bastard Greenwood had written all his appointments in it.

Steve's eyes devoured them, absorbed them, memorized them. Greenwood's life, all set out before him . . . the excitement was almost physical. In fact it was physical, and it was then that the best idea of all came to him . . .

Lying in Georgiou's sleeping bag, remembering, Steve gave a giggle into the darkness.

Ah, it had been a busy day. After leaving Greenwood's office he remembered he had a birthday card to send, and spent some time in the bookshop choosing just the right one. Then he got a stamp from the little post office − they had everything here! − and sent it off. Then he did some more exploring. He found a few vantage points, in a coffee bar, in the pool room of the Student Union building, where you had a reasonable view of the campus down below, looking like something made out of Lego with all these little figures scurrying back and forth over the terraces and walkways. It made him laugh to see them, they were so much like insects. You could imagine a big foot coming down and stamping on them. But they weren't the sort of places you could stay in for long, not without someone staring and sizing you up and trying to antagonize you; and you didn't get a clear view of the English Studies building. The best place for that, he had seen straight away, would be the weird pyramid-shaped place that directly faced it, but when he tried to get in there he found security doors barring his way. It was where the students lived, he had guessed. Pasted outside the security doors he saw notices about rape counselling and stuff, which made him laugh. You only had to look up at the windows of this place to see girls moving about, and they probably did that at night too, curtains open, half-dressed: if that wasn't asking for it he didn't know what was.

But now he was in! He had used his loaf and got himself a gaff here and it was magic!

One place anybody could walk in, though, was the pub. And it was there, this lunchtime, that he had seen Greenwood and his woman.

He wasn't into drink. It made him feel sick, and then superior, to see them all crammed in there tipping poison into their insides. He got a shandy and some packets of crisps and looked for someone to talk to. A lot of them gave him funny looks, but at last he sat himself down with a group who were talking about their holidays. One girl in a really short skirt — he wouldn't let her go about in a skirt like that if she was his girlfriend, but then the bloke sitting with her looked as if he was on drugs anyway — started talking about going to Paris, so Steve weighed in with, 'I've been to Paris', just to be friendly. He hadn't, but he had been to plenty of places, he'd been to Cyprus for Christ's sake, he'd seen some things there which was more than this lot had. The girl with the legs just said, 'Oh, right', and carried on talking, and he saw a few funny looks pass between them as he joined in the conversation which showed him that they were against him really, but he didn't care. He sensed that it didn't matter here, that there were all sorts of people and most of them were only interested in themselves. Here you could be just another face.

And the group he was with were just talking about this thing called Rag Week, which sounded pretty interesting, when he had caught sight of a face *he* knew all right.

Greenwood had come into the pub. He was making his way to the bar, and what with the size of the place and the crowd and Greenwood's being as blind as a fucking bat Steve realized there was practically no chance of him seeing him.

It was brilliant. It was so brilliant that Steve even found himself getting a bit of a hard-on as he sat there blending in with the crowd and looking through the blue cigarette smoke and the milling students straight at the figure of Michael bastard Greenwood. *Because Greenwood didn't know.* That was what felt so good. It made him want to laugh; yet in a way the pleasure was too deep for laughter.

It was the pleasure of strength.

Steve half turned his face as for a moment it looked as if Greenwood might come this way with his pint. But no, he had gone and sat down with some woman with short hair and dangly earrings. Steve disliked those earrings. He liked it when the women in his magazines wore some jewellery because that was different, that was glamour, but when women walked around like that — there was just something wrong about it. He supposed the woman was some smartarse doctor or professor or whatever they called themselves —

And then he had seen Greenwood and the woman kissing each other on the lips.

'You OK?' one of the students said.

'Yeah, I'm good, mate, cheers, great stuff,' Steve said. He wasn't thinking about what he was saying. He couldn't take his eyes off Greenwood and that woman. How many people were there in here? It was packed anyway. And there they were kissing in public. It was disgusting. And now the woman had her hand on Greenwood's knee as they talked.

He was too old! He was forty at least! And she must be getting on that way. Maybe he was all-right-looking, not that Steve knew anything about that, only homos looked at other men like that — but still, he shouldn't be doing it, not at his age. It was disgusting.

And what was more, Greenwood's wife had died. He'd told him so, on the train.

His wife was dead, and here he was snogging and feeling up some other woman.

Someone nearby gave a loud, yelping laugh, and Steve whipped his head round. Were they laughing at him? Because they were dead if they were, he wasn't going to put up with it any longer . . .

No. Just some studenty joke he didn't understand.

Christ, this lot laughed at nothing . . .

It was interesting though, Greenwood being a dirty bastard like this. It had possibilities. He watched them: they were talking with their heads close together. A new rage came up inside him, the rage that he had never done that and never could because women were even more against him than men if that was possible, but after a moment he directed the rage into his growing strength, which absorbed it and fed on it.

That was good. Control. He was in control.

At last Greenwood and the woman got up and moved towards the door. Steve got up and moved towards the door too, keeping at a safe distance. It was easy with all the people going backwards and forwards. Outside they parted and went different ways. But Steve kept his eyes on the woman. He knew where Greenwood was going: he had that all clear in his mind. It was the woman he was interested in for the moment.

He set himself to follow her. This was easy for him too, because he had experience. He had been doing it for a couple of years now: you picked someone out in the street, kept your eye on them, followed them everywhere they went, and ideally – it wasn't always easy, they might get into a car or taxi or something – followed them all the way home. Saw them go in at their front door and close it, thinking it was just a normal day and all unaware that someone had been watching them. That was the thrill – *they didn't know*. And now you even knew where they lived. You could even . . . Well, if you wanted to you could take it further. Not that Steve ever had, yet.

And this place was brilliant for following people

because it was so busy. Of course, even with a lot of comings and goings you could make yourself conspicuous to the person you were following, if you weren't skilful about it. Go down a few little byways of your own, that was the key: look in a window, nip into a shop, even turn and walk in the opposite direction for a bit if you could manage it. With this woman he hadn't got that much leeway; she was brisk, and he had to stick fairly close. First she went to the bank, then she went to the mini-supermarket. He followed her in there, and joined the queue at the till three places behind her. He bought himself a Mars bar, survival food, you could keep going for ages on snacks like these, in fact he seldom ate anything else. Outside again he shadowed her back down The Street and across a walkway and then up some steps into the Economic and Social Studies building. Would she have an office too? That might be interesting.

Inside she took the lift. Tricky. But surely she wouldn't use the lift just for one floor . . . He sprinted up two floors, looked into the vestibule. No sign. He pounded up to the third floor . . . Still not there. Shit, if he lost her –

No, there she was, taking something out of a row of pigeonholes that ran the length of the wall. Steve pretended to look at a notice board, watching from the corner of his eye. It was some sort of letter she had, but whatever it was she wasn't very interested: she crumpled it up and threw it into the bin next to the pigeonholes. Then she turned and walked down the corridor and straight into a classroom.

He couldn't follow her there, and God knew how long

these classes lasted. But the letter she had thrown away was lying right on top of the bin. Steve looked around. There were a couple of girls standing near the other end of the pigeonholes, talking in their la-di-da way, wrapped up in themselves. He moved swiftly and snatched up the letter and the brown envelope and made for the privacy of the toilets.

It was only some sort of form letter: *To all students taking the Liberalism and the Nineteenth Century course: please take note that the deadline for the final essay is May 22nd. Extensions only in exceptional circumstances* . . .

But the envelope was better. It had her name on it. *Christine Reed, School of Economic and Social Studies*.

Steve stuffed both letter and envelope into the pocket of his tracksuit bottoms, and flushed the toilet. He had the name of the woman Greenwood was knocking off. Good stuff. The telephone directory would tell him more.

And most interesting of all, it turned out she wasn't some sort of lecturer, as he'd first thought, but a student. At her age! She ought to be at home looking after the kids. She was probably one of these modern types who let them run wild while she was doing her own thing, which was how they ended up on drugs and being turned into homos. And meanwhile she was getting knocked off by a tutor! Were the teachers supposed to start screwing the students at this place? Surely not. And it wasn't as if there was any doubt that that was the situation. You weren't going to tell him that they were brother and sister, the way they were snuzzling up in that pub! Disgusting. But it was worth knowing. Well worth knowing . . .

Georgy-Porgy was snoring lightly. It didn't bother Steve. He let out another giggle as he remembered the best part of the day.

Divine inspiration, that was the word. He knew from Greenwood's desk diary that he was doing this lecture at three in Lecture Theatre One, so he had thought he'd make that his next port of call, check out the scene, see what was happening.

He'd got there early. The place − Christ, it was huge! − was just emptying from the last lecture. He went in − it was so easy, you just waltzed in, though he carried his notebook and pen for camouflage − and sat himself down and looked the place over. He had a thought of Greenwood standing up at the lectern there and how easy it would be to pick him off with a rifle from here, just like old JFK, and he thought of that wobbly piece of film where you see the top of the President's head coming off, and the thought made him laugh. And then he realized that the last stragglers had left the lecture theatre and that for the moment he was totally alone.

Divine inspiration.

In a moment he was up on the stage and drawing away, and it was the best drawing he had ever done, sometimes he had drawn pictures in his notebook that were so good he couldn't control himself but this was definitely the best one ever, it was just brilliant . . . And by the time the first students began filtering in he was sitting in a seat right at the back of the theatre and ready for the fun to start.

Steve couldn't remember the subsequent hour very well: he had gone away in his head so much with the pleasure of it. He had been laughing, but he couldn't let the laughter out, and so it all filled him inside like a funny gas; he felt like he was going to soar up to the ceiling. Greenwood's face! Greenwood's fucking blind-as-a-bat face, as he scrubbed the drawing off the blackboard and then glared up at the lecture theatre where Steve was sitting watching him!

Watching him. And he didn't know. But did he start to suspect? Steve had been so happy that sometimes a little snort of laughter escaped him even though he tried to stop it, and Greenwood seemed to think something was up. Luckily everybody was coughing and fidgeting and sniffing anyway, they weren't very healthy these students, probably all the drugs they took, they'd no respect for the bodies God gave them, just abused them with drugs and filth and homo perversion . . . And then when Greenwood went all red in the face and flipped! Steve had just sat quiet, knowing the bastard couldn't see him. And then that poor mare who thought he was getting at her coughing stood up and went out in a huff . . . It was joy. It was sheer joy.

So Steve had sat on till the end of the lecture. He didn't hear a word of it. He just looked at Greenwood, all on his own on the stage, sweating it, shitting it. Sometimes the thought of the rifle and the top of the head coming off like a lid occurred to him again, but that was just fantasy. Besides, that would just be an end. And Steve was enjoying this too much at the moment. He was totally, delightfully engrossed in what he was doing – what he had begun to plan from the moment that Greenwood had attacked him on the radio and pushed him that bit too far – and he was going to enjoy it even more as it went on. Especially now that he had concluded a brilliant first day's campaign by getting himself this brilliant gaff with Georgy-Porgy, right where he needed to be.

What he was doing was quite simple. He was going to make Michael Greenwood's life purgatory.

# FOUR

## 1

'Oh, Dad, you're *joking*,' Suzanne said. 'Walk to school with me? What *for*?'

'I don't want you going on your own, so I'll come with you.'

'Dad, don't *do* this to me,' Suzanne wailed. 'What if my friends see me? I'll just *die*.'

'No you won't.' Michael put his jacket on.

Suzanne stared at him. 'Bloody hell,' she said mutinously, 'if this is what it's like to be twelve, I wish I was eleven again.'

'And don't swear,' Michael said. And thought: what is this 'don't swear' crap? She effs and blinds like a docker when she's with her mates, you know she does, all kids do from about the age of five, it doesn't mean a thing . . .

But after the sight of that birthday card, *any* profanity connected with her seemed an outrage.

'Christine—' Suzanne appealed.

'Your dad's a bit worried,' Christine said, 'and so am I. So I think the best thing is if we all go in my van. We've got to go to the university, so I can drop you off at school on the way.'

'But it's only five minutes' walk,' Suzanne said. 'And I've told you, I don't even know any Steve.' She seemed mollified, however: getting a lift was crucially different, in cool terms, from being walked to school by your dad.

While she ran upstairs to get her bag Michael and Christine looked at each other sombrely.

'Steve isn't exactly an unusual name,' Christine said.

Michael shook his head. 'She doesn't lie. She says she doesn't know any Steves, none who'd send her a card.'

He, on the other hand, did know a Steve, God help him.

## 2

The day, Suzanne's birthday, had started out all right.

It hadn't been a good night, of course, because of that taunting phone call that had made Michael lose his head and start shouting abuse at his tormentor – a bad move, as he had agreed with Christine when they went back to bed, an unwise move. But it was done now: so they lay in bed and smoked and talked it through and agreed that he mustn't react again, assuming there was any more of it. And that if there was, and he had something tangible to show that he was being persecuted, then he would go straight to the police. So they had slept at last, and Michael had woken to surprising confirmation of the cliché that things did look better in the morning. It was morning, it was bright and hot again, someone across the road was going through the usual ritual of trying to kick-start a recalcitrant motorbike, Fred upstairs was playing his weird mood-music, and it was Suzanne's birthday. Not a set of circumstances conducive to the idea that someone somewhere —

*And where? Where was he?*

— was single-mindedly trying to make his life a misery. No. Life was just too *normal* for that.

And so they had gone downstairs and Suzanne had ripped open her presents and loved the beanbag and the Seal poster and the headphones and even the sunglasses and had gleefully accepted the money Michael gave her for those trainers she wanted (how *could* plimsolls cost so much?). And then she had opened her cards, from Michael, from Christine, from Fred, from Steph, from her grandmother in Cumbria enclosing record tokens — and from somebody signing himself *Steve*.

Suzanne was mainly embarrassed: bewildered, also; and seemed to wish to forget the whole thing. She couldn't think who could have sent it; whoever he was, he was a creep. She was most embarrassed of all at her dad's having to see the card.

*On your birthday*, the card read on the front, *it's nice to have a cup of tea in bed . . . or coffee . . . or cocoa . . .* and inside, *because you'll feel much better with SOMETHING HOT INSIDE YOU!* Beneath the printed message, in big, clear, swooping handwriting, were the words *All The Best From Your 'Mate' Steve*.

It had been chosen, it seemed, for maximum offensiveness and inappropriateness for a girl of twelve.

Michael fancied he could smell the malice coming off the card. A small square of cardboard, sent through the post; yet in its way it was as ugly an incursion as the pile of filth left on his office floor.

Only the recollection that this was evidence of some sort prevented Michael from ripping the card to pieces.

*Leave my daughter out of it*, he thought fiercely. *It's me you've got a grudge against, for whatever mad reason*. But that, of course, assumed that his persecutor was playing according to some gentlemanly rules: and was that likely? Especially after that drawing on the blackboard.

No, it was not at all likely.

Suzanne was cheerful again as they drove her to school: this was a day of double excitement, because it was the long-awaited play tonight, and she made Michael promise again that he hadn't forgotten and wouldn't suddenly say tonight that he'd got to go to some dons' meeting or other. When they dropped her off Christine said, unprompted: 'I'll pick you up from school this afternoon, Suzanne, all right?'

Suzanne seemed about to say something, then changed her mind. 'OK,' she said. 'See you later.'

Michael watched her gawkily running to the school gates. Poised between childhood and adolescence: give her a year, six months, and she wouldn't run, she'd slope, running would be uncool.

'Thanks,' Michael said as they drove on. 'Maybe I'm being paranoid.'

'It's no problem,' Christine said. 'This whole situation is, though, isn't it?'

He nodded.

'He must live in the city,' he said, half to himself. They were on the ring road, in the rush hour: thousands of people, speeding along the particular grooves of their particular lives, separate, mutually indifferent. That was the unwritten contract, anyway: the grooves might cross occasionally, but the contact should be fleeting, meaningless. Of course sometimes it happened otherwise — sometimes those blind, hurtling bodies collided significantly, resulting in a friendship, a partnership, a love affair. But for the most part urban modern life was, and should be, a matter of strangers.

Strangers on a train . . .

Except that once in a while maybe it didn't work that way. Many people, most perhaps, were familiar with those fortuitous collisions in which you first met your best friend or the lover who changed your life. Michael suspected that what had happened to him was the opposite: he had met hate.

*I have met hate and its name is Steve,* he thought wryly, grimly. And he didn't even know its surname. He knew next to nothing about the man who was handling his life with insolent, prying, obscene fingers.

'What have you got on today?' Christine said.

'Oh, seminar this morning, then that book signing, then another seminar. Got some advisees to see as well.'

'I'm free after one. I'll meet you for lunch.'

'OK. I've got something else to do as well. See about getting my phone number changed, go ex-directory.'

The day's schedule. He spoke of it casually: neither of them voiced the question — what unscheduled events might it have in store?

### 3

Steve had bad dreams, sleeping on Georgiou Sofroniou's floor.

The worst one, as always, was the desert dream. He was lost in miles and miles of sand, stretching away to the horizon. But this wasn't an ordinary desert. The sky wasn't blue as it was in films, nor was the sand that silky golden colour. The sky was dark, horribly dark, and the sand was grey and gritty like pulverized mud. Like dirt, like filth. It got into his shoes and under his clothes and into his mouth. No one was there: no one existed, it was just him and that filthy stuff all over him, smothering him . . .

He woke in a black mood. Georgy-Porgy was up, tiptoeing around, brushing his hair.

'I'm sorry, I didn't mean to wake you,' he said. 'Did you sleep all right?'

'Yeah,' Steve said.

'Would you like a cup of coffee? And some toast, maybe?'

'Haven't you got any tea?'

'No, I'm sorry, I don't drink it. Maybe I can borrow—'

'Oh, go on, coffee then.'

Steve rolled up the sleeping bag and then sat on it, hunched, smoking one of Georgiou's cigarettes. Bad dreams. Bad fucking vibes. He knew it, this was going to be one of those days when he couldn't do anything, when the only thing to do was sit and stare and stare into space, it was the only comfortable thing, it was the only thing that felt *right* . . .

It was all Greenwood's fault. He'd done this to him. He hadn't had this feeling, this *dead* feeling, for ages — well, for a while anyhow. These were the times when he saw clearly how bad the world was. How bad the people in it were. *Look* at them. You just had to look at them to know they would be better off out of it. And that wasn't his mind, like they'd tried to convince him at The Alders. That was reality. Thank God he'd seen it at last.

Georgy Girl was talking again. Jesus, he hated these chatterbox types, rabbit rabbit — 'What?'

Georgiou smiled timidly and gestured at the window. 'I was just saying it's a lovely day again.'

'Yeah.' Steve ambled over to the window. 'Yeah, beautiful.' He looked out. The sky was cloudless and blue, but there was something weird about it. Too bright, too sharp, it was threatening. They'd definitely mucked about with the weather lately, it wasn't right. Not that he cared really, they could do what they liked. He was just going to sit and stare and they weren't going to stop him, it was the only way, just sit it out and go far away in his head . . .

His eye fell on the building opposite. English Studies. English Studs. French Letters. *American Werewolf in London*, that was a good film, that was an ace film. He gave a small chuckle to himself.

No, English Studies. His feelings, the feelings God gave him, were tugging at him, telling him to resist the temptation to sit and stare. Because he had important things to do. Yes, he did. Maybe the people who were against him were trying to put him off, to stop him, and maybe the dead, dull feeling was part of that. Well, it wouldn't work. He had things to do, an aim in life. He remembered it now.

As if in answer to a prayer — *God is good!* — he saw a figure that he recognized climbing the steps of the English Studies building.

Was it?

Yes it was. There was Greenwood, going in to work.

Steve could see him, but he couldn't see Steve. It was brilliant! Elation filled him to the brim. The dead feeling was gone, it had never been.

'Oh-way, ohway-ohway-ohway. La la. La la,' Steve sang out. Now which would be the window of Greenwood's office again? Third floor . . . down the end . . .

Oh, yes! There the fucker was, opening up his window. Probably still stunk in there, yeah, stink-a-stink-a-stink, to Lily-the-Pink-the-Pink-the-Pink . . .

'OK?' said Georgiou, uncertainly, holding out a mug of coffee.

'Yeah, brill, cheers, mate, you're magic, nice one, good on you,' Steve said, seizing the coffee, keeping his eyes fixed on the window opposite.

'Mind, it's very hot — '

'Just the way I like it,' Steve said, gulping the scalding coffee down. He saw Georgiou looking at him in surprise. 'Cock-a-doodle-doo!' he said, making a trumpet of his fingers. 'Ah, I love the mornings, mate, just beautiful, I mean look at that sky, it's like the glory of God, all spread out before you . . .'

He resumed his study of the building opposite. Good lookout. Bloody good lookout. I'm watching you, Greenwood —

'. . . *stupid* . . .'

I'm watching you . . . Feeling good this fine morning? And how'd your daughter like her birthday card?

'You what, mate?' His host was chattering again.

'I was just wondering . . .' Georgiou hesitated, a loose-leaf binder in his hands. 'You see, I have a seminar to go to at nine, and—'

148

'Yeah, don't worry about me, mate, I'll be all right here, no problem.'

'Well. . . that wasn't really—'

'Ah, look, mate, I know you're a good one, else I wouldn't ask. It's just such a nice change to have a roof over my head, you know, little bit of comfort, little bit of company, do you see what I'm saying? First good sleep I've had for days. Just let me stay here for the morning, get my head down for another couple of hours, then I'll be on my way.' He watched Georgiou's face. This one was so easy to bully, he looked like a frightened rabbit half the time. 'Like I say, I wouldn't ask if you weren't a mate. And look, if you're afraid I'm going to nick stuff out of your room, well, you go and lock me in, I don't mind that at all—'

'Oh, no, I wasn't thinking that,' Georgiou said in a shocked voice. 'No, please, don't talk like that—'

'No, no, mate, no offence, you can't be too careful these days, can you?' Steve slapped his shoulder. 'What do you say, then?'

'Well . . . OK, if you'll be all right here—'

'Ah, it's a dream, mate, roof over my head, bit of peace and quiet, just while I get my head together, catch up on my sleep. Brill. Cheers. You're great.'

'All right then. There's the kettle, and coffee, and I'll be back about twelve.' Georgiou gave his little troubled smile. 'See you then.'

'Cheers, mate. You're a saint. Don't work too hard.'

Left alone, Steve windmilled his arms a few times, clapped and chanted, then went back to the window. He couldn't see Greenwood in his office any more, but that didn't matter: he had his timetable all written out in his notebook. Teaching, book signing, Suzanne's school play, he knew it all. He'd just give the greasy Greek time to get to wherever he was headed, then go out on the prowl. With a den to come back to. Ace.

He looked round at the study-bedroom. It occurred to him what a laugh it would be to trash it. Tear up the books. Maybe cut up those photos of his dago family, draw little additions on them, sticking out of their bodies. Piss on the bed. He could even smash the window with that great big lump of rock from dago-land, it wouldn't matter, nobody would take any notice in this place. They were all so wrapped up in themselves, a little friendless no-mark like Georgy Girl might as well not exist.

No. He wouldn't do it, because he needed this place, for now.

### 4

'No, I thought it a very disappointing choice for a school production,' Geoffrey Selby said. 'And in a sense rather worrying too, this perpetuation of the bourgeois respect for "classics", in itself a reactionary term, by imposing them upon children at an age when they're very susceptible to indoctrination.'

'Well, Suzanne's very excited about it,' Michael said.

'My point exactly. A child will be excited about the prospect of being in a play, and so will be all the more receptive to the ideology it inculcates, whether it be correct or incorrect. In this case, the reactionary ideology of a pederastic don, offering the child a vicarious escape into wonderland only in order that it may be more effectively enclosed within the power constructs of the society to which it returns.'

'I think it's *Through the Looking-Glass*, not *Alice in Wonderland*,' said Michael. The best tactic, when Geoffrey was working extra hard for the title of Wanker of the Year, was to outface him with statements of bland ingenuousness.

'Appalling unadventurousness on the part of the school, but I suppose it's only to be expected out in the sticks.' Geoffrey paused and searched his own remark for elitism, let it go. 'Anyway, I'll raise it at the next PTA meeting. I don't see why we can't have a school production of Brecht, for example.'

'You'd let Jake and Roz be in that, then?' Michael said.

Geoffrey Selby looked at Michael as if he had openly picked his nose. 'Michael, the day I *order* or *forbid* my children to do anything will be the day you make a name for yourself as a serious historian.' He turned and went into his office, on castors.

Oops, thought Michael. Shouldn't have done it. Shouldn't have let Selby needle him, shouldn't have bitched.

And he *wouldn't* have, if his nerves weren't stretched like piano wire.

He unlocked his office door: yes, he had made damn sure he'd locked it this time, but even so he paused on the threshold, senses strained and alert. Everything *looked* normal. Smelt normal too, apart from the lingering astringency of disinfectant from yesterday. He went in. Yes, of course it was OK. He opened the window to get some fresh air in. He really ought to unwind a bit. There were such things as locks and keys, and all you had to do was use them.

But how did you stop nutters sending you things through the post?

*From Your 'Mate' Steve.*

He wondered how Suzanne was feeling. The card didn't seem to have upset her unduly, but it was difficult to tell: she was good at hiding her feelings. It had certainly upset him. Upset, disturbed, angered him.

Which was precisely what it was meant to do.

How Steve had found out his address was no big mystery. The same place as he had found out his telephone number, of course. Still, it was the most disturbing thing of all, to think of this headcase knowing where he lived. He would make damn sure Suzanne was never alone in the house: it seemed that this Steve was one of those sickos who only dared to play his games from a distance, but he wouldn't take any chances. Luckily Fred was always home early in the afternoons, before Suzanne got home from school; and Christine was going to pick her up from the gates. And when she returned to the school to get ready for the play after tea, he was going to walk with her, whether she was mortified by his presence or not.

He collected his notes and went along to his seminar, and several of the students whom he passed in the corridors noticed that Dr Greenwood gave them a searching look, as if he were trying to remind himself who they were.

## 5

Chewing a Mars bar, Steve looked in at the window of Suttons, the campus bookshop. There was a notice: *Dr Michael Greenwood will be signing copies of his book* Anglian Voices *downstairs at Suttons from 2.00 p.m.*

I know, mate, thought Steve. I know all his little schedule. Me and Dr Michael fuckface Greenwood, we're like that.

'*. . . you stupid, cracked bastard . . .*'

We'll see about that, mate.

He went into the shop.

## 6

Georgiou waited outside the seminar room. He was slightly early, as usual: it was a habit he couldn't break, he had a fear of being late for things. Probably it was because he wanted so desperately to make a success of his time here. His family weren't really poor, but he was the first to go into higher education: it meant a lot to him and to them. He was aware that he lacked confidence, and it was still a daily surprise to him that he had managed to come alone to a foreign country and study here, miles from all that was familiar, surrounded by strangers. Sometimes it appeared to him that he had completely used up whatever confidence he had in making this huge step, for he didn't seem able to push himself forward at all here, to talk to people, to try and make friends. It was difficult, of course, with the cultural differences — all the British students had an immediate common ground — but he felt that it was at

least partly his own fault. He had lived in Borrow
Terrace for eight months now, and he still didn't know
any of the people on his floor except to say hello to. He
just couldn't seem to come out of his shell — though he
had to say, British people were extraordinarily difficult
to get close to. He didn't want to give credence to the
cliché about cold northern peoples, but he was afraid
there was a germ of truth in it.

He could always amuse himself on his own, because he
read a lot: but sometimes he couldn't deny that he was
lonely.

And that was how, he supposed, he had got talking to
Steve. Unable to face another evening looking at the
four breeze-block walls of his room, he had wandered
down to The Pub, realizing even at the time that it was
probably a bad idea — to sit sipping beer and observing
the laughing groups of students, who all seemed to know
each other. As Steve had said. That was what had been
refreshing, to meet someone who was open and friendly
and not part of some close-knit in-crowd. He had found
it a bit difficult to follow what Steve was saying at times,
but then he used a lot of slang and Georgiou didn't think
he'd ever catch up with all the English varieties of that. It
was just wonderful to chat with someone cheerful. And
what was more, he'd felt extremely concerned about
Steve's being homeless. Georgiou tried to be well
informed about the political and social situation in the
country he had come to, and sometimes he wondered
tentatively, whether as an outsider he didn't see a little
more clearly than the British themselves what their
society was like. He didn't want to be unpleasant; but
when British people said to him, on finding out he was

Greek, 'What was it like under the Colonels?' —
students almost invariably said it — when they asked
that, he was tempted to reply, 'As far as I can remember,
it was rather similar to your country now.' Under his
mildness he chafed a little at the patronizing implication
that his was some wobbly little country barely able to
sustain a democracy — whilst here people were sleeping
rough on the streets. If people were on the streets — and
he had seen them, not only in London but here in the
prosperous, picturesque capital of East Anglia — then
much, he thought, was wrong.

And so he had agreed to put Steve up overnight: it
seemed the least he could do. And in truth he was simply
enjoying company, enjoying having someone to talk to
about the home he missed so much (he hoped he hadn't
been a bore), and the unaccustomed extra couple of
drinks had done the rest.

The only problem was —

Well, it wasn't really a problem, leaving Steve in his
room for the morning. Just because you were homeless
didn't mean you were a thief, not that there was much to
steal — and besides, they had made friends. If Steve was
sleeping rough, it was very likely that he would relish a
lie-in in comfort. It was a bit awkward, but it was no
problem really.

Georgiou shyly nodded at the other seminar students
who were beginning to gather in the corridor.

No, the problem was . . . there was something
definitely not right about Steve.

If he hadn't really noticed it last night, it was because
he was simply so glad of the release from loneliness, and
had been chattering rather under the influence of the

lager. But even then there had been times when Steve's face had gone peculiarly blank — almost as if his soul or mind or whatever you wanted to call it had just gone out of his body, leaving it a vacant lump of flesh. And times, too, when he had started laughing and not seemed able to stop, laughing that didn't seem to have any point to it . . . But then Georgiou had suspected that it was probably some joke that he had missed, some pun or nuance that his rather formal grasp of English wasn't up to. Now he wasn't so sure. And last night when Steve had come back from the bathroom — his dark face had seemed to have darkened further, a really deep red, and his eyes had looked glassy for some minutes before he had started talking cheerfully again and got into the sleeping bag . . .

Drugs, Georgiou thought.

It would explain a lot. The way Steve's mood seemed to swing so abruptly . . .

Of course it was bad for him to think that. Just because the poor guy was out of work and homeless, that didn't mean he was a junkie. After all, anyone was entitled to be a bit moody in that situation.

Still, it worried him. That curious morose look Steve had had this morning . . .

Georgiou glanced at the faces of his fellow students, waiting to go into the seminar room. He wished he had a friend here, someone he could confide in and talk frankly to; someone who would tell him if they thought he had been foolish in putting Steve up. There was one guy on his course he sometimes talked to, who always seemed friendlier than the rest — a big good-looking guy called Fred Forbes. Georgiou had often thought he ought to make the effort to get to know Fred better, but shyness held him back.

Wasn't Fred here today? Wait, there he was, he was standing with his back to him reading something on the notice board. He did look like the sort of person you could talk to.

Georgiou gathered his courage and walked over.

'Hello, Fred.'

'Oh, hi, Georgiou, how are you doing?'

'I'm fine, thank you.' Georgiou looked up at Fred's amiably smiling face, wondering how to put it.

'What did you make of that thermodynamics lecture yesterday?' Fred said, trying to help him over the pause. 'Obscure or what?'

'Yes, it was very difficult to follow,' Georgiou said. 'I—'

'Morning, everyone, you all look like you're loitering with intent,' cried the tutor breezily, arriving with a great bustle and ushering them into the classroom. 'Do you know how long it took me to get here on the train from Cromer this morning? Over an hour. I could do it quicker with a horse and cart . . .'

Noisily they took their seats. The opportunity had gone: perhaps it was just as well, Georgiou thought. Fred might wonder what on earth he was talking about.

Oh, well, when he got back to his room he would give Steve something to eat, maybe some money to help him along if he would take it, and after that he would surely take the hint and be off. Georgiou would be alone again then, of course: but somehow now that didn't seem such a bad prospect.

### 7

When Steve left the bookshop he walked down to The Square, where something was going on. Several people were sitting on chairs reading aloud from books, while other people were doing things to them. One was having a bucket of bright green sludge poured over his head: another was having all his hair cut off, right down to the skull.

Lots of students were sitting and watching on the grass slopes that surrounded The Square. Steve sat himself down next to a couple of very trendy-looking blokes and said: 'What's going on?'

'Stunt for Rag Week,' one of the blokes said, after briefly looking Steve up and down. 'Sponsored Shakespeare reading.'

'Oh, right, and the others are trying to put them off, I get it,' Steve said. He yelped with laughter as one of the students in The Square solemnly continued to recite 'To be or not to be' while two girls painted his clothes with white emulsion. 'Yeah, it's like that thing on the telly, whatsisname Beadle. You seen that?'

'Uh-huh.'

'That Beadle, man, he's just a fucking nutter, it's unbelievable . . .' It was nice here on the grass, and Steve threw his head back and had a good laugh. When he came back he thought he saw the two trendies exchanging a funny look, but decided to give them the benefit of the doubt.

'Do us a favour, mate,' he said, seeing a packet of cigarettes in the first trendy's pocket, 'give us a fag.'

The trendy passed him a cigarette without comment.

Steve lit up and then picked up the book that was lying beside the trendy's bare leg on the grass. 'What's this, good book is it? Henry Fielding, *Tom Jones*. Oh, what, you're not telling me it's *that* Tom Jones, shit, "It's not unus-uhaaal . . ." '

'That's the name of the book,' the trendy said, sort of smiling.

'Yeah? "Bye, bye, my Deli-laah . . ." I'll tell you a book you want to read, mate, *Lord of the Rings*, that book, right, it's just *incredible*.'

'You can say that again,' the second trendy said.

Steve looked up. Was he taking the piss? 'You read it, then?'

'I got about halfway through it, once. I thought it was really awful.'

'What? You're kidding me, man, you read it and you're just *there*, I mean you are *there* in this magical *world* . . .'

'But Tolkien's such an old reactionary,' said the first trendy. 'All right, it's cleverly done, but what he's saying underneath really stinks. I mean, there are no women in this imaginary world except for a few unreachable glamour pusses who are dead from the waist down. Those hobbits who are always stuffing their faces and smoking pipes and yet manage to be incredibly brave and save the world as well are obviously Tolkien's idea of Englishmen, complete with servants who go ooh-arr and call Mr Bilbo sir and know their place. While the baddies are these nasty black foreigners who talk funny. And the dwarves, all greedy and secretive with cloaks and beards, are obviously an anti-Semitic portrayal of the Jews.'

Steve was shaking his head energetically. He just

couldn't shake his head enough, because this wasn't right . . . 'Listen, mate, I don't know what book you've been reading, Tom Jones or Val Doonican or whatever, but that's not the book I read, I mean it's got none of that in it . . .'

'It's there,' the first trendy said. 'Just depends whether you see it or not.'

Steve searched the two blokes' faces. He felt the blood rushing to his cheeks, burning and tingling.

'You saying I'm stupid?' he said.

'*I* never said that,' the first trendy said.

He had done it again, he had let his guard slip, he had forgotten that people were *all against him* and my God these two really were . . . 'Are you saying I'm stupid?' he said again. 'Are you?'

'Look, you said it, not me—'

'*Don't fucking try it!*' Steve bellowed. '*Don't ever fucking try it mister big smartarse . . .*'

He didn't know how it had happened, but somehow he had lunged forward and was crouching over the trendy bloke, his face an inch from his. There must have been spit coming from his mouth because the bloke was flinching away and screwing his face up – it looked really funny, he wanted to laugh.

'. . . Hey, hey, calm down, what's the big deal?' the other trendy was saying anxiously.

Steve got up. All the strength in him, the God-given strength, had boiled up to the top like milk in a saucepan. Thank God it hadn't boiled over. He needed that strength, for other things.

He looked at the first trendy, who was still flat on his back, his face all slack and pasty as he gazed up at Steve.

It did look funny. Steve laughed. He bent down and slapped the bloke's shoulder.

'Cheers, mate,' he said.

He walked away from The Square, where one of the reciting students was now having a hosepipe forced down his trousers. He was still in control.

It had been a warning though. A warning that they were all against him, that they would try and deflect him, sap his strength, provoke him. Luckily he had seen it in time. From the way the rage had surged up in him just now, the way his mind had just gone flying out into deep space, he knew it would be terrible if he lost control.

## 8

From fellow academics who had ventured into print Michael had heard grim stories about signing sessions. Who, after all, was going to buy a signed book, unless it was the new Jeffrey Archer doorstop, or maybe one of those novels by someone who was famous for something other than writing novels? Who, indeed, bought books at all? From what he had heard, the likelihood was that he would simply sit in the bookshop like a lemon, a pile of unbought books and a pen in front of him, to be occasionally nudged by an old lady and asked if he was famous.

So he was pleasantly surprised that afternoon in Suttons, insofar as some people actually did buy copies of *Anglian Voices* and present them to him to be signed. Of course, it was a rather artificial situation. It was the campus bookshop, and he was a tutor at the university, and he knew just about everybody who bought one. A couple of his students came along, including that incomparable study, Inigo, who seemed to be wearing two shirts, one on top of the other, and who knocked over the whole new paperback stand with impressive thoroughness. Peter Worrall bought one too, groaning at the loss of thirteen pounds.

'Wondered if I should wait for the paperback,' he said gloomily.

'Probably won't be one.'

'That's what I thought. Saving one for Geoff Selby, are you?' Peter grinned.

'Geoffist,' Michael said.

His mind had regained a sort of equilibrium. He had met Christine for lunch in the café at the Winfield Centre, and there amongst the desperately contemporary sculptures and feeble pastiches of Stanley Spencer they had talked some more about the situation. Somehow, with Christine's sturdiness, it had begun to seem less intractable.

'I hate to sound like Pollyanna,' she said, 'but I do think we're looking on the dark side a bit too much. I mean, there must be limits to this sort of childish nastiness. Boredom, for one thing. How long can he keep it up? It's not as if he's getting anything out of it.'

'No . . . that's true . . . I've just never come across anything like this before.'

'I have. Well — not exactly like this. But when I was going through the break-up with Phil . . . I've never told you this, but he got a bit funny. He knew it was finished, and yet he wouldn't let it go. One day there'd be flowers — the next day a letter full of abuse. Then he'd ring up and just listen to me say hello and put the phone down . . .' She rubbed her arms, as if a shiver had gone over her. 'It was frightening, in a way. To know that that was someone you'd been so close to. And yet it wasn't because soon I began to see, and he began to see, that he was making a fool of himself. The game just wasn't worth the candle. So he stopped. Sanity stepped in — or boredom, if you like. Perhaps they're the same thing.'

'And you think that's what will happen here?'

'I think so. I hope so. Or somewhere between the two. I thope so.'

She smiled at him, and he laughed. 'I thope so too.'

'By the way, what *is* that thing you're eating, Michael?'

He looked down at the grey slab on his plate. 'It's called a gala pie,' he said dubiously.

'Oh dear.' She was laughing. 'Doesn't look very festive, does it?'

And so . . . Nothing more had happened, and it seemed unlikely that this weirdo could continue his repertoire of nasty tricks without getting tired of it soon. Now Michael's tentative optimism was bolstered by the experience, undeniably pleasant, of signing his name with a flourish in shiny new copies of the book he had written.

Hilda, the faculty secretary, was standing beaming before him, hugging *Anglian Voices* to her angora bosom. 'I've nearly finished that lovely book all about dragons, Michael,' she said, 'and as soon as I do, I'm going to tuck myself up with your book. I'm looking forward to just gobbling it all up. I don't know how you do it, writing all these pages and pages. I think if I tried to write a book it would just about take me ten years, and then it wouldn't make any sense! I did have a go at Professor Rudge's latest one, but I just couldn't get on with it . . .'

As Michael took the book and opened it at the title page Hilda's voice dimmed swiftly in his ears, like a radio turned off at the socket. In its place he heard the roar of his own blood, as his heart missed a beat and jolted into life again.

A slip of lined paper was tucked into the opening pages of the book before him, and on it were scrawled the words I'M WATCHING YOU.

9

Hilda was still talking.

'. . . Of course, he does a lot of things for the television nowadays. The idiot tank I always call it, though perhaps that's a bit naughty. I do like those programmes with thingy, oh you know, Attenborough, where he shows you all the little animals running around . . . Are you all right, Michael?'

Michael stared up at her, the note crumpled in his hand. For the first stunned moment he had wildly seen Hilda as an agent of his persecution: but of course, he knew that big, looping handwriting, the pen-point pressed so hard into the paper that it almost dug through . . .

'Oh, have I got a torn copy? Oh, pooh, that's just my rotten luck—'

'No, no, Hilda, it's − it's nothing. Here you go, and many thanks.' He scribbled his name unseeingly, handed her the book, hardly noticing her expression of surprise.

Steve had slipped that note into the book. He had put it there, so Michael would see it . . .

Steve was *here*, somewhere. Or had been recently. There was no other explanation . . .

*I'm watching you* . . .

Michael got up, almost stumbling, knocking his chair aside. The manageress, at the counter, looked startled as he confronted her.

'Did you see anybody — was there anybody looking through these books today? My books, I mean. Somebody — a chap about thirty, dark complexion, black hair . . .'

The manageress was staring at him as if he had gone mad. 'I'm sorry, I couldn't say. There are browsers all the time . . . Is there a copy missing, do you mean?'

*I'm watching you* . . .

Where?

Where was he?

Leaving the manageress gaping, Michael ran, clattering, up the spiral staircase to the bookshop's upper floor. Browsing heads turned in surprise as he pounded, like some overgrown and uncontrollable child, round and round the tall stacks.

He wasn't here. Of course. Of course he wasn't.

But why *of course*? What did he suppose this Steve was — the invisible man? Some evil force out of a horror film, that couldn't be combated?

He was just a nutter with a ridiculous, misproportioned grudge. The Train Loony whom everybody dreaded having to sit next to.

*But what happened when the Train Loony turned out to be a real lunatic . . . ?*

Suttons was a split-level building, the lower floor opening on to The Street, the upper floor opening on to the main walkway leading to the library and lecture theatres. Michael flung out of the upstairs door, stood glaring about him, at chattering groups of students clutching books and folders, on their way to lectures, innocent, ordinary.

He ran down the flight of concrete steps to The Street, stood looking up and down it. He was panting, and not just from exertion. Pub. Buffet. Refectory. Launderette. Supermarket. Banks. Post Office. Little twiggy trees, caged in with chicken wire: wooden benches where students lounged. Now it looked more than ever like a coy parody of a high street, a mocking caricature of normality, hiding something twisted . . .

A memory of his childhood in rural Cumbria came to him. A couple of his playmates from the village climbing high up into the chestnut trees by the church, and then calling down to him through the leaves. 'Michael – coo-ee, Michael – can't see me – can't see me . . .' And himself standing at the base of the trees, head back, staring up through thick spectacles into the wavering, blurring mass of foliage, trying to pick out a comprehensible detail from all that vagueness, desperate to prove that he could see them, to put an end to their little taunting voices that seemed to come from the air itself. 'Can't see me . . .' The voices rang in his head as, beaten and bewildered, and with a feeling of stifling oppression upon him that he suspected was not going to go away, Michael turned to go back into the shop.

*Can't see me . . . can't see me . . .*

166

## 10

Steve could see Michael. It took all his self-control to stop himself bursting out laughing.

That was the brilliant thing about this place, all the split levels, all the plate glass — it was just full of lookout posts. He was on the upstairs level of the refectory, with a table right next to the window — cup of tea, cheese roll, and down below the floor show.

In fact he hadn't expected to see much. He would have got the best view from the upper floors of the library, but he couldn't get in there, not without one of those student cards that they flashed like coppers with their ID. He could see the bookshop clearly from here, even into it a bit in between the displays and posters; but mainly he had sat here so as to watch Greenwood going in and then to think about him finding his little message. The way Greenwood had popped out of the shop and run around like a headless chicken, staring in his four-eyed way, was a bonus, a terrific bonus.

He had gone back into the shop now, but Steve sat on in the refectory for a while, smiling to himself. He felt good. He had recovered from the knock-back he'd had when those two trendies had attacked him. (And hadn't one of them had a hammer? Surely he had something there in his hand . . . Jesus, it was terrible! What were the police doing?) And as he looked down into The Street, with the people walking about like funny little dolls, he thought again of how easy it would be to pick Greenwood off with a gun from somewhere like this.

*Bouf.* There goes his head.

But of course that was no good. Not that Greenwood

167

didn't deserve it — and remember, he'd brought it on himself — but it was too quick. The whole point was to draw it out. To enjoy.

All the same, he would have to pop back to the bedsit some time. It was getting dangerous here, the people who were against him were coming out into the open. Threatening him with a hammer, Jesus! Yes, he would have to nip back to the bedsit, before rejoining Georgy-Porgy, because there was something there he needed.

He needed his knife.

## 11

Georgiou returned to his room in Borrow Terrace at noon to find that Steve had gone.

No note saying goodbye or thanks: nothing but the faint odour of his roll-up cigarettes. All very abrupt. Still, he was a bit odd.

Georgiou hoped he would be all right. He didn't like to think of the poor guy sleeping rough again. But he was a bit of a strain to have around, and the room was very small for putting people up. In fact, Georgiou had to admit that he was intensely relieved to find his guest gone. Just as well, really, that he hadn't said anything to Fred.

He made himself a snack lunch in his room: aside from the fact that you couldn't leave any food in the kitchen refrigerator without it disappearing, he always felt shy about going down there — the other students stared so as they made their inevitable toast. He put the plate on his desk and opened out his work folder. The noise of other people's stereos, which sometimes

168

contended cacophonously throughout the block like a late Charles Ives piece, was fairly subdued for once, and the sun was shining into the room.

It was going to be a nice afternoon.

## 12

'So you think this young man could be one of your students,' said Dixon of Dock Green, squeezing his fleshy ear lobe.

'Not one of my own students, I mean not the ones I teach, obviously I know them,' Michael said. 'But it's a possibility that he's a student at the university, yes, though I wouldn't have thought it was likely. But certainly he must have been there, on the campus, to have done these things.'

'And you don't have a name for the young man?' Dixon said.

'Steve.' Michael shrugged. 'That's all he said on the train. I mean, it was just a casual meeting, you know, just making conversation.'

'Yet you seem to think he knows all about you, as it were?'

'He does.' Michael could feel fractious temper rising in him. 'I mean, he was one of these people who really pumps you, what do you do, are you married and so on. So he knew that I was at the university, and I dare say it was easy to find my number in the phone book. And so he's decided to — well, persecute me.'

Dixon of Dock Green, as Michael had mentally christened the elderly policeman, blew out a sigh and squeezed his ear lobe once more, as if it were some surprising and new piece of his anatomy that he had only just found. He looked again at Michael's rather pathetic little exhibits – the birthday card, the note slipped into the book. Somehow Michael had known, from the moment of entering the police station, that this was a mistake. After the book signing he had had another seminar to take, and had sat through it like a zombie, scarcely hearing anything his students said, knowing he had to do something. Christine was picking Suzanne up from school: he would ring home and tell them he'd be a bit late, and go straight into the city to talk to the police, and everything would somehow be sorted out. But when he had walked into the station and begun explaining to the desk sergeant he had realized at once how feeble it all sounded. At last the desk sergeant had fobbed him off with this avuncular character who had apologetically taken him into a little room like a broom cupboard – the place was being redecorated, he explained, and they were all in a bit of a mess at the moment – and now sat there doodling on a pad and looking – well, maybe not sceptical. Just a bit puzzled and bored.

'You say there was a drawing—'

'Yes, an obscene drawing, relating to me and my dead wife. It was on the blackboard – I mean, what was I supposed to do, take a photograph of it?'

What was it about policemen that made you both irritable and defensive? Dixon didn't seem to take offence, however. He sighed again and said, 'I do appreciate that these are rather unpleasant things to happen, sir. The card to the little girl, that's very nasty indeed. And the phone calls, you've every right to be concerned. Unfortunately we couldn't possibly deal with all the crank phone calls that go on even in a city this size. The best we can advise is that you do not react, do not try to get into a dialogue with this person, and if it continues, to have your number changed and go ex-directory. As for the card . . . well, it is an offence to send obscene material through the post, but that doesn't apply here, I'm afraid. You could buy a card like this over the counter anywhere, but I do see that it's a very inappropriate thing to send to your little girl. If this person should send anything genuinely obscene, then let us know about it. You see, sir, it's a question of an actual offence being committed. Has this person made direct threats to you or your family?'

*I'll give you fucking purgatory . . .*

'Not what you'd call direct threats,' Michael said dispiritedly. It was no good. Looked at from his point of view, the situation was disquieting, alarming, horrible, in its constant grinding upon his nerves. Looked at from Dixon's point of view, it all added up to doodley-squat.

And besides, Dixon hadn't met Steve. Dixon hadn't had those lidless, *peeled*-looking eyes fixed on him: hadn't heard that exaggerated, swooping laughter.

'Students do get up to pranks, don't they, sir?' Dixon said, for the first time giving him a watery smile. 'Even things like − well, the mess in your office.'

'Yes,' Michael said. He felt very tired, and a little nauseous from the smell of new paint in the station; and there was still Suzanne's play to go to tonight. 'Yes, they do get up to pranks.'

Dixon smiled genially and transferred his attention to his other ear lobe. 'I honestly think, sir, that if anybody is playing silly buggers they'll soon get fed up with it. But

I'll make out a report here, and if you do get anything more definite, then don't hesitate to let us know. I hope you don't think I'm being dismissive, but you must realize that unless an actual offence has been committed . . .'

*What do you expect us to do, give you an armed guard?* was what he was too polite to say, thought Michael. He thanked the sergeant and left.

His fruitless encounter with the Norfolk constabulary left him with a ten-minute walk back into the city centre to catch the bus home, and a feeling of childlike foolishness. The city was harsh in the six o'clock rush, a choked place of grinding gears and hurrying feet into which the lofty shapes of the cathedral spire and the hilltop castle seemed to have strayed by accident.

*I'm watching you.*

There was standing room only on the bus. Straphanging, swaying, Michael looked at his fellow passengers. How scrupulously they avoided eye contact, just as he had always done. Find a neutral space to stare into, keep your little piece of personal space inviolate, that was the rule. A good rule too. How else could people manage to live piled on top of each other in these communities of thousands and thousands?

A terrible, painful envy went through him, looking at these people reading newspapers or studying their knees or sunk into a temporary catatonia of boredom. They were going home to blessed ordinariness. No one had punched a hole in the protective shell of their lives. They might have problems, worries, deep distresses that waited to claim them when they closed their front doors . . .

But no one was watching them.

## 13

It had been, as Georgiou had thought it would be, a good afternoon. He had done lots of work, and now the declining sun was striking horizontally into his room and even giving a golden tint to the unlovely breeze block above his desk.

Often this was the sort of time when he felt acutely homesick: something about the hour was sad and nostalgic. But just now he felt positive. He would change his clothes, which always gave him a nice feeling of the working day being over, and then go down to the refectory for his main meal.

Someone was knocking at the outer security door. He sighed. It was hardly ever for him, but it always seemed to be him who had to answer it. But then, it might be someone who had forgotten their key.

He went down the corridor, past the identical closed doors of a dozen strangers, and out to the security door. The knocking was very insistent. He opened it.

'All right, maaaate, how you doing?'

Steve barged in, a fragment of a roll-up clamped between his grinning lips.

'Oh, hullo, Steve—'

'Sorry, mate, you must have wondered where I'd got to when you got back, should have left you a note. Bloke downstairs let me back in the block. Here, do us a favour, give us a proper fag, will you . . .'

Steve was already heading, with his strange rolling gait, straight for Georgiou's room. That walk was weird,

Georgiou thought. It was so *emphasized*, like the walk of an animated cartoon character.

'I thought you'd – er, gone,' Georgiou said, following Steve into his room.

'Went for a walk, mate,' Steve said, taking Georgiou's cigarettes from his desk and lighting one. 'Good long walk round, try and clear my head.' Georgiou noticed that he had a small canvas bag with him. 'Phew, that's better, got a decent fag at last. So how's it going, mate? You working hard, yeah, good, good.'

'Yes . . . thank you. I – didn't really expect to see you, I'm afraid I was just going to go out—'

'That's all right, mate, don't worry about me, I'll be all right here,' Steve said, prowling round and round the room, his insistent presence seeming to fill it to bursting.

Georgiou knew that he was not good at asserting himself at the best of times; and he couldn't think how to handle this situation, it was so peculiar, it had no precedents . . . 'Hey, Steve, I don't mean that it's not nice to see you, you know, but—'

'Listen, mate, I know how it is, you've got your own life, I'm not going to put you out, right? You did me a favour, and I appreciate it, there's not enough kindness in the world, and I'm not going to mess you about. You just get on with whatever you've got to do, I won't bother you.' He came and stood very close to Georgiou as he spoke. 'All I'm asking is, let me get my head down for a little while, just lay on your bed till this bloody headache goes off.'

'Oh – do you have a headache? I could get you some aspirin—'

'Nah, mate, I've always had 'em, they come and go,

aspirin doesn't do any good really. Just have to wait for it to go off. That's why I went out for a walk, you know, blow away the cobwebs, but it's no better. So look, I won't disturb you, a bit of rest is all I need and then I'll be off, see if I can stay with a mate tonight.'

Steve was already pulling off his trainers and settling down on the bed. Georgiou looked at him in perplexity. He didn't want this, he didn't want this at all. He had put the guy up for a night because he had nowhere to go, but to have him just parking himself like this, it was too much . . .

And yet he hated to think of himself as one of those cold, self-absorbed people that there seemed to be so many of here, who passed you in the corridors as if you didn't exist, and looked as if they would do the same if you were lying beaten in the gutter. He couldn't help feeling sorry for Steve, who was as alone as he was, and who did look as if he had a headache — there was a deep groove between his brows as he settled his head on the pillow, and his face was a hectic colour. There was no harm in letting him have a rest on his bed, especially when he had nowhere else to go.

'Well . . . OK,' Georgiou said. 'Have you — have you had anything to eat?'

'Yeah, mate, lovely,' Steve said vaguely, his eyes closed.

'OK, well, I'm going down to the refectory. If you're sure you'll be all right . . . I won't be long.'

Steve did not reply. He seemed to be asleep already.

*But you don't really* know *this guy*, a voice piped up in Georgiou's head as he descended the stairs.

True. But how could you get to know anyone, without

a little trust? That was why he didn't really know anyone at the university, because he couldn't break down that flimsy barrier of trust, and no one else seemed to want to. It was wrong that it should be that way between people. Coldness, barriers, separation. He didn't believe in that.

*But you are going to be so glad when he leaves*, said the sceptical voice. *You know you are going to be so glad when he's gone*.

## 14

Christine, having picked Suzanne up from school, had remained at Michael's house, and she greeted him with a displeased face when he got in.

'Thanks for staying,' he said. 'Everything been all right?'

She tolerated his kiss, nodding. 'I wouldn't mind seeing the inside of my own flat some time. What did the police have to say?'

'Not a lot. I'll tell you about it later.'

'Hello, Dad, Christine cooked tea, it was brilliant,' Suzanne said. 'Dad, I've got to go to the school and get ready, my costume takes ages to put on, you've not still got this thing about going with me, have you?'

Before Michael could answer Christine said, 'I'll take you in the van now. While your father gets something to eat and smartens himself up. Otherwise we'll be late for the performance.'

Christine had two pissed-off faces. One said I'm-Pissed - Off - Because - I'm - Just - In - A - Mood - So - Bear-With-Me. The other said I'm-Pissed-Off-And-I-Think-I-

Have-Every-Reason-To-Be, and was rare. She was wearing the latter as she left the house.

There wasn't much in the fridge – tomorrow was his shopping day – but Michael wasn't hungry. He made himself a cheese sandwich, swallowed half of it, then went up to the top floor to see Fred.

The bedsit room was filled with seasick music. Fred kept the place curiously spartan: the numerous books were his only concession to decor. They were an eclectic but solid selection – Dickens, George Eliot, Flaubert, Chekhov, Scott Fitzgerald, James Baldwin, V.S. Naipaul; it was an interesting but depressing fact that Fred the scientist was better read than most of his English students.

'Do you know, you're the only student I've ever known who hasn't got either a poster of Marilyn Monroe or *A Clockwork Orange*,' Michael said.

'Or that Escher one with a room reflected in a crystal ball,' Fred said, looking up from his desk. 'What was it when you were an undergraduate? Was it really Che Guevara posters?'

'Afraid so. Believe it or not, we really didn't see anything ridiculous about worshipping a man in a beret . . Any telephone calls, Fred?'

'No. I've been here since about half one. You still having weirdo trouble?'

Michael nodded. 'Bit of a cheek to ask this, Fred, but you will be here in the afternoons, won't you? I mean, I know it's silly, but I don't want Suzanne to be left on her own, and if I can't get back in time—'

'No sweat, I'll always be here. All my seminars are in the mornings.'

'Thanks.' It was reassuring to think of Fred here, big and dependable with his rich, clotted vowels.

Michael shaved and changed, and was just making coffee to perk himself up when Christine returned. Her expression had softened somewhat, but still he knew he must tread carefully.

'It doesn't start till half past seven,' she said. 'So come on. Tell me.'

He told: the note slipped in the book, the visit to the police station. And as he told he felt just as he had when faced with Dixon of Dock Green's vaguely sympathetic face — that it didn't amount to anything, that the hate he felt closing in on him was entirely insubstantial.

And he thought he saw that reflected, too, in Christine's face.

'Say it,' he said. 'I'm overreacting.'

Christine hesitated. 'This nutter's playing a very nasty game,' she said. 'I've witnessed enough of it myself to know that. But, Michael, it's all pieces of paper, you know? It's all kid's stuff. That's what you've got to bear in mind. Somebody who's really got it in mind to threaten you would do more than write nasty little notes and make nasty phone calls. It's just like something a kid would do, because a kid daren't do any more. If you were to meet him face to face he'd probably run a mile.'

'I wish to God I could meet him,' Michael said. 'I wish I could just confront him — ask him what the hell he thinks he's doing . . . But I don't know how to *find* him.'

'But that's just what I mean,' she said. 'Why should he be worth that effort? It only means you're playing his game.' She hesitated again over what she had to say

178

next, suspended, like a person holding a full plate and wondering where safely to put it. 'And it means in a way that you're − getting as obsessive about it as he is.'

Indignation rose, then faded. 'I know I am,' he said. 'That's what's so frightening.'

Christine sighed. 'Well, one thing's for sure,' she said. 'It's certainly screwing you up, isn't it? And it'll be screwing us up soon, too, if we're not careful.'

'And that's just what he wants,' Michael said.

Her sigh this time was different in quality: it touched exasperation. 'Christ, he's not all-seeing, all-knowing, Michael.'

He shook his head. 'I know.'

But a whisper inside him said: *Isn't he? Because that's how it feels.*

## 15

The school hall was nearly full when they arrived, but they managed to find seats near the front. The chairs were of that uniquely uncomfortable kind, metal-framed with webbing seat and back, and somehow odorous of plimsolls and changing rooms. The sheer persistent schoolness of schools amazed Michael. They hadn't changed at all since his schooldays, which he had hated: his mother was a teacher, he had been exceptionally bright, he had made his career in education, but still he had hated them. Comprehensiveness, co-education and computers notwithstanding, they were still the same wrong-headed places, full of things that children would never see or have anything to do with again for the rest of their lives once they left. Wall bars, for Christ's sake, and basketball hoops. Bunsen burners. T-squares. Contour maps. Squared paper. He still remembered his own bewildered, despairing impression that these things must have a crucial importance in life, and that his adulthood would revolve wholly around them.

Thankfully, at least, school plays had moved on a little since his day when, like Fred, he had had to mouth wodges of Shakespeare while wearing a cardboard crown. The Lower School's own adaptation of *Through the Looking-Glass* came on fresh, inventive and funny. There was a little wobble right at the very start, when the curtains, opening on Alice curled up in the wing chair with her kitten, refused to budge more than halfway, so that disembodied hands were presently seen tugging them back; but from then on Michael was absorbed, like the rest of the audience in the darkened hall. Alice, as Suzanne had suggested, had a tendency to overact, but what the hell, so did Kenneth Branagh. Suzanne's friend Steph was a triumph in the cameo role of the Tiger-lily — so he took careful note to tell her when he next saw her. The costumes and masks, mostly made by the children themselves, were excellent, and there were some sly contemporary references: Tweedledum and Tweedledee wore identical high-top fashion trainers, and the enamelled hair and hectoring tones of the Red Queen were surely inspired by a recent prime minister.

He had told himself not to go all gooey and parental when Suzanne came on, but in the end he couldn't help it. She was surely the best comedienne there — everyone must see that . . . He had forgotten, too, how many of the best lines the White Queen had. 'The rule is, jam tomorrow and jam yesterday — but never jam today.'

'It's a poor sort of memory that only works backwards.'
'Why, sometimes I've believed as many as six impossible
things before breakfast!' That got a good laugh, the way
Suzanne delivered it, all loopy eyes and dim smile. In
fact it was getting laughs all the way through, it was
going over tremendously, Geoff Selby didn't know what
he was missing; sometimes the laughter was so long
dying down you couldn't hear the next line . . .

In fact someone was disturbing the actors with his
laughter, someone right at the back of the hall. Michael
began to be conscious of it about the time Humpty
Dumpty came on. At first he had thought it was just
some overanxious relative determined to show
enjoyment; but soon he was listening out for that
laughter, his attention even wandering from what was
happening on the stage.

There it was again. It wasn't an amused laugh: it was a
laugh in the wrong place, just when everyone else was
quiet, a pointless giggle ringing out from the darkness.
He turned in his seat, but he couldn't see anything
beyond the people sitting immediately behind him.

'What's wrong?' Christine whispered.

'Somebody messing about,' Michael said. He turned
back and tried to concentrate on the performance. It was
the scene with the White Knight: the gentlest part of the
story, really, and the audience was quiet.

The boy playing the White Knight wasn't very
confident; and when the stupid giggle broke out again
from the back of the hall, he lost his thread and had to
be prompted.

This time Michael's wasn't the only head to turn. He
glared into the darkness, filled with a surprising fury.

That laugh wasn't just pointless, it was malicious. It mocked at what the children were doing so well and had worked so hard to perfect. It was a laugh like the casual trampling down of flowers, or pissing through a letterbox . . .

He did not know how long the suspicion must have been germinating in his mind, but suddenly it was there, fully formed. He seemed to feel the blood go still in his veins.

He knew someone who laughed like that.

The big final scene was beginning, the banquet, and Suzanne was on again, sitting at the head of the table alongside the Red Queen and Alice. This, he knew, was her favourite part, with the funniest lines.

There was that *damn* noise again. It was getting louder, it was a sort of idiot caterwaul, superior, spiteful, hateful . . .

'Can you do addition?' Suzanne was saying to Alice. 'What's one and one and one and one and one and one and one and one and one and one?'

*Wakwak*. A derisive kazoo noise. Michael craned round, incensed.

'Ignore it,' Christine hissed.

'I'll tell you a secret — I can read words of one letter!' Suzanne was saying.

A Bronx cheer brayed out above the general laughter.

Michael was out of his seat.

That crazy bastard was in here.

*In here*: spoiling something that meant so much to his daughter.

He struggled past obstructing knees to the end of the row, stumbled into the aisle. His heart was pounding.

Startled faces flickered his way as he stormed down the aisle. The emotion he was feeling was entirely new to him: it was white heat, it was possession.

He was going to break that bastard's neck.

*He was in here.*

He sensed rather than heard hesitations in the dialogue continuing on the stage behind him.

*In here . . .*

The *wakwak* noise sounded again. The very back row. He pinpointed it, headed for it. At the same moment he saw a furtive movement there in the darkness, right at the end, a ducked head. It was only the pounding sound of his own footsteps on the hall floor that let him know he was running.

*I'll give you fucking purgatory . . .*

The figure on the end of the row made a sudden darting movement, springing up from its chair, dropping the kazoo on the floor. Too late. An extraordinary exultation lashed through Michael as he lunged, seized the bastard by the shoulder, whipped him round to face him.

*Now . . . now we'll see, you lunatic . . .*

The chair fell with a metallic crash to the floor, stilling the performance on stage, as Steve struggled in Michael's grasp.

'I've got you, you little shit!' Michael's voice had become a bark. 'I've got you . . .'

The whole attention of the hall was on the fracas at the back.

'Get off — get off, you're not a teacher . . .'

Michael found that he was still grimly holding on to the struggling arms even as his mind perceived the truth.

That this was not Steve. That the source of the distractions in the hall was not Steve, but this thirteen-year-old boy shrugging off his hands and glaring at him with equal parts of resentment and shame. And that this thirteen-year-old boy was Geoffrey Selby's son Jake.

### 16

Steve slept on Georgiou's bed for two hours, into the greenish spring twilight.

He didn't move in his sleep, Georgiou noticed when he came back from the refectory. Most people sighed, wriggled, dug their heads into the pillow. Steve just lay on his back, breathing deeply, perfectly still. It was as if he did not so much drift into sleep as switch himself off.

Georgiou studied his face. Actually, with its dark complexion and crisp black hair and strong nose and chin it was quite a Mediterranean face — not unlike Georgiou's own brother back home, which was perhaps why Georgiou had felt that sympathy with him at first — at least while the eyes were closed. Open, they were unequivocally Anglo-Saxon in their blueness. More than that, in fact. Their blueness was unmixed. Most blue eyes had flecks, hints of some other colour. Steve's were pure, depthless, like mosaic tesserae.

Georgiou realized that those eyes were looking at him.

' "Good morning, good mo-orning, it's great to stay up late", ' Steve sang, not moving. He raised his hand up from the bed, slowly, in a sort of Roman salute. 'How you doing how you doing how you doing?'

'OK,' Georgiou said. 'Is your headache better?'

'It's gone, mate,' Steve said solemnly. 'It has fucking

gone I am telling you my son. Gone gone, gone gone' –
he intoned the words to the notes of a clock chime –
'gone gone, gone gone. BONG! Here is the news. The
Queen has done a big shit in the royal lavs. And it
stinks.' He laughed, stopped laughing abruptly, gazing
at the ceiling, then started laughing again.

Georgiou cleared his throat: it seemed to have got
clogged up somehow. 'Are you—'

Steve suddenly bounced off the bed and began pacing
the room. 'Do us a favour, make us a cup of tea.'

'I'm afraid I haven't got any tea,' Georgiou said.
'Steve, are you—'

'*Jesus* can you believe this guy?' Steve appealed,
wagging his head, pacing. 'What, you think tea's going
to *poison* you or something, is that what you're saying?'
He clutched his throat, making gagging noises. 'Aargh,
poison, eeargh . . .'

'Steve, listen, I don't mean to be rude but—'

'Ah, look, forget the fucking tea, I'm off.' Steve
yanked on his trainers. 'See you.'

Surprise for a moment took precedence over relief.
'You're – you're going?'

'Yeeeah, mate, going. A-follow the yellow brick road,
follow the yellow brick road,' Steve huffed, snatching up
his canvas bag and jigging to the door. 'Listen, you take
care of yourself, all right, mate? Cheers.'

He was gone, all at once.

Georgiou went to the window and watched him
crossing the walkway to the campus, shoulders hunched,
body rocking from side to side. His lips were moving,
but whether he was singing or talking Georgiou couldn't
hear.

He opened the window a bit, because Steve's socks had been rather stale. He savoured the solitude.

Never again, he thought, will I feel lonely.

## 17

'Oh, Jake Selby's a prat, he's always doing something childish,' Suzanne said. 'He didn't get to be in the play that must have been what it was all about. Trying to spoil it.'

Michael, about to speak, met Suzanne's unforgiving eyes.

'That doesn't mean I'm ever going to speak to you again, Dad,' she said. 'Not after what you did.'

'It was Jake Selby who was making those noises.'

'We could have handled that! It was you getting in a scrap in the middle of the school hall that ruined it Everybody was looking — Glyn Ellis forgot what he was supposed to say and we missed a bit out, and the ending all went wrong . . .'

'It wasn't noticeable,' Christine lied.

'Oh, it was all spoilt, you know it was!' Suzanne cried with real anguish in her tone. A few years older, and she might have laughed about the débâcle, it would have been a good story: but not now.

'Well, that's what I get for trying to be the hero,' Michael said. But it was no use trying to cross this gulf by the shaky bridge of humour. Suzanne's eyes were stony. Her mother's eyes, dear God, when he had let her down. Suzanne turned them away.

'It was so embarrassing,' she said. 'Everybody kept saying, your dad, what on earth was he doing . . .'

She tilted her chin. It looked like arrogance: Michael knew that it meant she was trying not to cry.

Her birthday too, he thought as Christine's van turned into Sheeps Hill Road. And her father throws a violent wobbly in the middle of the school play that meant so much to her, thereby disrupting the performance to the extent that it was pretty much a shambles by the time the curtain came down. With Geoff Selby's brat as well: there was bound to be comeback from that.

Thanks, God. If you've got any more days like this in store for me, at least space them out.

But he was being flippant with himself to no effect: he was dark inside, not just because Suzanne was hurt but because of the image of himself that this evening had showed him. A few pointless, needling harassments and look at him − he was practically assaulting a teenager, shouting, flailing − seeing threats in every shadow, persecution in every quarter . . .

Perhaps it was him who was the crazy one . . .

Christine drew up outside the house. Suzanne was out of the van in a moment.

'Would you like me to come in?' Christine said.

Michael shook his head. 'I'd better talk to her alone. Anyway, you've got an early start tomorrow.' Tomorrow was Thursday, when Christine worked at the Castle cafeteria.

'OK.' She lightly kissed him: it was one of those kisses that are like a gesture seen in the distance, trying to say something but conveying only ambiguity. 'Remember to see about getting that phone number changed tomorrow. And what I said earlier − I didn't mean—'

187

He shook his head. 'I'll see you tomorrow.' He started to get out.

'Oh — didn't you say there was that do at Peter Worrall's tomorrow night?'

'So there is. I forgot.'

She smiled lightly. 'That's not like you. Should be good, shouldn't it? I think that's what we need, you know. A really good booze-up. Things will look different then. Night-night.'

He found Suzanne sitting on the floor of her bedroom, with her new headphones on. He was going to say she ought to be thinking of bed, but realized that that wouldn't go down too well tonight.

'Do they work all right?' he said.

She nodded. 'They're really good.'

'Well, I've done something right today, anyway,' he said.

Suzanne gave him a look. It was exactly the look Kate used to give him when he was being self-pitying.

'I thought it was somebody else, you see,' he said after a moment. He didn't want to mention Steve to Suzanne, didn't want him brought into her life even by name . . . but of course, it was too late for that. 'Somebody who's been messing me about.'

Suzanne took the headphones off. 'Is that who sent me the birthday card?'

'I think so.' How much to say to her? He didn't want to alarm her, upset her even more. Especially when, as Christine had said, it was all kid's stuff. 'That's why I wanted you to be a bit careful. Going to school and so on.'

'You thought that was him in the school hall?'

Her tone of disbelief was understandable. How stupid it all seemed, when you brought it out into the light.

'God. What were you going to do to him?'

*Kill him.* The instant response of his mind was shocking, but he couldn't deny it. Now he recoiled from the violence that had possessed him as he had run down that darkened aisle, but at the time it had been real, frighteningly real.

*Perhaps I'm the crazy one . . .*

Suzanne was shaking her head. 'Men. They always have to try and be macho.'

'Me? I'm about as macho as Mr Magoo.'

Still she shook her head. 'They're all the same.'

Twelve, he thought. Only twelve. Yet she had touched upon an uncomfortable truth. He remembered that train journey — Steve insisting that Michael arm-wrestle with him, and Michael, against his will, doing it, pushing and straining as if it really mattered . . .

That was what was so dislocating about this bizarre experience: he was being made into another person, a person he didn't want to be. He was being drawn into a ridiculous sort of duel, and he mustn't start to accept it, he mustn't become involved in it —

'Dad.'

He came out of abstraction. 'What?'

Suzanne said, 'The phone's ringing.'

## 18

He took the call downstairs.

Irrelevantly, he noticed how messy the living room looked, as his hand reached for the receiver. He had most of tomorrow free, he ought to tidy up —

'Hello?'

A fragment of laughter. He closed his eyes.

'Dr Greenwood? What's happened, have you chickened out?'

For a moment he was speechless, half believing that Steve was doing some sort of ventriloquism to produce that cut-glass girl's voice . . .

'Dr Greenwood? You there? It's TJ. It's nearly ten o'clock, why aren't you here?'

TJ. Of course it was. Tracey, as she *didn't* like to be known. One of his students.

'Hello, yes I'm here — I'm sorry, what's up?'

There were others with her: he heard someone groan in the background: 'I *told* you he'd forget.' TJ made a shushing noise and went on: 'Don't say you've forgotten. We all sponsored you. For Rag Week? Knightsford Hall?'

'Oh, Christ, is that tonight? I thought . . .'

But he hadn't thought anything, really. He'd just forgotten about it. One of the Rag Week stunts was for tutors to spend an hour locked in darkness in the haunted gallery at Knightsford Hall, the historic annexe in the campus grounds. Several of his students — TJ, Neil, Rupert, Inigo, yes, he remembered now — had pestered him to put his name down, and he'd agreed. The sponsor money went to charity, and if he got spooked before the hour was up and had to come out, he had to pay a forfeit out of his own pocket. They did it every year: he remembered that last year Peter Worrall, to his own eternal disgust, had let himself be persuaded to do it.

It had seemed like a good idea at the time, and Michael had agreed readily enough. But he had forgotten all about it — with the Steve business on his mind, his already unreliable memory had given way completely — and he really wasn't ready, he was tired, irritable, this was just a very bad time —

'Look,' he said, 'I'm terribly sorry about this, but I really don't feel up to it tonight. Let's make it another night—'

'Ooh, he *is* chickening out!' TJ said laughing. 'It's not that scary, Dr Greenwood — maybe just a little bit creepy and spooky—'

'It isn't that,' he said, 'it's just that I'd forgotten, all right, I admit that, and it really isn't convenient just now—'

'Oh, but everything's all ready!' TJ said plaintively. 'The warden at the Hall's waiting — he has to give us the key — and there's a man from the local paper who's going to cover it as well . . . Oh, Dr Greenwood, don't be a spoilsport, you promised, and it is for charity. It's good fun really, Professor Hebb did it on Monday, and Dr Selby did it last night—'

'Geoffrey Selby?'

'Yes, and he stayed in there the full hour.'

Not like Geoff Selby to have any truck with charity: he said that, by ameliorating conditions, it delayed the revolution. But on the other hand, he wouldn't turn down a request from his students, because he liked to show that he was on the side of what he called The Youth.

Well, Christ, if Geoff Selby could do it . . .

'Look, OK, TJ, I'm sorry about this, but it's going to

take me a while to get there—'

'No problem, we'll pick you up, Neil's got his car,' TJ squeaked. 'Oh, super! Just give us the address and we'll be over straight away.'

Well, a promise was a promise. He didn't feel like going out again, he didn't feel like it at all, but he didn't want to let them down, and if Geoff Selby had done it . . . Suzanne's light was out when he went upstairs, so he climbed the extra flight to Fred's bedsit to tell him where he was going.

'Poor old you,' Fred said. 'You know they'll do something to try and freak you out?'

'I suspected that would come into it.'

Fred lifted the curtain at the window. 'There's the car now. Good luck.' He grinned. 'Look out for the hidden tape recorders.'

'Just like *Scooby-Doo*.'

'And don't worry. I'll be here. And if the phone rings, I'll make sure I answer it.'

'Thanks. See you later, Fred.'

He went out to the car. TJ and the priceless Inigo were in the back, Inigo with his knees somewhere near his ears and a smile like Disney's Goofy. Neil, at the wheel, raised his eyebrows. 'Better late than never. Thought you'd done a runner on us,' he said in his voice like the scratching of fingernails on a blackboard.

The more recent, Victorian wing of Knightsford Hall contained accommodation for the Climatic Research students, and some were leaning out of their windows and gave a cheer as tonight's victim arrived in the drive. The other wing comprised what was left of the original Restoration house: it was not very distinguished, but the long panelled gallery on the ground floor was intact, and it was the place where, on official visits, the Vice-Chancellor would have his photograph taken with whichever porcine illiterate was currently the Education Minister. It was also reputed to be haunted, though Michael suspected that much of the reputation was hype intended for just such occasions as these.

The reporter from the local paper, a suit with a beardless boy in it – it wasn't just policemen, Michael thought, *everybody* looked young nowadays – asked him a few questions. 'Well, no, I don't believe in ghosts, but I am a little bit nervous. You never know, do you?' Michael said, knowing that they would make up a quote anyway, but trying to say something close to what they were likely to invent.

'Great. That's terrific,' the boy said, scribbling down something which was probably *Yes I do believe in ghosts, but I am not at all nervous. You always know, don't you?* 'Now if we could just have a picture . . .'

Michael posed with his students on the steps of the Hall, at the photographer's request gnawing his nails and looking frightened. Across the park he could see the harsh lines of the campus, coldly lit against the warm night sky: the brute bulk of the teaching buildings which led the locals to call it the multistorey brain park, the outlandish pyramids of the halls of residence. It struck him that from here the place looked far more sinister than this genteel old pile.

'Right, I'm ready when you are,' Michael said.

His students escorted him inside, across a parqueted hall lit by hanging fluorescents to an undeniably old and weighty chocolate-brown door. The warden of the Hall, a dry, unamused, soldierlike man, was on hand with the keys.

'There isn't anything valuable in here I might break, is there?' Michael said to him, aware that his night vision was even more substandard than his day vision.

'All the good pieces have been moved into store. While this goes on,' the warden said, all disdain.

They saw him in with claps, cheers, and back-slappings. 'Remember, if you hear anything peculiar, it's just your imagination,' TJ said. '*Probably*.' They could hardly have made it more obvious that they were going to pull some prank or other.

The door closed behind him. The key rattled in the lock. There was a last muffled giggle from TJ on the other side of the door, then silence.

My God, it really *was* dark.

Michael stood for some moments waiting for his eyes to adjust. Slowly he began to make out some elements of the gallery. There were six tall sash windows along the left-hand side, their curtains open, which allowed in a faint chill light: at the end, facing him, there was a double window with arched mullions. The room must have been some eighty feet long, though no wider than his living room. Along the right-hand side he could see what looked like bookcases, and low shapes that were probably settees, on either side of a marble fireplace. Two branched shapes depended from the ceiling: chandeliers.

He began carefully to walk down the length of the room. Floorboards protested beneath his feet. There was a smell of wax polish and beneath it that old, salty, secretive odour that he always detected in such places.

The past was his province, but he had no enthusiasm for the stately-home enclave of it. Architectural historians gushing about the exuberance of hideous plaster ceilings seriously pissed him off: he remembered reading one such delinquent who solemnly proposed that the widespread poverty, malnutrition and human misery of the eighteenth century was a fair price to pay for the possession of these dismal mausoleums.

He put his hand on the settee by the fireplace. Even in the dark he could tell it was modern: as the warden had said, all the valuable stuff was in store. He walked to the end of the room, peered out of the double window: must give on to the lawn at the back, but he couldn't see anything. There was another stout door to the side. He tried it: locked. He retraced his steps, sat down on the settee, which made a scrunching noise. He checked his watch.

An hour. With nothing to do. In a way it was like a sensory-deprivation exercise.

He listened (mouth open, Michael, you can hear more) and could hear faint sounds, but they were distant, probably coming from the other wing of the house where the research students lived.

Weird end to a weird evening. He took off his glasses and rubbed his eyes, feeling weary. Actually it wasn't unwelcome to sit here quietly in the darkness, thinking, trying to put things in perspective. Problems with Suzanne and Christine, both alienated from him. Geoff Selby would have something to say about his nearly beating the shit out of his son — or autonomous differently aged gene-sharer, or whatever it was correct to call your offspring. And all because of Steve, bloody

Steve whom he didn't even know, who simply wasn't part of his life, who was out to get him . . . But wasn't that classical paranoia? Grimly postulating some external malevolence for everything that went wrong in your life – a conspiracy, something in the water, a radio in your head planted by aliens . . .

Maybe everybody had it to a degree. Geoff Selby, for instance, quite seriously believed that his phone was tapped and his mail read because he was active in the AUT; as if the government really gave a tinker's damn for some powerless tinpot union. *Ve haff a very dangerous enemy, Herr Reichsminister. He must be closely vatched. He is Geoffrey Selby of the Association of University Teachers* . . .

Michael shifted in his seat, and the settee groaned again. The noise seemed very loud: he could almost feel his ears pricking like a dog's. He ought to stay alert really, in case a rubber skeleton came dangling from the ceiling or something. The trouble was, readying yourself so you wouldn't jump only made you jump even more. He remembered a toy Suzanne had had some years ago – a little plastic frog with a sucker underneath, mounted on a spring. You pressed it down, so that the sucker held on to the base, and there the frog innocently sat, sometimes for minutes at a time, until the force of the compressed spring suddenly sent it shooting up into the air. How Suzanne had loved it, and how he had hated it: she would creep up and put it on his desk, and there was nothing he could do – try and ignore it, stare fixedly at it, nothing was any good, it was always just when you weren't expecting it that *Boing!* up it went and you had jumped out of your skin once again.

Michael put on his glasses, then turned quickly. Was that a movement he had seen at the window?

He listened.

Probably not. That was the whole point of shutting you up in a dark, spooky place: you were bound to start imagining things. Like when that newspaper offered a prize to anyone who would spend the night in Madame Tussaud's. Christ, now that *would* be creepy. If you stared at any object in the dark long enough, it seemed to waver and distend; he remembered as a small boy being terrified by the sight of his own white shirt lying on a chair at the end of the bed, which he was sure was moving, shifting . . . So imagine those waxworks!

He cleared his throat loudly – realizing as he did so that he just wanted to hear some comforting noise. God, it was quiet. *Too quiet*, they would say in pulp thrillers. He remembered reading somewhere that the most frequent line in Hollywood movies (who compiled these statistics?) was *Let's get out of here*. What about television? he wondered. If you just took American programmes, it would surely be *You want to talk about it?* Yes . . . He invented one of his little theories. 'It is an invariable law that in any given episode of any given American comedy series – *M\*A\*S\*H\**, *Cheers*, *The Golden Girls*, whatever – one of the characters will say *You want to talk about it?* in the twenty-first minute of running time.'

He looked at his watch. Twenty-five minutes gone. It occurred to him for the first time that there might be a double-bluff: that the idea might be to keep you in suspense for a trick that never in fact came, so that you were a gibbering wreck by the end of the hour. Clever, that.

His stomach rumbled. He hadn't eaten much today: he was hungry.

And more than a little bored.

He tested the upholstery of the settee for comfort. It would be quite a coup if he were to be found fast asleep in the haunted gallery. His father had been a man of such imperturbable temperament that he had once fallen asleep in the dentist's chair. Kate, on the other hand, would start chewing the scenery over a lost earring. Only near the end had that horrible calm come over her, showing how ill she was. He would have given anything for one of her rages then.

Experimentally he lay down on the settee. Within a second he sat bolt upright.

Breathing.

He could hear breathing in the room.

Come on, Michael. It's your *own*, for Christ's sake. Listen: hold your breath for a second, and it will stop.

He got to his feet.

No. Someone else was breathing.

Now don't make a fool of yourself, he thought. This is the game, this is what you were expecting.

*Isn't it . . . ?*

He turned slowly, a full circle, trying to locate the quarter of the darkness which that sound was coming from. It was quite close, it had to be close . . .

But how on earth could anyone have got in here? There were two doors, either of which he would have heard opening. Ditto the windows, the six along the left-hand wall and the one at the end.

Unless they had been in here from the start . . .

Impossible.

But then his investigation of the room on entering it hadn't been very thorough.

The breathing was louder. Faster. In, out, in out in out . . .

Feeling a little foolish as well as tense, he bent down and peered underneath the settee; then made his way down the room, screwing up his damned inadequate eyes, feeling with his hands. The bookcases . . . shallow, nobody could hide there. Hidden passages? Ridiculous, that was for horror films, and the house was too late for a priest-hole. Unless there was a cupboard or something in the panelling that he couldn't spot in the darkness —

His fingers lit on something, down on the skirting board. A very thin wire. At the same moment he remembered Fred's friendly warning.

He followed the wire with his fingertips. He knew what he would find: the only surprise was that it was right where he had started from. A small speaker, hidden at the side of the marble fireplace. He put his ear to it: there was the breathing all right, complete with amplifier hiss, which he should have noticed. Showed how easy it was to get spooked in spite of yourself.

The speaker was freestanding. He picked it up. Pretty basic trick really. If he laid it face down, that should blot out any further sound effects they might try —

'AAAAAAHHH!'

He dropped the speaker, with a thunderous impact on the floorboards.

*Jesus*. His hands were trembling. He recognized the

drama-student tones of TJ in the deafening scream that had rung out from the speaker — but as with the toy frog, it was impossible not to jump. Nice timing, Trace.

He laid the speaker face down. Good job old Muriel Weeks hadn't agreed to do this stunt, with her dodgy heart.

Well, they had certainly signalled it now. What would be next? What would — ah, wasn't that a movement outside one of the windows?

He steeled himself for some sort of ghost-train frightener. But all he saw was a black shape flit past the window. Then nothing.

He could hear breathing again. No, wait, that was definitely his own.

He moved closer to the window. Perhaps he hadn't seen anything after all —

'*Christ*—'

He was cursing himself even as he stepped back — but it was just impossible *not* to step back . . . The black shape had flitted by again, this time briefly turning a white-cowled face in his direction. He couldn't tell which of his female students was dressed up in the nun's habit; possibly Laura, the TV personality's daughter, but it was bloody creepy whoever it was.

They're getting to me, he thought, with shaky amusement. They really are getting to me. He sat down on the settee, hearing the boom of his pulsing blood in his ears. Still, there was a sort of fun in it, as TJ had said. Exhilaration almost.

He froze.

Something was moving underneath one of the floor-length window-curtains. It made jerky, scratchy noises.

*They wouldn't have put a rat in here, would they? A real live rat? They wouldn't have —*

The thing came out from under the curtain and began cautiously, hesitantly moving along the floor, keeping close to the skirting board. Humped. Greyish. Tail trailing.

*My God it is a rat they've put a rat in here!*

Without knowing it, he had brought his feet up on to the seat: very Tom and Jerry, very comic if you could see the funny side, which he couldn't just now. Hell, it was one thing to spook you, another to put a real live rat in the place, he didn't know *anyone* who would fancy being locked in a dark room with a rat —

A rat which was heading straight for him.

'Get away,' he murmured. 'Get away . . .'

A rat which was getting closer, back hunched, little button eyes gleaming —

*It's no good, I'm going to have to shout, I'm going to have to get out —*

A rat which was apparently blind, because it had just fetched up against the leg of the settee with a *clunk*.

If he was wrong he was going to scream, but if he was right —

He reached down. His fingers still flinched as they touched the fur, even though his mind knew that that was no live animal . . .

He scooped it up, and felt the rubber wheels still whirring round underneath.

Good one. He had to admit, that was a good one.

He took the thing to the window where there was more light. Pretty crude really: it seemed to have been fashioned from a fluffy glove puppet. Button eyes, indeed. The furry rat-shape had been stuck on to some sort of model car, one of these remote-control jobs. He wondered who was working it from the other side of the door: Neil probably, it seemed like his sort of thing.

Effective though, undeniably effective in the dark, the way it nosed along. He laid the contraption upside down on the floor and looked at his watch. Thirty-eight minutes now. Well, he hadn't cracked up yet.

He turned to the row of windows, and burst out laughing.

That sketch, Inigo, was standing outside the window covered in flour or some such, wrapped in a sheet, and making the most unconvincing ghostly gestures since Bela Lugosi. He looked as if he were waiting for his underarm deodorant to dry. The fact that he still wore his little granny-glasses added to the hilarity. Michael was so doubled up with laughter that he missed Inigo's exit. It was a pity, he would have liked to have seen his attempt at a ghostly glide.

An idea came to Michael when the white shape reappeared at the double window at the end of the room and began tapping at the glass. It would be funny if he could make *Inigo* jump . . .

He dropped to a crouch, and crawled the length of the room, keeping below the level of the sill. Directly beneath the window he paused, listening to the soft tapping. Now if he popped up suddenly, the enfloured and terminally unwary Inigo would surely leap out of his skin. Turn the tables . . .

He sprang up, making the same Bela Lugosi gestures that Inigo had —

Except it wasn't Inigo on the other side of the window.

202

The figure pulled back the white sheet that hooded it, and the grinning face of Steve was six inches from Michael's.

The comic-horror noise that he had been about to make died in Michael's throat. A croak came out instead.

He couldn't hear the words being formed by Steve's lips, but he could read them.

*All right, MATE . . . ?*

Steve pressed one hand flat and white against the window. Michael saw that the other hand was holding something, something long, bright and sharp that he waved slowly back and forth, metronome-like, in front of his wildly smiling face. A knife.

*All right, MATE . . . ?*

Michael stumbled backwards. Another croaking sound came from his throat.

*Bam*. Steve's free hand struck the window so that the frame rattled. The whites of his eyes formed perfect circles around the pupils. That face, unseen since the train journey, yet so horribly familiar, more wooden and puppet-like than ever, like the face of a ventriloquist's dummy with all those symmetrical teeth and the deep-carved grin lines . . . Yet Michael saw something else in that face that he hadn't seen, or had refrained from seeing, the first time. That was the face of a seriously crazy man. That man was not right —

*Bam*. The window shuddered again. Steve had put the knife in his mouth, clamped it between his teeth: it ought to have looked absurd, shades of Zorro, but it was terrifying because Steve didn't care about having that wicked blade next to his lips, you could tell he wouldn't notice if it sliced half his face off —

*Bam*. Steve was attacking the window with both hands. His grin, clenched around the knife, was more dizzyingly manic than ever. *Bam. Bam. Bam bam bam . . .*

Michael was paralysed. He was caught in the glare of Steve's shadowless eyes like a rabbit in the headlights of an oncoming car.

*Bambambambambambam . . .*

He moved. With a wrench like the tearing open of a wound, he turned and ran for the door.

'Let me out! For God's sake, let me out!' He pounded at the panels of the door. 'There's a bloody lunatic out there, for Christ's sake!'

He could hear them laughing in the hall. Neil's voice came through: 'Hey, I thought you didn't believe in ghosts, Dr Greenwood . . .'

'I thought you were going to stick it out.' TJ's voice. 'You'd have to pay the forfeit, you know . . .' More laughter.

Michael rattled at the handle. Locked. He glanced over his shoulder, saw that Steve was pushing at the old sash of the window, trying to heave it up.

'For God's sake, this is serious, open this door!' Pounding with his fists, bellowing. 'Open the door, you — open the door!'

They weren't going to let him out, they thought he was just spooked, and Steve was going to get in with that knife and he was crazy enough, he was crazy enough to —

'OPEN IT!'

A key rattled in the lock. Michael flung his head round

again, sweat running down into one eye.

Steve had gone.

Laboriously the key turned in the lock, and the door opened.

Michael looked back to the window again, blinking the sweat away. Steve wasn't there.

## 19

'Hey, are you all right?'

The others were still laughing and cheering, but TJ looked concerned. She took his arm. 'Do you want to sit down?'

The light and noise were disorientating. Michael swayed a moment, then pushed a way through them, ran across the hall out to the front door.

A blinding light exploded in his face as he came out on to the steps. The photographer.

His arm was taken again: the fledgling reporter. 'OK, could you just stand there for another picture, Dr Lockwood — and can we have your students standing round you, in their various outfits . . .'

He cast a wild, half-blind glance round at the students gathering about him. Laura in the nun's habit. Inigo covered in flour. Neil was wearing a monk's cowl, no doubt that would have been the *pièce de résistance* . . . Could he possibly have been wrong? Had he mistaken one of them for Steve?

With a *knife*? Come on . . .

'Was it the rat?' TJ was saying. 'I told them that was a bit much — that wasn't fair—'

'Who else was with you?' Michael seized Neil's arm.

'There was somebody else at the window, now who?'

'Oh, that guy, yeah, he wanted to join in. Said he knew you. Inigo lent him his winding-sheet—'

'Where is he?'

'Don't know . . . Did he go? Did you see him, Inigo . . . ?'

Michael was already running down the steps. There was a whole crowd of students from the Hall milling about in the drive, watching the fun. They gave him ironical cheers: one made a mocking ghostly noise.

He pushed through them, ran round the side of the building, past the long row of windows, round the corner and on to the lawn at the back. TJ was skittling after him. 'It was all just kidding, Dr Greenwood,' she called anxiously. 'Are you sure you're OK . . . ?'

*Or am I going mad?* he thought. Because the prospect of Steve still lurking at the back here was no worse than the thought that he couldn't trust his own perceptions, his own mind . . .

There was the double window. No Steve. Beyond, the lawn: then the fenced enclosure where the Climatic Research people kept their strange instruments. Trees, greenhouses, long corrugated-iron sheds, cultivation plots, a whole world of doubtful shadows.

He could be anywhere now.

*But he was here . . . He* was *here . . .*

Wasn't he?

Michael felt beaten. Beaten, exhausted, scared. Like a hunted animal.

'Come on, Dr Greenwood,' TJ said timidly. She began to lead him back to the front of the Hall. He went unresisting. 'We've got a bottle of fizzy stuff, it's not

real champagne, you know, but it's nice. Come and have
a drink with us. You've been ever such a good sport.
None of it was real, you know.'

## 20

Although Steve smoked — whenever he could get hold
of some fags, which wasn't often, people were so *stingy*,
you asked them for a few fags and it was like some *big
deal* — even so, he reckoned he was in pretty good
shape. He didn't poison his system, he didn't stuff
himself with food, and he'd stayed fit since leaving the
army. Look at how far he'd cycled, right out into the
country where there were no people and it was all just
*magical* — before the bastards took his bike . . . Yet he
was out of breath when he got back to Borrow Terrace
that night, having legged it from Knightsford Hall all the
way across the park to the campus.

He'd had to go a bit of a long way round, of course —
making for the cover of those greenhouses and stuff
behind the Hall as soon as Greenwood threw his wobbly,
then coming round by The Broad and entering the
campus from the back where all the boiler houses were.
He'd ditched the sheet in The Broad. Fancy calling it a
broad! He'd *been* to the Norfolk Broads, and they were
nothing like it. People were always trying to put one over
on you. Luckily he was a bit too fucking fly for them.

Still, he shouldn't have been this out of breath. But he
knew why that was. It was the adrenaline. And the
laughter. He was on a high. It was just so good . . .

Greenwood's desk diary had mentioned Knightsford
Hall, 10 p.m., Wednesday, but Steve hadn't known

what it was all about. He just went over there to scout out what was happening. The students gathered there were happy to tell him all about it. He supposed they thought he was a student too . . . Christ! Did he look as if he was a homo, or on drugs? It was handy though. That was the brilliant thing about this place, the way you could just blend in with the crowd.

And then when Greenwood was shut in and the students were getting into their gear he'd simply asked if he could join in. Simple as that. It was a fucking gift. And when he'd found that rear window and stood there – and seen Greenwood's face – oh, shit, his *face* . . .

Steve let the laughter burst free. The laughter went to the sky but it wasn't enough, he had to run up and down the pavement outside Borrow Terrace, swinging his canvas bag, whirling it round his head . . .

'Zigger zagger zigger zagger zigger zagger OY OY OY . . .'

Greenwood's face!

He must be bricking it – absolutely bricking it. *Where am I, Michael bastard Greenwood? You don't know where I am . . .*

God, he needed a piss. And a cup of tea wouldn't go down badly either. He'd better rouse old Georgy-Porgy.

He knocked for several minutes at the outer door without success. These lazy sods wouldn't come down for anybody. At last he stepped back into the parking space in front of the building, looking up at Georgiou's window. Yes, his light was on.

He scooped up a handful of gravel. Good aim, he'd always had good aim. In the army the sergeant-instructor had said what a good eye he had . . . And remember that time at home — that hedgehog behind the garage? He'd hit it every time. With darts too. *One hundred and eighty!* Steve giggled. It was so funny the way it just curled up in a ball . . . Christ, if things couldn't *survive* they were better off out of it.

The gravel struck Georgiou's window. A moment later the window opened, and Georgiou put his head out.

'All right, mate? How's it going?' Steve called up. 'Come on, let us in, will you?'

'Steve . . .' Georgiou's voice was faint. 'It's past eleven . . .'

'What, you going to turn into a pumpkin, are you?' Steve couldn't help laughing again. 'Fucking pumpkins, man . . . Come *on*, mate, let us in.'

'Look, Steve — like I said, you're going to have to find somewhere else to stay tonight, I really can't—'

'*Listen*, man, all I want to do is use the loo, scrounge a cup of tea off you, then I'm off, right, is that fair? Yeah? Deal?'

Georgiou hesitated.

Steve hoped he wasn't going to have trouble with this one. Georgiou hadn't *seemed* particularly against him, but you could never tell with foreigners . . .

'Well, all right,' Georgiou said. 'But you can't stay long, I've got to get to bed.'

'Cheers, mate. You're brill.'

Georgiou's head went in.

'Got to get to bed, got to get to bed, that's what he said, Zebedee said,' Steve sang, running on the spot.

Georgiou appeared at the security door. 'Keep it down, will you,' he said, admitting Steve. 'There are people trying to sleep.'

'What, at this time?' Steve said. Taking drugs and screwing each other, more like, he thought. He skipped past Georgiou and began sprinting up the stairs.

'I really wasn't expecting you, Steve,' Georgiou said, following him. 'After what we said today—'

'All right, mate, all right, keep your hair on!' Steve said. 'What there is of it.' He laughed. Georgiou didn't smile. All right, he did have plenty of hair, but it was still a fucking good joke. What could you do with these miserable people? They had no get up and go. Steve felt like he could keep going all night.

He had a piss, and when he came out into the corridor Georgy-Porgy was standing outside his room, hand on hip. Ooh ducky.

'I can give you a cup of coffee, and then you're really going to have to leave,' Georgiou said. 'I've got an early seminar tomorrow—'

'Yeah, yeah, yeah, no worries, mate.' Steve darted into Georgiou's room. Christ, he was knackered. He plonked himself on the bed. Music was thumping through walls and ceiling, and he clicked his fingers to the beat.

Georgiou said nothing as he made the coffee and handed the mug to Steve. Steve didn't care. He felt like talking. Noticing Georgiou's books, he talked about *The Lord of the Rings*, swallowing his coffee down. Such a brilliant book! He would have to fetch it here, he thought to himself, have a book to read in his little hideaway . . .

Georgiou was looking stroppy. Steve didn't like the way he was looking at all.

'Cat got your tongue?' Steve said. '*Meee*-ow.'

Still that look.

'I've got to go to bed,' Georgiou said. 'I'm sorry, but—'

'Yeah, know how you feel, mate, I'm shagged out myself. Look, just get your sleeping bag out and I'll kip down here for the night, deal?'

'Steve, I can't put you up again. I told you—'

'Listen, mate, I wouldn't ask you, but you've got to help me, right, I can't go out there again, there's these men who've got it in for me and I'm scared, that's the truth. There's this one with a hammer, and I know they're out to get me—'

'What men?' said Georgiou, frowning.

'Little green men. Bee-bop bee-bop.' Steve put his hand above his head like an antenna and laughed –

But all of a sudden he didn't feel like laughing. Not with the way Georgy Girl was looking at him. And he'd decided, hadn't he, that he wasn't going to let anyone look at him that way any more . . .

He felt one of his headaches starting, like a nail between his eyebrows.

But his mouth was still laughing, because laughing helped, it cheered you up . . .

'Listen mate, I'm not going to stick it up your bum, if that's what you're worried about,' Steve said. 'Bum-biddy-bum-biddy-bum-biddy-bum . . .'

That *look* Georgy Girl was giving him . . .

Georgiou shook his head. 'You're crazy,' he said, moving to the door. 'This, this is *stupid*, I want you out of here, I mean this is really crazy—'

He didn't say any more, because Steve sprang up and with his whole weight behind the blow punched him in the mouth, knocking him to the ground.

211

### 21

Georgiou opened his eyes.

Had he blacked out for a moment? He must have, because he was on the floor . . .

Yes. Steve had hit him – my God, so hard . . . felt as if his jaw was broken . . .

And Steve was still crouching over him – and *yelling* into his face, he could feel the spittle spraying on his cheek . . .

*'Don't ever try it! Don't ever – don't ever fucking say that . . . ! You fucking greasy homo dago, you fuck with me like that and you fucking get what you deserve . . . !'*

The scarlet, screaming face was a couple of inches from Georgiou's. God, the pain in his jaw was terrible, he could hardly move . . . and that face so close to his, the squat neck with veins standing out, a nightmare face . . .

'I'm sorry,' Georgiou said. Abject, grovelling – yes, he would say anything if that face would just get away . . .

*'You think that makes it all right?'*

'Steve . . .' Talking was agony. 'My wallet's – on the desk. Take what you want and . . . go, and I won't say anything—'

Steve slapped him across the face. Georgiou's cheek bloomed fire. He couldn't speak.

Suddenly Steve was across the other side of the room. He opened the wardrobe door, began flinging clothes out, grunting.

Georgiou tried to lift himself off the floor. His head

was swimming, and he felt sick. 'What are you—'

'Shut it.' Quieter this time. Steve was breathing heavily.

'I told you . . . take – what you want—'

*'Shut it!'*

Steve came back, bearing Georgiou's ties.

*Oh my God no he's going to strangle me this man is going to kill me –*

He yelped with pain as Steve turned him over and shoved him on to his face. He felt the roughness of the carpet tiles against his bruised cheek.

Steve was straddling him, and had hold of his wrists behind his back. Georgiou began to struggle, to protest, but Steve's grip was like iron.

His mind was protesting too. Like some refined old gentleman, it wouldn't accept what was happening. *How has this happened? What has suddenly gone wrong with the world? This nuisance of a guy comes around again, wearily you let him in telling yourself that this is definitely the last time, he starts acting weirder than before, maybe it's drugs, who knows, and . . .*

Steve was tying his wrists together.

Georgiou thrashed weakly, opened his traumatized jaw, cried, 'Help . . .'

'Say it once more, and I kick your head,' Steve muttered in his ear.

*. . . and suddenly you're in this insane situation –*

Georgiou tried once more to get up. Steve knocked him down, and this time the explosion of pain in his face almost sent him unconscious again.

His wrists were tightly bound together, and now Steve was starting on his ankles.

*— this insane situation . . . But Steve wasn't sane, was he? Oh God, no. This man was not sane.*

An image came to Georgiou of his mother and father, at the airport back home, saying goodbye to him. The night before, his father had said how proud they were of him — for he had always been a little on the shy side, not so good at getting to know people . . .

'Steve . . .' Reason. Talk reason —

*With a maniac?*

— talk reason because it was the only way, and he was a reasonable person, look at the Panandrakis family, their neighbours at home, always having terrible rows, throwing furniture into the street sometimes, and Georgiou was the only one who could calm them down, act as the peacemaker . . .

'Steve . . . there's no need for this, you can stay, I'm sorry I didn't understand — '

'Well, of course I'm *staying*, my old mate,' Steve said, tightening the knot around Georgiou's ankles. His tone had taken another one of its bizarre swoops, it was chirpy and friendly again.

'OK . . . let's talk then . . .' Though talking was agony. His whole body was agony, and he felt like passing out every moment. But if he could get free, then maybe he could summon the energy, ignore the pain sufficiently to make a move, a run . . . 'Untie me, and we'll talk about it—'

Steve's big fist thumped down into the small of Georgiou's back, knocking the wind out of him.

'You are *joking*.' Steve was laughing. Could it be? Yes, he was actually laughing. 'What, and you're not going to run to the fucking headmaster or whoever you have here? You're telling me you're not going to fetch them all, send them all after me, all the bastards, all of them, it's always been the same, in the *army*, at *Tesco's*, you've all done it, you've all ganged up on me—'

'Not me, Steve, not me,' Georgiou groaned breathlessly.

Steve didn't answer. He flicked Georgiou's right ear lobe with his forefinger, painfully. Something about that childish gesture terrified Georgiou more than anything else that Steve had done to him.

'No, no, mate,' Steve went on, his weight pressing Georgiou down on to the floor. 'You'd be fetching them all on to me first fucking chance you got. That's why I've got to do this. It's your own fault, sunshine. You've brought this on yourself, do you hear? You've brought this on *yourself*!'

Georgiou tensed himself for another blow as Steve's voice rose; but instead Steve turned him over on to his back. The refined old gentleman that was Georgiou's civilized mind was babbling now: *this isn't happening, you know this isn't really happening, these things don't happen all right this country you've come to is rather a nasty seedy place in many ways but this CAN'T BE HAPPENING . . .*

Steve dug his hands under Georgiou's arms and dragged him up on to the bed. *My God he's so strong he's like an ox . . .*

'Now lay there,' Steve said, standing over him, a vein like a squiggle of lightning standing out on his red forehead. 'And don't give me any more trouble.'

Groggy with pain, his bound hands underneath his body already going numb, Georgiou lay still, watching

Steve. *What's he going to do? Is he going to go, and leave me here? All right, that will be all right. I can lever myself off the bed somehow, get to the door . . . Supposing he takes my key and locks it? All right, then I'll hammer on the door somehow, I'll bang on the window somehow, I'll get help . . .*

But Steve was giving no signs of leaving. He was pacing up and down the room, muscled shoulders high and tense, arms swinging. His face worked as if he were having an internal debate with himself: sometimes his features creased in a rictus of anguish, sometimes his eyebrows went up and he emitted a light-hearted, breathless titter. Fragments of speech escaped his lips, and all the time he was shaking his head, shaking his head.

*How can he go on shaking it like that?* Georgiou wondered.

*You know how. This man is crazy, dangerously crazy.*

Georgiou remembered his mother and father at the airport, kissing him goodbye. He felt like weeping.

*Should I scream for help? Scream, right now? I don't know if I can open my mouth enough, it feels like my jaw's broken . . . Maybe if I scream he'll panic and make a run for it.*

*Maybe if I scream he'll panic and do something else . . .*

All of a sudden Steve stopped in his pacing. He looked at Georgiou, as if he had forgotten he was there, and frowned deeply.

'We're going to have to do something about you,' Steve said.

216

## 22

It wasn't fair, Steve thought.

He'd had a really good evening, a real laugh. That Knightsford Hall thing had given him a real buzz. And then this stroppy foreigner had to go and spoil it all.

Well, he'd brought it on himself, that was all he could say. The time was past when Steve let people say things like that to him.

*STEVE SHITFORBRAINS* . . .

Georgy Girl had started it, he'd just have to take the consequences, there was nothing Steve could do about it. It wasn't his fault. Georgy Girl shouldn't have made such a fuss about him staying here again – then he wouldn't be lying there all tied up, with his face all bruised, looking up at him as if –

Well, he'd better stop looking at him that way, or else he was going to be in even more trouble.

He'd brought it on himself, there was no more to say. Selfishness, that was this guy's problem. That was the trouble nowadays, everybody just thinking of themselves.

The thing was, Steve *needed* this little lookout place. Look at that Knightsford Hall crack, and the book signing. And the thing in the lecture theatre. And the little pile of do's in the office. Steve laughed. And being able to *see* Greenwood, watch him, keep tabs on him, and all the time he didn't know. It was just brilliant. And it was *important*. This thing he was doing to Michael bastard Greenwood, the fucking captain of all the do-Steve-down bastards of the world, this thing was *vital*. At last he was getting his own back, at last he was in control. He felt more alive than he'd ever done in his life, doing this. But fucking Georgy-Porgy, like all the rest of them, had to stick his oar in and try to stop Steve doing what he wanted, the old old story, come on everybody let's get Steve, that's what it came down to but it was just *not on* any more and the greasy dago had found that out now and it served him right.

The trouble was, now he'd got the little spic tied up and lying on the bed so he couldn't threaten him any more — and what else could he do, for Christ's sake? — now he'd done that, he was starting to get one of his headaches. God, it was a killer. And his tablets were back at the bedsit, thanks a lot, world, nice one. And he couldn't think straight. He couldn't think straight at all.

Hang on though. Wasn't that just what they wanted? Let's give Steve a good thumping headache so he doesn't know what he's doing . . . Oh no, he wouldn't fall for that one.

But he definitely had a bad feeling growing on him as he paced Georgiou's room. The feeling of something going wrong. Everything had gone so well so far, and now this had to happen to spoil things. Of course, it wasn't his fault, but it was a bad omen.

He stopped and looked at Georgiou lying there. That was no good. That wasn't enough. Not if he was going to keep his secret hideout. The spic wasn't secure enough. These innocent-looking ones were the worst; he was probably planning something against Steve right now.

'We're going to have to do something about you,' he said.

He began rifling through the wardrobe and the drawers, hurling on to the floor things he had no use for.

He found something that might do, bundled up at the bottom of a packing-case. String, but of the thick, twined, hairy sort you used to tie down a trunk. He couldn't see a little shrimp like Georgy Girl breaking through that. And there was lots of it.

He turned back to the bed.

## 23

Georgiou's mind was racing. As Steve turned round to him, running the string through his hands, a mad steeplechase of thoughts hurtled through his head. *Ignore the pain and the giddiness and try and fling yourself off the bed. Fling yourself at him. Bite him. Try and get to the window – curtains closed though – open them then – how – teeth? Head then – window closed anyway, who's going to notice you? Scream then – try and scream over the thump of the hi-fi's, scream*, Help, in number ten, help, *someone might hear you, just do something* . . . But first in the race of thoughts, the clear winner, was *But he'll kill me . . . he'll kill me . . .*

'Steve,' Georgiou said. His voice was cracked. 'You don't have to do this. This is—' He nearly said, *This is crazy*, managed to stop himself in time. 'This is not necessary, Steve. We can talk about it. Whatever the problem is, we—'

'*I – haven't – got – a – problem!*' Steve bellowed. His fist came pounding down like a piston with each word, repeatedly hitting the pillow an inch from Georgiou's head.

'OK – OK,' Georgiou gabbled, fresh sweat breaking out on his face. But Steve had already whirled round and was extracting something from a drawer. The next moment Georgiou found one of his own socks being rammed into his mouth.

'Just remember,' Steve said, hunting in the drawers again, his movements more jerky and frenetic than ever, 'just remember you brought this on yourself, sunshine . . .'

Georgiou, nearly gagging from the cotton filling his mouth, found his head yanked up off the pillow by Steve's brown hands. A ripping sound –

Tape. Sellotape. Steve was winding it round and round Georgiou's face, over the sock and round the back of his head. A gag. Steve was breathing hard, his tongue poking from the corner of his mouth, like a child concentrating on an absorbing task. Georgiou began to struggle, to thrash, heaved himself with a lurch off the bed, got on to his knees on the floor, tried to lever himself up to his feet.

Steve stood back, watching. He had taken something from his canvas bag.

'Lay on that bed now,' he said quietly, 'or I stick this fucker in you.'

He simply showed Georgiou the knife, as you would show somebody a new pen or cigarette lighter.

Georgiou heard himself whimpering. It seemed like the final degradation to start to cry, but he couldn't help it.

Steve put his hand to Georgiou's chest and with the gentlest push toppled him back on to the bed.

The beds in the campus residences were of a narrow cot design, with a metal sprung frame on short legs topped with the thinnest of mattresses: the joke among the students was that they had been expressly designed to make sexual intercourse an impossibility. The design also made it relatively easy for Steve to tie Georgiou to the bed, winding the twine round and round the frame like a cotton reel, pinning Georgiou flat to the mattress. As he worked he held the knife clenched in his teeth, his mouth forming an unholy grin around the blade.

He tied the string tight. It dug into Georgiou's stomach, but he was hardly aware of that: it was just a detail in a comprehensive nightmare.

Steve suddenly laughed, stepping back to look at his handiwork. 'You know what this is like?' he said. 'You know them old silent films, where they tie some girl to the railway track? You know what I mean? It's just like that.'

Georgiou gazed up at his captor. *Someone will come*, his civilized mind cried, the refined old gent making a last protest. *Someone will surely come . . .*

But who? No one ever came to Georgiou's room. Only the cleaner, once a week. On Tuesdays.

Today was Wednesday.

Georgiou felt a tear trickle down his face.

*What's going to happen to me . . . ?*

'Them old films, mate, they're just like brilliant, you've got to admit it, you've got to laugh,' Steve was saying. He was prowling about the room again, and whirling his arms round and round in their sockets, and stopping to throw an explosive laugh at the ceiling. 'That Laurel and Hardy, man, and Charlie Chaplin and what's that one, Buster Langdon, you're not telling me they weren't fucking geniuses, I mean, *what*?' He began to sing the Laurel and Hardy theme, clapping his hands

221

above his head football-crowd style. 'Ner-ner-ner, ner-ner-ner, nunna ner-ner, nunna ner-ner . . .' Faster and faster he chanted it, pounding up and down the room, turning with a little hitch step when he reached the door, over to the window, back again . . .

This man . . . Georgiou seemed to see the craziness rising in him like mercury in a thermometer. He wanted to close his eyes, to shut the sight out; but he knew that he would see Steve behind his closed lids, that that awful hulking presence would not go away from him, that those naked blue eyes and peg-like teeth and hunched shoulders and wrinkled trainers and long-nailed hands were all that his world was going to contain for ever and ever just as if he had been nailed into a coffin with Steve and buried in the earth . . .

Steve suddenly stopped and dragged the sleeping bag from the heap of things he had thrown out of the wardrobe. 'Better try and get some fucking shuteye,' he said. His face was suddenly morose, sullen. His eyes flicked to Georgiou. 'Any trouble from you and you know what you'll get. So just catch some zeds, all right?' He giggled, snatched at the air. 'There's one! Here, catch!' He made a tossing gesture. 'Ah, missed it.' His face suddenly fell again, and he shook his head as he laid the sleeping bag out. 'Fucking . . . it's fucking not right,' he muttered.

He turned the light out. Georgiou listened to him getting into the sleeping bag, muttering and sighing.

Georgiou stared upward into the darkness.

*Someone will come . . . Someone must come . . .*

222

# FIVE

## 1

'So this baby polar bear goes to his mum and says, "Mum, I am a polar bear, aren't I?" She says, "Of course you are, son." He says, "I mean, I'm not a koala or a grizzly or anything?" She says, "No, you're a polar bear." So the baby polar bear goes to his dad and says, "Dad, I am a polar bear, aren't I?" His dad says, "Yes, of course you are." The baby says, "I mean, I'm not a koala or a grizzly or anything?" His dad says, "No, you are a polar bear." So the baby goes to his grandad and says, "I am a polar bear, aren't I, Grandad?" His grandad says, "Of course you are." The baby says, "I'm not a koala or a grizzly or anything?" His grandad says, "No, son, you are a polar bear. Why?" And the baby says, " 'Cos I'm bloody freezing!" '

'Oh, *Fred*,' Suzanne groaned, slapping Fred's big knee.

'They can't all be gems,' Fred grinned. 'Right, you ready for the off?'

'Chauffeur-driven again, blimey,' Suzanne said, picking up her school bag. She darted over to Michael, gave him a peck on the cheek. 'See you later, Dad. Oh, are you going shopping today? Can you get me some dried mixed fruit, we've got to have it for home economics tomorrow.'

'I won't forget,' Michael said.

She raised her eyebrows at him.

Well, the peck on the cheek surely meant he was partly forgiven for the débâcle of the school play last night. Only partly. He recognized in her something strongly reminiscent of Kate when she was displeased with him – a sort of conspicuous refraining from comment. An expression that said, I'm-carrying-on-as-normal-but-don't-think-I've-forgotten.

Strange: the school play, only last evening, seemed years ago. He knew why, of course. It was what had happened later, at Knightsford Hall, that occupied the central place in his dully beating mind.

Or rather, what hadn't happened. He couldn't really doubt that he had seen Steve at the gallery window, brandishing a knife –

*Could he?*

– but the fact remained that as far as anyone else was concerned *nothing had happened*. There was no Steve to be found outside the Hall; there had been no act of violence against Michael; and his students, a little abashed and uncomfortable that he had reacted so hysterically, as they saw it, to a harmless Rag Week stunt, hadn't been able to tell him much about the dark guy who had asked to join in the fun.

They probably thought he was mad, Michael reflected. And who was to say they were wrong?

Only himself. That was the point. He knew what he had seen. The significance was for him alone. It was

Steve versus Michael, an insane duel of wits that had as
its object —

What?

The knife. That was what he couldn't stop thinking
about. The lunatic had a knife . . .

And yet he hadn't used it. He hadn't smashed his way
into the house and stuck the knife in Michael's ribs, he
hadn't leapt on him in the university corridors and
planted it between his shoulder blades —

*But who's to say he won't?*

— and Michael knew that that same thought would
occur to the police if he should be foolish enough to go
back to them. You saw this man where, sir? He was
doing what, sir? Are you quite sure, sir?

No, officer, I don't know what he's trying to do.

Well, in fact I do have a fair idea. He's trying to make
my life hell.

*I'll give you fucking purgatory . . .*

He didn't even know if he could tell Christine. Not
after what she had said last night. Was Steve the one
with the obsession, or was it Michael?

And now it was Thursday morning, and the tactless
sunlight pointing out the grime and clutter of the kitchen
made the events of last night seem an unlikely dream,
and strangely enough Michael had managed to get some
sleep last night, and stranger still —

Nothing had happened. No phone calls. No letters.
Nothing.

All he could do was wait, and wonder. Wonder about
Steve. What was he doing? Where did he live? Did he
live alone? Did he work?

*Where was he?*

'This, my friend,' Michael said to his reflection in the shaving mirror, 'is a sure way to send yourself round the twist.'

The only thing to do was behave normally. Crazy, but true. The more abnormal the situation, the more the mind fled to the foxhole of the everyday. Evening dress on the *Titanic* . . .

But besides that, it was a question of fighting. This lunatic wanted to screw his life up; therefore he would carry on his life as normal. It was the only form of retaliation open to him. And it *was* a fight, now, he had no doubt of it. He did not relish it. He had never in his life been in any sort of fight, unless you counted that time when he was six and he had hit the boy next door on the head with a glass marble. As far as he knew, he had not an aggressive bone in his body.

But he did have stubbornness. Stubbornness had carried him through his postgraduate research, when his short-sight had struggled to cope with masses of scarcely legible documents. Stubbornness had carried him through his bereavement after Kate's death, when for two years he never, even in the darkest moments, touched a drop of alcohol for the simple reason that that was a way of alleviating pain and towards the end nothing had been able to alleviate Kate's pain. And stubbornness was what had taken possession of him now.

Tempting to take sick leave, whisk Suzanne up and be off to Cumbria for an impromptu holiday. But that would show that his antagonist had disrupted his life, so in his stubbornness he refused. And though he had talked just yesterday of getting his phone number changed, now that it came to it his stubbornness reared up. Why should he? It was a nuisance, a pain. Friends wouldn't be able to ring him until he'd let them all know. It was a disruption. No, he wouldn't do it.

And as Thursday was the day when he cleaned the house and did the shopping — he had only one seminar to take, late in the afternoon — then that was what he would do.

In a spirit of mild penance, too, he elected to clean out Suzanne's rabbits, letting them out in their wire run whilst he shovelled shit. From time to time he shifted the position of the run: it would get the lawn cut too after a fashion.

The back door stood open, so that he could hear the telephone should it ring: but all was quiet.

## 2

Georgiou fended off madness by trying to pinpoint the moment of sunrise.

He must have slept at some point in that endless night, but he was aware only of drifting up from a whirlpool of confusion, passing from nightmares to a nightmare reality. He lay in the pre-dawn greyness, his eyes, fixed on the square of curtained window over the bed, flicking occasionally to the red dial of his clock radio. His head was a mass of pain: the pain originated in his jaw, but it seemed to be marching out, colonizing the rest of him. Earlier the sock stuffed in his mouth had made him retch, and bring up bile that he could only try to swallow down again, filling his mouth with a filthy taste: but now his mouth was so dry that he could not taste anything.

His hands, bound beneath him, might not have been there: he was numb below the biceps.

So he looked at the square of curtained window, and at the clock radio, and tried to pinpoint the moment when the sun came up above the horizon. And when he realized that there was light in the room, and that the dawn had happened gradually without him being aware of it, he was as disappointed as if it were something that mattered.

All the time he had refused to turn his head and look at the sleeping figure on the floor. Sleeping: because Steve had been snoring for part of the night.

The sleep of the just. Georgiou realized – though his brain mutinied at having to accept the fact – that Steve really believed that none of this was his fault.

*You've brought this on yourself* . . .

Perhaps, Georgiou thought, he really had. A fastidious sense of fairness had always characterized him – disabled him, some might say: his brother back in Athens, who had his own catering business, often told him that he let people walk all over him. Maybe he had done something horribly wrong, and this was his punishment . . . How else could you rationalize what was happening to him?

*No,* he told himself. *You can't rationalize it. Because what you are dealing with here is a maniac. You have let a psychopath into your room and you know what? No one knows or cares. You are a thousand miles from home. You are in a place where you have no friends. You are in a place where it is common knowledge that one first-year student killed herself with a bottle of sleeping tablets and left a note explaining that she hadn't*

*exchanged a word with a living soul in two months.*
*These are the facts, Georgiou. Reason doesn't come into*
*it.*

Another fact was drilling its way into his brain. He
needed to pee.

From outside there came the faint sound of footsteps.
Going along the concrete walkway below, clip clip clip.
He listened until they had become inaudible, still
straining to hear even then, unwilling to let that sound of
blessed normality go.

Pretty soon there would be lots of footsteps, voices,
music. The campus would come to life, and go about its
business. All unaware of what was going on in one of
those rooms, behind one of those countless identical
windows that rose in glassy pyramids.

His heart gave a lurch as the figure in the sleeping bag
stirred and groaned.

Would Steve wake, or go back to sleep?

Georgiou didn't know which he feared more.

### 3

Matt and Luke safely back in their hutch and doing their
usual ecstatic tunnellings in the clean straw, Michael
started on his own hutch. He scrubbed and Ajaxed,
pondering at the same time on the semiology of product
packaging. Cleaning products always came packaged in
cool colours, blues and lime greens: you never saw a
toilet cleaner in a brown bottle. The signal was pretty
clear − though what was particularly clean and fresh
about blue? Mould was blue. He remembered too, from
when Kate had a cat, the different coloured labels that

went with the various flavours of tinned cat food. Salmon was pink — fair enough. Liver was dark brown, ditto. Tuna was blue — suggestive of the sea, he supposed. But why was rabbit green? Suggestive of meadows? And what about heart? It seemed somehow right that the label should be red, but why? Heart's blood?

Righteous, he cleaned down the sides of the cooker. Determined, he hoovered in all the corners. Absorbed, he only noticed with a start the knocking at the door penetrating the roar of the Hoover.

The door was set with those frosted panes of glass that make a sinister featureless silhouette of anyone standing on the doorstep. *He wants you to be scared to open the door*, Michael told himself. *Therefore, don't be.*

He flung open the door with such abrupt emphasis that it was the young man on the step who looked scared. Some poor get-them-off-the-jobless-figures helot who was going round selling household items out of a suitcase like in the thirties. His face was marked with a thousand snubs. Michael did his bit for the enterprise culture and bought a bath towel and a pack of dusters. The poor sod babbled his thanks, eyes lighting up at the thought of his four pence commission.

Michael broke for coffee, making out his shopping list. The pristine house, astringent-smelling, was silent around him.

He found that his shoulder muscles were bunched like pretzels. He willed himself to relax, with the inevitable result that he grew tenser. He remembered again Suzanne's toy frog. Waiting for it to jump.

Waiting.

*4*

Someone was knocking at Georgiou's door. He was sure of it.

*Oh please . . . oh please . . .* A sunburst of joy broke over him, the heavens opened —

And closed again as he listened.

He had been caught by that before. It was the sound of knocking at the door of the room next to his. Sometimes you could swear the knocking was at your own door: especially when you were lonely, or bored, or homesick.

Or in fear of your life.

He was not the only one to hear the sound. Steve had sat up in his sleeping bag and was looking blearily, suspiciously round.

His eyes fell on Georgiou.

*'Christ, mate, what the hell did I think I was doing last night, I'm sorry, it was the booze, it was the smack, I was out of my head, let's get you out of that, I'm so sorry . . .'*

Georgiou so fiercely imagined him saying this that it seemed impossible that he should not do so.

Steve, however, merely looked at him. Looked *through* him.

Georgiou didn't know what Steve was seeing. But he knew he was not seeing what he had done. He knew Steve wasn't seeing the reality of this hellish situation. He was far, far away. *Out to lunch,* as the Americans said. Steve wasn't just out to lunch. He had packed up and gone. He had moved to another planet.

Steve got up, scratched himself, yawned, farted loudly

and giggled at the sound of it. He went to the window and opened the curtains. Then he turned and walked out of the room.

Leaving the door unlocked. Georgiou's keys were on the desk.

*Gone for good?*

No, because there was his canvas bag, where he kept the knife. He wouldn't go without that. He had probably just gone down the corridor to the toilet.

*And, oh God, I need to pee*, thought Georgiou. The need had crossed the threshold into a pain in his bladder, a pain outscreaming the one in his head.

*Down the corridor surely he'll meet someone down the corridor and they'll think . . .*

What? Nothing, probably. If anything, they would merely think he was visiting someone.

And besides, he wouldn't look furtive, not Steve. Georgiou could just see him cheerfully greeting someone in the corridor. *All right, mate?* That down-to-earth matiness: it was convincing. After all, he had fallen for it himself.

A spasm went through Georgiou. He did not recognize it at first. Then he realized it was hate.

Hate of Steve. Absurd, perhaps, that he had not felt it before: but sheer fear, sheer *disbelief* had held it at bay. Now he tasted this new and bitter flavour, and was shocked by a vivid image of what he would do if he could get hold of that knife.

He had never thought of such a thing before. Steve had not only humiliated and brutalized him: he had changed him.

'On the goo-oo-od ship, Loll-i-pop,' Steve was singing

as he returned. He put the kettle on and switched on the radio. He clucked his tongue and chuckled and shook his head through the news, and then tensed for last night's football results.

'Whoa yes!' he cried. 'One-nil, one-nil. One-nil, one-nil.' He clapped his hands over his head, clicked the radio off. He switched off the boiling kettle, made himself a cup of coffee.

Georgiou watched him. All this time Steve had not even looked his way.

*I don't exist . . .*

Steve had taken a spiral-bound notebook from his bag and was looking through it with deep attention. Georgiou gathered his courage. He vocalized, moaned through the gag, wriggled around.

Steve's head slowly turned until his eyes met Georgiou's.

'Knock-knock,' Steve said. 'Who's there. Tife. Tife who. No thanks, I prefer PG Tips.' He wheezed with laughter. 'Fucking PG Tips, man . . .'

'Mmm—' Georgiou opened his jaw wider, almost blacking out with the pain, managed to articulate: 'Mm-*teve* . . .'

'WHAT?' Steve slammed the notebook down, stood over Georgiou glaring down at him.

*Don't let him see tears . . . maybe that antagonizes him . . .*

Georgiou tried to articulate again, could only moan round the gag.

'Oh, for *crying* out loud,' Steve stormed. He wrenched the sock out of Georgiou's mouth, ripping and tearing at the Sellotape.

Fireworks of pain went off in Georgiou's jaw, but he tried to concentrate. 'Steve . . . I'm sorry . . .' He struggled to moisten his parched mouth. 'I have to — I have to pee . . .'

'Oh, JESUS . . .'

Georgiou watched as Steve prowled around the room, head clutched in his hands, eyes squeezed shut, mouth contorted.

'Jesus . . . Jesus . . . oh, Jesus . . .'

*Am I supposed to feel sorry for him?* Georgiou's mind cried in outrage. *Does he expect me to feel* sorry *for him?*

Steve stopped suddenly. He regarded Georgiou from a distance.

'I'll do something for you,' he said, 'if you do something for me.'

Georgiou stared into the protruding blue eyes. It was like looking into an airless vault.

'OK,' he croaked.

Steve stood still for a few seconds, like some stalled mechanism. Then he left the room. He came back after a moment carrying a plastic bucket. It looked like the one the cleaner kept under the sink.

Steve put the bucket on the floor by the bed. Then he took out his knife and cut through the string binding Georgiou to the bed. Georgiou barely had time to savour the relief of not having that twine cutting into his stomach before he found himself being shoved to a sitting position, his head almost between his knees.

Steve's hand gripped the back of his neck.

'I'm going to untie your hands,' he said. 'You make one single move and this knife goes in your back. You try anything and I cut your balls off and break them on your face. Deal?'

'Yes. Yes.'

Georgiou meant, indeed, to try something, he didn't know what. Lunge at Steve with his bare hands? He would probably have got himself killed in two seconds flat, but as it happened the question was academic. He could only just tell when his hands were freed, they were so numb; and the pain of the blood flowing back into them was excruciating.

Steve, meanwhile, had the blade of the knife a couple of inches from his face.

'Go on, then,' he said. 'I'm not going to hold it for you, I'm no fucking homo.'

Georgiou's feet were still tied. He had to roll to the edge of the bed, fumble in his fly, and try to aim his stream into the bucket. The relief was so great that it practically overcame the humiliation of having to urinate in front of his tormentor.

'God, you're disgusting,' Steve said.

Mutely Georgiou struggled to tuck himself back into his fly, his numb hands as clumsy as hooves. He felt dizzy from the change in position, which sent the blood rushing to his swollen and agonized face. *And you were going to lunge at this brute with your bare hands? You can hardly move . . .*

Quick as lightning, Steve had wrestled him over to his face and was sitting on his buttocks, jerking his arms behind him. Georgiou cried out.

'You're a whinger,' Steve was saying, 'that's what you are.' He was tying Georgiou's wrists again: one big, sharp-nailed hand was enough to clamp them together.

'There's too many of your sort around nowadays. Always want nannying. Always making excuses . . .'

His voice was muffled: Georgiou guessed he had the knife gripped between his teeth.

'I'm sorry,' Georgiou found himself saying, he didn't know why.

'So you should be.' Steve flipped him over on to his back like a doll, grinning round the knife. 'Now I'm going to tie you to this bed again, sunshine. And what I said just now still applies.'

'Don't,' Georgiou groaned, 'please don't—'

Steve slapped him an open-handed blow across his cracked jaw.

The agony went on so long, buzzing and reverberating round his head, that Georgiou found he was tied down to the bed by the time the pain had dimmed enough for him to be lucid. As his vision cleared, he thought that Steve had gone . . .

No. He was sitting in the desk chair, with his notebook and pen. Like some insane *secretary*. A giggle that was itself close to insanity sounded in Georgiou's bruised mind. Take a letter, Mr Psycho . . .

'Right, now I've done my bit,' Steve said. 'You do yours. You're Mr big clever smartarse brainbox student. You tell me this. Suppose somebody's dead, right?'

Georgiou stared. *He means me . . . He's talking about my death . . . He's going to kill me . . .*

'Look, are you listening?' Steve said. 'Jesus, bastard foreigners . . . Somebody died, right. Six years ago. How do you find out about that?'

Georgiou didn't dare not answer. 'I — I don't know what you mean,' he slurred.

Steve gave an exasperated sigh. 'Look, man, it's simple, right, somebody I knew, his wife died six years ago, that's all I know, and I want to know more, you get what I'm saying? I want to pay my respects and all that, you get me? So when somebody dies, it must be like written down somewhere, how old they were, what they died of, were they cremated or what, all about it . . . Oh, Christ, why ask a fucking foreigner, you don't know shit.'

Terrified by the deep brick colour of Steve's face, Georgiou kick-started his brain. 'Deaths,' he stammered, 'they are − local newspaper. There is always a column in the local newspaper − reporting the deaths − and when the funeral will be held—'

'Oh, come on, man, I'm talking about six years ago, not this week.'

'Yes, that is what I mean,' Georgiou gabbled. *Let him keep his temper − just don't let him attack me again.* 'Local newspapers − they have files. Going back through the years. You could look there.'

'What, and the local paper's going to let you just go in and look through all their files?' Steve looked uncertain for the first time.

'Maybe. But − there is a local studies unit here. In the university library. I think − I think they have newspaper files too.' He knew the library well, having spent many solitary hours exploring it; he was pretty sure about the local studies unit. But what. if he was wrong? What would be his punishment if he led Steve wrong . . . ?

Steve looked intent as he lit one of Georgiou's cigarettes. 'Yeah?' he said, sounding interested. 'Whereabouts is this place in the library then?'

'In the basement,' Georgiou said. The cigarette smoke was attractive, but what he most longed for was a drink of water. His tongue felt like cotton wool. Dare he ask . . . ?

Steve smoked for some time, his eyes, normally so staring, withdrawn and heavy-lidded. Then he snatched up Georgiou's wallet from the desk and began searching through it.

*Yes*, Georgiou thought. *Take my money, bank card, the lot. Because that at least makes sense. Just do that, and go . . .*

'Wahey!' Steve said happily, producing Georgiou's student ID card with a flourish. 'This is what gets you in, innit?' He held the card up next to his face a moment. 'Tell that's not me on the photo?'

It was true, Georgiou thought: from the cursory glance that was usually accorded the ID, you wouldn't notice that the photograph laminated on to the card wasn't of Steve. A dark-complexioned, curly-haired young man with a strong nose . . . The old jobsworths who manned the library turnstiles were unlikely to spot anything.

But then again they just might – and that – *oh please God* – might be his salvation. A stolen ID card, investigations . . .

'No, you can't tell,' Georgiou said.

'And this' – Steve held up another card – 'this is the library card, yeah? Nice one. Good stuff, mate. We're there. We're on a roll. We have lift-off. Beam me up, Scotty.'

He was on his feet and making for the door with his weird cartoon pugilist's walk. And he was taking the

cards with him. Tucking them into that canvas satchel
along with the knife and the notebook and Georgiou's
cigarettes. He had the keys too.

His hand was on the door handle: he was leaving . . .

'Steve,' Georgiou said.

'Yeah?'

'I'm . . . let me have a drink of water, please . . .'

Steve was totally still for several seconds, the stalled
automaton again.

'Yeah, sure, mate,' he said.

He walked over to the bed, and before Georgiou knew
what was happening Steve had picked up the plastic
bucket and was tipping the urine between Georgiou's
parched lips.

'Had enough, mate?' Steve said, standing over him,
watching him. 'Good.' He put the bucket down and
picked up the sock he had used as a gag and rammed it
into Georgiou's mouth. 'Now put a sock in it.' He burst
out laughing, and was still laughing as he went out and
locked the door behind him.

It was only when his own choking and retching had
subsided that Georgiou realized that, had he not spoken
out just then, Steve would have forgotten the gag.

5

Look at the tits on it, Steve thought as he passed a girl on
the walkway from Borrow Terrace to the teaching
buildings. They were all bloody women's libbers, yet
they went around with their tits half out like that. They'd
get a shock one of these days and it would serve them
right. They were all at it anyway. He was willing to bet

she'd had a few pearl necklaces in her time, with a pair like that.

It was another beautiful day, cloudless and blue, the goodness of God written all over it. He'd had a good night's kip and he was raring to go. Lots to do today, always supposing Georgy Girl had set him on the right track. There'd be trouble if he hadn't. He didn't allow anyone to mess him about any more, they were finding that out now and they didn't like it. He had to stop himself laughing at some of the people who passed him. He had that feeling that he often got when he roamed around town and looked at people's faces, that they were dead, they were zombies, and he was the only one who was alive. More fool them.

Steve squeezed the bridge of his nose. Still that headache lurking there. It was that bloody Georgiou's fault, he was doing Steve's head in . . . He had to admit, he had gone a bit wrong there, his plans had taken an unexpected turn, though it wasn't his fault. But it was always the way, there was always one spanner in the ointment. He mustn't be too surprised, because after all they were all against him. Fortunately he was one step ahead of the lot of them. He used to wonder if his term in the army had been a bit of a failure − though not his fault, of course: but now he could see otherwise. God moved in a mysterious way, there was a time for everything. And he saw now that his army training had been to prepare him for this very task he was undertaking now.

Shop first, get some food inside him, crisps, chocolate, quick and easy. And then the library, to get down to some serious business.

### 6

The old city had for many years been the second in size in England. You only had to look at the number of large and fine flint churches within a small radius of the Castle to know that this place had always mattered. The trouble was, a twentieth-century city population — not to mention most of surrounding Norfolk — did not fit easily into its historic boundaries, and so you had to put up with a certain amount of congestion when you went shopping.

Normally this did not bother Michael. Myopia and absent-mindedness led him through the ancient crowded streets like a sort of holy fool, with a minimum of wear and tear — whereas Christine, for example, barely avoided getting into fist-fights when she went shopping. But today it was different.

People seemed to step out in front of him a lot, and then dawdle, or even stop dead, staring into a shop window at something they patently didn't want and weren't interested in. Or else they would drift towards him, talking to a companion and not looking where they were going: or, worse, simply walk at him head on as if he didn't exist, so that he had to stumble into the gutter. After a while he got tired of walking in the gutter, and simply met ignorance with ignorance, and jousted shoulder and hip; but still he seemed to come off worse. They let shop doors swing shut in his face. They ran pushchairs and shopping trolleys against his legs. They monopolized the shelves where he wanted to be.

It was almost, he thought, as if they were all conspiring to get at him.

And this alarming thought led on to another, as his impatience and annoyance seemed to break out on his body like itching hives: how easy it would be to snap.

How easy it would be to flip. What a simple matter it would be to just lose control, and the next time that gross slob with the beer belly stood in your way, lash out at him. What a short step it was from simply sighing and biting your tongue when that piggish woman collided with you, to losing your head and sticking a knife in her guts.

Once you looked at it that way, madness was no more than turning a different corner in your mind.

The horror of this thought made him stop in the street — just like the people who had been annoying him — and take deep breaths to calm himself.

*My God. I'm becoming like him.*

But maybe not. Because at least he knew now why he was glaring round at the milling shoppers as if they were a bunch of assassins bent on his destruction. He knew now that all his resolutely chirpy normality today was no more than the most desperate of fronts, and that the hours since waking had been like a slow winding of an already tight string. He was staring at every face he saw because in every face he expected to see the grinning features of Steve. He was flinching at every car horn and every crash of till register and every snatch of laughter because he was waiting for Steve's next move.

And because *nothing had happened*.

Laden with bags, sweating in the heat, he began to barge his way through the crowd in earnest. He needed to get out of this, he needed to sit down, he needed to pull himself together. Because a feeling was coming over him that if he just looked hard enough amongst these stampeding herds of people he would see Steve amongst them: that if he just turned round at the right moment —

*Now!*

— he would see Steve's hulking figure just darting into a shop, ducking into an alleyway, hurrying round a corner, flickering out of sight.

Which was crazy.

Yet he caught himself doing it. Just as he entered Jarrold's department store he whipped round . . .

No. The woman directly behind him looked at him as if he was —

*Crazy.*

In the top-floor cafeteria he found a table by the window. A crow's nest: a lookout position. He drank tea thirstily, though he wished it were alcohol, and looked out at the city, the awnings of the market stalls like a patchwork quilt, the extravagant church of St Peter Mancroft like a medieval rocket about to take off, the vast functional drabness of the City Hall, the people, people, people, threading their way around the traffic-choked streets, weaving in and out, a myriad anonymities.

And he thought, with a tightening across his chest: *Where are you? Show yourself. Show yourself.*

7

Georgiou had been pleased to get a room at the end of the corridor: he thought it would be quieter. For the same reason he had put his bed against the outer rather than the party wall. He had never foreseen a time when he would be beaten, abused and tied to that bed, with his only apparent hope in being able to get his neighbour's attention.

By twisting, and ignoring as long as possible the pain of the twine cutting into his stomach, he was just able to kick at the outer wall. But he hadn't been wearing shoes when Steve had attacked him, and his stockinged feet made only dim thumps on the breeze block. Dim thumps on an outer wall, three storeys up. Despair broke over him in waves.

But he kept it up. It might be audible in the room below, perhaps. And if it went on long enough and monotonously enough perhaps the person in the room below would be irritated enough to complain . . . or go to the Resident Tutor of Borrow Terrace and say, Excuse me, I'm worried about the occupant of the room above me . . .

He mustn't think of these hopeful scenarios: they distracted him, made him want to weep, like the sight of the photographs from home on the pinboard. Like the idea that had briefly sustained him, of his absence being noticed at the seminar he should have attended this morning: people were always missing seminars, you could miss a whole term's if you liked. No. He must simply concentrate on those repetitive kicks.

But the pain in his jaw, which now seemed to be swollen grotesquely, was shatteringly amplified with each kick that jarred through his body: he had to stop every now and then to let the pain subside to manageable proportions, and when it did the terrible thirst demanded his attention again. Plus another feeling, a creeping, inescapable feeling that made sweat prickle on his forehead.

Yet the main trouble was precisely that this block *was* so inhabited. It was one great honeycomb of noise. The noise of amplified music, beating through the breeze block like a hectic pulse. The noise of doors and windows opening and closing, room doors, security doors, bathroom doors. The noise of feet ascending and descending stairs. The noise of portable televisions. The noise of clumsy student cookery in kitchens. The noise of hundreds of yards of plumbing in constant gurgling use. Normally you didn't really notice any of this. Now Georgiou's ears heard and picked out every single sound.

*Concentrate on kicking the wall. Don't think of what's going to happen. Don't think of Steve returning . . .*

No, he mustn't think of that. Because that made worse the awful feeling in his guts, the cramps and pains that meant his body needed to take a crap, and soon.

And he mustn't look at those photos of his mother and father on the pinboard. Because that made him wonder if he would ever see them again.

### 8

It was early afternoon when Steve arrived back at the bedsit.

His headache was worse, from poring over all that print he supposed. He felt good though. Good inside. Good feelings.

Nice to be back in his own place for a bit. He put Taylor Dane on the stereo and lay on the bed. As he lay there he read over what he had written in his notebook and soon his laughter was rising to the ceiling. Brilliant laughs, echoing, rebounding . . .

He needed to move around. He got up and walked round and round the room, because the energy was all itching and struggling inside him. The room wasn't big but there was a fair bit of floor space and sometimes, if he needed to, he could tire himself out this way, starting at the bed, walking right round the walls clockwise, round the back of the hi-fi, step over the electric lead, back to the bed, then same thing anticlockwise, and so on for as long as you liked. Occasionally he found himself still doing it when dawn broke.

Of course, he thought, it was here, in the bedsits, that it had all started. Though he hadn't known it at the time. But he was seeing things more clearly now. Thank God.

It was the theft of his bike that had triggered it. That, and the man with the hammer. That the two were connected he was sure, though exactly how was hidden from him. His feelings had just told him so, and now he trusted his feelings, in spite of what the people at The Alders told him.

*Remember you don't have to listen to those voices, Steve,* the doctor had said. *You are your own person. You make the decisions.*

But then the doctor had been against him too.

Pacing, Steve remembered the bike.

The bike had been important. On the bike he had made long trips into the countryside, ten miles, fifteen miles, twenty miles. The other lads in the house couldn't believe he went these long distances. 'What for?' they said, and the expression on their faces made him laugh so much he couldn't stop. Sometimes people's faces, the things they did, they just made him laugh, he couldn't help it. And laughter made the world go round, didn't it? Sometimes he laughed on his own, in the bedsit; if it was a wet Sunday afternoon or something he laughed to cheer himself up. It didn't always work: sometimes the world was just too bad, and he felt sorry for the creatures who lived in it. Like the kitten. So you had to act for the best, and that was what he had done. God had it all planned, sure, but sometimes you had to take a hand in things. But the bike — they didn't understand that. How it took you out to places in the fields, where it was just green for miles around, and sky, and it was just *good*. And mainly it was good because man wasn't there. Without man, the world was beautiful, the way God had made it.

And then the bike took you back to the city, too, because you needed to talk and tell people all about it. And talking was good, too, you could just talk for hours if people would stop being against you and let you do it, and if one or other of the lads in the house was back from poisoning his system in the pub then often they wouldn't mind having a chat, even far into the night. Sometimes they would turn against him, and pretend they were tired, and he *knew* they weren't because he wasn't tired and he'd just cycled to Aylsham and back. He never got tired. It was just an excuse to get rid of him when he was only trying to be friendly. But he didn't care, he'd go down to his bedsit and play his music because the alive feeling was still pulsing round his veins. He'd play Belinda Carlisle or Cher, and think about the singers, maybe that was bad but he didn't think there was any harm in it, same as the magazines under his bed. It was different if you actually messed about with yourself and polluted yourself because that was dirty and what did God give you a body for if not to keep it clean? There was enough filth in the world.

He always used to leave the bike round the back of the house, in an old falling-down shed there. The landlord always said he was going to build a proper shed but he never did. Some of the lads in the house called him a thieving old bastard because the house was in such a bad state of repair, and when their housing benefit was overpaid he just pocketed it. One of the lads said when he left this fucking hole he was going to take the miserable furniture with him and flog it for what he could get to make up for being ripped off by the old bastard. Steve didn't go along with that. He thought there had to be law and order, and respect. There wasn't enough respect nowadays, that was why the world was in such a sad state. And that was why people went around stealing other people's bikes. Christ, if you couldn't leave your bike safely . . .

It just happened that that night he had left it at the front of the house, leaning against the wall. One or two of the lads – the ones he had always suspected were against him! – said if he left it there, then what did he expect, but they didn't understand . . . He'd had a bad day, really bad feelings kept coming to him, it was the weather or something, the weather wasn't *right*, there was just something sinister about it and if people couldn't feel it, then that was their problem . . . and so he'd just left the bike there . . . he'd just . . . What was it coming to if you couldn't leave your bike outside?

What were the police doing, for Christ's sake?

He hadn't seen anything actually sinister in it at the time – he hadn't made the connection yet. But he was certainly lost without the bike. He couldn't get around, and if he stayed still for too long bad feelings started creeping up on him. In the end he'd walked out to the countryside. It wasn't the same, and his feet were covered in blisters by the time he got back to the bedsit. They were funny those blisters in a way, he'd started to laugh because they looked just like when you blow bubble gum, and he just had to go and show them to the other lads. They didn't seem to think they were that funny, but that was because they wouldn't look, they just wouldn't *look* . . . With hindsight he could see that they were all ganging up on him, but it wasn't easy at the time. That was the trouble – people kept things hidden from you. They were treacherous.

No bike. It was terrible. Other people didn't get their bikes nicked: that was what made him begin to realize that there was more to it – that he was being singled out, and that they were out to get him. Of course, he did get another bike; Tommo, one of the lads in the house, got hold of one for him from a mate of his. But there was something about it, something about the way it steered, it just wasn't right, you could tell with certain objects that they were just no good. So he had left it somewhere in town, he couldn't remember where. And Tommo had got really stroppy about it when he found out. Steve couldn't believe it! He'd always thought Tommo was supposed to be his friend. But then the friendly ones were the worst, underneath.

Then he'd got the kitten. Someone he knew had a

litter, and he went and picked one and brought it home in a cardboard box, and named it Jack.

The kitten had been good at first. Steve had really thought they were going to get on. But then he'd started to notice the way the kitten looked at him. It really glared. It was like it was full of hate. And then there was the stink it made when it crapped on the newspaper Steve put out for it. Jesus, that stink! And there was Tommo, who was supposed to be a mate, going on at him saying he ought to get a litter tray and then it wouldn't stink, for Christ's sake, didn't he see that the kitten was doing it deliberately? And then it was always wanting food, and the thing was, Steve thought that these creatures should be independent, they should fend for themselves. After all, they'd taught him how to survive in the army, animals should be able to do it, but there it was whining for food all the time even though he shouted at it to shut up . . . And then the way it cowered, that was even more annoying, really no one could have expected him to put up with it. He tried throwing it outside, but it was so cunning, it was always crawling back in. That cunning wasn't natural, in fact. Some people didn't take the idea of possession by the devil seriously, but Steve knew that the devil could enter into anything, any time, for real, never mind all that *Exorcist* stuff.

Hadn't his father told him about the way the devil worked, right from when he was a tiny kid, long before he could read the texts on the walls? Hadn't he met the devil in his first childhood nightmares, shouting out from his bed in terror, until his father had come in and made him quiet with the slipper or the belt?

He knew about the devil, and the kitten had it inside,

there was no doubt about it. 'You've brought this on yourself, Jack,' Steve had said as he'd filled the sink with water, 'you've brought this on yourself, it's not my fault.' And the way the thing scratched him as he drowned it *showed* it was evil. So Steve knew he was doing the right thing.

And after all, the kitten was better out of it. He was doing it a favour, with the world the way it was. Same as with those baby birds he'd found in that nest in the hedge, back when he was a kid. He'd known then they were better out of it, and that he was doing the right thing, absolutely the right thing: the only thing that had worried him was having the box of matches, because his father would have punished him if he'd known about that. And it was pretty funny to see the way they wriggled when they were on fire. It sometimes made him laugh now to think about it.

But it was not long after he'd put the kitten out of its misery that his real troubles started. It was all so connected! Thank God he'd begun to see it now, begun to see the trap they were closing round him! He was just sitting in the bedsit one evening, and there was a football match on. England v. Poland, and he'd really wanted to see it, but he couldn't because his portable TV was broken. It wasn't his fault, he'd smashed the screen the other night because of this stupid programme, God it was so stupid there was nothing else he could do. Christ, what did they think they were doing, putting on such stupid programmes? He could have gone and watched it in Tommo's room, but Tommo had gone out − surely on purpose, surely yet another sign that Tommo was turning against him. But even if he couldn't watch the match he was in a football sort of mood: so he put on his favourite record, 'Tell it to my heart' by Taylor Dane, and did a bit of cheering and chanting. He liked to make up his own chants, you could take any word, like 'ashtray', and just make no end of variations on it. And some of them were so funny, you sounded like a Zulu or something, you just had to laugh. And when 'Tell it to my heart' came to an end he lifted the stylus arm and put it on again, and again, because it was so brilliant he could hear it any number of times, and he was having himself quite a good little time chanting and clapping.

And then *he'd* turned up. The one with the moustache, Kevin or whatever his name was. He'd not long moved into the house, and the other lads said he kept himself to himself, though as far as Steve was concerned he was just ignorant. He wouldn't stop long in the hall to talk, and after the first few times he stopped giving Steve fags when he asked. Only a few fags, for Christ's sake! It wasn't his fault if he had no money, he was on the dole, and all right, there was the money his mother gave him, but he'd bought that magazine, and he couldn't help it if those things were so dear . . . Actually he wouldn't have been surprised if this Kevin bloke had been a homo, with that moustache, and he knew what the Bible said about homos. Some blokes in the army had had moustaches, but that was different, you knew where you were in the army. And this Kevin had the room directly above his! Christ, he didn't want some pervert living above him . . . But that wasn't the worst of it. The worst of it was this Kevin came knocking on his door and told him to keep the bloody noise down or else he was going to complain to the landlord.

It made Steve's head swim to recall it: this bloke standing there, having a go at him, looking at him like he was a piece of shit. Threatening him. Coming out with some crap about being on shiftwork and needing his sleep, or something . . . Steve's memory was a bit vague on the details of what had happened after he'd answered the door, which wasn't his fault, his mind was so blown by this bloke threatening him and revealing all the hate that the world had always been storing up for Steve, right from the word go, his dad and the army and that job at Tesco's that they'd thrown him out of and the doctors at The Alders when he'd had that bad time and the whole lot, there it was all coming out in the shape of this bloke having a go at him . . . But what Steve did know was that this proved what he had always suspected about the attitude of the world to him; because if you couldn't play a bit of music without some homo coming down and threatening you with a hammer . . .

Tommo didn't believe him about the hammer. 'Oh, come on, Steve, Kevin might have complained about the noise, all right, but where would he get a hammer, for fuck's sake? And where you get this idea he's queer I don't know.' Which just went to show that Tommo had joined the other side. Maybe Steve was a bit unsure about the details, but his *feelings* told him that there had been a hammer, and he was going to trust his feelings from now on, never mind what the doctors had said. God created everything, so God must have created those feelings. And after all that bloke might as well have had a hammer, he was *getting at* Steve so it came to the same thing.

It was all that bloke's fault, Steve hadn't felt right since. Though in a way it was a good thing, because it had opened his eyes. Opened his eyes to the way they *all* hated him — Tommo, Eddie, all of them. The fuss they made over that business with the fridge! It had started when Steve had thrown out all his coffee and tea. It just occurred to him that his body didn't need this crap. It was probably poisoning him slowly, you could never tell. So he threw it all in the dustbin. And then he had looked round his bedsit with one of those bloody *headaches* coming on and had seen that fridge humming away in the corner and — there was something about that hum, it just wasn't right. There was only one thing to do and that was get that fridge out of there, get rid of it.

It was raining when he dragged the fridge outside and into the front garden. To hear the lads go on you'd have thought it was Steve's fault that it was raining. They didn't see it there till the next morning: Steve had spent the night walking round his room. Tommo went through the roof when he saw the fridge. 'The landlord'll go spare if he sees that there,' he kept saying. 'For fuck's sake, Steve, what are you doing?' In the end the expression on Tommo's face just made Steve burst out laughing. He had a really good laugh, he thought he wouldn't be able to stop.

The rain had all got into the fridge and it was useless. Tommo got one of his mates with a van and he took it down to the dump. And then he got all stroppy because Steve had to keep borrowing milk from him. But what was the point in him buying his own milk now he hadn't got a fridge, for Christ's sake? Not that it was any good saying that to Tommo, he was just against Steve now and that was it. A drop of milk, for crying out loud. It wasn't as if Steve asked a lot of him.

That Kevin bloke moved out soon after that. Thank God. Except that now Steve was left with the worry of when he was going to come back to get him. His feelings told him it would happen some time. At night he sat on his bed with a screwdriver in his hand, waiting. He could take care of himself if the bastard came for him. The trouble was, he had a feeling there would be more of them. He remembered now when he'd left the army, four years ago, getting into a quarrel with a couple of blokes in a pub in Huntingdon, it wasn't his fault, there was just something about them he didn't like; someone had broken it up before any damage was done, but they definitely had it in for him. What if they came looking for him now? In fact he had a very deep feeling that they *were* going to come for him, and he knew he ought to be ready. The screwdriver wasn't enough, so he took a good steel carving knife from Boots, and kept it under the bed, sharpening it every night. He was totally against thieving, but this was a matter of survival, it was kill or be killed, you learnt that in the army and it was true in civilian life too — more true, it was more true, because at least the IRA or the Argies or whoever were open about wanting to kill you, whereas the people you met now hid their intentions, they were two-faced, you had to watch them really carefully for when they betrayed themselves and revealed what they really thought of you.

Like Greenwood. Who was just one enemy too many

for Steve. The time had come to fight back, and that was what he was doing . . .

He stopped pacing, came back to himself. Things to do. Life had never been so busy.

He went upstairs — past Tommo's room, he was finished with Tommo, Tommo was against him — and entered Adrian's room.

'Fucking hell, Steve, don't you ever knock,' Adrian grunted, jumping out of his manky old armchair.

Steve tittered. What had he been doing, tossing himself off? Dirty bastard, it was disgusting. The curtains were drawn too, which was just as well with the state of the room, TV blaring, empty milk cartons and dead teabags and a jammy knife sticking to the newspapers on the table. It was sick the way some people lived, Steve thought.

'And if you've come to cadge any more fags off me, forget it,' Adrian said, sullenly sitting down again. 'I've only got ten to last me till my next Giro.'

Steve just laughed. He knew Adrian would have another packet hidden somewhere. People were so obvious! He could see right through them. He was feeling stronger than ever today. The strength was building up inside him.

'You still got that dog?' Steve said.

'What do you think that is?' Adrian gestured to a blanket in the corner of the room, where the mongrel puppy cocked a wary eye through wrinkles of loose skin.

Steve went over and picked the puppy up. It wriggled uncertainly in his arms, half-scared, wanting to trust. Its paws, with funny fringes of hair, looked too big for its skinny body.

'Wish I'd never got it,' Adrian grumbled. 'Bloody thing's always either pissing on the floor or scratching to go out or whining or wanting food. Gets on my tit.'

Steve scratched behind the puppy's ears. Poor thing. 'You want me to take it off your hands?' he said.

Adrian looked surprised. 'Do you want it?'

'Yeah, man, I'll have it. I love animals. I've always wanted another one since I lost my kitten. You know what, I reckon somebody came along and nicked that. Just like my bike.'

'Wish somebody would nick that dog,' Adrian said. He took out a cigarette and, after a hesitation, passed Steve one too. 'You really want it?'

'Yeah, mate, I'm telling you, she's beautiful.'

'She's a right pain, I'm warning you.'

The dog, squirming, licked Steve's hand. 'Nah, she won't bother me. I've got patience, I can put up with all that.'

Adrian made an open-handed gesture. 'You want her, you've got her. Mind you, I don't think the landlord's going to be too keen when he finds out. Not that I cared, I was just going to tell him to fuck off, but you know what I mean.'

'That doesn't matter,' Steve said. He carried the puppy to the door. 'Cheers, Adrian.'

The puppy looked up at him, whiskery and inquiring. Poor thing.

9

Michael came home by taxi. An extravagance: somehow in his childhood he had absorbed an idea that taxis were an impossibly effete luxury, like the Orient Express and peaches, and even as a non-driver in a world of drivers he had never quite lost it. But it would have been unwise in his present fraught mood to attempt a bus journey laden with six bags of shopping.

Fred's fantastic chariot was in the drive. Michael sprinted straight up to his bedsit.

'Any phone calls, Fred?'

'No. Good God, you look terrible.'

'More terrible than usual, you mean?'

'More terrible than usual.' Fred smiled, but he looked concerned.

'Oh, well, you know. Stress of modern living. Supermarketitis.' He shouldn't have run up those stairs so fast, he was winded. God, he was out of condition. 'By the way, got you these.' He placed on Fred's desk a jumbo-sized tin of salted peanuts, which he knew Fred loved to munch into the small hours as he pored over impenetrable physics.

'Cor,' Fred said. '*Wow*. Thanks, Michael.'

'Well, it's to say thanks to you, really. Having to be around to keep an eye on Suzanne, and so on. Must be a bit of a pain. Afraid it's a bribe too. If you're going out tonight—'

'Which I'm not. So don't worry, I'll be here.'

'I won't be late. It's just we've been invited to Peter Worrall's, and—'

'Do you good, I reckon,' said Fred, opening the peanuts and pausing to inhale the released odour, eyes closed. 'Cor. Magic. Have you — heard any more from your crank?'

Michael shook his head.

Fred tossed a peanut into the air, caught it in his mouth. 'Do you know, my grandad used to say that if you ate the pips in an apple core you would end up with an apple tree growing inside your body. I believed him for years . . . Perhaps he's stopped.'

'Your grandad?'

'Your crank.'

'It's a possibility.'

And as he said that, Michael was assailed by a memory of the time when Kate began to be ill. The time when she still had good days, good weeks even, and they would both allow that treacherous hope to steal over them: *Perhaps it's stopped.*

Downstairs he unpacked the shopping, turning the hope over in his mind, looking at it from various angles. Perhaps Steve had grown tired of it. Perhaps something else had supervened. After all, Steve couldn't devote his whole life to harassing Michael.

Could he?

Fred was calling down. 'You want me to go and pick Suzanne up?'

Could it have stopped?

Not worth the risk.

'No, it's OK, Fred. I'll go and meet her.'

Suzanne only did a brief pantomime of despair when he met her at the school gates. For the benefit of her mates he had prepared a loud speech to the effect that he just happened to be passing the school, but it turned out that she needed to keep him sweet anyway: she had this English homework, it was grammar, she couldn't understand what it was all about, would he . . . ?

Thank God for English homework, he thought,

feeling needed as he spread the exercise books out on the kitchen table. Very sensibly, Suzanne elected to go upstairs and refresh her ears with Seal, leaving him to it: the point was to get a decent mark, not to understand it.

*I will never*, Michael thought as the telephone shrieked into life, *I will never again be able to hear the telephone ring without jumping*.

It was Christine.

'How's things?' she said. He could tell her voice was guarded, even on the phone.

'Quiet,' he said. They had parted after the school play last night, and she knew nothing of the Knightsford Hall affair. He wouldn't tell her about that over the phone: the instrument made bad news worse. 'How was work?'

'Knackering. Had three parties of French students going round the Castle today. Why do a people who had that brilliant revolution treat humble café assistants like serfs? "Cheeps, cheeps, give me cheeps." Well, lovey, are we still on for the booze-up tonight?'

'Deffo,' he said — a phrase of Suzanne's. Yes, a drink. By God, yes. He had never felt more like a drink in his life. 'I'll call round for you, shall I? About eight. We can walk it to Peter's.'

'Good good. Don't want to be driving tonight . . . So everything's all right, Michael?'

She was anxious about him, but anxious not to show that she was anxious. It was bad enough, he thought, him having to put up with Steve: she shouldn't have to worry about it too.

'Everything's OK,' he said. 'Did you know that OK comes from the slogan "Old Kinderhook" used by the

Van Buren party in American presidential election campaigns in the 1830s?'

'You old fart,' she said fondly. 'I'll just nip out and get a bottle of plonk. See you later.'

### 10

The sun had moved round, and was striking low and full into Georgiou's room. It made a glare on the glossy surface of the photographs on the pinboard. Georgiou was glad: glad he couldn't see his parents' faces.

Glad they couldn't see him.

He couldn't help it. He hadn't been to the toilet since yesterday morning, and what with the sickening pain in his head . . . He couldn't help it.

He had given up kicking the wall. His stockinged feet were bruised raw.

Earlier in the afternoon he had passed through a stage of gnawing hunger that had even taken precedence over the thirst: but that was gone now. Nausea instead, and the ever-present pain.

And the terror. Growing.

### 11

Steve left the bedsit around tea-time. He had changed his clothes, and repacked his canvas army-surplus bag: it was heavier now.

Things to do. He had to go and see Mrs Greenwood — just a brief visit: he would pay his respects later. But while he was out and about, he thought he would make a detour and check out where Greenwood's current piece of meat lived. He had the address in his notebook, and it seemed a pity not to use it.

It was in one of the old streets of red-brick terraced houses that the ring road had surgically separated from the city centre. Steve, approaching the house with a casual step, saw that there was a little old disregarded church just a few doors away. He was willing to bet she never went in there. It was disgusting really, her shagging that bastard and living near a church. He'd noticed, when he'd followed her round the campus that day, that she wore no wedding ring; so she was probably a lesbo anyway, he thought, she just liked it up her now and then, they all did if they'd only admit it.

The street was empty: he paused in front of the house. Fifteen A, a flat, he'd thought as much. Ground floor though. A tiny paved front garden, a bay window without nets: if he opened the gate and stepped up the little path he might even be able to see in. Tempting.

He opened the gate. A tabby cat appeared and rubbed round his legs, then sniffed up at his bag, nose wrinkling.

He could just see into the front room: bookshelves, the corner of a coffee table —

He froze as he heard the sound of an engine behind him, brakes, slam of a car door —

God reached out and touched him. He put his hand up and calmly knocked at the door of the flat.

He heard footsteps coming up the path, turned and smiled. It was her. She was carrying a bottle of wine, wrapped.

'Can I help?' she said.

'Yeah, sorry to bother you—' He indicated his bag.

'Just selling kitchen goods, you know, if you need any oven gloves, tea towels, you know . . .' *Divine inspiration*, he thought. *God is good.*

'No, I'm sorry,' she said. 'I really don't need anything.'

'Righto then. Cheers anyway,' he said. He turned back down the path and – *God is good* – opened the next gate, went up that path to the house next door, knocked, all in full view of her as she got out her keys and went into her flat, calling the cat in after her.

Nobody answered next door: he didn't have to do a repeat performance. A good job too, because he was going to laugh and laugh, he could barely hold it in . . .

He took a quick note of the registration number of the car she had drawn up in – a van, in fact, typical, she must be a les – and hurried off down the street.

Once round the corner, he let his laughter free.

Pity she hadn't said yes, really. He could have shown her what he really had in his bag.

## 12

Michael and Christine walked to Peter Worrall's house in the suburbs, leisurely in the mild, soft evening air that made malice and madness seem impossible abstractions; and he told her about the episode at Knightsford Hall.

She breathed, 'My God . . .' and squeezed his hand tightly, almost painfully, but then was quiet for some time. They were crossing a children's playground, and she urged him to sit down with her for a minute on a brightly painted roundabout. They had a cigarette.

'Have you thought about talking to a psychiatrist?' she said.

Michael stared at her. 'You think I'm going round the bend,' he said dully, without protest: he half believed it himself.

'Not you.' She laughed briefly. 'This weirdo. I mean he's obviously got a slate missing somewhere. You can't tell what's going on in his head, but a psychiatrist might be able to give you a few pointers. Maybe – maybe if you can start to understand what makes him tick, you won't feel as if you're at his mercy quite so much.'

Michael conjured up the image of Steve's grinning face. A face from a totem pole, vivid but insensate . . . Did he really want to know what was going on inside? Somehow he didn't fancy examining the bats in that particular belfry . . .

And yet it was a damned good idea. One of the worst things about this week was the sensation that he was facing something blank, amorphous, incomprehensible. Yet it was only one man's warped mind, and that was no more inaccessible than a book in a foreign language. There was always a key somewhere. And as Christine said, it would surely make him feel less powerless.

'There's the Psychology School at the university,' Christine went on. 'I don't know whether there are any clinical psychiatrists attached to it, but I'm sure you could find someone there who could give you an expert opinion. Why not try it?'

'You know, I think I will.' He nodded. 'Yes. Tomorrow . . . There's just one thing that's bothering me.'

'What's that?'

'Why didn't *I* think of it?'

She laughed and pulled him to his feet. 'Come on.

There's the plan then — tonight, pour a few drinks into you and try to forget about it: tomorrow, Psychology School.' As they went on, arms linked, she shook her head and gave a low whistle. 'Seeing him at the window like that . . . my God . . . I thought you were a bit *too* calm today.'

' "It was quiet — too quiet",' he said. 'No, you see, it's partly that as well. That's what I can't understand. Nothing else has happened. It's as if it's stopped.'

'And you can't tell if it has until — until something else happens?'

He nodded. 'Catch-22 . . . I wonder how we managed before the expression "Catch-22" entered the language.'

'Now I know you're feeling a bit better,' she said, squeezing his arm, 'you're working up one of your theories.'

'I always feel better when I'm with you,' he said. It was true: but it came out so cheesy that they could only look at each other and burst out laughing. Yet all at once a renewed warmth existed between them.

Peter Worrall's was not a standard-issue university lecturer's house. No monkey-puzzle tree outside it, no yucca plants filling the windows, no children's school paintings on the fridge, no photomontage of friends and holidays on the kitchen wall, no spaghetti measure, no jars of pesto. The mantelpiece was not stacked with books, and there was no framed collection of cigarette cards hanging above it, nor were there any Steve Bell cartoons slipped into clip-frames. Nor was the house old or interesting or impossible to heat. It was newish and square, and set in a neighbourhood of minor executives and clipped lawns and Sierras in carports. Peter Worrall clearly detested studentdom so heartily that he could not bear to be reminded of it in the slightest when he went home from work.

All the same, the guests that evening were virtually all academic, as Peter apologetically mentioned to Michael as he took his jacket. Peter's wife taught at the technical college: so who else did you ever meet?

'Friend Geoffrey was asking if you were coming, by the way,' Peter whispered.

'Oh, balls, is he here?'

Peter shrugged ruefully. 'How can you keep him away?'

It was true: in the back-scratching faculty world such a snub simply could not be delivered. Familiar faces thronged the big lounge: Hilda, sweet sherry in hand, Paisley square pinned round her shoulders; Muriel Weeks, pissed as a newt already but still disarmingly articulate; Geoffrey, alas, Selby smiling his self-righteous smile over a glass of dry white.

'Pull your horns in, Michael,' Christine whispered as they saw him.

Hilda was coming over, with the peculiar slinking, playful walk that some people assume to show that they are at a party and not at work.

'Now, Michael, what is this I hear about you getting the willies when they locked you in Knightsford Hall last night?'

Michael grimaced, and felt the tension that was still coiled inside him tighten a little more.

'I never thought of you as the superstitious type,' Hilda said, tapping him with a plate of Twiglets as an eighteenth-century lady would have tapped with her fan.

'Mind you, I should be no good at all in that situation. I go all goosey-bumps just reading a ghost story.'

'Michael has an active imagination,' said a soft voice behind him. 'He doesn't let the facts of the matter get in his way.'

How *did* Geoff Selby manage to appear noiselessly at your elbow like that? Could he dematerialize like some bloody alien?

'Hullo, Geoff. How's things?'

Geoffrey made a shrugging gesture, conveying that it was irrelevant to consider his own personal wellbeing when people in the Third World were walking twenty miles to get a drink of contaminated water. 'Apparently the school play was quite a success last night,' he purred.

'It went very well,' Michael said stiffly.

'So Jake told me. Listen, Michael, I'd always had you typed as basically a well-meaning liberal — an untenable ideology under late capitalism, but there could be worse — and yet now I find you're an advocate of corporal punishment in schools.' He paused to take a bird-like sip. 'And not administered by the teachers.'

Christine had slipped away to talk to Muriel Weeks: she knew better than to hang around when Michael and Geoffrey got together.

'Jake was disrupting the performance,' Michael said. 'Or somebody was. I didn't know it was him until . . . So I stopped him. I certainly didn't clout him, if that's what you mean.'

'Disrupting the performance? What can you mean?' Geoffrey said with an amiably puzzled smile.

'Giggling. Catcalling. Making stupid noises—'

'Oh, come on, Michael. Good historical precedents

for an audience being candid about what it thinks of the performance. If you didn't like the new *opera buffa*, you threw orange peel. Far more healthy, performers and audience as equals, instead of the hegemonic elitism implicit in the audience sitting obediently and clapping in the right places.'

'It was a school play, for Christ's sake, not a sixties happening. Anyway, he was putting them off.'

Geoffrey's composure became even more infuriatingly seamless. 'That's not the way I heard it,' he said.

'Well, consider the possibility that you weren't told the truth,' Michael said. Meaning, *your brat of a son's a congenital liar*.

Geoffrey shook his head. 'I know you've always had a bit of a down on The Youth, Michael. But don't lay your authoritarian power games on Jake, please.'

'I wouldn't have to if he'd been brought up right,' Michael said. The spring was tightening.

Geoffrey made the soundless nodding movement that passed in him for laughter. 'Brought up. I haven't heard that phrase in ages. What next, Victorian values?'

'You can't get much more Victorian than Marx.'

'Now what are you two cooking up between you?' said Hilda, interposing herself. 'Honestly — you boffins can't stop talking shop for two minutes . . .'

### 13

In the mild early evening Steve made his dogged way to the campus, singing under his breath.

God, that had been difficult to find. He never realized these places were so big: his dad had been cremated, and had his ashes scattered over Lake Windermere where he used to go on holiday! What a twat. Steve chuckled.

Anyway, he would be able to find it again when he went back later. He had even taken note of a gap in the holly bushes where he could climb over the wall. He was knackered: he'd been on the go with this business all day! Still, it should be worth it. It should be the best yet.

*Shitforbrains* . . . He'd like to see *them* carry through a complicated operation like this.

The campus lights were coming on: the place looked huge, eerie. It was a pain, but he'd better see what Georgy Girl was up to; he just couldn't be trusted on his own. If the dago was quiet he might manage a bit of a kip in the sleeping bag. He could set that smart clock radio to wake him at twelve.

God, this place did look spooky with the orange lights on those blank concrete walls, and the sky all bluey-black behind it . . . Surely the sky shouldn't be that colour. It wasn't right. Steve rubbed his temples as he crossed the walkway to Borrow Terrace. That headache again . . . Bad feelings. The feeling of things being *not* right. It was all to do with that Georgiou − everything had been going right till he'd stuck his oar in. Whingeing, fussing, complaining . . .

Some bloke gave him a funny look as he climbed the stairs to the third floor. Who did he think he was looking at? He had to stop himself having a go. The bastard deserved it, but it might cause problems.

*I'm in control. I'm in control.*

He put the key in the lock of Georgiou's room, turned it, opened the door.

The smell hit him.

And suddenly Steve wasn't in control any more.

## 14

At the sound of the key in the lock Georgiou's whole body went rigid. He had never known such fear in his life. In fact there were no comparisons — this fear was unique in quality, it was everything, it filled the world, it filled eternity —

Steve came in. And some small part of Georgiou's brain that was not quite paralysed said, *Look at him — that red face, those absent eyes — that man is getting worse — that man is going downhill* . . .

Steve paused, lip curling over his teeth. Smelling. Looking.

'*I couldn't help it!*' Georgiou cried. '*I'm sorry, I just couldn't stop it!*' That was what he tried to cry, anyhow, stretching his shattered jaw round the gag, but only a strangled moaning came out.

Steve slammed the door. And came at him.

'You dirty *bastard*! You fucking dirty little homo *cunt*! You shat yourself! You did that on *purpose*!'

He was shaking Georgiou by the shoulders. Georgiou closed his eyes to shut out the sight of the yelling, bursting crimson face and readied himself for the blow. *Just let it be quick* . . .

Steve let go of him.

Georgiou opened his eyes, saw the flash of the knife.

The faces of his mother and father appeared to him again — kind, loving . . .

Then he felt a slackening of tension at his stomach. Was this what it felt like to be —

Steve was slashing through the twine tying him to the bed, grunting and whimpering as he did so. He flung the twine aside, clamped the knife in his mouth, and then gathered the soiled blanket around Georgiou, still bound at wrists and ankles, and –

*Oh my God the strength of him!*

– picked him up in it, heaving him off the bed. For a moment it was like a grotesque parody of a comforting embrace, a mother swaddling a child in a towel; and then Steve kicked open the wardrobe door and –

*Oh God, no!*

– shoved Georgiou inside.

Georgiou's head hit the back of the wardrobe and he slid down on to his buttocks. He was dazed for a few moments, but he could feel Steve grabbing his feet and squashing them into the confined space, could hear him grunting, 'You don't fuck with me any more, man, it's too late, you just can't do it any more—'

And then the wardrobe door swung shut on him, the key turning in the lock.

Georgiou fought for breath against the swelling panic in his chest. It was so *small* in here, he was squeezed in like a foetus, he couldn't move . . .

A shadow moved on the louvred door four inches from Georgiou's nose. Steve's face. He was yelling again.

'You've brought this on yourself! You did it! It's not my fault!'

Bound, gagged, covered in his own excrement, half-concussed, racked with pain and thirst, in darkness, Georgiou felt something lift from him. For a moment he thought it was his soul leaving his body. But that relief was denied him. What had left him, like a haggard bird taking wing, was hope.

## 15

Steve paced the evil-smelling room, rubbing his temples, hearing the feeble struggles of Georgiou inside the wardrobe.

His fucking *head* . . .

It wasn't *fair*. Why was the world so horrible to him? Why was everybody against him?

He had known, though, hadn't he? He'd had a bad feeling on the way here. At least his feelings hadn't let him down. God hadn't deserted him.

Well, one thing was for sure. He wasn't staying in here. God, that *stink* . . . just like when he had had that kitten. Well, the kitten had brought its punishment on itself, and so had Georgy Girl, he'd just have to take the consequences. Steve was off. Out of here.

He hurried out, locked the door, ran down the stairs. He felt as if something was pursuing him, he didn't know what. You got that feeling sometimes when you went far out into the country, it was all just beautiful and glorious and then suddenly you would sense this *presence* in the middle of it all, this evil presence . . .

Halfway along the walkway he stopped dead.

Two figures were blocking his way. Devils, with horns.

*Punishment.*

One spoke to him.

'Contribution for Famine Relief?'

He couldn't find his voice.

The other devil rattled a bucket full of coins. 'Go on, anything will do.'

*Girls they're just girls dressed up in devil costumes it's that Rag Week crap again . . .*

But though his mind knew that, his heart still pounded. Just the way they were standing there, blocking his way, looking at him as if –

'Fuck off,' he said.

'All right, no need to—'

'I said fuck off!' he bellowed, and pushed his way between them.

He calmed down a little when he reached the service road that led away from the campus. An idea had come to him. He shouldn't have been surprised at those whores trying to stop him – because that was the pattern, wasn't it? Why else had Georgiou done that filthy thing except to divert him, put him off his stroke, spoil his plans? He had something important to do, the most important thing of the campaign so far – it was only to be expected that the bastards would try to stop him.

He breathed deeply, even managed a little chuckle. Yes, people were so obvious. He knew what they were up to all right. Well, they'd have to do a lot more than that to stop him. It would be full dark soon: he'd go and do the important business, make a thoroughly good job of it too, and then get back to the bedsit. The plan was still operational. He was in control.

But he wished this damn headache would go.

## 16

Michael checked his watch. Past ten: so twenty-four hours had gone by since the last manifestation from his persecutor.

What was going on?

Had it really stopped?

He disengaged himself from Muriel Weeks' sozzled brilliance and sought out Peter.

'Peter, is it all right if I use your phone?'

'Sure. Use the one upstairs, it'll be quieter.' The party was loud now, though only with the yapping of people who loved the sound of their own voices — an academe gathering was always an ensemble of monologues. The mild jazz coming from the stereo couldn't compete. 'Michael, what music should I like?' Peter went on, swaying.

'*Should* you like? Well, what do you like?'

'Well, I sort of like jazz. But I don't want to be like one of those right-wing farts like Larkin and Kingsley Amis, you know, droning on about jazz with loopy pop-eyes. I can't like pop or rock or whatever you want to call it, I mean I don't want to be some pathetic specimen like Geoff, forty years old and desperately trying to keep up with The Youth. I can't like classical because I'll end up like one of those dinosaur judges, you know, who've never heard of the Beatles and quote Latin. I can't like Indian ragas and Armenian folk songs and nineteen-twenties German cabaret and old fat dead blind black blues singers because that would make me like a student. Do you see my problem?'

'You can get sound-effects records — you know,

trains, seagulls, donkeys braying,' Michael suggested. Peter's eyes lit up.

Upstairs Michael found the phone in Peter's bedroom. It was a relief to get away for a moment, because down there he was being haunted by Geoffrey Selby, who was determined to pick a quarrel with everything he said, and the tight-wound spring inside him was close to breaking point. He dialled his own number. Fred answered.

'Hallo, Fred. Michael. Just seeing if you're OK.'

'Yes, fine. Suzanne's just gone to bed. She beat me at Scrabble.'

'Did she indeed? So much for the English homework.'

'Yes, beat me hollow. Mind you, I'm not sure there is such a word as quazox . . . How's the party?'

'Fine. There haven't been any . . . phone calls?'

'Not a dicky bird.'

'Oh . . . OK. See you later. I won't be late.'

He put the phone down, absently noticing on the dressing table a graduation photograph of Peter, looking very studenty.

Nothing had happened today. For the first time since he had met Steve on the train, nothing had happened.

Could it have stopped?

Laughter floated up from the room below.

Or was this just a lull, meant to make him relax his guard? Give him a false sense of security that would be abruptly shattered?

Worse thought: supposing nothing happened, and nothing happened, and nothing happened . . . Would he be able to convince himself that it had completely stopped? Wouldn't he *always* be waiting, tense, wary, expectant, just in case . . . ? Wouldn't that be the worst torture of all?

*Not knowing*.

Normally a few drinks relieved tension. But it wasn't working tonight, though he had had more than a few. That spring inside him was dangerously overwound.

He rejoined the company downstairs. He found Peter and Christine talking about the homeless.

'. . . It stands out even more here,' Peter said. 'I know it shouldn't but it just seems to hit you more when you see these poor sods sitting in the doorways of pretty timber-framed listed buildings.'

'They're so young as well, a lot of them,' Christine said. 'That reminds me, I felt awful today. One of these young chaps came to the door selling bits and bobs, you know how they do — and I was in a hurry and I just wanted to get in the shower and get ready, so I said no — and afterwards I thought, you mean cow, I mean I usually try and buy something, they always look so fed up.'

'I had one of those round this morning,' Michael said. 'My mother used to talk about men coming to the door with a cardboard suitcase full of bootlaces in the Depression. Is that what we've come back to?'

'And no doubt you bought something,' Geoffrey Selby said, materializing (or did he come up out of the floor like a pantomime devil?). 'And so perpetuated his exploitation.'

'What else should you do, then?' Christine said.

Geoffrey made his open-handed, Comédie-Française gesture, which any jury would admit was an incitement to murder. 'Don't buy. If no one buys, these government schemes fail, the system slowly begins to fall apart, in time it is completely overturned and something better put in its place.'

'And in the meantime,' Michael said, 'the poor sod with the bagful of tea towels earns even less, and feels even more useless.'

'You can't make an omelette without breaking eggs, as Lenin is reputed to have said,' Geoffrey sighed.

'Who cares what Lenin said? I thought that degree of hero worship went out with the Pharaohs,' Michael said. 'Or Nietzsche. The ideal of the superman. And we know where that led.'

'Liberal scare tactics,' Geoffrey said. 'Always the same when real change is postulated. Like your hero Cobbett. Very strong on the injustices done to the poor, but balked at the idea of the real redistribution of wealth. Rather like the Labour Party.'

'Well, apparently you won't redistribute *your* wealth to the extent of buying a few tea towels,' Michael said.

'Of course we should redistribute wealth,' Peter said, 'starting with the royal family, which at least won't be too long now, thank God.' Peter was an ardent republican, and had told Michael that the whole aim of his life was to live long enough to see the Electress of Hanover and all her idiot kin get their long-overdue comeuppance, in particular that witless brood mare the Princess of Wales. 'But how are we going to redistribute it? The traditional Communist model hasn't got much of a track record.'

'What Communist model?' Geoffrey said. 'Real Marxist socialism hasn't even been tried. It would work if somebody tried it.'

'Yes, that's always the get-out, isn't it?' Michael said. 'Just like religious freaks. Suggest to a Christian that his co-religionists have not exactly increased the sum of human happiness over the centuries, and he says, oh, they weren't *real* Christians. And no doubt if we have a Marxist revolution and it goes wrong, we can say, oh, they weren't *real* Marxists.'

Geoffrey wore an expression like an operatic tenor holding a *sotto voce* falsetto. 'You're a bit early with this speech, Michael, the Tory Conference isn't till October,' he said.

Michael saw Peter and Christine exchange a *trouble* glance. 'I am not a Tory,' he gritted.

'Mainstream Labour then,' Geoffrey said, shrugging. 'Pretty much the same thing.'

'Yes, I suppose I am.' The internal spring twanged shrilly. 'I thought you were a member of the Labour Party, Geoffrey?'

'Nominally,' Geoffrey said. 'I stay so as to work for change from within, to make it a genuine socialist party.'

'Why? It never has been a socialist party on the Continental model. In power, out of power, it never has been and isn't designed to be. There aren't going to be any more Marxist revolutions in Europe. Revolution is a nineteenth-century idea. We're not going to order our lives according to the dictates of a nineteenth-century German-Jewish philosopher any more than we're going to go back to riding about in stagecoaches and sawing off legs without anaesthetic.'

'Quite an interesting little theory,' Geoffrey said. 'But how will you get it into one of your picturebooks, I wonder? Or would it make a pop-up book, perhaps?

*Michael Greenwood's Wonderful World of History*? I don't think it would do your reputation as a scholar any harm. Mainly because you don't *have* a reputation, Michael.'

The spring snapped.

## 17

Well, it had been one hell of a day, and he was tired from all the tramping around; but he had done the business and made a good job of it. At the end of the day you could only do your best, Steve thought, and that was what he'd done, even with this damned headache. He felt satisfied and proud as he unlocked the door of the house and switched on the hall light. He could hear music coming from Adrian's room: Christ, it was gone eleven, some people just had no consideration.

'Steve?'

He whirled round. It was Tommo, who had the back downstairs room. He was poking his head round the door. And giving Steve a very funny look.

'You scared the shit out of me,' Steve hissed, 'what the fuck are you trying—'

'Just listen, will you,' Tommo said. 'The landlord's been round tonight. He took a look in your room.'

'What?' Steve seemed to feel a weight crashing down on him. '*What?* He can't do that, he can't, it's not right, shit, you're lying, man, you're *lying*—'

'He looked in everybody's rooms,' Tommo said, 'he was just snooping round the way he does.' Still he gave Steve that funny look: still he craned round the door and didn't come out. 'Christ, Steve, I don't know what

279

you've been doing in there, but he went mad when he came out. I mean he went apeshit, he wanted to know where you were, he said he was going to have you out of here, he said he'd be back here first thing tomorrow and he'd probably have the police with him—'

'You are *lying*, man, you are *lying* . . .' Steve didn't know how many times he said it: the rage had control of him, and inside his head he was howling down long corridors of panic.

Tommo kept looking at him. 'My God, Steve,' he said, 'what did you do in there?'

He flinched as Steve pointed a shaking finger in his face.

'You did this,' Steve said. 'You planned this. All of you. You set me up. You're all out to get me . . .'

Tommo shook his head and started to close the door. 'Steve, mate,' he said, 'you need help. Get it quick.'

Steve stood for some moments staring at the shut door. He gave an absent laugh, because it occurred to him that Tommo didn't know how close he'd been to death just then. Steve could have opened him up just like that, just like gutting a fish. Only the fact that he had more important things to do stopped him –

Plus the fact that it was no good here. He was in danger here. The bastards had counterattacked in his own home, and his plans had gone wrong again. Not that it was his fault – he had a lot of things to do, he just hadn't had time to clean up the mess, and after all the dog was his, Adrian had given it to him . . . But when the bastards had it in for you, it was no good expecting them to listen to reason. Once the conspiracy got moving against you, the only thing to do was fight or retreat.

And he was going to have to make a tactical retreat from here, that was for sure. He knew Tommo hadn't been lying to him (though of course he would if it suited him) for the simple reason that it all fitted the pattern. The landlord was inevitably on their side, and inevitably he would try to deflect Steve from his purpose. Or even worse. The police! But he hadn't done anything! Why weren't they out catching criminals? But there again, that proved his point: if they were out to get you, they didn't bother with reasons.

He paced round the dingy hall, trainers squeaking on the bare tiles, the pain in his head sharpening. There was another thing — God alone knew what lies Tommo and the others might have told the landlord about him. They had probably cooked up all sorts of stories to get him into trouble . . . Jesus! It wasn't fair, the way people ganged up on him.

Well, one thing was for sure, he wouldn't stay here and wait for the landlord to come and get him in the morning, he'd have to be stupid to do that. Tommo had really slipped up there, giving him that warning: he must be cursing himself. Yes, he was getting out of here. He had another gaffe where he could get his head down, no problem.

The landlord snooping in his room! God, it made him feel dirty. Nobody respected privacy any more.

He left the house, closing the door quietly behind him. Lucky he was in good shape, because he had another long walk back to the university ahead of him . . .

Trouble was, there was that whining dago to reckon

with when he got there. Just his luck. Why did
everybody make things so difficult for him? It just
wasn't fair. Well, if Georgy Girl gave him any more
trouble, he'd regret it. You could only push Steve so far:
that was what Greenwood was finding out. And he'd
find out more in the morning. Steve gave a laugh at the
thought of it, and the laugh echoed round the empty
street. The bastards were trying to keep him from his
prey, but that only made him more determined. More
strong.

More raging.

### 18

'Peter was very good about it,' said Christine in the taxi.

Balefully, Michael stared at his reflection in the dark
mirror of the taxi's window. Had that face always been
so angular, so pitted with shadows, so — alarming?

Ridiculous, to be alarmed by your own face.

Yet he was not the only one. He had seen expressions
ranging from unease to downright fear on the faces of
Christine, Peter, Hilda, others, in those moments when
they had dragged him away from Geoff Selby.

His knuckles stung. So it really did hurt when you
punched somebody in the face. Or at least, when you
punched in a moment of incandescent fury, blind and
deaf. *Transported by rage.* He understood the truth of
that expression now. He had indeed been transported:
for several seconds he had gone away from himself, and
only when he came back did he really see what he had
done. See Geoff Selby staggering back with blood
running from his nose.

A drunken brawl. A not terribly successful university lecturer, resentful of a more successful colleague, boozily hits out at a faculty party. Dear God. Sordid and half-comic. Stuff of the campus novel.

Except it wasn't like that. Peter Worrall, as Christine had said, had been good about it: at their premature departure from the party he had said aside to Michael, 'About time somebody planted one on the little shit'; but Michael knew, and Christine knew, that it wasn't like that at all. He had really meant to hurt. He was unfit and forty, but he was not a small or delicate man, and when he had thrown the punch he had put his weight behind it.

It had been, in fact, brutal. And that was why Christine was looking at him with eyes full of hard, withdrawn doubt.

'I'll see Peter tomorrow and apologize,' Michael said.

'And Geoff Selby?'

'And him.'

'It's a good thing it was Geoff Selby, in a way,' Christine said. 'Somebody else might have hit back and we'd be ending the evening in the casualty ward. Or the police station.'

He nodded. There was nothing to say. How could you explain that an intolerable pressure, like the tightening of a spring, had been building up all day – all week – and that something, no more than the wrong word at the wrong time, had made it break?

A silly, taunting, off-the-cuff remark, scarcely worth noticing, had produced a violently over-the-top reaction . . . Now where had he seen that pattern before? And who did that remind him of?

He knew very well who it reminded him of before

Christine spoke the name both had been avoiding.

'It wasn't Geoff Selby you were really hitting out at, was it?' she said. 'It was that Steve.'

'I suppose so.' Because he couldn't reach Steve, couldn't find him, couldn't see him.

'I don't like the Michael I'm seeing,' Christine said. 'I hope it's not the real one. Geoff Selby isn't Steve, Michael. And neither am I.'

He turned to look at her. Her face was pale, smooth, and distant.

'Do you see what I'm saying?' she said. 'If you keep getting wound up by this Steve so much that you have to lash out, what if it's me who's in the way next time?'

He shook his head. He wanted to reject that argument: but his own belief in himself had been horribly shaken. He thought about the situation he was in now. Work would be unbearable, with Geoffrey in the office next door; his relationship with his daughter and, even more, with Christine, was troubled; his mental state was such that he could hardly apply himself to even the most trivial of everyday tasks. What sort of person was who had got himself in this situation, and had rounded it off with that disturbing loss of control tonight?

He had always thought of himself, or liked to think of himself, as reasonably easy-going, tolerant, sane. And now the fear had come upon him that it was all a lie. With his self-image so crucially undermined, he was wondering how much else was false. His happy marriage to Kate, his (usually) good relationship with his daughter, his feelings for Christine, his work . . . Was it all just a sham, covering darkness and crude futility?

*My Fairy Palace . . . it's gone . . .*

Darkness. It was all around him as he rode home with Christine silent, a few inches, a few miles away from him in the back of the cab. It held his grim reflection on its surface: it swathed the city on all sides.

And somewhere in its velvety expanse, there was a man who was slowly driving him crazy.

### 19

As Michael rode home in darkness, Steve unlocked the door of Georgiou's room in Borrow Terrace on the university campus. He put down his bag, switched on the desk light, and ignoring the weak sounds coming from the locked wardrobe, began to write Michael a short letter.

# SIX

## 1

Georgiou drifted up into consciousness, and immediately longed for oblivion again. Enemies attacked him all at once — the thirst, the pain in his head, the cramp in his limbs and haunches, the struggle for breath, the claustrophobic terror.

Directly in front of his face were thin bars of light, like a glowing music stave. His numbed brain was slow in comprehending. Morning, of course: the light was filtering through the louvred door of the wardrobe.

Then his brain wasn't numb any more as he realized that it wasn't the light that had roused him but the sound of a voice.

There was a voice in the room, and it wasn't Steve's.

## 2

'So, how was the party?'

Fred popped his head into the kitchen on his way out. Michael, sitting over his third cup of coffee, blinked blearily at him.

'That good, eh?' Fred said.

'That bad,' Michael said. He had risen early, not so

287

much hungover as sick with self-disgust. He had insisted on walking Suzanne to school even though Steph had called for her — a humiliation which she bore only with a thunderous silence.

'Was that the phone I heard just now?' Fred said.

'Yes, it was OK, Christine.' She had rung to see how he was. They had somehow arranged, through a mutual screen of coolness, to meet for lunch at the campus.

'Going to be a scorcher again,' Fred said.

Michael looked up and noticed for the first time the bright sunlight. He had hardly been aware of the continued hot weather this week, except as a minor aspect of the mounting pressure that was squeezing him out of shape.

'You teaching this morning?'

'Seminar at ten thirty.'

'I'll give you a lift.'

'Thanks . . . What's wrong?'

Fred was peering out of the window at the back garden and frowning. 'Did you let the rabbits out, Michael?'

Michael leapt to his feet.

The door of the hutch was hanging open. The rabbits were not inside.

'Oh, my Christ, Suzanne's going to be heartbroken if they're . . .' Michael scanned the long-overgrown garden. 'How on earth did they get out? I put a brand new catch on that hutch not so long ago . . .' His mouth was talking, but his mind wasn't with it. His mind was saying, *You know how they got out. You know.*

A flash of white amongst the long grass: Michael let out a cry of relief. It was Matt, the bigger of the two rabbits, loping towards him. 'Thank God for that,' he said, scooping the animal up and hustling it back into the hutch. 'The other one must be around somewhere—'

'Michael.'

Fred called him over to a patch of weeds. They looked sickly down at all that remained of Luke, the smaller of the rabbits.

'Oh no,' Michael said.

'Cat,' Fred said. 'They'll take them if they're not too big . . . Jesus.'

'Are you sure?'

Fred looked surprised at Michael's feverish tone. 'Pretty sure,' he said. 'See a lot of it out in the country.'

They buried the remains at the foot of the garden, marking the spot with a stick. There was nothing more to do.

Fred kept silent until they were on the road in the bilious Zodiac: then he said, 'Maybe Suzanne didn't shut the hutch door properly – maybe that's how they got out—'

'They didn't get out, they were let out. Somebody came and . . .' The thought of Steve creeping around his garden at night turned Michael cold to his bowels.

'How can you prove that?' Fred said.

'I can't.' Michael smiled bleakly. 'That's exactly it. That's exactly the way it's done. You see? Everything he does can always be seen as something else . . . And so you can never pin him down.' He saw his eyes in the sunscreen mirror. Haunted eyes. God, he thought, poor Suzanne. How was he going to tell her?

'Just who is this bloke who's been bothering you?' Fred said: then, misinterpreting Michael's expression, he added, 'Or should I mind my own business?'

'No, no. It's . . .' Michael sighed. It was no good pretending he didn't want to talk about it — or rather, didn't need to. 'His name's Steve, that's all I know. I met him by chance on Monday, on the train . . .' He gave Fred an abbreviated account of what had happened. Edited highlights of a week of —

*Purgatory.*

— tension, craziness, paranoia. Fred listened attentively.

'Maybe it's stopped,' Michael concluded. 'How am I to know? I don't know anything about him, though he seems to know so much about me. I just can't tell what's going to happen. I don't know what's going on in his head.' Then, remembering Christine's idea last night: 'But I'm going to try and find out.'

### 3

Georgiou listened, heart jerking in irregular beats, little involuntary grunts escaping his gagged mouth. That voice — that voice was not Steve's . . .

'. . . and the good news for those of you who like it hot, some do you know, is that there'll be unbroken sunshine for the rest of the day, except in some coastal districts, where it will also be slightly cooler with a fresh north-easterly breeze. Top temperature inland, twenty-four degrees. BBC Radio Norfolk . . .'

Georgiou bit into his gag, dug his nails into the palms of his bound hands; but nothing could stop the tears coming.

**4**

Steve stirred his coffee. This crazy weather, it just wasn't right! Not in May. And they tried to tell you there was a new Ice Age on the way. They were always trying to pull the wool over your eyes. Something big was coming to the world, all right, he had long thought so, but it was more likely to be Armageddon. Not that he would shed any tears for that, it would put the world out of its misery.

Not just yet though. He had a purpose in life, and he wanted to see it through.

He'd had a reasonable night's sleep after all, after legging it back from the bedsit, in spite of that lingering smell of filth in here. And the headache that was still lurking between his eyebrows. And the noises from the wardrobe, where the little spic still wouldn't be quiet. Christ. The things he had to put up with. This everlasting coffee pissed him off as well: he preferred a nice cup of tea first thing in the morning.

He wondered if the landlord had turned up at the bedsit yet, expecting Steve to be there, expecting to lord it over him, threaten him, get at him. Ha ha, too smart for you, mate. Thinking about it in the light of morning, Steve doubted now whether the landlord would really bring the police. He was running too much of a dodgy operation himself to want to have too much to do with them. That house was a firetrap for one thing. Still, he had to make a living, and it was his property. You had to have free enterprise, look at the state of these Communist countries. All the same, Steve knew he had done the right thing, keeping away from there. He was

still one jump ahead of all the bastards, no danger
there —

'Oh yes!' he cried, as Taylor Dane's 'Tell it to my
heart' came on the radio. Brilliant! That was the trouble
with this place, he hadn't got his stereo.

He pounded round the room to the beat of the record,
clapping his hands above his head, making up chants to
go with it. His favourite record — perhaps that was a
good omen. Perhaps everything would start swinging his
way again.

He thought of last night's work, and had to laugh. It
was a beauty. It was magic.

In fact, he'd better get back to work now, before
Greenwood arrived at the campus. He drained his coffee
and snatched up the note he had carefully written last
night. Did it say enough, though? He considered it.
Yes . . . it was just right. He found an envelope in the
desk drawer, wrote DR MICHAEL GREENWOOD on
it, slid the note in.

Georgy Girl was making a noise in the wardrobe
again. On his way out Steve gave the wardrobe door a
kick and said, 'Shut up.' He hated these whingey people.
And this headache was getting worse.

He kept his eyes to the ground as he crossed The
Square. There were a lot of girls in shorts and skimpy
dresses — at nine o'clock in the morning! — and he
knew better than to look at them, these lesbos would
scream rape at the first glance, even though they were
asking for it. God, it was so hot, so glary with the sun
bouncing off all this plate glass! It was making his head
worse. Just his luck.

Nice and cool, though, in the grey corridors of the

English Studies building. He kept his eyes peeled as he approached Greenwood's office. He knew from his timetable he wasn't due in yet, but you couldn't be too careful.

There were some pins on the board next to the office door: maybe he should pin the envelope up. But no, someone might take it off. He bent down, slid the envelope under the door.

He chuckled, thinking of Greenwood's face when he read it.

He was halfway down the corridor when a noise made him look back.

What the hell . . . ?

There was a fat bull terrier sniffing round the door of Greenwood's office, pawing at the crack underneath. Steve had left the note peeking out slightly, and now the damn dog had got hold of it and was dragging it out . . .

He ran back.

'Leave it,' Steve said. 'Fucking leave it—'

'Is there a problem?' said a voice.

Steve started and turned. A man with a silvery beard had come silently out of the office next door, and was watching him.

*Shit . . . oh, shit, man . . .*

'No . . . no problem, mate, it's . . .'

*He's rumbled you . . . and you left your knife in the dago's room . . .*

'Nono, leave that,' the man with the beard said. He bent and picked up the envelope. 'I'm sorry, is this yours?'

*Deny it? Admit it? Attack . . . ?*

293

Christ, his *head* . . .

'Yeah, mate — I was just — just leaving it—'

'I can give it to Dr Greenwood, if you like,' the bearded man said.

'No — no, mate, no worries, it doesn't matter . . .'

'All right then. I should push it right under the door if I were you. Nono doesn't mean any harm, he just likes to play. Nono, here.'

He called the dog into the office and closed the door.

Steve could feel sweat cooling all over his body.

Hadn't that bearded guy looked at him strangely? He was probably an ally of Greenwood's. Greenwood probably had friends everywhere, looking out for him, ready to corner Steve as soon as they got the chance.

Hastily he shoved the envelope right under the door and got out of there. No real harm done, he told himself, he was cool, he was in control . . . But this *headache* kept coming and going, he was going to have to take something for it if it got any worse . . .

He hurried back to Borrow Terrace: there were a lot of students about now, in trendy shorts and T-shirts, and they all seemed to be giving him funny looks. And he didn't feel safe without his bag. It was just too dangerous now, the enemies were drawing too close.

At least the dago in the wardrobe was quiet again when he got back to the safety of his lookout. Was he trying to make Steve think he'd snuffed it in there? What a laugh. He was only sitting on his arse, that wasn't going to do him any harm. He should try being in the army, then he'd know about endurance.

Steve found bread and some sort of dago cheese on Georgiou's shelf. He placed the desk chair by the window, snacked, watched. His eyes never left the entrance to the English Studies building even when he rolled himself a cigarette.

His patience was rewarded. There was Michael bastard Greenwood, in his sights. He was with that lodger of his, the one who had the puke-green car. They paused for a while at the foot of the steps, talking. Probably up each other's arses, Steve thought, it was disgusting. Then they parted, the lodger crossing The Square, Greenwood going up the steps.

Steve waited. His roll-up, gripped between his teeth, went out but he didn't notice. He looked at the girls going up and down the steps in their teasing summer gear, but he tried to stop himself thinking about what he'd like to do to them, it was distracting.

And there he was again! Coming out of the building at a fucking *run*! *Haring* down the steps!

'AAAH! Watch it, mate, watch you don't go arse over tit you blind FUCKER!' Steve cried, laughing, clapping. He just had to get up and jump round the room, it was so brilliant. 'Glory glory hallelujah, glory glory hallelujah, youareshit youareshit youareshit. ONE nil one nil, one nil one nil . . .' For the moment he forgot his headache, forgot everything.

Greenwood was going to see his handiwork. And he'd have to give it ten out of ten.

### 5

Michael arrived at the campus heartened by the thought of consulting a psychiatrist. It was action at least, it was doing something. He talked some more with Fred about the situation before they parted at the steps of the English Studies building.

'Right, back to the grind,' Fred said. 'Have a good day, Michael. Listen, if you need to talk again, I'll be in the library all morning, ground floor.'

'OK. Thanks, Fred. See you later.'

Now to face the faculty, Michael thought. Even those who hadn't been at Peter's party and seen him planting one on Geoffrey Selby would have heard about it by now. There was nothing to do but brazen it out.

Luck was with him, it seemed: he got to his office without meeting any faculty. Nor, thank God, did Geoff Selby pop out of his own office on hearing him unlock his door. Now, if the day would just continue as serendipitously . . .

He looked down: he had trodden on an envelope addressed to him. Well, who was asking for an essay extension this time? he thought, stooping for it. TJ probably, a notorious defaulter.

He drew out a sheet of paper on which were written, in a looping script that he recognized, the words *Go and see your wife.*

## 6

'What the hell is that supposed to mean?' Fred breathed, staring at the sheet of paper that Michael had thrust before him.

'Christ knows,' Michael said. He clutched at the stitch in his side, leaning one hand on the table where Fred was working. 'But there's only one place he can mean . . . Fred, I'm sorry, will you—'

'Hold on,' Fred said, gripping his arm. 'Hadn't you better sit down a minute, get yourself together?'

Students at tables all the way along the library, glad of the diversion, were turning their heads to observe them. Michael shook his head. 'I'm all right,' he said. 'I've got to go, Fred.'

'OK. I'll take you. Will he be there, do you suppose?'

'No.' Michael helped Fred gather up his books. 'No, that's not his style.'

The Zodiac took them to the cemetery within minutes. As Fred parked outside the Knightsford Road entrance Michael thought of his visit here earlier this week. How the sound of accelerating footsteps on the gravel walk behind him had sent him into a fugue of panic.

A false alarm then. Just paranoia. But somehow he knew, as he retraced that path between the marble angels and the urns and the crosses, Fred following silently behind, that this was not a false alarm. Somehow he knew that this was for real, and that when he had wondered whether the persecution had stopped he had been way, way off.

He knew all this, but he was still unprepared for the sight that met his eyes when they came to Kate's grave.

'Oh, Jesus,' Fred whispered.

Even as the sickness rose in his throat, even as his mind spun out of control, Michael noted that there were flowers on the neighbouring graves, and reproached himself for not bringing flowers more often. However, Steve had placed his own little tribute on Kate's grave. On the turf just in front of the headstone lay a mongrel puppy, decapitated. Its head, trailing a bloody trachea, had been placed six inches from its body. Flies caroused about the corpse, creating a momentary illusion of movement.

The crowning obscenity was the headstone itself. A red spray can had been used to daub on its smooth white surface, in huge sprawling capitals that obliterated Kate's name, the words SHE WAS A DOG.

### 7

'I know it doesn't help,' the WPC said to Michael, 'but we have had a lot of cemetery vandalism in the city in the last couple of years. Mainly in the Mallory Park cemetery, but this one too. Often it's kids, younger than teens sometimes. I know, it's unbelievable, it's sick, but it happens. You must appreciate it's not an easy thing to track down.' Her soft Norfolk burr was in uneasy contrast with the hectoring constabulary inflections. 'Often people feel they've been targeted in some way, but usually it's just mindless vandalism.'

'But there was a note,' Fred said. 'A note telling him about it. This guy who's been playing him up—'

'Yes, so you said,' the WPC said. 'And that'll be looked into. You say you reported this man who's bothering you when, Mr Greenwood?'

Michael, who was leaning on the bonnet of Fred's car outside the cemetery gate, tried to think. 'It would be Tuesday — no, Wednesday . . .'

'Can you remember the name of the officer who took your statement?'

'I — no, off hand, I can't . . .'

'Well, it doesn't matter, does it?' Fred said impatiently. 'The report was made. And now this needs adding to it—'

'Yes, well, you leave the procedure to us, we know a bit more about it than you do,' the WPC said, looking at Fred without favour. 'In the meantime you can rest assured that the council staff will have everything cleaned up in no time.'

'Everything?' Michael said.

'Well,' the WPC said, not looking at him, 'the groundsman tells me the headstone may have to be replaced, it depends what sort of paint was used. But they'll do all they can.'

Michael nodded. He looked over at the cemetery gate, where a male constable was talking to the groundsman. The trees around the gate were breaking into blossom.

He had managed not to vomit: but still he felt empty, drained, without will. And defeated. He hadn't been able to keep Kate alive: but at least he should have been able to protect her in death.

Empty. Useless. It was Fred who had gone to a call box and phoned the police, Fred who had done most of the talking when they arrived; Fred too who seemed more frustrated at their inability to help. Michael had already been through all this with Dixon of Dock Green, and he hadn't the energy to do it again.

Besides, what the police did or didn't do seemed fundamentally irrelevant. In that hideous desecration there had been a message for him alone, a message that might as well have been written too in red spray paint. *This is between me and you.*

Yes, it was. And he was going to have to see it through to the end.

'. . . so if you can take the time off, Mr Greenwood, I'd advise you to go home and rest,' the WPC was saying, closing her notebook. 'We don't need you any more just now, and if we do we'll be in touch. And if there's anything more you want to talk to us about, just pick up the phone. Will you do that?'

There must be a course at police college called 'How to talk to the public as if they were kids', Michael thought idly. 'I will,' he said. 'Thanks very much.'

'Patronizing cow,' Fred muttered as he started the car. 'Sorry, Michael, I wasn't much help there, it's just the way they talk, oh, we'll make the usual enquiries, sir, pat pat, it gets my goat—'

'No no,' Michael said. 'You've been a big help, Fred. All along . . . You won't say anything of this to Suzanne, will you?'

'Christ, Michael, what do you think I am?'

'Sorry. Of course you wouldn't.'

'Listen, I've got a seminar at eleven, but I can skip it if you like, if you'd prefer some company in the house—'

'Oh, I'm not going home,' Michael said. He looked bleakly at Fred. 'Go home and hide my head? What would be the point?' The tremble in his hands was down to manageable proportions now, and he managed to get a cigarette alight. 'No, let's go back to the university. I've got teaching to do. And I'm going to go to the Psychology School and find someone to talk to about this. I want to know what he thinks he's playing at.' His voice was flat: the flat surface of dark, unfathomable depths. 'I want to know what sort of mind could do a thing like that. And what else it's capable of.'

*8*

Steve had been laughing and chanting for a long time: he could tell that because his throat was sore. But now that feeling of magical exultation had left him. It had just died away, and the bad feelings were creeping up, along with the headache. He found he was sitting in Georgiou's armchair and just staring at the opposite wall, without knowing how long he had been doing it.

He ought to be moving, planning, getting on with things. But it was no good, that old dead feeling was taking hold of him, he recognized its onset. It was like seeing everything on a black and white TV set. Just sit and stare, rocking slightly backwards and forwards because that was what felt right, and feel yourself dwindling away inside your body as if you were retreating down a long deep cave, sights and sounds fading away because they weren't real . . . they just weren't real . . .

From time to time he would start to come out of it, stretching and shifting his position, and an emotion would rear up and challenge the dead blankness. Jubilant triumph was first: for just think of what he had done! And off his own bat too, no one to help him, only bastards trying to obstruct him. Yet he had succeeded: armed only with the knowledge that Greenwood's wife croaked six years ago he had gone to the local studies unit in the university library, combed his way through every local newspaper for that year, reading all the Deaths columns, and finally found what he was looking for. *GREENWOOD, Kate. On 6th May, after a long illness. Dearly loved wife of Michael, mother of*

*Suzanne. Interment at Knightsford Road cemetery, 11.30, 9th May. No flowers by request. Donations to Cancer Research.* That was what he needed to know: where they had planted the bitch. But then, of course, there was the problem of finding her — the place was so big. But even that hadn't defeated him. He'd got talking to some no-mark who was weeding the grass and found out which were the newer plots, and so he had tracked the grave down at last. A lot of legwork, but a lot of brainwork too. Fuck you, Dad! And fuck you, Mister Doctor Professor Smartarse Greenwood! Who was the shitforbrains now? And then of course there was the matter of Adrian's dog. It had not only taken brains to think of that idea, it had taken guts and a steady hand to put it into operation. Christ, all that blood, and the way the thing had shat itself under the knife — not everyone could have done it. No wonder the landlord had thrown a wobbly at the mess, which Steve just hadn't had time to clear up — but anyhow, it was his room, wasn't it? And the dog was better off out of it.

The best stroke of the campaign: he was right to be proud of it. The way he had kept his cool, even climbing into the cemetery at night with the dead puppy in his army bag (that stupid Christine bitch! if only she'd known!) and doing the business by torchlight. It was bloody creepy in there, but his nerve had held. A job well done, and the thought of Greenwood seeing it . . . well, it was just magical. In fact the thrill had been so great that he had just had to go over to Sheeps Hill Road and think of Greenwood in there, all unknowing. And God had even given him a little bonus by showing him the alley to the back gardens, and the rabbit hutch. Joy, sheer joy.

But then that emotion was swallowed up by the blankness too; and after a long interval of drifting another one rose up. Fear and trouble. It was something to do with this room, and something to do with the bedsit, and there was a headache mixed in with it too. And a sort of question groped at him through the black and white inertia. *Where now? What now?*

He stirred, trying to grasp the question, set his mind to it. The campaign was moving into a new phase: he could feel the forces being ranged against him.

If only he could snap out of it . . .

Steve sat and stared, fingers pressed to his temples, rocking. He kept thinking of his dad today, he didn't know why.

He drifted. He was a child again, and his dad was gripping his upper arm to hold him in place as he used the slipper.

'You've brought this on yourself, Steven,' he was saying. 'You've only got yourself to blame.'

It was true, it was right. People had to take responsibility for what they did. Look at that girl who'd worked at Tesco's, the one who'd made him lose control that day in the stockroom. She must have known that what he did to her was her fault, because she never went to the police. She'd brought it on herself, and that proved it. They said these women often didn't go to the police because they were frightened of not being believed, but Steve didn't think much of that, he trusted the police. If you didn't have law and order, where were you? Though it was probably her in the end who said things about him to the manager and got him sacked, which proved another thing – you couldn't trust people. They were always covering up. They acted normal and all the time they were out to get you.

Authority was the key. Authority was what people *needed*, or they just ran amok. Because God was at the top of everything, and He was the ultimate authority. His dad had taught him that, and Steve was grateful. His dad knew all about God. And maybe the other kids at school had mocked and said, 'Your dad's a Creeping Jesus' and laughed at him still having to go to Sunday school when they were going to discos but what did they know? They were all against him anyway.

His dad knew all about God; he had taught Steve that God would sort it all out in the end. Indeed, for some time Steve had thought of God's authority and his dad's as one and the same. But at last he had learnt otherwise, and it was God who had shown him it.

He was sixteen: that time when they were always going on at him about what he was going to do with his life. His mum was at work, but his dad had been feeling poorly and had stayed at home in bed. He thought it was probably those cold meat sandwiches he had eaten as a snack last night, and he said he was going to send a stiff letter to the supermarket about their produce: he was always sending off stiff letters, because he said these places were always looking for a chance to do you down. He had got up for a while and pottered about the kitchen in his pyjamas, getting at Steve, complaining about the pains in his chest, before going back to bed. Steve had looked at his dad's white, wrinkly old legs and feet sticking out of his pyjamas and had felt disgust. His parents had waited for years before having children, because they hadn't been sure that the world was fit to bring them into; and now for the first time Steve questioned what had always been to him incontrovertible wisdom. Look at him there, all old and shrivelled and horrible. Steve felt like being sick. In fact he had half a mind to go in the toilet and stick his fingers down his throat and make himself sick, as he sometimes did when he kept thinking about the meal he'd eaten, thinking about it lying in his stomach and then shifting round his intestines, inside him, and the only thing to do was get rid of it, get the filth out of him . . . But this time he didn't because he heard his dad shout from upstairs, calling his name.

When Steve went up he found his dad lying all in a heap, half in and half out of bed. He'd knocked his cup of tea over and his pyjama sleeve was all soaked in it. It looked funny really.

His dad's face had gone a weird colour like porridge. That was quite funny too. And his voice was different. It wasn't strong any more. He could hardly get the words out. It sounded like an old crow cawing.

'Steven . . . get the doctor . . .'

His veiny old hand went to his chest again, gripping the front of his pyjamas. His lips went back in a sort of grin, showing his false teeth and his pale pink gums. A bit of snot ran out of his nose and he said 'Ag' which Steve thought was even funnier. Imagine saying 'Ag'!

'Steven . . .'

His dad's eyes stopped rolling about and fixed themselves on Steve. The whites looked yellow, and the rims of his eyelids were a sort of meaty colour. His expression was one that Steve had never seen on his face before. It was as if he was begging.

'Ring for an ambulance . . . quick . . .'

He said 'ambulance' in a funny slurred way. *Annmblnce*. Steve wanted to laugh.

'Steven!' A high, thin, cracked sound.

Steve looked at his dad. Authority. You obeyed your dad as you obeyed God.

Ah, but they weren't the same thing. He saw that, all at once. His feelings were telling him not to obey, and who gave him the feelings but God? God knew what He was doing.

He looked at his dad.

After all, the world was awful. Man had spoiled it because he was full of filth. You were better out of a world like this, really.

He looked into his dad's eyes. Begging.

Steve gave a gurgle of laughter, and walked out of the room.

He went downstairs, and switched on the television, turning the volume up. He was still watching it when his mum came home from work, and they both went upstairs to find that God had gathered his dad's soul to rest.

*Just stupid, Steven . . .*

Not stupid enough to ring the ambulance when you were fucking croaking though dad not that stupid!

Steve rocked, drifting, remembering. That time in the army when he had found a graffito about him on the barrack toilet wall. He couldn't remember what it was exactly —

*SHITFORBRAINS it said STEVE SHITFORBRAINS*

*over a picture of a crazily grinning man in a strait-jacket.*

— but he knew they were getting at him, publicly. Just like Greenwood —

*And he knew who'd done that graffito, though of course they all had it in for him anyway, but there was that one guy who just wasn't right, who was funny with him, but Steve hadn't done what they said he did to the guy, he must have done it to himself somehow — he didn't know how, how could he? the ones who were against you could do anything if their mind was set on getting you into trouble — anyway, the guy had brought it on himself, it was his own fault — but of course it was Steve who got disciplined, it was all a set-up job so they could discharge him saying he was unfit . . .*

Bad memories. Bad vibes. Get rid of them. Concentrate, concentrate on Greenwood. He must snap out of it. He had things to do.

Steve rocked, drifting.

## 9

Fred drove Michael back to the university without comment. Privately he thought Michael was taking this a little too well: he wondered how close the poor guy was to cracking underneath that surface calm, and whether the WPC hadn't been right in suggesting he go home.

On the other hand, Fred could understand *Michael's* need to understand. Quite a few questions were nagging at him too as they arrived at the campus. Such as — how had this sicko found Michael's wife's grave? Michael just seemed to take that as read — as if there were nothing that his persecutor didn't know, nothing he couldn't do. But that ghastly display in the cemetery had taken *effort*. That was what baffled Fred. The little incident in his first year that he had told Michael about – the harassment from that meathead in the Young Conservatives – had been perplexing enough in that regard: that that guy had felt malice enough to actually go out and *buy* a jar of Vaseline and wrap it and send it through the post, that he had taken that *trouble* . . . But this was worse. It suggested total absorption in the task.

A dismaying thought – that people's capacity for malevolence was only limited by their laziness. It challenged Fred's view of human nature, which was fundamentally tolerant.

'Now are you sure you're OK?' Fred said, as they crossed the service road to the campus.

Michael nodded. Fred felt that he was miles away.

'All right then. Don't worry about anything,' Fred said. 'I'll be at home this afternoon.'

He went to his seminar, where his mind took in practically nothing. He was still woolgathering at the end, when the tutor said, as the group was leaving, 'Oh, by the way, anybody know Georgiou Sofroniou?'

Head-shakings. 'Yes,' Fred said. 'Well, I know him slightly.'

'You don't know if he's ill, or anything?' the tutor asked him. 'Only he's missed a seminar and a tutorial. And there was some lab work yesterday that he specifically asked to be in on, and he didn't turn up. He's usually one of these conscientious types, which made me wonder. If you see him, could you ask him to drop by my office some time?'

'Yes, sure,' said Fred.

He went down to the student common room and got himself a cup of coffee from the vending machine. Various Nordic physicists were conducting an umlaut-strewn argument from the depths of the nineteen-seventies extruded-foam chairs. Fred sipped at the cup of scalding nothingness and felt guilty. He hadn't in fact noticed Georgiou's absence from classes at the time, though he realized it now. The guy was so quiet and solitary, and when you did talk with him it was difficult to break down his shyness . . . It was bad, though; he should have noticed. That was the trouble with this life, you could just drift along in your own little world . . . His guilt was sharpened because of what had happened this morning. Until then he had not taken Michael's problem too seriously, hadn't given it much of his attention. Wrapped up in himself, he supposed: it was the student's occupational disease.

He abandoned his coffee and went out to the lobby where the pigeonholes were situated. You received internal mail through these, and most people checked them daily. He looked in the S pigeonhole. There was several days' worth of internal mail addressed to Georgiou Sofroniou.

Fred picked up his own mail, thinking. Of course, absence from classes usually meant that the student had gone home to patronize his parents for a few days, but that was hardly practical in Georgiou's case . . . He remembered a time in his own first term, when he had lived in halls of residence. Shy and lonely, he had gone down with flu, and had spent a wretched week entirely alone in his room, sneezing and listening to the extroverts haw-hawing their way down the corridors outside. If Georgiou was ill, he was probably doing the same.

Where did Georgiou live? Fred was sure he remembered him once saying it was somewhere in the campus halls of residence; but then there were so many of those awful barracks. Was it Fry Buildings, Browne Terrace, Sewell Terrace . . . ?

He looked again at Georgiou's uncollected mail. Most bore only the faculty name, but he noticed one from the Overseas Student Society that gave Georgiou's address too. 3A, Borrow Terrace.

Fred's stomach gave a growl. Yes, all right, it was time for lunch. But it wouldn't hurt just to nip over to Borrow Terrace first and see if Georgiou was all right.

## 10

It was, thank God, Inigo's turn to present a paper to the seminar that morning, so Michael was able to sit back and let him get on with it: Inigo's presentations always lasted an hour and were practically Ph.D. material. He let Inigo's Prince Charles tones flow over the surface of his mind while he concentrated on that abomination at the cemetery this morning. Concentrated on it, because he knew he must. At the first sight of it his brain had somehow pulled down a shutter that had stayed down ever since. A refusal, a denial. But that was dangerous: the outrage would surely break out, the stronger for being suppressed.

Think of it. Face it. Stop pretending that normal life can go on despite it. Normal service is not going to be

resumed. This *is* your life now. And it is —
*Purgatory.*

— going to stay that way. Until you can confront the man behind it.

He met Christine in the refectory for lunch. She surprised him by jumping up and seizing him in a warm hug as soon as he appeared.

'Hullo, what's this?'

'Been thinking about you, that's all,' she said. 'How have you been?'

He drew a deep breath. Best to postpone telling her until she had finished her lunch. 'Fine.'

'You haven't seen Geoff Selby?'

'Eh? Oh! No. Managed to avoid each other.' It all seemed a long time ago now.

He picked at a plate of chips while she talked, rather nervously, about her morning's work. Then she fell abruptly silent, leaned across the table and took his hand.

She said, 'You've got something to tell me, haven't you?'

It didn't take long. He kept his eyes on the congealing mess of tomato sauce on the plate in front of him, as if daring himself to be sick. He felt Christine's hand tighten around his until the blood had almost ceased to flow in it.

'Oh, Michael,' she said. She swallowed. Her face had turned completely white. 'Oh, Christ, Michael—'

'You can't hurt the dead,' he said suddenly and harshly. 'I know that. I know that perfectly well. But it seems like that. It feels like that. Do you see?'

Christine could not answer. She covered her eyes with

311

her hand, biting her lips. It hurt him to know that she was trying not to cry.

'Bastard,' she got out at last. '*Bastard* . . .'

Michael merely nodded, tightly: he couldn't trust himself to say any more about it. He waited until she had forced herself back under control, then said, 'There's a meeting of the Interdisciplinary Committee this afternoon. Shouldn't take long. After that I'm going to follow up your idea − go over to the Psychology School and talk to somebody there about what this man's doing. Try to get a fix on him. See if I can get into his mind.'

'God . . . I know it was my idea, but is this the right time? I mean, do you *want* to know just now?'

'But that's just it. All the time I've been thinking, I don't know this man, he's nothing to do with me, I don't want to know. But really I've got no choice. He *is* in my life. He's taken it over.' He paused. 'It's like a challenge that I've got to take up.'

She released his hand, though gently. 'It isn't fair you should have to,' she said.

'No. But I haven't got any choice − have I?'

She shook her head. 'If I ever see this man . . . Well. I'm free this afternoon, how about if I picked Suzanne up from school?'

'Be great if you could. Thanks, Christine.'

'And say I meet you back here about five? Then you can tell me if you've learnt anything.'

'OK.' He got up, kissed her. 'Take care.'

She squeezed his fingers, a world of trouble in her eyes. 'You take care too.'

## 11

Fred stood for some time knocking at the security door of Block A, Borrow Terrace. At last a bleary young man in pyjamas opened up.

'Oh, hi, is this where Georgiou Sofroniou lives?'

'Jaw-what?'

'Georgiou Sofroniou. Greek guy, smallish—'

'Oh, yeah. I think so. Right down the end, top floor. Haven't seen him lately.' Yawning, the pyjamas shambled back to his room.

What horrible places these halls were, Fred thought, sniffing that well-remembered odour of burnt toast, patchouli and institutional disinfectant that haunted the corridor. Musical heartbeats throbbed through the walls. He came to the room at the end and paused, wondering if he were being nosy. Perhaps Georgiou wouldn't like being disturbed: perhaps it would be better to leave him a note. But then if he was ill, that wouldn't be much use to him. And after all, the tutor had asked him to pass on a message, so he had a legitimate reason for calling.

Fred knocked at Georgiou's door.

## 12

The dead feeling had left Steve at last. Thank God! It had lasted a long time, and there was always the fear that it would just carry on and you could sink deeper and deeper, never to come to the surface again . . . Still, it was gone now. He boiled the kettle and switched on the radio and windmilled his arms a bit to perk himself up.

Things to do, must get on. If only this *bloody* headache would go . . .

He was just stirring his coffee when there was a knock at the door.

Steve froze. For the first moment he thought it was the dago in the wardrobe playing up, but no . . .

Panic leaped and capered in his head.

*Jesus no go away . . .*

He reached over and switched off the radio.

The knocking came again, louder.

*Shit shouldn't have done that they must have heard it go off now they know they know someone's here . . .*

He stifled a whimper. The pain drilled deeper between his eyebrows.

*Go away go away go away . . .*

A voice on the other side of the door. 'Georgiou? Hello? It's Fred Forbes.'

Steve could hardly breathe.

And it was then that the dago in the wardrobe really did start playing up.

Banging, rattling at the wardrobe door, moaning through his gag, going crazy – *shit*, whoever it was was going to *hear* that –

'Georgiou?' came the voice. 'You OK? I just came to see – Are you ill or anything? Georgiou? Do you want me to call a doctor?'

*Jesus he's not going to go away.*

Stifling another whimper, Steve flung open the wardrobe door –

*Christ, that stink!*

– grabbed Georgiou, hauled him out. Dragged him across the floor, heaved him on to the bed on his back.

Threw the blanket over him and pulled it up to his chin. Grabbed his knife and put it against the spic's face.

'Say one word, make one move, and you die,' Steve hissed into his ear. 'Promise.' He yanked out the gag, then slipped the knife into his pocket and went to the door.

He opened it cautiously, halfway.

Stared. *Greenwood's lodger he'd sent him they were coming to get him . . .*

The tall guy was staring too. 'Oh – hi – I've come to see Georgiou.' Frowning, and poking his head into the room –

*Pushy bastard!*

– to see past Steve . . .

'Yeah – yeah, mate, he's not too well,' Steve said, stammering, jerking his tongue into motion, 'not too well at all, you know, I'm a mate of his, been looking after him a bit—'

The pushy bastard had slipped into the room. He was staring at the bed, at Georgiou.

'Georgiou . . . my God . . .'

'Yeah,' Steve said, 'looks a bit rough, I know, but he's on the mend, mate, no worries, he'll be all right. Thing is, he's still infectious, so if I were you I shouldn't hang about . . .' Good one, good thought, don't panic, you'll get through this –

And then Georgiou, gazing up at the tall guy, opened his mouth and began to scream.

*'Fred help me he's crazy he's tied me up for God's sake help me—'*

For a moment Steve was mesmerized by that yelling mouth, so wide, so red . . . . *screaming* . . .

*'He's locked me up help me!'*

The tall guy seemed paralysed. Then he took a step towards the bed.

Steve pulled his knife out of his pocket –

And it snagged. Caught on a loop of cotton that snapped, so that the knife went clattering to the floor and skittering under the desk –

*Jesus . . . .*

The tall guy started at the sound of the knife. He began to turn, but not quickly enough, because Steve had seized the lump of Aegean rock from the shelf –

Georgiou screaming, *No Steve no Steve don't no!*

– and brought it crunching down on the back of Fred's skull.

## 13

The tall guy went down with a grunt, buckling at the knees. His head hit the floor a few inches from the bed, a few inches from Georgiou's face.

Georgiou was silent a moment, mouth open and gasping.

Then he began to scream again. A different scream, a thin, shrill note, on and on like a football whistle, like a boiling kettle, a sound that seemed to drive the headache agonizingly into Steve's brain.

'Shut . . .'

He fumbled under the desk.

*'Shut – up . . .'*

He stepped over the tall guy's body, gripping the knife.

*'Shut – up—'*

The sound shriller, more piercing.

'You've – brought – this – on – yourself,' Steve moaned, and pressing down on the screaming face with his left hand, he brought the sound to an end by cutting Georgiou's throat through to the windpipe.

## 14

'I'm a bit worried about the behaviour of someone I know,' Michael said, and thought: that must be the understatement of the century.

'So am I. But there, the electorate voted him in, what can we do about it?'

Because all the teaching buildings at the University of Broadland were built to the same plan, the common rooms of the various faculties were all identical, which had a disorientating effect when you entered one that wasn't your own. Going into the Psychology/Philosophy common room Michael half expected to see Peter Worrall lounging over the *Times* crossword or Geoffrey Selby morosely pinning an ANC poster to the wallboard. But the Psychology faculty seemed a genial lot, including Roger, the temporary lecturer who had agreed to talk to him. In fact he knew Roger slightly, having met him at some university bunfight, though he had had some idea that he was a geologist. So much, again, for his memory.

'Someone close to you?' Roger said, gesturing him to an armchair. As befitted his name, he was a breezy, *Boy's Own*, young-looking character.

'Not really. It's a bit difficult to explain. It's someone who's – well, who's got a grudge against me. And is behaving very strangely, frighteningly . . . am I allowed to say crazily in here?'

Roger gave a blast of laughter. 'What would we do without the crazies? No, of course, I wouldn't expect my students to talk about loonies in their term papers, and you'll find chaps here who'll argue that to set any kind of dividing line, however tentative, between sanity and insanity, mental health and mental illness, normal psychology and aberrant psychology, is to impose an artificial and basically political structure on the endless variables of the human mind. It is a serious point. I mean, it's a commonplace that there are people out there in positions of power and influence who are every bit as "insane", whatever you want the word to mean, as many people who are confined in mental institutions. On any given day you probably pass ten mad people in the street; and I don't just mean that old chestnut statistic that says one in five people — or is it three now? — will be treated for mental illness at some time in their lives. But look here: you know I'm no psychiatrist. What we mainly do here is quarrel over the translation of a word in Freud's laundry lists. I can't talk to this person, I'm just not qualified.'

'No,' Michael said. 'You can't talk to him anyway. That's just it . . .'

## 15

For some minutes Steve gazed at the arc of blood that made a rainbow shape on the breeze-block wall. Some of it had gone on the curtains too. And there were even splashes on the photographs pinned to the board above the desk.

. . . Like a *fountain*, man . . . it just went up like a *fountain* . . .

There was some on his clothes too. On his pullover. Even spots on his trainers, shit, look at the *state* of them . . .

At least the dago had stopped jerking and twitching now.

At least he had stopped that noise. Jesus, that *noise* . . . What else was he supposed to do? It wasn't his fault . . .

He looked down at the tall guy, stretched motionless on the floor. The back of his head was a mess. Mess everywhere.

But that wasn't his fault either — Jesus, Greenwood had sent the guy to get him, they were in it together, they were probably homos together. All he'd done was fight back.

'Weee-are going to-win the league,' Steve sang under his breath. He didn't really feel like singing, but it was good, it cheered him up, and he needed cheering up, because there were some very bad feelings coming over him . . . And that *headache* too, that headache was *unreal* . . .

'It's not fair,' Steve groaned, holding his head.

But he had won through here, hadn't he? The enemy had counterattacked — but he was still in control, wasn't he?

Yes . . . but the game had changed. Everything was different from now on. His plans were all overturned.

*Oh God what do I do what do I do . . .*

*Carry on.*

Yes, carry on. His heart leapt in thankfulness: that voice of authority still hadn't left him. God is good.

After all, his aim was still the same, wasn't it? And wasn't all this mess in here *designed* to make him lose sight of that aim? Christ. The bastards were so cunning.

Steve windmilled his arms. Initiative. When your plans went wrong, you responded with initiative. Basic training.

He looked at the tall guy. Greenwood's lodger, the one with the puke-green car. There was a bulge in his jeans pocket.

Initiative . . .

Steve dug his hand into the pocket. He didn't like doing it, he was nearly touching the tall guy's groin and that was disgusting, it meant you were a homo, but it was important —

Got them.

Keys.

'Glory glory halleluuu-jah,' crooned Steve, and flinging on Georgiou's jacket to cover his bloody pullover he hurried to the door.

It was a different game now. Time to strike. Strike where the enemy was most vulnerable.

### 16

'But that was all there was,' Michael said. 'One little wisecrack at the end of a radio interview. I keep thinking I must have done something else to antagonize him—'

'Not necessarily,' said Roger. 'A schizophrenic personality may not perceive any hierarchy of significance. Their nearest and dearest may suffer a terrible accident, and it doesn't affect them. They get a leak in the plumbing, and it's the world's worst tragedy. And it's specifically *directed at them*. You're English Studies, you'll know that passage in *Middlemarch* about the scratches on a polished surface. Hold a candle to any spot on the surface, and all the scratches seem to converge on that spot. George Eliot's using it as an image of the way any individual sees the world. But take it to the *n*th degree, and you've got a fair image of paranoid schizophrenia. There *aren't* any little things, in that world-view. Life teems with threatening meaning. The merest glance from a stranger can set off an excessively defensive reaction.'

'Or a word on the radio,' said Michael.

'Very possible. A personality like that − and look, I'm only theorizing here, but from what you tell me the guy is certainly violently unstable − a personality like that is continually alert for what he sees as signals of malicious intent. The defensiveness may have much to do with his image of himself − seeing himself as misunderstood, despised, mocked, generally persecuted.'

'But in a way I did mock him,' Michael said.

'Oh, well, in a way that's the least of it. You could have said he was the greatest guy in the world, and he would have seen that as taking the piss out of him. Remember we're talking about his perception of the world, not the world as it is, which is a very debatable concept anyway.'

'Do you think he may have done things like this before?'

'Hard to say. From what you've told me about him, he has probably had persecution delusions for a long time, and regularly makes these inappropriate emotional responses. But such a condition can go up and down. Or suddenly escalate. I mean, nothing's fixed. You can describe to me, as you have, what seem to be the actions of a paranoid schizophrenic of a particularly nasty kind, but we're only playing pin the tail on the donkey with labels. There's no such thing as a classical paranoid schizophrenic that you measure all the variations by. You've got hebephrenic schizophrenia, where the behaviour is bizarre and clownish, catatonic schizophrenia, which is how it sounds, trance-like — I could go on and on. And any mixture of these can occur in any individual. I'm sorry, I'm not really giving you any answers, am I? Ask me about Melanie Klein and primitive infantile wishes.'

'No, no, you're being a great help,' said Michael. 'You see, I've just been trying to rationalize the way this man's behaving, and maybe I've been starting from the wrong end . . . But what gets me is, how can he show such persistence? I mean, if he's mentally unstable—'

'That may not be the same as mental infirmity. Delusions can occur with a tremendous strength of conviction, I mean, really unshakeable. That is, if what we're talking about is genuine psychosis and not neurosis, which can show broadly similar symptoms. A person suffering from obsessional neurosis can be quite unshakeable in some pursuit that is fundamentally pointless. But the guy who can't stop washing his hair or counting to ten knows what he's doing and doesn't like it. He hasn't made the psychotic's leap into the void.

Your guy may not have done so. It all depends.'
   'On what?'
   'Well . . . . on what he does next.'

### 17

Consciousness returned to Fred as a mixed blessing.

It brought with it pain: a pain so amorphous, so universal that he could not at first establish where it was coming from. It just seemed to inhabit him entirely. It brought with it, too, memory; but a memory so fragmented and phantasmagoric that in grasping at it he seemed rather to be groping amongst faded dreams of an immeasurably long sleep.

Something flowed in between his fluttering eyelids: vision, wavering and strange and somehow shocking, as if it were a faculty he were experiencing for the first time. Other senses filtered their way through the greedy pain. Smell, and taste: his own vomit, pooled around his face on the floor. Touch: the roughness of carpet tiles against his cheek. And hearing: a muffled booming sound of amplified music.

Kaleidoscope chippings of memory drifted together, and at last formed something that made sense. The image of a dark red face with staring blue eyes.

But no, that didn't make sense. It wasn't a face he knew. Yet it had something to do with him. Something momentous.

His vision was still blurred, but he was pretty sure that the jagged lump on the floor was a piece of rock. Why did it have something sticking to it, something like blood and hair?

The image of another face was emerging from the jigsaw of memory. He did know that face. Terribly pale, bruised and swollen, deathly even, but recognizable as Georgiou's. Yes, and its mouth had been open. It had been screaming, yelling something, a plea, a warning . . .

'. . . *he's crazy* . . .'

And suddenly the memory all came together, clear and perfect.

The image of perfect horror.

Fred knew where he was now. And he was afraid that he knew what he would see if he moved and looked at the bed in front of him.

If he moved . . . Because he was beginning to locate the source of that pain that was filling him. Vast and incredibly potent as it was, it came from one place – his head. And these tricklings on his neck and cheek were not sweat or vomit but blood. And this was where the wall of terror loomed up because he feared that he was not going to be able to move, that that incubus of agony fastened to the back of his skull was not going to let him move. It was going to keep him here, immobile, helpless. In a place where no one knew he was.

And if he didn't fight it, he was going to die here.

## 18

'Well, if you're talking about treatment, there are phenothiazine drugs, psychotherapy, various rehabilitation strategies, but it depends on how far down the slope the person's gone, and if you're moving into the area of psychopathic behaviour, then you're in a different ball game, where medicine meets criminology,' Roger said. 'But you're talking about how to handle this fellow, right?'

'Right.'

'Don't handle him, Michael. That's my advice to you, simply person to person. Listen, a relation of my wife's got into a quarrel with his neighbour. Over mess in the garden or some such silly thing. The neighbour took it badly. Poisoned the family cat with paraquat, set light to their garden shed, and came after the man with a tree-feller's chain saw. The neighbour was a respectable insurance salesman and for all I know still is. Was he mad . . . ? Do you see what I'm saying? Dangerous people are dangerous people. Enumerate their complexes, write a textbook about them if you like, but don't think that gives you a magic key to dealing with them. If we had that, we wouldn't need high-security institutions.'

'So I can't fight him?'

Roger shrugged. 'The only guideline with people like that is — expect the unexpected.'

### 19

Christine parked the van opposite the school gates and watched the first detainees come hurrying out to freedom. Was she beginning to suffer from Old Fart's Disease like Michael (or like Michael pretended to), or were fashions really getting more weird? Eleven-year-olds looked like miniature denizens of a pop video. And didn't teenagers have spots any more? Some of the older boys looked like Apollo in a blazer.

But then people in the past always looked ugly — whether Henry VIII and his piggy-eyed crew or 1950s holidaymakers with their ashen faces and shapeless legs. And to Christine her own past was no more attractive. She preferred to forget it: the present was where it was all happening, where life became worthwhile. For her the world had finally become, in the last couple of years, a place that it was reasonable to expect happiness from. That was why, at the beginning of this trouble, her instinctive, buried impulse had been to deny, to reject. She had wanted to think that Michael was overreacting: how *could* the everyday world around them be the place of teeming threat and danger that he now saw? Look at this sunlit street, these carports and privet hedges, these kids stampeding out of school. Impossible.

And yet she hadn't convinced herself. So life was just a bowl of cherries, was it? Why then the self-defence classes? Why the flashes of memory, like pains from an old injury, of the end of her marriage, when the man whose bed she had shared had hit out at her like a boxer with unreasoning hate in his eyes?

No, it was wishfulness, not realism, that had made her want to deny the significance of the events of this week. But the wishfulness was understandable: her life with Michael was good. And what was more, it was the opposite of her marriage, with its sullen suspicions and lurking resentments: the warm, bright place that she and Michael had found together seemed the last place in the world to be vulnerable to the dark encroachments of violence and unreason. Misplaced confidence, it turned out. Yet she still had faith in that warm, bright place. She was determined that she would not see it destroyed.

She sounded the hooter as the unmistakable long-legged form of Suzanne appeared. Remembering Michael's account of the desecration in the cemetery, Christine felt a fierce protective pang that she realized, to her surprise, was maternal. The kid's air of light self-confidence only made her appear more poignantly young. A very nice kid, a very nice father. They were worth fighting for.

'Hi, Christine. I thought for a minute it'd be Dad waiting at the gate and trying to look casual.'

'Nope. The VIP limousine today. How was school?'

Suzanne clambered in. 'Double geography this afternoon, yawn yawn. We watched this really antwacky film about sheep farming in Australia and then drew diagrams of the Ardmona fruit farm, I mean how is that going to help me be an air hostess?'

Christine smiled and started the engine. 'I get the feeling you think your dad's being a bit of a pain, meeting you out of school and so on.'

'Oh, I know he's always been a bit protective like that, since Mum died anyway. And now he's got this thing about this bloke who's got something against him. But it is a bit of a drag.'

'It's because he cares about you, though,' Christine said.

'I know.' Suzanne chewed her hair, then realized she was doing it and hurriedly stopped. 'I feel a bit rotten really. Especially throwing a wobbly over that school play business. I mean, I was pi— annoyed, but there was no need to act like a *kid*.' She said the word with scornful disapproval.

'It's been a bit of a stressful week for all of us,'

Christine said. And thought: you can say *that* again. 'None of us have been at our best, really. Except old Fred, maybe. I wonder if he ever feels stress?'

'Never seems to. Must be all the sponge pudding. Weighs him down sort of thing.'

'I think I'll have to try it then . . . Tell you what, how about we all go out tonight? For a pizza or something. And the pictures too. We'll drag Fred along. It can be a sort of belated birthday treat for you. And a treat for your dad: we'll fuss him up a bit, yeah?'

'Brilliant, yeah! Let's go to that place down Tombland, where they have those pancakes for afters. Oh, bum, I've got maths homework. I'll do it straight away when I get home, get it out of the way. I can ask Fred to help me, he does it so easily, he's a genius.'

'Well, your dad's got a fair brain on him too, you know.'

'Oh, I know. Mustn't let him know I know, though. It might make him bigheaded.'

They drew up outside 134 Sheeps Hill Road. Fred's Zodiac stood in the drive, so he was home: it was all right to leave Suzanne, she wouldn't be on her own. 'Right,' Christine said. 'Your dad's at the university, he's got a meeting. I'll just pop home and change and then go and pick him up. So I'll see you later. Wear our glad rags tonight, eh?'

'OK.' Suzanne got out of the van. 'See if you can get Dad to wear something decent. See you soon.'

Christine watched her go up the path and into the house. Then she beeped the hooter and drove away.

### 20

'Well, I'm sorry I couldn't be more help,' Roger said.

'Not at all,' Michael said. 'You've been very helpful. Really. Just sorry I kept you talking so long, I didn't realize the time.'

'Talking's the thing I do best. Anyway, you could say it's an example of interdisciplinary co-operation, couldn't you? Are they big on that in ES?'

'Fitfully. It works better in theory than in practice. Drama students chafe at having to take history courses, historians can't understand why they have to do linguistics, that sort of thing.'

'Well, I hope you don't have any more trouble from your weirdo. Of course, there is one simple answer to this sort of thing.'

'What's that?'

Roger grinned. 'Never speak to anyone. Lock yourself in a bunker, never have anything to do with any other human being except strictly known quantities. Beware of everyone you meet – because, after all, you never know, do you?'

### 21

Fred clung on to consciousness.

There was choice in the matter: because he was aware of a sort of side turning offering itself to his mind, which offered relief and oblivion if he took it. The pain devil, gnawing at his head, wanted him to go down that turning.

But he refused to. Because he had an idea where it would lead.

With an effort that seemed to wrenchingly displace his guts, Fred lifted his head.

The pain set up a siren wail, but such was the sight that met his eyes that he was hardly aware of it.

Halloween. That was the word that flashed in his mind. The gaping mouth-slit in a Halloween pumpkin.

That was what Georgiou's slashed throat looked like.

*Yes, shut your eyes, Fred, but it's no good, you know you are going to see that sight in your dreams for months to come, the walls too, you noticed the walls, didn't you, the blood* . . .

If he *had* months to come . . .

Fred groaned, and the sound of his voice seemed to bring him back from the edge of insanity.

Georgiou's little study-bedroom in Borrow Terrace was a slaughterhouse. Some day his mind was going to have to find a way to deal with that hellish fact, but not now. The only fact that mattered now was that he was in it. And he was injured and losing blood.

He had to get out.

With dinosaur slowness, he began raising himself to his hands and knees. There seemed to be some strength in his arms, but his legs juddered and trembled wildly. He could hardly control them. Turning himself around demanded prodigious amounts of grotesque effort, while supernovae of pain exploded in his head.

He was facing the closed door at last. Now there was just a vast desert of carpet to cross to get to it.

Through the walls the amplified music boomed, echoing the roaring in his head.

He began to crawl forward.

The man who had done this was insane, of course.
And an insane person wouldn't think to lock the door
behind him. Surely.

*What if he came back . . . ?*

No good thinking of that. Of course he wasn't going
to come back. He had done –

Christ, what *had* he done? Killed Georgiou – half
killed Fred.

What for? Had he stolen something?

He couldn't tell whether his wallet was gone from his
back pocket, but a familiar friendly friction was missing
from the right side pocket of his jeans. Keys.

*STEVE Georgiou shouted the name STEVE – come
on Fred you know who this is – unless there are two
crazies called Steve running around with knives then you
have just had a run-in with Michael's maniac and he is
crazier even than that business in the graveyard
suggested –*

*And oh God he's taken your keys . . .*

The hi-fi thunder came to an end. A brief moment of
quiet, and then the music started up again.

Fred was near the door. The handle was within reach.
If he could only lift his arm high enough . . .

It felt as ponderous as the arm of a crane. His muscles
seemed to squeal like tortured girders. It was no good –

His fingers closed around the handle. Slipped. Closed
round it again, and pushed down.

Locked.

Drums and electric guitar meshed in a barbed fence of
noise. Fred slumped to the floor, eyes squeezed shut.
After a moment he realized he was moaning aloud.

'Help me . . . help me . . .' He tried to raise the

croaking voice he heard issuing from his own mouth. '*Help* me . . .'

He beat on the base of the door with the palm of his hand: he couldn't make a fist. The effort racked him, but the sound was as weak as a dog's tail wagging on the floor.

'*Help me* . . .'

The pain devil dug in its claws.

The music pounded.

## 22

The music pounded through the ceiling as Suzanne ran into her bedroom and flung down her school bag. Fred playing his weird modern classical stuff again — it was nearly as bad as those antwacky symphonies and operas that her dad listened to, though at least it had a beat. Why was she the only one in the house who had any taste in music? Though Christine had some good stuff. Christine was smart. When Christine was around it proved to her dad that you didn't have to be totally out of it just because you were past thirty. Though she knew her dad put it on a lot. It was a wind-up when he called her trainers plimsolls; and the sunglasses he'd bought her were spot-on.

She dragged her maths folder out of the bag and looked at it with distaste. It was a pain having to think about this on a Friday afternoon . . . maybe she should leave it till Sunday . . . But no, Fred was in, and he would rip through it in a matter of minutes and then it would be done.

With the folder under her arm she sprinted up to the

top floor. Fred's door was half-open; the weird music came pulsing out. She tapped on the door, and pushed it all the way open.

'Fred – would you mind having a look at my maths—'

It was the shadow of the figure behind the door, elongated in the afternoon sunlight, that she saw moving; and even before the arm grabbed her round the neck she knew that it was not Fred.

### 23

Michael sat in his office, pen poised over a blank sheet of paper. He was trying, and failing, to make notes for next week's seminars on Carlyle and the Industrial Revolution. Instead everything that Roger had said was revolving in his mind, endlessly revolving and getting nowhere.

*Don't handle him.*

But what if he had no choice?

He looked at his watch. He would be meeting Christine again soon. He wished he had something more positive to tell her.

But then what had he been expecting a psychologist to tell him? A magic word that would immobilize Steve, like Mr Spock touching the Vulcan pressure point on your neck?

And after all, he had said the magic word that had started all this.

*Purgatory.*

For the first and only time in his life Michael experienced a fleeting wish to be a citizen of the United

States of America. Then he could have gone out and
bought a gun.

### 24

Gasping with the effort, Fred managed to fumble the
fountain pen off the desk. Georgiou's pen: dear God.

'. . . *he's tied me up* . . .' How long, then, had he
been a prisoner here? A prisoner released only by
death —

He mustn't think of it. And he mustn't look round at
that horrific sight on the bed, because he could feel
himself growing weaker and he needed all his strength
and if he saw that gaping throat again . . .

Concentrate. Fight the pain and the sickness and the
moving shapes of blackness fluttering across the mind.

He hauled himself nearer to the wall and began
rapping with the pen on the pipe that fed the radiator. It
made a deep clanking sound. Surely audible to someone
in the room below . . . ?

He listened to the reverberating music. Downstairs,
next door . . . ? Probably both . . . *Christ*, why did they
all have to play their music so *loud*?

Perhaps he should rap in Morse code. Like Richard
Hannay or Bulldog Drummond . . . Hysterical laughter
seemed to sound in his mind. *Jesus, Fred! What the hell
are you doing? Tapping on a hot-water pipe in the hope
that someone will hear you and come galloping to the
rescue! It might work in a Saturday morning serial, but
it's not going to work in real life!*

The pen dropped from his trembling fingers.

*I know. I know. But I don't know what else to do. I can't stand, I know I can't stand, I can't get to the window past — past Georgiou . . .*

Face resting on his hands, beaten about by wings of darkness, he looked through rippling vision across the expanse of blood-spattered carpet. And saw the lump of jagged rock.

## 25

Steve hoisted his burden on to his shoulder, fireman-style, and began to negotiate the stairs. Three flights down, shit, just his luck.

Fortunately she was quite light. Thin as a rail, though she was getting tits already, he'd noticed them poking up through her school blouse when she went down to the floor. They all matured so young these days, she'd probably had a cock up her already, they were all at it. But one thing was for sure, it wasn't the lodger who'd put it to her. Steve had had a good look round his room, having driven here in his car and used his keys to get into the house —

*Stupid! Fuck you, Dad! And fuck you, Doctor Professor Smartarse Greenwood! Was that stupid? Just walking in here, making myself at home in your own fucking house! It was a piece of piss! Call me stupid now!*

— and he'd seen definite signs in that room that the lodger was a homo. Pictures of male film stars. And a newsletter from something called GaySoc. It was disgusting. Well, he'd got what he deserved. Steve

335

shuddered to think he'd had to put his hand into the homo's pocket to get his keys. He might have caught something . . . But he hadn't got time to worry about that now. He'd used his initiative and he was *back in control*, it was going his way —

*Except for this headache this bloody headache!*

— but he had to be alert. Greenwood might be back any time, and he needed to get his daughter away. He'd knocked her out, having made himself a nice little cosh from one of the homo's socks and a few pebbles from a bowl on his desk — initiative! — but he'd gone easy on her, and she was whimpering a bit and twitching around. The belts round her wrists and ankles would do for now, but he must get her into the car quick.

*Jesus!*

In the hall he stopped dead.

What was he going to do — go waltzing out to the drive with the bitch over his shoulder, in full view of the whole street?

*Shitforbrains.*

He muttered and moaned, looking around him. The headache tightened.

'Come on, come on, come on . . .' He struggled into the living room, laid her down on the settee, checked her face. She was breathing all right: her eyelashes were fluttering. He sprinted upstairs and dragged the duvet off the first bed he found, nearly tripped on it bringing it downstairs again. *Stay in control . . .*

It was much harder bundling her up in the duvet than he had thought. Her legs kept poking out. Once he got a look at her knickers, and that distracted him . . . no, that was for later . . . He had just got her satisfactorily wrapped up when her legs slid out again. One shoe came off, and he couldn't get it on again, it just wouldn't go . . .

Wailing, he put his hands to his head and pounded round the room. It was all going *wrong*, it was all going *wrong* . . . 'Oh, God,' he pleaded, 'it's not fair . . .' He clapped his hands and chanted, trying to cheer himself up. Then he tried laughing. For a moment it didn't seem to work. The headache throbbed . . . Then, like an engine that was slow to start, he got a good laugh going. The laugh went up and up. God is good! It was all right. Fuck the shoe. She wouldn't be needing it.

He hoisted her on to his shoulder again. Out the front door, calm, calm. There was nobody around, and if there were any snoopers looking out of their windows they'd just think it was a roll of carpet or something. People were so thick! It made him laugh.

He opened the boot of the puke-green car — typical homo car, shit, he should have realized it from the start — and laid her down in it. For a minute he thought the legs were going to stick out again, they were so long, but he managed to bend them at the knees and get the boot shut.

Would she suffocate in there? He didn't want that. That was no good. No . . . these places weren't airtight, especially in an old rust bucket like this. She would be hot — it was crazily hot today, it just wasn't *right*, there was something wrong — but she wouldn't be in there long.

He got behind the wheel.

*I've got her, Greenwood. I've got her.*

He put the key in the ignition. Trouble was, he had no

gaff now. Georgy-Porgy's room was out. The bedsit was out.

The headache tightened.

But shit, he had wheels! He could go miles! He could go out into the country, out to all those beautiful magical spots he'd found before Greenwood had stolen his bike. All quiet and remote . . . He could get those knickers down first, and then finish the job.

He started the engine.

Jesus, the things he'd had to do today! But he'd had no choice. The dago . . . and the homo . . . and now the girl . . .

The engine idled. Steve thought of the things he'd done today. The things he'd done . . .

He put his hands to his temples. God, that sun was so glary, the way it flickered through the new leaves on the trees, it just made his headache worse and worse . . .

He shook his head, and reversed the car out of the drive. It was all right . . . it was all right . . . he was in control . . .

But he was going to have to get something for this headache.

## 26

Fred hoisted himself up on to his left arm, while his right hand closed around the lump of Aegean rock, felt its rough texture.

His head was more than spinning now: it seemed to be moving on a wild, up-and-down merry-go-round of pain, and vision was too strong a word for the shimmering impressions on his retinas. He struggled to bring one of them into clearer focus — the square of brighter light to the left of the bed.

One last effort.

He dredged up the last lees of strength from his numbing body, lifted the rock high in the air, and flung it at the window.

### 27

Michael saw Christine through the refectory window as he approached it from The Square, and was struck by how beautiful she looked. Pensive, and pale, but beautiful was the only word for her. He had been talking and thinking of sickness and ugliness all afternoon, and the sight of her was like an eruption of colour in a monochrome landscape.

He hurried in, put his arms round her and kissed her. 'Have you been waiting long?'

'Few minutes. God, it's good to see you. How did it go with the psychologist? Do you want a coffee?'

He shook his head. 'I'll tell you about it. Let's go home.'

### 28

Halfway down Knightsford Road there was a small shopping centre — a supermarket, a fish-and-chip shop, a launderette, a chemist, an off-licence — with a covered walkway. Here Steve slewed the Zodiac to a halt on the opposite side of the road and buried his head in his hands.

His prescription painkillers were at the bedsit . . . but he could get some Migreze or something. He didn't believe in pouring all that poison in your system —

— but shit, this headache was the worst ever. It wasn't fair. Why today of all days?

He slammed his hands on the steering wheel, then shouldered his army bag and leapt out of the car and ran across the road. It wouldn't take two minutes . . . He still had some of the spic's money in his pocket . . . It would be all right.

There was a fat woman in the chemist's, dithering between two brands of hay-fever tablets. 'Thass hard to know what to dew, isn't it?' she kept saying. 'Thass hard to choose.'

Steve paced the floor, sweating. So hot . . . He peeped between the tall blue jars in the window to check on the Zodiac parked across the road. It was all right. And it wasn't as if she could get out . . .

The headache jabbed and twisted.

'I dunno . . . Thass hard, isn't it?'

The fat woman turned to look at Steve. He glared back. What was that look supposed to mean? Did she suspect? Was she one of them? Were they after him already?

The fat woman turned back. 'Well, I doon't knoo . . . I reckon I might as well take that one, do you think thass best . . . ?'

Stupid, stupid cow! He had his bag with him — there was something in there that would put her out of her misery if she wanted it! He'd soon spill her fat guts on to the floor —

The headache hammered at his brain.

'Noo, wait, I got the right money here, somewhere, I know I got some change . . .'

Stifling a moan, Steve peeped between the jars again. There was the Zodiac . . .

And there were two men looking at it. One was a traffic warden.

The other was a policeman.

'Oh, God Jesus . . .'

Panic hit Steve like a cudgel. For several seconds he was in blackness, emptiness. The headache disappeared into the void along with everything else.

'Oh, Jesus . . .'

The warden and the policeman were walking round the car, talking, nodding. The policeman looked up in the direction of the shops.

*This was it.*

*They were after him.*

'I say . . . I say, dair. I've finished now, I'll get out of your way.'

Steve stared at the fat woman, lips trembling.

'Are you all right, dair?'

Steve bolted.

There was an alley behind the back of the super-market that cut through to a side street. Steve ran along it, leaping cardboard boxes and pallets, slipping on refuse and nearly falling. His heartbeat boomed in his ears.

*They were on to him. It was all up.*

He should never have taken the car . . .

*Stupid!*

He came hurtling out to the side street, darted straight across it, a van braking behind him with an enraged blare of the horn. They were all against him! His legs pumped, his lungs burned, sweat laved him. Every moment he expected to hear himself pursued, shouts, whistles, yells, sirens . . .

*He had lost! It wasn't fair!*

But as he tore down the leafy suburban streets, not slowing his pace until at least five minutes had gone by, he began to hope that he had given them the slip, and allowed himself to look back. No: no police in sight, though of course they could be watching, lying in wait anywhere.

He jogged on, with no direction in mind, only the single imperative of flight pushing on his tired muscles and seared lungs. Rage and terror subsided just a little, and allowed him to be thankful to God for having told him to look through the window at that moment. His enemies had been so close to capturing him then – so close! Well, they had the car –

*And Greenwood's little slag of a daughter fuck it fuck it it wasn't fair* . . .

– but they didn't have him. The tide hadn't quite turned against him yet.

It was no good, he was going to have to slow down. The headache was back.

He looked round again. No one was on his trail . . .

But it was only a temporary respite. He knew that now – that he only had a limited time left. After what he had done. It wasn't his fault, of course, he'd had no choice, but it was no good expecting people to understand that and it never had been: they were too busy ganging up on him.

He was hunted now –

*They're after me!*

– but after all that was nothing new really. They had just come out into the open.

One thing was for sure, he was going to finish the job. Sooner than he'd planned, but it couldn't be helped. He had found a purpose in life, and he was going to see it through.

He might be the hunted – but he was still the hunter as well. And the rage inside him was going to be tremendous when it found its outlet.

But first he needed somewhere to go.

## 29

'No,' the PC said, climbing back on to his bicycle, 'you don't see a lot of these nowadays. What was that other one with a Z – a Zephyr, was it?'

'Thass right,' the traffic warden said, taking off his cap to wipe his brow. 'Zephyrs and Zodiacs. Funny old names they give cars then, weren't they? Nice old cars though. Shame about the colour.'

'I know, like a gret ole tin of peas, isn't it? Probably one of them students' cars. Look at the way it's parked. Loopy lot.'

'Ah, well, my ole booty, I shall have to give you a ticket do you leave it there much longer,' said the traffic warden, patting the Zodiac's bonnet. 'Phew, fry an egg on that.'

'Scorcher, isn't it? More like August than May. No, it's bad for parking here, they really want a proper car park for them shops.'

'Goo on, thass it, put me out of a job,' the traffic warden said laughing.

'See you, Ron.' The constable waved and wobbled away.

The traffic warden walked round the Zodiac once more, then sighed at the heat and ambled across the road for a snoop around the shopping centre before he knocked off for the day.

The faint whimpers that came from inside the boot of the car went unheard.

*30*

Michael and Christine were on their way to the campus car park when their attention was caught by the commotion in front of Borrow Terrace.

'Rag Week?' Christine said.

'Don't know.' Suddenly Michael understood the term *gut feeling*. Something quivered unpleasantly in his stomach. 'Let's go and see.'

Two police cars and an ambulance were drawn up in the forecourt outside the pyramid-shaped building, and already a clump of rubber-necking students had gathered, despite a PC urging them to keep back with the infallible ghoul-attracting formula of 'There's nothing to see.' A WPC was talking to a girl who, half-tearful, half-indignant, was pointing up at one of the windows of the block. '. . . it just came crashing through the window, I mean it was a bloody great lump of rock, it could have *killed* somebody, not to mention the glass, I mean I was really lucky it didn't hit me but it shook me up, you know? You're just walking along the pavement minding your own business, you don't expect to get hit by flying rocks, I mean I know it's

Rag Week but I just get fed up with these sick jokes, so I went to the Resident Tutor and he went up there and knocked and then used the passkey and – and – oh, God, I'm sorry, you just don't expect to see anything like that . . .'

Michael pushed his way through, scarcely aware whether Christine was following, the feeling in his guts growing stronger.

'. . . University campus . . . name of the building is Borrow Terrace, B-O-R-R-O-W, it's a hall of residence . . .' A second PC, leaning on the open door of his cruiser, wiped the sweat from his face with his sleeve as he spoke into the radio. 'Yes, we've got a fatality, looks very nasty I'm afraid, also wounding, they're bringing him down now, over . . . No, no firearms as far as we can tell . . .'

The other PC was still ushering people back. He put his hand on Michael's chest as he broke through. 'Please keep back, sir, let people do their job . . .'

Michael was sure he knew, several seconds before the ambulancemen emerged through the security door bearing the stretcher, several seconds before he saw Fred's grey-white face and bound head upon it.

The PC caught his arm as he lunged forward, and he heard Christine echo his own cry of 'Fred!'

'You know this man, sir?'

'He lives in my house, he's my lodger – Christ, what happened?'

The PC hesitated, then signalled to his younger colleague with the radio.

They wouldn't let him go near Fred, who didn't seem to be conscious; he and Christine could only watch as the stretcher was lifted into the ambulance, as the doors were closed, as the vehicle, siren keening, was driven away. The young PC made him sit down on the passenger seat of his cruiser while he took his name and Fred's name.

'Is there a family we can contact, sir?'

'They're in Somerset — I've got their number at home somewhere. My God, what happened to him?'

'Do you know the gentleman who lived in the room where Mr Forbes was found, sir?'

Michael shook his head. 'Friend of Fred's, maybe . . . I don't know . . .' A second ambulance was drawing up, manoeuvring with difficulty through the milling students: the WPC was starting to set up a cordon round the entrance to the block. 'Someone's been killed, haven't they?'

The young PC didn't comment. 'Mr Forbes was conscious when he was found, sir, and kept saying something about his keys being stolen, can you shed any light on that? Would he have had a car?'

'Yes, yes, he loved his car — it would have been in the car park — an old Ford Zodiac, weird thing, green, registration number — oh — TFL 334—' My God, did it take something like this to make his damned memory work?

'All right, we'll check the car park in case, but I'll put out a stolen vehicle description. As I say, he was very concerned about his keys, and he kept repeating the name Steve, now whether you know . . .'

Again, the knowledge was instantaneous, complete. In fact he had known from the first sight of the ambulance: *Steve*.

Fred's keys taken. His house. The implications hit him like a bomb blast.

'My God, Suzanne – my daughter, she's at home—'

'Your house key will have been stolen as well, is that right? Would there be any identifying address on it?'

'No, no, nothing like that—'

'Well, in that case, I wouldn't be unduly alarmed, sir, it's unlikely that—'

'Listen, you don't understand – ' he gripped the constable's sleeve ' – I know who must have done this, it's this man, this Steve, he's a lunatic, he's been harassing me, I put in a complaint about it and then this morning there was a, he desecrated my late wife's grave, look, your lot will have a report on that too, for Christ's sake, he's a lunatic—'

The PC reached for the radio, frowning. 'You say your daughter's at home, sir? On her own?'

Christine gave a sob. Michael looked at her.

'When I – when I dropped her off – Fred was there then.' Her face was a mask of anguish, mouth square, hand up as if she was going to be sick. 'At least – his – his *car* was there . . . Oh, Michael, I just saw the car parked outside the house, and I assumed . . .'

They stared at each other.

'When was this, madam?' the PC said.

'I don't know . . . twenty minutes . . .'

The PC grabbed the radio. 'Give me your address again, sir.'

347

*31*

The phone call to his own home had elicited no reply. Michael didn't expect it to. Another knowledge was seeping into his mind: and this one was intolerable.

*Suzanne.*

Their first impulse, to get in the van and hurtle back to Sheeps Hill Road, was not allowed by the police: he hadn't expected that to be, either. They were allowed to travel in the van, but sticking close behind the police car that led the way. Christine, somehow, had regained control of herself. He could only guess at what lay beneath her white calm.

As for himself, what kept repeating in his head was a memory: a memory of when Kate was desperately ill, and they had both known it, and he had said to her, 'I'll take good care of Suzanne.' And she had said, 'I know you will.'

They had to park some way down the street from his house, and wait in the van while the PC who had escorted them talked on his radio. Trying to overhear something that made some sense from the radio's static gargling, Michael peered up ahead at the tree-lined street. He could see police vans there, more figures in uniform. Christ, did they have marksmen? You read about these sieges in the newspapers, you wondered how they happened, how they ever got started . . .

'If he's in there . . .' He stopped: he hadn't meant to speak out loud.

'They know what they're doing,' Christine said.

Neither of them could say any more. They sat and waited, eyes fixed on the young PC leaning one hand on the roof of the cruiser in front while the other grasped the squawking radio.

Michael closed his eyes. The PC was coming towards them.

'Mr Greenwood. Sir.'

He looked into the young brown eyes.

'There's no one in the house.'

## 32

Pogo had been sitting on the windowsill of the fish-and-chip shop observing the bright green car ever since the traffic warden had moved on.

His real name was Graham, but his mates knew him as Pogo. Sometimes, he knew, they referred to him by other names as well; but he chose to turn a deaf ear to it because you were a sad case if you couldn't put up with the odd piss-take. And besides, he didn't want to lose his mates, because when it came down to it he hadn't got a lot else. He was nineteen years old.

Pogo screwed his chip paper into a ball, kicked it into touch, and stood up, digging his hands into the pockets of his letter jacket. Moving casually, he walked over the grass verge and stood at the kerb, waiting to cross the road.

The bloke with the red face who'd left the car hadn't come back yet. He'd seemed to be in a hurry – looked as if he didn't expect to leave the car for long. He was on a single yellow line. Maybe got caught short – there was a toilet in the shopping centre.

So Pogo would have to decide quickly.

Some of his mates on the estate reckoned Pogo was a

bit of a mummy's boy. Oh, they never came out and said
it to his face — which made it worse in a way. It was just
hints. Maybe it was because he'd bottled it that time they
did the newsagents over Sprowston way. Well, he'd just
had a bad feeling about it, that was all. Which turned
out to be right because Gary got caught and now he was
on remand. But his mates didn't see it that way. They
had him marked down as a bullshitter, a chicken. It hurt.
They never expected him to do anything like Lee had
done, lifting that car from outside the Chinky and
burning it all the way to Yarmouth and back and doing
seventy right round the estate and then trashing it in the
old shoe-factory car park. That had been well wicked.
And not the sort of thing you'd expect Pogo to do.

Well, with a bit of luck their opinion of Pogo was
about to change.

He crossed the road, walked round the back of the
bright green car, on to the pavement, a quick look
round . . . then allow your eyes to glance inside . . .

The keys were in the ignition.

*Ho-ly shit.*

The door handle gave in his hand, willingly,
welcomingly.

Pogo was in.

He started the engine. Crazy sort of car, but all the
better. Wait till they saw *this* . . .

He was away.

## 33

Suzanne had often had nightmares of being in some
stifling, enclosed space: usually when you woke up you

found you were trapped under too many bedclothes. That had been her first thought when she came to.

Then she found that her head hurt and she couldn't move her arms and legs. Couldn't see. Could hardly breathe in the thick, rubbery heat.

And then she remembered the arm going round her neck in Fred's room.

Still she didn't panic, not quite. Some strong part of her mind found solid ground amidst the quicksands of terror and stood fast on it. She knew what her suffocating prison was; she knew from the smell, from traffic noises; she had seen *Crimestop* on the TV just the other week, where someone — a bank manager she thought — had been tied up in the boot of a car and driven somewhere . . .

But they weren't moving. Had they been moving before? How long had she been passed out?

Her mind was struggling to keep its footing on that solid ground. Because the heat was pressing down on her so unbearably, and when she opened her mouth to shout it was so dry she could only whimper. The heat . . .

Dogs died locked in cars. They died of the heat.

She tried to cry out again, feeling as if she were breathing warm cotton wool. Someone would come, someone would release her . . .

Her mind began to slither and tumble from the firm ground. She was remembering more about that *Crimestop* programme. It *had* been a bank manager, and they'd taken him so that he would unlock a safe for them.

But whoever had her couldn't possibly want her for anything like that. Nothing like that . . .

There was a bang, a jolt, and her prison shifted on its springs. Then the noise of a gunning engine drowned her gasps as the car began to move.

### 34

They took Michael into his own house. The place seemed to be full of police, as if it had effectively ceased to be his.

Christine was still unnaturally calm, but he wasn't. He was frantic now, with a feeling that his head was going to break loose and fly off into the sky like a kite.

A WPC was questioning him now. Why did they assume these were automatically more soothing?

'Are you quite sure that Suzanne hasn't just gone out somewhere on her own? A friend calling round for her, maybe?'

'She always leaves a note,' Michael said, hearing his voice come out as a gibber. 'Always. And anyway, she wouldn't just go out, not at the moment, with this crazy bastard bothering us, she knows I wanted her to be careful—'

'Mr Greenwood?' The plain-clothes man had a ragged handlebar moustache and a faint Scots accent. 'Would you come up to the top floor with me, please? I understand that's your lodger's room?'

'Yes – why, what have you—'

'Just come and look, please, sir.'

He climbed the stairs to Fred's bedsit. There was another PC in uniform there, examining some mud on the carpet.

'We haven't touched anything, this is just as we found

352

it,' the Scots detective said. 'Now how does it look to you?'

Fred was normally very neat. But his desk chair was knocked over, and the desk was disturbed, the pebbles he kept in a bowl scattered.

'Someone's been in here,' Michael said.

The Scotsman nodded, and steered Michael downstairs again. He sat him down at the kitchen table with Christine.

'Now we've searched the house, Mr Greenwood, and your daughter's not here and there are signs of an intruder having entered. Maybe using your lodger's stolen keys as you suggested. We're questioning the neighbours to find out if anyone was seen coming to the house after Ms Reed dropped the wee girl off from school. *But*' – he held up his hand – 'we want to look on the bright side too – I mean the chance that Suzanne simply went out of her own accord. So. We've put out the description of your lodger's car that was taken from the university and every officer in this city and in the county of Norfolk is going to have his eyes peeled for it. Whatever crazy bastard's going around, whatever he's up to, we're after him. So what I want you to do is think hard of any place your daughter might have gone to. Any friends, anyone from school, just any possibility whatsoever. And either you or Ms Reed ring round all the possibilities. OK?'

'OK,' Michael said. And he thought: *They're just giving me something to do, to keep me occupied.*

*They know that maniac's got her.*

## 35

Steve sat in a brick-built bus shelter, holding his head. He was trying to think his way past the headache.

He didn't know this part of the city. Concentrating on putting as much distance as possible between himself and Knightsford Road, he had ended up in a dingy post-war council estate. The bus shelter looked out over a muddy green and a junction to a school with boarded-up windows. There was a condom near his feet. He kicked at it. It was disgusting, they should be shot.

The air was cooling at last, but it wouldn't be dark for a long while yet.

He needed somewhere to go.

The police would surely be swarming round Greenwood's place. He could probably take a couple of them out, but . . . No, no good.

An underfed cat came timidly sniffing into the bus shelter. Steve reached out and tickled its cheek. A memory came to him of another cat that had sniffed round his legs, just the other day.

And suddenly he knew where he could go.

## 36

Pogo twirled the knob of the radio till he found some decent music. Shit, Vanilla Ice − well, it was better than nothing. He powered up the sound as high as it would go, which wasn't much. Crappy system. But still, he had *done* it! He was there! He was fucking there!

Lee's jaw would hit the ground when he saw what he'd done. He could hardly wait.

He got on to the ring road at Farrow Road, but it was crawling with tea-time traffic and he could hardly get above twenty. Shit, this was no good. He wanted to be bombing along, windows down, music blaring, heads turning . . . The steering on this old crate was a bit ropy, but he liked the rough sound of the engine. It was smart. After dark this thing was just going to *roar* round the estate.

Traffic lights now. Shit. He slowed the car to a halt and waited, jigging up and down in his seat, fingers tapping out rhythm on the steering wheel. Oh, well, once he got over the old railway bridge he could turn off towards the airport, take the Cromer Road out, there would be loads of elbowroom there, he could really open her up –

In the wing mirror he thought he saw a checkered shape move out from a side road behind him.

A siren groaned into life and howled out over the sound of the radio.

Pogo started shaking.

The traffic lights were still red.

*Fuck it, that couldn't be for him* . . .

He looked over his shoulder.

That was a filth wagon all right –

– and it was edging between the tailback lanes, blue light flashing, siren screaming . . . *Coming for him* . . .

'Shit!'

Pogo put his foot down.

The old car bucketed forward and slewed across the junction, missing an oncoming bus by inches. Pogo shrieked his exhilaration and fear, bouncing in his seat, swinging the big sticky old steering wheel. Another car crossing the junction from the opposite direction braked and hooted, and Pogo gave him the finger. 'Waa-hoo, fuck you!'

He had made it across the junction and the pig wagon was still stuck on the other side behind the stalled bus –

'Wooo-hooo!'

Just wait till he told the lads about this one –

Shit, the traffic was practically creeping along here too . . .

He swung the Zodiac out and began moving along between the tailbacks, laughing to see the faces of the straights sitting inside the cars as he accelerated past them. One more junction ahead, and then –

A blue flash in his wing mirror.

Christ, they were on his tail again – and *fast*, how were they coming so fast?

The other traffic was falling away from that pig wagon, that was why, creeping out to the edge of the road –

They'd do it for him then too. Pogo put his foot down again.

The siren shrieked after him. Gaining.

He was practically grazing the doorhandles of the adjacent cars as he hurtled towards the next junction –

Red, shit, red again!

The pig was right behind him, oh Jesus –

Here was the junction . . . Second time lucky . . .

'Yeee-haah!' Pogo yelled, as he gunned the Zodiac across the junction. He swung the wheel to avoid a motorbike and *yes*, he was there, this car must be made of elastic, man, it was wicked –

Then the side of a lorry as big as a house came rushing

towards him and everything went dark red.

## 37

It was astonishing what your mouth could do independently of your mind. Michael had been engaged for what seemed like hours in making phone calls to the parents of every friend of Suzanne's he could think of, and with each one he somehow managed the same everyday tone, the same assurance that no, it was nothing to worry about. He even found himself speaking as if they were the ones who were on the brink of insanity with worry over their child rather than he. He even found himself dialling the numbers and putting down the receiver with delicate care, as if he were being filmed in close-up. Perhaps at such times the body simply took over, functioned without the mind. It must have, because his mind had given out. It had tortured itself with hellish imaginings and then just shut down. If anyone had asked Michael his name at that time he would have stared blankly and not for the life of him known what it was.

Christine sat next to him, silent, as he made the calls in the living room. A WPC was with them. She kept pressing them to have a cup of tea. The Scots inspector had looked in and gone away again: Michael dimly understood that he had gone to take a look at the scene at Borrow Terrace.

He had tried the last of Suzanne's friends he could think of, and was dully staring at the telephone, when it rang.

The WPC was by his side as he snatched it up. 'Mr

Greenwood, remember—' she began.

'Hello?' Michael said. And thought, his mind stirring to life: *This is how the nightmare began.*

*I'll give you fucking purgatory . . .*

'Hello, Michael, I couldn't help but ring you back — I was a bit worried after your call, and so's Steph, I mean is everything really all right . . . ?'

It was Suzanne's friend Steph's mother, the first person he had rung. He shook his head at the WPC.

'Yes, Jean, it's OK.'

'Only you will let me know, won't you, when she turns up . . .'

Michael started to say something and then the receiver fell from his hand. The inspector was back and had his hand on his arm.

'Mr Greenwood — some good news. We've found the car. And Suzanne. Your daughter's safe.'

Suddenly Michael understood the impulse that made people drop to their knees.

Instead he wept.

The WPC was patting his shoulder. She looked as if someone had given her a present.

Christine spoke for him. 'Is she — is she really all right?'

The inspector looked at them both, as if sizing them up. 'The guy who took her tied her up and put her in the boot of the car.' His clipped Scots made it sound like a gentle, dainty action. 'So she's pretty shocked and a wee bit bruised and suffering from the heat and she's been taken to hospital. But I believe she's basically unharmed. You can go see her straight away.'

Michael was on his feet. 'What about — him?'

'One of our patrol cars spotted the car on the ring road and gave chase. Trying to get away the guy jumped a red and went head-on into a goods lorry. So when I say Suzanne's a wee bit bruised I mean she's taken quite a knock—'

'Christ—'

'*But*, I repeat, she's basically all right; it may sound a curious thing to say but she was probably in the best place in a collision like that. The bonnet went under the lorry bed like a wedge under a door and the driver's in pretty bad shape. They had to cut him free.'

Michael thought of Steve. 'I wish—' he began, then stopped. The violence of his feelings shocked him even now. He met Christine's eyes: she knew what he wished.

'Well, as I say, he's in a bad way, and he's being taken to hospital too. From what I hear he'll be in no fit state to get up to any more of his tricks for some time, if at all. As soon as his condition's such that we can question him we will of course do that, but it won't be just yet. In the meantime, you get off to the hospital and see your wee girl.'

'Thanks.' Guilt struck Michael a light blow. 'Oh – my lodger, Fred, have you any news?'

'I'm afraid I don't know anything about that, Mr Greenwood. You can find out at the hospital – WPC Marshall here will go along with you and help you find out everything you need to know. I'll be along there later myself to talk to you, and perhaps you can help us get some idea of what this freak thinks he's been doing.'

*I know what he's been doing*, thought Michael. *Making my life purgatory.*

But now, thank God, it was over.

## 38

Steve knew he was running a high risk trying to break into Christine Reed's flat. Not that he had any doubt that she wouldn't be there: she was sure to be with Greenwood, holding his hand and soothing his fucking brow while they looked for his little slag of a daughter. But it still wasn't dark — just a sort of deep pink in the sky, beautiful really, a gift from God, not that the bastard human race appreciated it — and as there was no question of trying to get in from the front he had to go down the path at the back of the terrace and walk up the back garden in full view of everybody in the other houses if they chose to look. Plus there was the upstairs flat to consider . . .

But this was his last idea. And one thing he had learnt was that if you looked confident, if you didn't lurk and skulk, then it was amazing what you could get away with: people were so stupid.

And so he waltzed up the garden path, bag slung over his shoulder, as cool as you liked. There was a sort of conservatory effort at the back and without hesitating or looking around him he stuck his elbow straight through the glass in the door.

These were the crucial moments. If anyone spotted him now, he had had it.

But God hadn't quite deserted him. He poked his arm through the broken glass and found the conservatory door was only bolted.

He was in.

Getting into the flat proper took longer. The door leading into the flat from the conservatory was a proper

door, if not particularly strong, and he had no jemmy.
Luckily it seemed as if Greenwood's tart was quite a
handywoman, or a les anyway, as he had thought: there
were all sorts of tools in here. He broke one screwdriver
trying to force the door, but by breaking the handle off a
garden fork he made a reasonable jemmy that finished
the job.

In the kitchen he found a bottle of milk and swallowed
it down. The bitch's cat came timidly sniffing round
him, but it ran off when he kicked at it. These fucking
animals, treated like royalty while everybody was out to
get him. It wasn't fair.

Formerly he would have been interested in having a
good look round the bitch's flat, but it was too late for
that sort of finessing. It was a hideout; and it was as
close to Greenwood as he could get at the moment.

And it had a phone. And people, including
Greenwood and his tart, had to go home at some time.
And whichever place they went to, he would know about
it.

### 39

Michael and Christine drove to the city hospital in the
van. When they parked in the underground car park
Christine sat for a few moments looking at the keys in
her hand and then turned and hid her face in Michael's
shoulder.

'If I—' she began.

'No,' he said. 'No. If I could bloody well drive instead
of being a useless article depending on other people's
kindness, then I would have dropped Suzanne off from

school and said, Ah, Fred's in, and gone away, and nothing would be any different.'

She touched his cheek: then sat up, wiped her eyes.

'Do you hope he dies?' she said.

'Steve?' He considered. He had created the image in his head, several times, of Steve driving head-on into a lorry. He didn't know what it made him feel: he only knew that the feeling, frighteningly maybe, but definitely, contained no element of pity. He said, 'I hope he suffers.'

WPC Marshall was waiting for them in the main lobby, and took them up to see Suzanne.

Hospitals only meant one thing to Michael: they were forever associated with Kate's illness, with despair, with a slow spiral of hopelessness. The very cheeriness of the children's drawings pinned to the walls of the long corridors spoke to him of death. It was perhaps because of these associations that when he saw Suzanne his first thought was: it's all right. She looked pale, she looked bruised, her head was bandaged, she was only very dreamily conscious from the sedative they had given her – but she looked like a person who was going to be all right quite soon.

She didn't say much to him: only held his hand and smiled and murmured, comfortably, 'You all right, Dad? Yeah . . . I wonder if I'll be on *Crimestop* . . .'

He stayed holding her hand for some time, watching her sleep. With her hair scraped back like that she didn't look so much like her mother. Perhaps it was the resemblance to him that came out. Poor kid.

He spoke with a doctor, a genial Indian woman with a long braid down her back.

'We'll keep her in tonight,' she said. 'The physical problems aren't much. Just bruising, and heat exhaustion, that was the worst of it. She should be fit to go home tomorrow, though that's not a promise. She seems very contented now, but that's the drugs. It's when the memory of her ordeal hits her that we need to take care. She may need counselling to see her through that. But don't worry. Someone from the counselling service will talk to you tomorrow.'

The report on Fred was not so good. They were keeping him under close observation, and Michael couldn't see him. Even now Michael's feelings about hospitals were such that he took some convincing that a fractured skull didn't mean Fred was going to die or even suffer brain damage. 'He's getting the very best care, Mr Greenwood, and his condition's comfortable. His parents are driving over tonight. I really don't think you need to worry. You may be able to visit him tomorrow when you come to see Suzanne.' The doctor smiled at Christine. 'He's a worry-gut, your husband, isn't he?'

Christine smiled.

They went back to sit with Suzanne, who was sleeping. After a while Christine said, 'Fred will be all right, you know.'

He nodded.

'And Suzanne,' she said.

'Yes.' He took her hand. 'I just keep thinking — you know — if he hadn't crashed that car, if they hadn't caught him—'

'Don't think it,' Christine said. 'Because it didn't happen. You know, when I was a kid and I used to go to the pictures, I always used to wonder what would happen if the cinema caught fire. I spent all that worry on a thing that didn't happen. And what you're thinking didn't happen. And now it won't. It's finished.'

Michael took off his glasses and rubbed his eyes. 'I know. But I keep thinking of something else as well. The fact that – *he's* in here, in this hospital.'

'It's good,' she said vehemently. 'We know where he is.'

He nodded again. 'Yes. For the first time since it started.'

After a while the inspector arrived, and asked to speak to them in the corridor. Looking at his watch, Michael was surprised to see it was past nine. It must be dark outside: the windowless, artificially lit environment of the hospital made you lose track of time. Of course, he should have remembered that.

'They tell me the wee girl's fine,' the inspector said, his moustache looking more hangdog than ever under the fluorescent light. 'That's great. Can't say the same for our man. He was pretty badly smashed up. Severe chest injuries. They're going to have to operate. So obviously I can't say when or if we'll be able to talk to him.'

Michael closed his eyes a moment. He felt as if he were trying to fight off the devil – the devil saying *gloat, relish, be glad*.

'Anyway, I suppose the main thing is he's not going anywhere. The trouble is, neither is the student who was killed at the university. Overseas student, from Greece. That's going to be one big slice of hell that someone's going to have to give his family . . . We've been talking to the other residents of the block where it happened. It seems your lodger may have disturbed this bastard in Mr Sofroniou's room, maybe in the act as it were. Mr Sofroniou's body was bound, so we assume . . .' The inspector shrugged. 'All I can say is that lorry did everyone a favour. Listen, Mr Greenwood, obviously I'm going to have to talk to you at some length about what's been going on, but I don't imagine you fancy that just now any more than I do. Like I say, we've got him, he's not going anywhere, so I suggest that we leave it till tomorrow. You must be done in.' Turning, the Scotsman paused and looked beadily at Michael. 'D'you know it appears that Mr Sofroniou may have been held in that room against his will for some time. Maybe several days. In a block full of thirty-odd people. And no one knew.'

'That's the trouble,' Michael said wryly. 'We're all strangers nowadays.'

### 40

Darkness had fallen as Steve sat waiting in Christine's living room.

It wasn't the dead feeling that had come over him. He was simply still. The only movement to be seen was the blinking of his eyes.

Nor was he thinking. He was simply gathering himself.

At last he moved, as if physically prodded by an idea. He switched on the radio in the midi hi-fi, tuned it to a local station, listened.

It did not seem at all odd that they should be talking about him on the radio. It seemed natural. The great conspiracy against him that he had long suspected — how long? It seemed to him now that he had known right from a little child his own unique position in the world — was out in the open.

'. . . Police are waiting to question a man in connection with several offences, including the attempted abduction of a twelve-year-old girl from the Sheeps Hill area of the city. The girl is safe and unharmed and is currently recovering in the Norfolk and City Hospital . . .'

Steve clicked the radio off. He walked over to the phone and dialled Michael's number.

He listened to it ring for a couple of minutes, to be sure. Then he put the phone down.

### 41

'Put it this way,' the Indian doctor said. 'You can sit in that chair all night and then when she wakes up in the morning she'll see a zombie instead of her dad. Or you can go home and get some sleep and be here first thing in the morning looking nice and human for her. Take your pick. Also I think you'll be needing treatment yourself if you don't get some rest, but what do I know, I'm only a doctor.'

'You're right,' Michael said. 'Of course you are . . .' He peeped back into the room where Suzanne was sleeping. 'You will let me know if—'

'If she starts flying around the ward on a broomstick, yes, but it's not going to happen and neither is anything else, so don't worry!'

'I'll get him out of your way,' Christine said, taking

Michael's arm. 'Come on, husband. Let's go home.'

He gave Suzanne a last look, called a thank you after the Indian doctor who was already gliding away at speed, and allowed Christine to steer him away.

'It's going to be weird in that house,' he said as they descended to the car park in the lift. 'No Suzanne. No Fred.'

'You could come to my place.'

He thought about it. 'Thanks. But I'd better be home — just in case they need to ring me.'

The lift disgorged them into the forlorn concrete spaces of the car park underneath the main hospital building. Overhead orange lighting somehow wiped out the different colours of the rows of cars, turning them all a sickly grey. The subterranean place still held the heat of the day: the warm, tired mustiness of the air reminded Michael of tube stations. Service lifts could be heard clanking and humming somewhere in the mass of concrete overhead.

'Suzanne's an unusually mature kid,' Christine said as they walked to the van, footsteps echoing with a sound like the drip of water. 'She's got the strength of mind to come to terms with what happened. I'm sure of that.'

'And make sense of it?' Michael said.

'Maybe we've just got to face the fact that it *doesn't* make sense. Asking yourself why is a bit like having the torture twice over.'

'You tend to think senseless things happen on the grand scale, in exceptional circumstances. Death camps, wars. Jack the Ripper flourishing his cloak. But there must be bits of that grand senselessness floating around everywhere, every day, walking down the street, travelling on a train . . .' He swallowed. 'And suddenly it's there, in your life.'

She rested her hand on his shoulder a moment. 'It can only happen once. Law of averages.'

They got into the van. Christine put the key in the ignition, then stopped.

'Damn,' she said. 'I had a jacket, didn't I? I've left it in that waiting room.'

'I'll go.'

'No, it's all right. You're done in. Won't take me a minute. I'd better get it, it's got my ID card in it.'

She got out and he heard her footsteps clipping away into the distance. The cab of the van was hot and stuffy, filled with the musty heat of the day: he opened the passenger door to let in some air. He became aware of how sweat-soaked and grubby he was, at the end of a day that seemed to stretch back to the beginning of time. A deep, scalding-hot bath was what he wanted, to wash it all away. To wash Steve away, scrub and sluice him away for ever. There was a grumbling tension-ache in his lower back: he felt forty and more. *Drained* was an insufficient word for how he felt: he was emptied, scoured, bled, a husk inhabited by a spark of consciousness.

He took off his glasses and massaged the bridge of his nose. He needed, he thought, a long holiday. But then after this every day would seem like a holiday.

He reached over to pull the van door shut, and a hand grabbed him.

Many things telescoped into an instant: the sight of the long-nailed brown hand clutching at him; a grin of tombstone teeth; shallow blue eyes; a glint of sharp steel, moving; a hot pain and wetness in his left shoulder —

— his glasses skittering out of his grasp and smashing on the concrete . . .

He didn't know if he was crying out as he tried to slam the van door on the intruding arm, or whether it was his assailant. There was a yelling somewhere. He felt the dull thudding impact as he trapped the arm between the door and the sill, but the hand still clutched at him, writhing and lunging like some blind, sinuous creature —

He flung the door open wide, hitting Steve in the face with the edge of it, and swiftly slammed it back shut, and this time he felt the crunch of fingertips caught in it. He heard the scream of pain as the hand was snatched back. He banged down the door lock.

*My God that is Steve he's here how can he be —*

And then Steve's face was pressed to the passenger window, not just red now but a terrible dark mottled colour like something overripe, rotten, full of putrescence; and he was gripping the knife between his teeth —

*Knife with my blood on it he stuck it in me my God . . .*

— and pounding on the glass with both fists, drawing them back behind his head to strike harder, BAM again BAM again BAM, the glass shivering . . .

Naked eyes riveted to the staring blue eyes on the other side of the glass, Michael slithered over to the driver's seat. He clutched his shoulder, felt the warm stickiness, began to mutter under his breath.

'Oh God . . . oh, Jesus . . .'

He looked wildly at the dashboard, blinking like an

owl through his myopia. Keys in the ignition — you turn that, and — Christ, he'd never driven, he didn't *know*, how did you . . . ?

*Come* on, *you've seen Christine drive it a thousand times, just think, it's simple —*

BAM. The glass rattled.

*He's going to get in here . . .*

*But how can it be Steve how can it be it was a head-on smash he's in intensive care —*

*Never mind how, they got the wrong man somehow they got the wrong man and STEVE IS HERE —*

He started the engine. Its sound gave him hope. *Now, think, there's the handbrake, and the gears . . .*

Through sheer fumbling chance he found reverse. The van gave a jolt and a lurch and then bucketed backwards, out of control, he couldn't stop . . .

The van hurtled in reverse the whole width of the car park, tyres screeching as Michael wrestled with the wheel. His foot found the brake too late: the van cannoned into the bonnet of a parked car with a brilliant percussive shimmer of broken headlights, tossing Michael about like a doll. The collision of his chest with the steering wheel knocked the breath out of him for some moments, and he thought he would pass out. At last he got air into his lungs, and the dancing spots cleared from his vision . . . but that still didn't leave much vision, without his glasses. He put his face close to the windscreen, peering into the bilious orange vagueness, just making out the symmetrical shapes of cars, concrete pillars . . .

*Where the hell is he?*

His groping fingers mapped the dashboard, came

upon a switch he recognized. He flipped on the headlights.

Better. The bleaching beam cut a broad swathe through the dimness, sharpening the fuzzy images that moved on his retinas. He puckered his eyes, feeling them achingly adjust —

And saw Steve. Moving deliberately into the acid thoroughfare that was the headlights' beam, stepping slowly forward . . .

Not alone. As Christine had promised, it hadn't taken her long to fetch her jacket. She was wearing it now, as Steve pushed her forward into the light, one arm gripping her waist, the other round her neck. The knife at her throat glowed like something at white heat.

'*Come on!*' Michael could hear Steve's voice only faintly, though his mouth was stretching wide to yell the words, the jaw yammering as if on a hinge. '*Come on come on come on . . .*'

Michael heard himself give an animal grunt. He couldn't make out the expression on Christine's face, but his mind supplied the nightmare picture. His hand moved instinctively to the doorhandle —

And then Christine reacted.

Michael had seen it done on TV, in self-defence displays — never in real life. It was so quick. A flex of the body, and she dug her elbow backward like a lightning piston, slamming it into Steve's groin, and lunging free of him as he doubled up like a dropped marionette.

Michael could hear her screaming something as she darted away to the side out of the headlights. Some atavistic part of his brain responded, directing his fumbling hand to the gear lever, his foot to the pedal . . .

Steve was still doubled up right in the centre of the headlight beam, like a soloist on a spotlit stage. He was just rising from his agonized crouch, still clutching his knife, as Michael found the gear, and his eyes looked full into Michael's as the van roared forward, straight for him.

'*You – bastard* . . .' Michael's voice rose above the engine, high, exultant, terrible.

The accelerating van hit Steve squarely before he could move and tossed him up on to the bonnet. His face struck the windscreen and stayed there, staring straight into Michael's eyes with a sort of explosive astonishment, as he was carried forty yards and then slammed right into the concrete wall of the car park.

The impact threw Michael forward; his head struck the windscreen a glancing blow, and his vision blackly swirled again. When at last he looked up at the windscreen Steve's body had slid down out of sight, leaving a bloody stripe on the bonnet.

Michael closed his eyes a moment. Forced down the urge to be sick. He tried to open the driver's door, but the crash had buckled it, and he had to slide over and climb out on the passenger side. Glass was tinkling musically to the ground, and there was a drip of oil.

He heaved the door shut, put his hand gingerly to his bleeding shoulder, and looked blearily up to see Christine, a dozen yards away. She was gesturing, but his eyes couldn't make out what the gesture meant.

'*Michael!*' she screamed.

*Pointing.*

Pointing behind him.

He whipped round, and Steve came moaning at him out of the dark.

It was Steve's weight, simply thrown at him like a punchbag, that knocked him off balance. He went down with Steve on top of him. One of Steve's arms was hanging loosely, at an impossible angle, and he was bubbling blood; but with the other arm he pinned Michael's throat, the long nails digging into the tender flesh, and he had the knife clamped between his teeth, blood spraying over the blade. The terrible empty, carved face on its bull neck, eyes popping, drew nearer to Michael's as Steve bore down on him.

Michael struggled to free his right arm from the dead weight of Steve's body. He was gasping, choking — the billowing clouds were closing over his vision again . . .

He wrenched his arm free, brought it round in an arc, and hammered his whole forearm straight in Steve's mouth. A cry of sickness broke from him as he drove the knife sideways into the hellish face like a razor into an orange; and he closed his eyes against the rain of lifeblood and against the sight of Steve slumping to the ground, his face split in two.

# SEVEN

## *1*

'Dad, what have you done to your arm? And your head!' said Suzanne, sitting up in the hospital bed. 'I don't know, when I'm not around you go all to pot. Hi, Christine. What's he been doing?'

Michael hugged her. 'It's nothing much,' he said. 'How are you feeling this morning?'

'Loads better. Can I go home today? Anyway, where were you, I've been awake for ages?'

'Sorry, love. More confabs with the police.'

He had just come from a long session with the Scots inspector − who it turned out had been hurrying on his way to find Michael when the attack in the car park had happened. Fred had recovered consciousness, and the description he had given the police of his attacker, together with their swiftly establishing the identity of the young man who had crashed the stolen car, had ignited the realization that they had the wrong man. It was unlikely, the inspector told Michael, that there would be charges. Not against him: and Steve was beyond all that now.

It occurred to Michael that he still didn't know Steve's surname.

'Dad,' Suzanne said quietly. 'What about the man who – you know . . . ?'

Michael held her hand. It felt wonderfully young, full of potential. 'He died,' he said. He shook off a brushing shadow and smiled. 'So how did you sleep?'

'Really well. I didn't have any nightmares, like I thought I might . . . Did you?'

'Only one,' Michael said.